Cover art by Elizabeth Best. See her art on Instagram

@artoferbest

Logo and Chapter Headings by Omni Jacala. See his art on Twitter

@artsyomni

Copy edited by Beth Cantwell. See her work on Twitter

@beththedork

LICENSE NOTES

Dedications

To my son, my daily challenge, my wild ball of energy, my goofy, nerdy, cuddlebug, who gives me a reason to continue on every day.

To Joe Meenan, husband, friend, world developer, and my biggest fan, for supporting me through all the difficult parts of this. You were never short of the support and encouragement I needed while writing.

To Omni Jacala, friend and artist, for forcing me to write the very first draft of this book. If you hadn't insisted this take place on Zyearth, there would be no book.

To Mom and Dad, who instilled in me a love of reading and passed on their love of creativity to me. Dad, I know you're watching over me and cheering me on. Mom, I could never have gotten this far without you.

To my amazing, talented, wonderful writing group, Linda, Randy, Chris, Jim, Jill, Victoria, Andrea, Missy, and Heather, who guided me as I grew as an author, who unabashedly pointed out my massive plot holes, and who supported me as I set out to write and publish this book. You're all amazing people and I love you all.

You are all the lights of my life. Thank you from the bottom of my heart.

"Don't make fame your goal. Make your goal doing what you do to the best of your ability, and that's something no one can take away from you." – **Dan Avidan**

Shadow Cast

Book One

From the Guardian Archives

By R. A. Meenan

Starcrest Fox Press

FATE

"I can't believe you have me out here running in forty-degree weather," Izzy Gildspine groaned, leaping from one foot to the next on the cold, wet sand. She flattened her ears against her golden-brown quills. "I should have brought a jacket."

Matthew Azure ignored Izzy's complaints and glanced out over the ocean as a gentle breeze blew through his blue-tipped ears and quills. Zyearth's sun peeked a thin line of light across the surface of the water, streaking the dark sky with blue and orange.

The perfect setting for his normal morning run.

He slipped his shoes off, tied the laces together, and slung them over his shoulders. He dug his bare, white-furred toes into the wet sand, testing his grip with his toe claws, then glanced at the Defender cliff face and the ocean around him, his stiff quills rustling in his ears.

Izzy wrinkled her short snout and snorted. "Did you hear me, Matt?"

7

Matt rolled his eyes, tilting a catlike ear back. "Running is good for you."

"Sure, it is," Izzy said, rubbing the golden-brown fur on her arms and shaking herself. The quills on the back of her head waved softly and she splayed both catlike ears. She carefully twisted the silver, sapphire-studded wedding coil on her wrist, as if trying to coax some warmth into the cold metal. "But running doesn't have to be done at six AM in weather so chilly I'll freeze my ears off. I'm tired, cold, and definitely not happy." She pointed to Matt's shoes. "You're not expecting me to go barefoot, are you?"

"Not if you're going to be a wimp about it," Matt said. He stretched slowly, spreading his toe claws and working the muscles in his legs and arms. His quills bounced on his head as he moved.

Izzy crossed her arms. "I am not a wimp."

"Tell that to your feet."

She narrowed her eyes. "Really, Matt? We're going to play this game?"

Matt finished stretching and gave Izzy the side eye with a smirk. "Rosemary will be disappointed."

Izzy shivered. "Don't start that. We're fully fledged Defenders now and we outrank her." She crossed her arms. "I swear to Draso, I'll never live down her bootcamp eye-peckings."

Matt laughed. "I hear you, but I don't think she'd appreciate the species stereotypes."

"Are you kidding me? She's the one who *started* the whole chicken-taunting thing. And she's threatened me so many times with eye-pecking, especially when she finds out I've been slacking off in training."

"You never slack off in training."

"Rosemary would say different."

"I think she'd be happy to see you running with me. She likes taking the new recruits running barefoot at six AM too. That's where I got it from anyway." He pointed at her feet. "Except that you're still wearing shoes."

8

"Fine! Shoes off!" Izzy kicked off her boots and slung them over her shoulder. "Happy?"

Matt grinned. "Very. Wanna run through some Gem exercises too?"

"Why not?" Izzy said. "Hit me with your best shot, airhead!" She took off down the beach, leaving behind one rocky crag and heading for the next, some five miles alongside the water. Their rules had always been simple – If Izzy got to the other end of the thin beach before Matt stopped her with his magic, she won.

Matt mentally reached for the white, blue-trimmed Lexi Gem on his belt. A surge of power rushed through his body and little twisters of wind formed at his feet.

"You'll never catch me being that slow, Matt!" She sped up and increased the distance between them.

Let's see her dodge this. He dashed after Izzy, toe claws extended for better grip in the hard, wet sand. Calling on the power from his Gem, he tossed a small twister at her feet.

Izzy leapt over the twister and rolled on the sand. "Gotta do better than that!"

"That so!" He formed a larger twister and threw it at Izzy. It picked up sand and debris as it gathered speed.

Izzy held out a hand and in a quick shimmer of green and purple that quickly faded from view, she created a full body shield and fought off most of the rubble. "Keep trying!"

They kept up their exercise all the way down the beach. Matt kept his powers weak during the spar. Using his full-strength magic against someone who wasn't also an elemental user could be deadly, despite Izzy's prowess with shielding. Izzy was a healer, but Gem magic never worked on the user. Helpful to keep fire users from catching their tails on fire, but useless to healers who couldn't heal themselves.

9

Using his power at half strength also helped boost her confidence in battle, he reminded himself.

And they both needed every boost possible.

As they neared the end of the strip of land between the two craigs, Matt pulled out his final attack. A thick tornado that he kept above the beach to avoid it gathering any sand. He ran through the waves and harder sand, until he hit full speed and nearly caught up with Izzy.

"Heads up!" He tossed the tornado toward her.

Izzy shielded again, but it didn't do much good. Matt's tornado lifted her a few inches off the beach and skipped out into the shallow waves.

"Matt!" she called, though her voice was nearly drowned out in the wind. "*No fair*. Put me down!"

"As you wish." He pulled the power back and dropped Izzy into the drink.

"*Matt!*" Izzy scrambled to her feet and shook her arms. "You *ass!*"

Matt ran up to her, grinning. He had won. Again. "Well, you're awake now, aren't you?"

"Yeah, but I'm even *more* cold and my unhappiness has evolved into unbridled rage!"

"At least I got one out of three," Matt said. "You can shower and take care of the other two."

"After I climb the cliff stairs with soaking wet clothes," Izzy said. She checked to make sure her golden brown Lexi Gem hadn't fallen out of its holster at her hip, then crossed her arms. "You're such an asshole. I should sic Roscoe on you after this."

"I could kick Roscoe's tail and he knows it," Matt said.

"You're not taking into account Roscoe's raw anger," Izzy spat. "He's gonna be pissed at me for dripping sea water all over the carpet. We just had that cleaned."

Matt rolled his eyes. "Here." He ran into the ocean and dove into an oncoming wave. The cold water hit his ears and quills, sending shocks up his body. He swam up and burst through the surface of the water, then stood and shook himself. Water flew off his fur. "Happy? Now we're both soaked. You can tell Roscoe I'll pay for the carpet cleaning in both our suites."

"You should have been born a polar bear instead of a quilar," Izzy said, shivering.

Matt laughed. "Fair enough." He gripped Izzy's shoulder. "Let's get breakfast. My treat. Roscoe can join us if he's awake."

"Shower first."

"Deal," Matt said.

They walked toward the cliffs. Matt's gaze trailed the rocky escarpment until he caught sight of the Defender Academy towering over the edge. The tall glass buildings shined above them, gleaming in the sunrise.

Izzy glanced up at them too, pasting one ear back and frowning. "Think we'll get the Golden Guardianship today?"

Matt flattened his ears. Golden Guardians. Third highest ranked in the Defender military. It was a place of honor. A high rank designed for those willing to put their lives on the line for the good of others. Both Matt and Izzy's fathers and grandfathers had been Guardians before them, leaving behind a legacy that their children felt they needed to live up to.

Both previous pairs of Golden Guardians had died on the job as well. Matt still had nightmares of his father's final screams, images burned in his memory of red quilars, called the Omnirs, destroying his home.

But he refused to let that get in the way of his desire to be a Guardian. He needed to be one. It was his legacy. And more than that, he needed to succeed where his father failed.

Master Guardian Lance Tox had been excited at the prospect of them becoming Guardians when they'd first brought it up, but as they went through

11

training, he became more and more reluctant. So reluctant that he hadn't been willing to induct them into the Guardianship without extra training and experience.

Matt and Izzy had twenty years of training, nearly twenty more as a ranked soldier, with countless war games, missions, and skirmishes under their belts, and, by Lance's standards, they had just barely qualified to apply.

Three applications in three years. All three rejected with vague explanations as to why. This was their fourth, and since not much had changed since his application last year, he suspected he'd lose this one too.

Lance had some hidden reason for refusing them Guardian status. Maybe he thought Izzy and Matt lacked the necessary experience. Maybe the governing Assembly had convinced him they weren't ready.

Izzy had confided in Matt that she thought Lance was afraid to lose another Guardian pair.

"I don't know if we'll get it this time, Iz," Matt said. "Especially if Lance really is paranoid about losing us, like you think."

Izzy eyed him. "He's not paranoid. He's lost two pairs already. That's unheard of in a single Master Guardian's rule, especially when they weren't even in war. All of them died on what should have been simple missions. Hell, our dads weren't even *on* a mission when they were killed. They were just in the wrong place at the wrong time."

"But it's part of the job," Matt said. "Guardians take on some of the most difficult and dangerous tasks the Defenders face. They die. It happens. We accept that when we sign up for it. And whether he likes it or not, he's not going to be able to go much longer without appointing someone. The Assembly won't stand for it."

"They have for over sixty years."

"Yeah, but even the old slugs have limits to their patience," Matt said. "And we're not getting any younger."

"You're only sixty, Matt."

"Fifty-nine."

"Water *below,* Matt, " Izzy said. "You haven't even hit your first century yet, and you've got four to live, assuming Guardianship doesn't take that away from you."

"It'll never have a chance to if Lance doesn't appoint us."

"Matt."

He met Izzy's eyes.

"Don't be in a hurry."

But he was in a hurry. And Izzy should be too. They were wasting precious time sitting idle while they could be doing a Guardian's work.

"You know," Izzy continued. "It might help if you'd actually listen to command instead of charging into everything you do like a moron."

Matt shot her a glare. "I listen."

"Not well enough," Izzy said. "We've all noticed it."

Matt crossed his arms. "If I need to take an unusual action on a mission, I'm not going to wait for authority to approve it. That's one of the perks of being a Guardian."

"But you're not a Guardian yet," Izzy said. "And it's not just on missions, Matt. You question a lot. You need to follow orders. You're a soldier."

Matt shrugged. "I'm a Guardian."

"Not yet you're not."

"But I will be."

Izzy sighed. She gripped Matt's shoulder, squeezing water out of his shirt. "Come on, Matt. I need a shower and you owe me breakfast. We'll figure out where we stand at some point today. No sense in worrying about it too much, right?"

He glanced at her. "You brought it up."

"And now I'm dropping it. You're too stubborn to listen anyway." Izzy turned toward the carved stairs in the cliff. "Breakfast?"

"Fine, fine," he said. "I'll be right there."

Izzy smiled, then started up the stairs.

Matt turned back to the beach and let the waves lap at his still-bare feet. Should he even hope for Guardianship anymore? It seemed so far out of reach. And if Lance really was worried about losing his third pair of Golden Guardians, the idea that he'd ever fill that role was pretty much nonexistent.

It was in Draso's claws now. If the dragon god really wanted him in this position, He'd give it to him. If not...

Well. No use in thinking about that, right?

"From my thoughts to Draso's ears," he said, tilting his head up to the sky in prayer to the feather-winged dragon. Surely He would bless Matt's willingness to sacrifice for the greater good. Then Matt jogged after Izzy.

Time to learn his fate, whatever it was.

CHAPTER 02

CHANGE OF PLANS

"This isn't really what I had in mind when you promised me breakfast," Izzy groaned. She wore her full Defender uniform now – black with white and gray accents, indicating her Gem magic specialty as healing. She also wore her personal battle hammer, more for decoration than anything. Eying Matt, she slipped her Defender pendant around her neck. The brightly polished, black, legless dragon held a red Gem in its coils.

The pair stood at the entrance to the Academy's cafeteria, known as The Grill. Normally The Grill was quiet at this early hour, but now it buzzed with activity. Today was the annual Defender Advancement and Open House, and the whole campus was up early to prep for the event.

An event that Matt and Izzy would hopefully be a part of today, if they got the Guardianship. But that seemed less and less likely, considering the Advancement Ceremony was only a few hours away and they still hadn't heard from the Master Guardian one way or another.

15

A mix of soft feral barks, meows, growls, chirps and other assorted animal sounds hovered over the visitors. The room smelled of hot breakfast – everything from eggs to cooked meats, to waffles, oatmeal, fruit, and coffee. The light entering the big picture window on the far end cast long shadows over everything from the tables and support pillars.

More than a few Defenders lifted their heads at Matt and Izzy's entrance. Matt tried to ignore the stares, though he was careful to return a salute should anyone give him one. He and Izzy were top-ranked Defenders – just below the highest class of ranks. That, on top of the well-known fact that they were applying for Guardianship meant they generally got a lot of stares and salutes when they entered a room, especially when they were in uniform. While Matt didn't technically have to salute back at his high rank, he always made sure to return the courtesy. All soldiers should be respected, regardless of rank or power.

"Your hubby didn't join us today?" Matt said, ignoring Izzy's protests. He returned a salute to a Defender recruit.

"Roscoe is already with Darvin and Sami prepping for the Open House," Izzy said, also returning the salute. The recruit smiled sheepishly at them then ran after her friends.

"His loss." Matt grinned. "Hey, the cafeteria is having a special on Tioka toast this morning." His black, teal-lined elemental specialty uniform carried the wrinkles of something slightly neglected, though his identical Defender pendant had been shined to a mirror sheen.

Izzy flattened one ear and stuck out her tongue. "Bleh. They dip that stuff in raw egg and then *fry* it. You know I hate fried foods. And eggs."

"You put eggs in your homemade pasta."

Izzy crossed her arms. "That's different."

"If you want to believe that."

"Matt."

16

Matt laughed. "Fine, just get your usual oatmeal-flavored wallpaper paste." He handed her a tray. "Or indulge a little and get a waffle."

"I should break your bank account and get one of everything since you're paying," Izzy said, dropping a yogurt on the tray.

"Grandis Regini Azure and Gildspine," a voice said behind them. "May I trouble you a moment?"

Matt turned at the mention of his name and rank. A black, blue streaked wolf with a white muzzle stood at full attention behind him, not quite meeting their eyes. His blue-tipped ear twitched as he watched them.

Cix Terrill, Matt's dear friend and weapons-specialty partner. Cix wore a uniform identical to Matt's, indicating his fire-wielding Gem specialty. The Gem at his side was jet black with streaks of white through it, catching the early morning light. The blue-dyed fur was strictly non-regulation, but since Zyearth was at peace, regulation breaks often slipped by unnoticed. And hey, the touch of rebellion was one of the things Matt liked about him anyway.

Matt eyed Cix. "'May I trouble you a moment?' Using our full rank names? Come on, Cix. You never talk like that. Especially with me."

Cix shook his head and eased himself a little, though he didn't smile. "Normally I wouldn't, but when the Master Guardian himself sends you with orders, you tend to take yourself a bit more seriously."

"*You* do, maybe," Matt said, though a flood of adrenaline shot through him. Orders? Was the Master Guardian summoning them to his office? Were they finally going to get the Guardianship?

Cix frowned, bending his ear back. He fiddled with an official-looking envelope in his black, white tipped fingers. "From the Master Guardian. Obviously I haven't looked at this myself. You nervous?"

Matt eyed the paper hungrily. "Anxious."

Cix passed it to him. "Good luck, you two. Hope to see you in the ceremony with me later today."

17

Matt forced himself to be social, though the anxiety ran through his bones. "You're being promoted, aren't you?"

"Finally hitting Captain." Cix perked his ears, smiling, his tail swishing slowly from side to side. "I wish Mom and Dad could be here, but Dad got stationed in the Archipelago and can't get the leave yet and Mom is having a hell of a time getting Robert adjusted. She didn't want to drag him out here, and I don't blame her."

"Your brother's what, seven now?" Izzy asked.

"Eight next month," Cix said with a grin. "Already got leave to go visit them. We'll celebrate my promotion then. At least I've got Pasadena, Griffon, and the twins coming, though they've joked that it's because they're loyal Defenders rather than loyal family members."

Matt faked a laugh, but failed to keep his ears perked and couldn't manage a smile.

Cix flicked one ear back. "You'll get the Guardianship soon enough, Matt. Today or otherwise. But I hope to see you up on stage with me. Maybe you could come visit the family for a day or two with me next month. Robert would love you."

He managed a smile now. "Thanks. Let's plan for it."

"Later, partner." He flashed a quick salute, a sweep of his fist across his chest, then left.

Matt's hand shook as he opened the envelope, praying it was a summons to the Master Guardian's office.

The envelope held a half-sheet of paper. Words littered the page in a dull black.

Matt gripped the paper, shock racing through his body.

What the hell was this? A *rejection letter?* He couldn't bother to tell them face to face? He just sent Cix? When he knew Cix was going to be promoted today? Water above, what a kick to the gut.

And what the hell did he mean by "thank you for your service"? That was practically a dismissal. And nothing, literally nothing, about *why* they were rejected or what they could do to improve. Just a simple form letter. A *form* letter. Lance couldn't have been ruder, which really wasn't like him.

Izzy pasted her ears back, but she shrugged. "I can't say I'm surprised."

"I can," Matt snarled. "This isn't right, Izzy. A form letter sent along with another Defender? He can't even meet with us directly?"

"Well, the Open House is today. . ."

"That's not an excuse," Matt said. "This is too important to dismiss with a damn form letter. He should be meeting with us, or at least calling. He's avoiding us."

Izzy pinned her ears back. "He doesn't think we're ready."

"You say that like you don't think we are either."

Izzy frowned, but she didn't say anything.

Matt frowned then hardened his features. He folded the paper and stuffed it in his pocket. "I'm sick of this cat-and-mouse game. I'm going to go find him myself and get to the bottom of this."

Izzy wrinkled her snout. "You can't just go marching into his office."

"We'll see about that, won't we?" He picked up a pair of apples, paid for them, and tossed one to Izzy. "Are you with me?"

Izzy's fur bristled. "No real breakfast then."

"This is more important."

Izzy bit into the apple. Juice dripped down a long, sharp incisor.

"Izzy?"

Izzy sighed. "Fine. Let's get going."

Matt led the way out of The Grill and ran for the offices, Izzy trailing behind. They jogged through The Meadow, the large grassy square where the Open House was going to be held later that day. Booths and shops had already been set up and while the faire portion didn't technically open for another hour, Defenders and civilians alike wandered about.

It didn't take long to get to the main entrance to the offices. It was quieter than the rest of the campus, since most zyfaunos were off for the day and getting ready for the Open House.

So it took Matt by surprise when he found Domini Defender Larissa Hobbes waiting inside the lobby.

Matt stood at immediate attention. "Ma'am!" Izzy followed Matt's example.

The old silver and maroon badger stood, standing a few inches taller than Izzy. She left her cane on the chair, a necessity after a battle injury to the leg that she frequently ignored and openly hated. Experienced and cunning, DD Larissa led the entire Defender army, being ranked just one step below the Master Guardian himself. She was getting on in years though, nearing the middle of her final century of life, and there were rumors that she was thinking of retiring.

Larissa's wife Viriandia, a silver-gray, floppy-eared rabbit, sat in one of the chairs next to her, nose buried in a data slate. Viri lead the Defender's weapons development and had no intention of retiring, despite being nearly as old as Larissa. Matt had always thought her manic need to work would drive her to her grave. Larissa didn't seem bothered by it though.

Larissa glanced at Matt and Izzy over her glasses before nodding acknowledgement. "Azure, Gildspine. At ease. What brings you here today? I would expect you to be getting ready for the Open House."

Matt pressed his lips together and flipped his ears back. "Ah, we were hoping to catch Master Guardian Tox." Viri finally put the data slate down and lifted her head at the mention of the Master Guardian.

"Ah, yes," Larissa said. "I suspect this is about the Guardianship. I'm sure he's sorry he couldn't tell you himself, but he's a busy zyfaunos, what with the Open House and all."

Viri smiled. "And speaking of, congratulations!"

Izzy blinked. "I'm sorry?"

"On earning the Guardianship!" Viri said. "The Assembly finally approved your application last month. About damn time too. Larissa told me all about it, though it was technically supposed to be Vaulted until Lance told you himself. Top secret and all that."

"I know Lance was waiting to sign the final approval closer to the Open House. He insisted we all keep the whole thing under wraps or I would have told you sooner," Larissa continued. "I suspect he waited a bit too long which is why he told you through paper, but he was never as organized as Lovetta. We always joked that she was the real Master Guardian in her time." She trailed into a story about Lovetta and Lance.

21

But Matt didn't hear any of it. The Assembly had *approved* their applications? But Lance's letter had rejected them! Technically he had that veto power, but the letter made it sound as if the Assembly had rejected them as well. Had the Assembly approved their other applications over the years too? What the hell was going on here?

Izzy shifted. "Ah, DD Hobbes, if you wouldn't mind..."

"Izzy? Matt?" The baritone voice stood Matt's fur on end. He turned.

The Master Guardian, Lance Tox, walked into view. He glanced at them through thin glasses, his yellow eyes neutral and his white wolf ears perked straight up. His black, teal-accented uniform, indicating his ice fabrication magic, also bore gold accents along the seams, as did his jet-black Defender pendant, identifying him as the Master Guardian. He stood straight and tall, though he tilted his head curiously.

Matt stood stiffly at attention, despite his frustrations, and Izzy, Larissa, and Viri followed suit. This was the Master Guardian. The leader of the country of Zedric, the Defender army, the Assembly... everything. The zyfaunos responsible for Matt's future.

This was also the wolf that had rejected his application four times, despite at least one Assembly approval.

Lance cleared his throat, his inner ears slightly pink against white fur. He immediately took on the voice of a leader of many. "At ease, Defenders." Everyone eased their positions. He adjusted the glasses perched on his snout. "What brings you here? I expected you to be preparing for the Open House."

Matt frowned. "Sir, if I may--"

"I'm sure they were just coming to talk about their new positions as Guardians," Viri said suddenly.

Izzy shifted, bending both ears back. Matt cleared his throat.

Lance pinned his ears back as well and wrinkled his long snout. "I didn't grant them the Guardianship."

And there it was, straight from the lion's mouth. Lance hadn't approved their applications. Lance, the doting uncle who had been training them for this position the moment Matt and Izzy joined the Young Defenders, who had pushed them to be the very best they could, who told them again and again that their fathers would be proud, had betrayed them. Matt's insides churned.

Larissa raised both eyebrows and her fur stood on end. She exchanged a glance with her wife. "You didn't?"

"No," Lance said, studiously avoiding Matt and Izzy's gaze. "I don't believe they're ready."

She looked at him incredulously. "But the Assembly--"

"Is not privy to their training and experience like I am," Lance said, still looking away from Matt. "If I say they're not ready, then they're not. End of discussion."

Larissa frowned. "But--"

"End of discussion, Larissa," Lance said. He finally met Matt and Izzy's eyes. "If you would like to talk about the rejection, it can wait until after the Open House."

"Can't you say anything about it, Lance? Just a hint?" Matt blurted. Izzy kicked his shin, but he ignored it.

"Another time," Lance said. "But right now, we have a job to do, and I better not hear any more objections. Do I make myself clear?"

Every bone in Matt's body screamed at him to object, to yell, to demand an explanation right here, right now. Where was the Lance he knew? The wolf who had been training him since the moment his Gem broke and he got his powers? The Master Guardian who couldn't wait to induct them into the Guardianship and see them as peers, rather than just average soldiers? But he bit his tongue. Like it or not, Lance's word was law, and he wouldn't be proving himself Guardian material if he let his anger get the better of him. "Yes, sir."

23

"Yes, sir," Izzy repeated, her voice strained.

"Good," Lance said. "Today, go mingle in the crowd and get some good PR in. Matt, I believe your sister is supposed to be here soon anyway."

And Matt's sister Charlotte would be perfectly happy hearing Matt hadn't gotten the Guardianship. She meant well, but she'd never approved of Matt's bid for it, considering the way their parents had died. "Yes, sir."

"Coward," Larissa muttered before heading out of the building. Matt stared at her. Had she seriously just said that? Did Lance hear? He looked over. Viri and Izzy wore shocked looks, but Lance didn't even acknowledge it. Maybe he hadn't.

Damn, that was cold. Matt watched her a moment before saluting one more time to Lance, begrudgingly, and leading Izzy out of the building. At least one person had the guts to say what they were all thinking. Lance watched them, his face unreadable.

What had they done wrong? What was keeping them from Guardianship?

"This would not happen if we were at war," Larissa grumbled. "This life of peace has made kits and cubs of us all."

"La-La, don't say that," Viri said with a frown. "That's bad luck."

"Hrmm."

Izzy stared at Larissa, shocked. "Pardon me, Ma'am, but you can't seriously be wishing we were at war."

"All I'm wishing for is something to prove we still need our Guardians. If you want peace, prepare for war. I think Lance has forgotten that." She looked at the two of them and sighed. "We will make your fathers proud, one way or another. Mark my words." She walked off, standing straight, brandishing her cane like a bat. The limp was hardly noticeable. Viri let out an exaggerated sigh and followed.

Izzy crossed her arms. "That's just the words of an old badger used to war. She didn't mean that."

24

Matt frowned. That was quite a declaration. But she had a point. Not about preparing for war, but… maybe the life of peace was too much. Maybe Lance worried they hadn't faced enough difficulty. Maybe he thought they were too soft.

Draso's horns. Something better happen soon to prove they weren't before they lost the Guardianship completely.

CHAPTER 03

OURANOS

A tall, black quilar with bare feet, short quills, and long, ribbon-wrapped spines flowing off the back of his head drew stares as he wandered among the tents, tables, and conversations littered around the big grassy knoll. His long red pants dragged around his feet and the wind tickled the fur on his bare chest. The air smelled of indiscernible meat cooking, mingling with sweets and spices, some familiar, most foreign. The alien accented speech mixed with a variety of barks, mews, chirps, and other animal sounds. Bits of fur, down, and various hairs danced on the wind around him.

The group of zyfaunos was far more diverse than he expected. One would think that the diversity would make it easier for him to hide, but perhaps he should not have been so optimistic. After all, he was the only Athánatos quilar on the entire planet.

And he was lucky to be that, after the crash a full week earlier. The artificial intelligence piloting the ship had had enough power to mask their decent and subsequent collision with the planet's surface, though he was running low on energy. No doubt the A.I. would have to drop the mask soon, lest he whittle his digital essence away from power withdrawals.

Once the mask dropped, it was only a matter of time before these Defenders discovered him. And yet, he still had not found his target. The white and blue Zyearthling who carried a dragon.

He flattened one cone-shaped ear against his head and stopped. Various Zyearthlings watched him, some disturbed, most curious.

His thoughts warred. On the one hand, finding the correct Zyearthling granted his enemy a powerful tool of destruction.

On the other, he needed the Zyearthling to achieve his own goals and finally be free. And he had to be free if he wished to resume his campaign to save the Athánatos under his rule.

Ouranos, a voice echoed in his mind. A powerful force pushed through his limbs and forced his feet forward. *You will find the white and blue Zyearthling.*

Ouranos winced at the words. His father, Theron, Basileus ruler of the Athánatos quilar, occupied him body and mind, despite the distance between the planets they currently occupied. Like a string puppet awkwardly guided along on a tiny stage, he moved onward, unable to help himself.

His father's control was absolute, both with his control over Ouranos' body and his control over the Athánatos quilar at home.

But he did not control Ouranos' mind.

Though that was a relatively recent cure. He shook his head. Less cure, more makeshift bandage over a still-bleeding wound. A strange zyfaunos he had met at home had somehow bridged the gap between his body and the soul his father stole from him decades ago. While it did not allow him full control over his body, it did grant him the ability to once again build and recall memories.

Whether this was good or bad was left to be determined.

27

Natassa, his sister, had told him to seek out a blue and white Zyearthling. That they would be willing to help Ouranos. Though he was skeptical.

Could his soul be returned? Could he truly be free of his father's control? Or was he doomed to forever live this waking nightmare as the Basileus' tool for destruction? These thoughts haunted every waking moment.

There was one method for returning the soul of the still-living soulless, but the means were vague. The process, forbidden. With good reason, considering the cost of such a thing.

Prínkipas, his father spat Ouranos' royal title. *Eyes forward. Remember your goal.* He forced Ouranos forward, making awkward steps through the crowd. Several zyfaunos stared, but others purposefully looked away, clearly not wanting to get involved.

"Your goal, Father, not mine," Ouranos mumbled, though it fell on blocked ears.

It always fell on blocked ears. Ouranos, Prínkipas of the Athánatos, a marionette played by his father in the theater of war.

Prínkipas… By all rights, a ruler of Athánatos. And it was this claim that pushed him to free himself from his father. He needed that right as prince if he were to save his people from their warmongering king.

Ouranos knew three things about his target.

One, the Zyearthling had white fur and blue tipped ears and carried a dragon. He was not sure what that meant, but he assumed it would be obvious. Dragons were a rare sight.

Two, based on the Basileus' knowledge, his target had the ability to produce a liquid which, when properly refined, allowed for the creation of the Shadow Cast. He shuddered. Images of the broken, ruined, stolen shapes that made the Cast flooded his mind. He shook the memory free.

To your task, Ouranos.

Ouranos took a heavy breath.

28

Three, the Zyearthling supposedly had the power to allow Ouranos to escape the Basileus' puppetry control, a fact he had managed to keep from his father. How Natassa knew this, and how she had been able to pass the information to Ouranos without informing their father, he knew not.

But it did not matter. Not if he could get that power.

Only he was unsure of how to acquire it. Natassa had not provided a means.

Your TASK Ouranos. NOW.

Ouranos winced again. Surely his strange body tics drew even more stares. Thank Draso his father no longer had access to his thoughts.

A chill drove up Ouranos' spine. Everything stiffened at once and Theron directed Ouranos' gaze to the left.

He froze.

There, hidden among the crowd, surrounded by zyfaunos wearing similar outfits, was the first white and blue Zyearthling he had seen since invading this strange campus. His prey.

The Zyearthling, a quilar, masculine, stood taller than he expected, almost nearing Ouranos' height, which was practically unheard of outside the Athánatos subspecies. His bright green eyes stood out against his white fur, and the blue tips on his ears were unmistakable. He looked… angry, perhaps, or at least upset. Ouranos saw no dragon, but who else could this be? There were no other white and blue Zyearthlings.

Ouranos licked his lips, though he was unsure if he or his father had performed the action. Finally. But how to get to him? The crowds made it difficult to approach already, and the zyfaunos following him did not disperse. A bodyguard perhaps? Not likely, as the golden-brown female did not even look his equal, let alone his superior. Though she did carry an air of strength about her, and looks could be deceiving. How could Ouranos get her away from his quarry? Perhaps--

The Basileus pulled at Ouranos' body. *Take him now.*

Ouranos fought back. *Father--*

Now!

He is protected! Ouranos hissed back. *I need a diversion.*

Summon the Phonar.

Adrenaline quickened Ouranos' heart. The Phonar summons would certainly distract the Defenders… but summoning them would give Theron control over them. And while Ouranos feared for the innocent lives they might destroy, the Basileus had no such worries.

This is not a suggestion, Prínkipas. You will do as I command.

No. I will not. He pressed all his energy and thought into controlling his body, desperate to push his father out.

You will not win! A spike of pain burst through him, dragging him to his knees. He bit his tongue, desperate to keep silent. More bystanders stared at him, though no one came to his aid. *I alone control you. You know this. You will do as I say. Now stand.*

Ouranos did. Still a puppet. Still controlled.

His only hope lay in his prey.

He must succeed in acquiring that prey before it was too late.

CHAPTER 04

PROOF

Matt trudged behind Izzy, fiddling with his Defender pendant. By now, the Open House had started proper and the Meadow was full of booths, greasy faire food, music, and loud conversation. Defenders and civilians alike walked about grinning, stuffing their faces with caramel popcorn, and buying trinkets like plastic Defender pendants, homemade scarves, and stuffed dolls that they'd forget about in a week.

Matt ignored the crowd, meditating on Larissa's words. *Something to prove we still need our Guardians...* But what? A chance to prove his prowess in magic? He had heard a few people discussing some rumor about wild air magic in Corinth Woods. Wind magic was his specialty and he might be called on to do something about it. Maybe that could prove something to Lance. But from what he'd gathered, it had already faded and it hadn't been anywhere near a civilian population anyway. No need to bother with it. Damn.

Not that Matt needed to prove his prowess with magic anyway. Lance already knew how powerful he was.

So what then? An impossible battle? Full-on war? An invasion? As much as Matt might agree that one of those would allow him and Izzy to prove themselves, he couldn't bring himself to wish for one. He wasn't stupid. War wasn't a game to prove yourself. That was dangerous thinking, no matter how much he wanted the Guardianship.

So what did Lance want from them?

His thoughts wandered to his conversation with Izzy that morning. Maybe she was right. Maybe Lance was afraid of losing another Guardian pair.

Matt formed a fist. Maybe he really was just being a coward.

Izzy shoved a stick of fried dough covered in cinnamon and sugar under Matt's nose, breaking his thoughts. He reeled back a minute before meeting Izzy's gaze.

She eyed him. "You're brooding."

"I am not."

Izzy shook the treat, raining cinnamon and sugar on the grass. "Then eat this. It's a better breakfast than just an apple."

Matt pinned one ear back. "You hate fried foods."

"I'll make an exception today," she said. "Just take it."

He sighed, then gingerly took the pastry. "I thought I was supposed to buy breakfast."

"I guess you buy lunch then," Izzy said. She took a bite out of her own treat. "I'd ask what's on your mind, but clearly I already know."

Matt sighed. "Yeah, it's--"

"Hey, Matt."

Matt turned and saw his sister, Charlotte, walking up, ears pinned back, no smile. She wore a simple gray shirt with a short white vest and black pants. Her long, blue-streaked white quills hung low on the sides of her face. She had a black cloth Gem pocket wrapped around her waist. The Gem in the pocket hung heavy at her side.

32

It wasn't her Gem, sadly. The Gem Sanctum hadn't been able to match her with a Gem when she came of age, so she shared a Gem bond with their Uncle Walt, allowing her to still have long life.

Gem sharing wasn't unusual – sometimes the Sanctum's Dragon Seer simply couldn't find a Gem "willing" to bind to a zyfaunos. Those who couldn't be bound could share a temporary bind with a family member until a Gem could be found, usually within the next few years.

Charlotte and Matt had visited the Dragon Seer every year after that, looking for a Gem for her. Forty years later and they still hadn't found anything.

Walt had passed away just two weeks ago, after his own bind with their shared Gem finally ended. Matt had never been that close with him, but for Charlotte, it was like losing a parent all over again.

It didn't help that she had to carry his Gem with her wherever she went. The only way she could still keep the benefits of their shared bind was to keep the Gem close by. Salt in the wound, Charlotte had told Matt.

Matt mentally pushed aside his own troubles. He tucked his Defender pendant under his shirt – she hated seeing him wear it – and hugged his sister. The Guardianship would always be there, but this trouble was more immediate. "Hey sis."

She hugged him back a moment before letting go. "Any news about the Guardianship?"

Matt raised an eyebrow and perked his ears. "Getting right to the point, huh?"

Charlotte rubbed her arm. Her pink eyes gleamed as if she was holding in tears. "Honestly, I'd kind of just like to know. Get it over with."

Matt frowned, reminding himself that Charlotte had every right to be thankful that he hadn't gotten the Guardianship. She had already lost so much family and she didn't want to lose more. "We ah, didn't get it. Lance said he'd talk about why after the ceremony."

Even though he knew it was coming, the relief on Charlotte's face felt like someone had ripped one of his fingerclaws straight out at the root. She immediately schooled her face. "Sorry, Matt, I know you really want it, and I shouldn't be happy that you didn't get it, but--"

"I get it, I get it," Matt said. "You don't have to explain each time. Especially after... after Walt."

Charlotte shifted her weight, staring at the ground with her ears flattened. "Thanks for understanding."

"Hey." Izzy handed Charlotte an extra pastry. "I know there's not a lot I can say to help ease your hurt, but hopefully a tasty snack will do a little something."

Charlotte smiled weakly and took it. "Thanks."

"Hey, Matt!"

Matt turned, catching a glimpse of a black stag with silver antlers. Darvin Polttarit, in full uniform, navy blue accents for his cloaking abilities. Darvin's brother and Izzy's husband, Roscoe Gildspine, jogged up toward them, his gray fur and copper antlers gleaming in the light. He had his left sleeve rolled up, revealing his gold, ruby studded wedding coil. Sami Girsougon, an arctic fox, followed behind. Both wore the teal accented uniforms for elemental magic.

Izzy smiled and gave her husband a kiss. "Hey, hun. Missed you at breakfast."

"Sorry about that," Roscoe said. "I had to get an early start."

"It is what it is," Izzy said. She turned to her brother-in-law. "How's that eye doing, Darvin?"

"So-so." Darvin pawed his left eye. The normally deep-green eye had odd white spots in it -- a souvenir from his last mission which had earned him a splash of Lexi acid in the face after his Gem overloaded and formed an acid mist around it. A product of him using too much Gem power for too long a time. "The doctor says I'm lucky I didn't lose the eye. I can basically only see spots out of it, though the doctor's hopeful for a full recovery."

"That's good news, honestly," Matt said. "Lexi acid is no joke."

"So, are we talking to the Defender's newest Golden Guardians?" Darvin said, punching Matt's arm playfully.

Matt flattened his ears.

Darvin frowned, his large ears twitching. "That's a no then."

"We got our rejection letter this morning," Izzy said.

Sami's tail stopped its slow swish. "Wait, a *rejection letter*? He didn't tell you face to face?"

"No," Matt said, crossing his arms. "We had to go hunt him down just to get a confirmation. The worst part was that Larissa told us that the Assembly had approved the application."

Roscoe's jaw dropped. "You're *kidding.*"

"If only," Matt said. "Viri even said it was about time. Makes me wonder if Lance has been pushing for them to deny it and when he couldn't get them to, he just vetoed it." He growled. "Burns me up."

Darvin twitched his nose. "Did he say why?"

"Apparently we'll be talking about it after the Open House," Izzy said.

Roscoe wrapped his arms around his wife and muttered his condolences. "I'm sorry, hun. I know how much you want that. Hopefully Lance will actually give you a legit reason today that you can actually work toward. The whole thing is so damn unfair."

Matt furrowed his brow. "Izzy thinks he's afraid of losing another Guardian pair."

Darvin perked his ears and exchanged a glance with Sami. He wrinkled his long snout. "I mean, I suppose I can't blame him, considering his history."

35

Roscoe clutched Izzy tighter. Izzy gripped his arm.

"That's not an excuse," Matt said, ignoring Izzy and Roscoe. "We need our Guardians. Even Larissa said so. He's just being a coward."

Everyone stared wide-eyed at Matt.

He shrugged. "Larissa said it first."

"And he didn't court martial her?" Roscoe said.

"I don't think he heard her," Matt admitted. "But it doesn't mean she's wrong."

Izzy furrowed her brow. "Matt…"

"Can we please end this conversation?" Charlotte said. Matt frowned at her, opening his mouth, but he couldn't bring himself to say anything. Charlotte hugged herself, flattening her ears. "Please?"

The group fell into awkward silence, but no one continued.

Darvin eventually broke it. "I think they're going to start the advancement ceremony soon. We should head to the Arena."

Matt sighed. Great. One more year standing in the crowd, watching his friends and fellow soldiers advance while he missed out on the Guardianship. Again. He shook his head. What right did he have to think that way? He should be happy for his fellow soldiers, dang it.

But the loss still stung, especially after learning the Assembly had approved their applications.

Izzy gripped his shoulder. "Next year."

"I doubt it," Matt grumbled. Izzy didn't protest.

"I think I'm going to check out the booths," Charlotte said. "I'd rather not see the ceremony. Meet up for lunch?"

Matt nodded, warring with wanting his sister to be happy and wanting the Guardianship. "Sure."

Charlotte forced a smile again and headed deeper into the faire. Matt pressed his lips together, making a mental note to do something nice for her later. She could definitely use it.

He followed Izzy and the others to the large open-air stage carved into a massive rock near the edge of the Meadow. The stage was sunk into the ground, and surrounded by tier seating, sculpted out of the hills and paved with grasses and stones. Small pine trees pockmarked the edges of the stage and seating, filling the area with the trees' sweet scent.

The stands were quite full already, but the crowds parted when Matt and Izzy approached. Those in uniform usually saluted since they outranked nearly everyone there, but the civilians tended to avoid them, eyeing them suspiciously and muttering to themselves. One word fell from their mouths constantly -- Black Bound.

Matt kept his expression neutral and his gaze forward while they walked, though he couldn't help but hear the murmurs around them.

Fire and ice, he hated that.

While Black Binding was a rare occurrence, it wasn't that amazing. It just meant that Matt had bound himself to his Gem instead of someone else binding him. Izzy had also bound herself, and while the fact that they both bound themselves at the same time and both survived was unusual, it wasn't impossible.

But to most Defenders, that meant they were practically gods. Black Bound individuals were rumored to be the most powerful bound jewel users in history.

For others, though, it meant they were broken, unpredictable, and dangerous. The polarizing responses made it difficult to cope at times. Especially since neither Matt nor Izzy believed Black Binding made them special. They certainly hadn't shown themselves to be the godlike powerhouses that the rumors painted them as.

Roscoe gripped Izzy's hand while they walked, and Darvin and Sami were perfectly at ease around them, chattering away about some book they were both reading. At least a few Defenders didn't treat them any different because of their Black Binding.

Normally Matt would insist on being front and center for an Arena event, but he had faced enough disappointment that day. He didn't feel like subjecting himself to more by sticking himself in a place where everyone could see he hadn't gotten the Guardianship. Instead, he found a spot near the top of grandstands in the far-left corner and waved at the group to join him. Darvin raised an eyebrow in confusion, but Matt's gaze shut down any questions. The group found seats on the cool grass and waited.

The opening ceremony was always a bore at these things. Talks about the ideals of the Defenders, their original creation, their current advancements, that sort of thing. Then, the introduction of new recruits. Matt liked to pick out which ones he thought had the best chance of making it through their first year – the Defender boot camp was brutal and weeded a lot out – but today, he couldn't summon the enthusiasm.

Then came the commissioned officers, receiving medals, insignia, and swearing their new oaths to the Defenders. The Defenders were a relatively small army, given the size of their planet. Only about 25,000 strong, and most on other bases or at home awaiting orders. No need to keep everyone on campus during times of peace. As a result, commissions were rare these days, so only fourteen Defenders were ready to receive honors.

And in Matt's mind, the only one who really mattered was Cix. At least one Defender should get the position they deserved today.

When it was Cix's turn, Matt gave the wolf his full attention, clapping at all the right places, enjoying his friend's excitement. Cix beamed when Larissa pinned the Captain's insignia on his freshly pressed uniform. He then held up his hand and began his oath of office.

"I, Cix Terrill, do solemnly swear to serve my country and Master Guardian. I will support and defend the Assembly Papers of Zedric against all enemies, both foreign and domestic…"

Matt's thoughts wandered away from Cix's oath and to a very different one - the Guardian Oath. One he had had memorized for years, just waiting for the chance to swear it and live by it. He closed his eyes and whispered the Guardian Oath while Cix finished his.

"…I solemnly swear to support my fellow soldiers, protect the innocent, defend all creatures, and uphold the Defender Spirit. I swear to put my charges and my mission first. I understand and am willing to put my life on the line to abide by the code of the Guardian. I take this obligation of my own freewill and will faithfully perform to the best of my ability from now until the end of my service or until death takes me. I swear this before Lord Draso, and his sacrificial offspring Kai. *Tel rasta separit vasa bayfore--*"

Someone screamed.

Matt flashed his eyes open and he leapt to his feet. The crowd flew into a state of panic, some pushing each other aside, others frozen in place, most staring at the sky. Matt followed their gaze.

A large lightning bolt streaked just inches above the trees surrounding the Arena, branching into tiny bolts, catching the treetops on fire. It moved far too slowly to be natural. It almost looked like it was flapping wings…

That meant it was magic. Matt's heart raced. *Magic.* They were under attack.

They were under attack!

"Defenders!" Lance bellowed. "To arms! Find the source and end that thing! Get the civilians to safety! Water fabricators, get those fires out!"

Matt's training kicked in and his body buzzed with adrenaline. "Everyone, with me!" he said to his group. No, not his group. His *pack.* They were in battle. The Guardian Oath flashed in his mind.

Protect the innocent. Support his fellow soldiers. The best way to do both was to take charge and eliminate the problem.

Time to do this.

"Let's get whatever's causing that electricity!" He ran for the odd, flapping streak of lightning on the other end of the Arena. Darvin, Roscoe, Sami, and Izzy followed behind.

The earth violently shook as they ran, throwing everyone to the ground. Matt rolled to a kneeling position. "Earthquake?"

"No," Roscoe said. He placed a hand on the earth, scratching the dirt with his finger hooves, and his features hardened. "That's not natural."

A loud crack sounded in the middle of the Arena's seating, and rock and sand burst up from the ground. When the dust settled, a tiny bird hovered over a fissure in the stands, blowing away huge clouds of dust with its strangely large wings. It held its place in the air surprisingly steadily, considering how little it flapped its wings. It must be flying with magic.

Matt couldn't tell for sure what it was – the thing was shrouded in dust - but it looked like a miniature owl. Only it was off, considering the impossibly long feathered tail and unnaturally large flight feathers. As they neared it, a distinctive, musky smell of earth assailed his nose.

The bird let out a high-pitched hoot and twirled into the air, leaving the ground shaking like mad and scattering dust and rocks.

Roscoe tensed, pinning his ears back and forming fists. He pressed his hands to the dirt again and with careful control, calmed the earthquake the bird had caused. He stood and glanced at Matt. "I need to go after that thing. We don't have a lot of earth manipulators to fight it."

"Take Darvin and Sami with you," Matt said. "You'll need the support."

Roscoe nodded. He squeezed Izzy's hand. "Stick with Matt and get this thing. Lance may not think you're Guardian material, but I know better. You've got this." He ran off after the bird with Darvin and Sami behind him.

Izzy watched them run off. She pinned her ears and wrinkled her snout, looking around. "I… I should go find the healers. Kole or Kiara or Jordan. Help them."

Matt frowned, twitching his short tail. She couldn't do this now. This was their chance. "Izzy, I need you with me."

Izzy turned. "You don't need me."

"Yes, I *do,*" Matt said. "This is our chance to prove ourselves. I need my partner. We're going to be Guardians."

Izzy chewed her bottom lip. "Matt… I'm just a healer."

Ah. Back to the core of it again. He gripped her shoulders. "You're a *soldier.* This is what we've trained for. I know we can do this, but I need you with me."

Izzy furrowed her brow. "Matt, I…" She squeezed her eyes shut. "…Okay, fine."

Matt fought the urge to smile. He turned and ran for the flapping lightning, Izzy at his shoulder.

Time to prove himself.

CHAPTER 05

PHOENIX

Izzy raced after Matt as he chased the flying lightning. Damn it! Couldn't he slow down?

This was stupid. Utterly *stupid.* She was *support,* damn it. She shouldn't be fighting, she should be with the other healers. She wasn't a Guardian yet. Hell, she didn't know if she'd ever trust herself to be a Guardian, no matter what the Assembly said. Or Roscoe.

Lance was right to deny them. Her, at least.

This was so damn *stupid.*

Damn it all, what was Matt thinking? She couldn't back him up the way he wanted. He needed a partner who could actually support him, and she wasn't it.

She sucked in a breath as she ran. But he needed someone. She'd have to make do.

She slipped her war hammer out of her beltloop, both grateful that she had it and worried she'd have to use it. Memories flashed by. It hadn't been that long since the fight to get her Gem powers, and the battles clung to her, one big one in particular on the same beach she and Matt had run down that very morning. She found herself trapped in that memory.

Lance blasted ice at her and she dove into the water to escape.

Sea water rose around her. Her hammer dragged her under.

Roscoe's Gem broke. He chased Lance with earth spikes.

Lance panicked and stabbed him with ice. Blood gushed from the wound. *She was going to lose him.*

Her Gem finally broke giving her healing -- healing *-- but she saved Roscoe... just barely.*

"Izzy, eyes up!" Matt called.

Izzy turned her gaze up, the memories vanishing in an instant. The lightning bolt jolted toward them before letting loose a barrage of electricity among the stands. Somehow it missed everyone. Oddly missed everyone... almost like it was on purpose. Izzy shook her head. That couldn't be right.

It might have missed all the zyfaunos, but it connected with the ground, sending chunks of hardened debris in the air. As it whirled around, it almost "flapped" two wedged cages of electricity, like wings.

Like *wings*.

"Matt, that's got to be a bird too, like that other one," Izzy said. "What are these things? Elementals?" But they seemed way too strong to be elementals. And they usually only lasted a few minutes before the magic left whatever animal it had possessed.

Matt snarled. "I don't know, but it's about to get a dose of wind. Cover me!"

Izzy brandished her hammer. Matt formed a tight tornado, kicking up dust, grass, and small stones. She held her hand out and projected a shield in front of him. The air around him popped and a curved slab of light flashed green, then purple, then faded from view. Hopefully the shield would hold if

43

the bird thing hit him with a strong bolt, but Izzy had no idea. Her shields were stronger than average, but there were too many unknowns.

Draso's wings! Why couldn't she have gotten elemental magic? She'd be much more useful if she had. Matt would have the partner he needed.

Matt aimed his twister at the mass of electricity. It connected and sent the wild ball of electricity flying out of control before the it all but dissipated.

A tiny predatory bird with red tail feathers and gray spotted wings plummeted toward the ground before righting itself and alighting on a pine tree. It had a few impossibly long tail feathers with red peacock plumage scattered among normal feathers, similar to the other bird. A strong smell permeated the area. Izzy wiggled her snout, trying to place the scent. It was like a thunderstorm – cold, wet, with the sharp smell of electricity, accompanying an almost bitter taste on the tongue.

The bird's feathers crackled with solid bolts of electricity. With a loud shriek, it set itself ablaze with lightning again and rained it down around them.

Izzy shielded herself and attempted to strengthen Matt's shield, but a particularly large bolt smashed into her. She fell hard and her shield splintered, wedging pieces into the dirt before vanishing.

Matt's shield held, though, and he retaliated with another twister. But the bird leapt into the air and flew swiftly out of its path toward the shelter of trees.

Izzy snarled. It wasn't going to get away that easily. She scrambled to her feet and lifted the war hammer over her head with two hands, then sent it flying at the bird.

The hammer sailed through the air and caught one of the bird's tail feathers in the back spike before lodging itself in a nearby tree. The bird shrieked and crashed to the ground. It spread its wings and keened at Matt and Izzy, shooting tiny bolts at them.

Izzy hopped about to avoid them, but one hit her foot.

The Prinkipas needs help!

Izzy nearly fell over. What the hell was *that?* That was most definitely a voice in her head. Where did it come from?

Matt stood stunned as well. "Did you hear that?"

The small bird, a kestrel, Izzy decided, now that she could really see it, shrieked again and rained down more tiny bolts around them. Izzy reached for one this time. The bolt buzzed against her fur and skin, but didn't hurt or even leave a mark.

But that same voice echoed in her head.

The Prínkipas needs help!

"What the hell is a Prínkipas?" Matt said. He stared up at the bird. "Did that thing just talk to us?"

What kind of elemental spoke telepathically? That didn't make sense.

The bird keened again. It leapt into the air, tugging and pecking at its trapped tail feather until it finally pulled free. It left the tail feather buried and crackling in the tree with Izzy's hammer, then circled Izzy and Matt once, staring strangely at them, before tearing off toward the booths.

Izzy's skin grew cold. "Matt, the faire! The civilians!"

Then someone screamed, followed by a pained stag bellow.

Izzy froze. Roscoe. That was *Roscoe.* She glanced around the stands, frantic, but she couldn't see her husband anywhere for the dust and debris in the air. Memories crashed down again. Ice shard to Roscoe's gut, broken leg, damaged antler, nearly drowning-- *"Roscoe!"*

Matt hesitated, too. He turned back and forth between the stands and the bird, apparently unsure which to follow. He chewed his lip and turned to Izzy. "I'm going after the kestrel."

Izzy perked her ears. "What?"

"Go help Roscoe."

Izzy frowned. "But--"

45

"Just go!" Matt ran after the bird. "Send Sami and Cix my way when you can!"

Izzy stood in place, shaking. *Move, damnit!* She forced the memories away and rushed back toward her hammer.

The bird's tail feather was still alight with electricity. And Izzy's hammer was metal. She couldn't touch it without getting a massive electric shock.

Roscoe bellowed again.

Izzy abandoned the weapon and ran toward her husband instead, hammer be damned. She'd have to do this without it. Damn it, why did she get stuck with healing?

Draso, please protect Roscoe until I can get there!

SUMMONS

Izzy rushed toward the stage amid the cloud of dust and debris. Spectators flew by, covering their faces. She pulled up a shield, hoping it would keep her lungs from filling with sand.

Roscoe. Where was Roscoe?

"Izzy!" Cix jogged up, shielding his own face and coughing. He let out a low wolf whine, shaking his black and white fur free of dust. "Are you okay? Where's Matt?"

"Headed for the booths," Izzy said. "Have you seen Roscoe?"

Cix's face grew dark. "Not since Lance took off to put out fires."

She didn't wait to hear more. She dove into the dust. Cix followed. After a hard minute of pushing through the wall of sand, they emerged near the stage into a pocket of air, free of dust, like the eye of a hurricane.

The bird, a tiny owl of some kind, hovered in place, ducking and dodging fireballs and ice shards. But Izzy couldn't see where the fire and ice came from. Whose magic was that?

Cix pointed. "There."

A gleam of silver caught bits of light near the edge of the stage. Darvin. He kneeled down, hovering an arm over something invisible and his Gem was lit up. He must be cloaking Sami and Lance... and likely Roscoe, if she read his protective arm position correctly. Someone in any case. He clenched his teeth, bending both ears back, clearly strained. The stage wasn't great protection, but so far, the bird hadn't noticed him. Izzy wished for the thousandth time that Gem powers worked on their users. He'd be much safer if he could cloak himself too.

"He must have Roscoe," she said. She found a path along the edge of the sand wall and sprinted toward Darvin. Cix followed.

Roscoe flickered into view next to Darvin. He reached for his brother, who had collapsed with exhaustion.

She needed to get to them *now*.

"Sami, it sees you!" Lance shouted. "Shield up!"

Izzy turned. Both Lance and Sami were visible now too. The owl spat a dark *hoot hoot hoot* and a row of earth spikes chased Sami down.

But the earth rumbled, and the spikes stopped as quickly as they'd started before sinking back into the ground. Izzy chanced a glance at Roscoe and Darvin. Both were slumped over, but Roscoe had a hand pressed to the dirt to counter the bird's magic. Darvin huffed, waving a hand around his face. He must have overloaded his Gem's power and couldn't cloak them anymore.

Cix growled. "I've got to go help them. Get to Roscoe. He's in a bad way." He rushed toward Sami. Izzy continued her sprint along the sand wall, keeping one eye on the battle.

The owl snapped its beak and spread its wings wide. Its feathers shook, then hardened into jagged spikes of earth. It dove at Sami. Sami shrieked and shielded, but the shield remained stubbornly green and weak. Cix got there in time to block the bird with an invisible shield of his own.

48

Izzy tore her gaze away from them. She needed to help Roscoe. They could take care of themselves. She raised a hand to catch his attention.

"Cix, Sami, down *now!*" Lance shouted. Then he screamed.

Izzy stopped in her tracks and turned back to the battle. Lance never screamed.

He lay on the ground, gripping a very bloody arm, eyes shut, ears pinned back, teeth clenched. Sami was at his side, pressing her jacket to the wound. Cix hovered over them both, projecting a purple shield in front of him.

Izzy's ears grew cold. He'd never fend off an attack with a purple-level shield. And Lance...

But Roscoe...

The bird circled around, hardened its feathers into spikes again, then dove at Cix's shield. He snarled at it as it hit. The shield held, but cracked and the edges splintered and broke apart.

Izzy hesitated. Heal Roscoe, or help Lance? Her husband, or her Master Guardian? Play support... or play the Guardian?

The bird spun about for another attack.

No time. She ran toward Lance and the others. "Hey, owl!"

The owl stalled in midair and turned toward Izzy. Its musky dirt smell ripped through her senses.

What the hell was she doing? She didn't have a weapon or an element or anything. But she had to keep the thing from Lance. She picked up a rock. Probably useless against an earth elemental, but she might distract it.

The owl glared and the rock exploded in her hand, raining dust on her palm. And in the dust... words. *You were with the white and blue Zyearthlings.*

Izzy perked both ears, eyes wide. "What?"

The owl hovered and waved a wing, spraying her with a fine dust. *The quilars. Which one carries the dragon?*

49

"I…" Izzy tensed, perplexed. Was that thing talking about Matt? And Charlotte? "I don't know what you're talking about."

More dust. *The one who carries the dragon is the Prínkipas' savior. The Prínkipas needs help.*

Izzy took a step forward. This thing was talking to her. If she could keep it distracted… "The electric bird mentioned a Prínkipas too."

She is Jústi, the bird said. *And I am Pax.* It dropped to the ground by her feet. Izzy resisted the urge to step back. *The Prínkipas needs help. The Basileus holds him and holds us. He commands us.*

Izzy's jaw dropped. Commands them? Did… did that make them… summons? Old lessons sprung in her mind from her Academy days. Mythical creatures, born of magic, sentient, intelligent, powerful, who bound themselves to a summoner of their choice by oath. So rare that most planets had never even seen one. Did Zyearth even have summoners anymore? "Who is the Basileus?"

A blast of fire smashed into the bird and it vanished in a cloud of dust. It rained on Izzy's feet and she got one more sentence. *Seek the Black Cloak.* The dust storm around them ended immediately, dropping dirt and debris over the stands. Izzy glared at Cix, her fur bristling.

"Cix, I was talking to it!"

"Well, while you're having imaginary conversations with bird elementals, the Master Guardian is bleeding out!" Cix snarled, bristling the fur on his tail.

"I'm fine." Lance stood, still holding Sami's jacket to his arm. Sami walked next to him, her face a mask of worry. "Or I will be once someone takes care of this."

Izzy let out a little gasp and rushed to Lance's side. She peeled back the jacket and examined the wound. Superficial, though it bled like hell. She held a hand to the arm.

50

Lance's white fur rapidly flashed to Roscoe's gray in a bizarre hallucination. Her skin buzzed and her fur all stood on end as memories of her husband's first major injury while fighting to get his powers flooded her mind. She yelped and leapt back.

Lance frowned. "Izzy?"

A flap of wings echoed in the arena and a zyfaunos secretary bird landed beside them. She saluted with a taloned fist across the chest, her long black flight feathers brushing dust into the air. "GR Gildspine, with your permission, I'll handle Guardian Tox. PD Gildspine needs you. Kiara and her team are headed this way as well."

Izzy blinked rapidly at the senior healer. "Um. Yes. Thank you, Kole. Please." She turned toward Darvin and Roscoe without waiting for Lance's permission.

The bird... the owl... had a name. Pax. And the kestrel was Jústi. Latin, Izzy thought, remembering from her education, for "peace" and "just." Odd names for the destructive things.

But were they really summons? Summoners were almost unheard of. There were probably only a few thousand in the entire span of the universe if she remembered her history correctly. Maybe only a few hundred. They almost never appeared on Zyearth. How had one gotten here?

One thing was certain though. If Pax and Jústi were summons then the real enemy was their summoner. The Basileus or... the Prínkipas. She couldn't tell which, or what they were.

She reached Roscoe and Darvin.

"Thank Draso," Roscoe said. "I don't know what you did with that owl, but it worked a treat."

Izzy dropped the façade of the Guardian and took on the role of the healer, relaxing a little. She looked over Roscoe's injuries. Cuts, bruises, and a busted

51

ankle, but nothing like some of the injuries she saw when they'd been trying to get their Gems to break. She sighed. Thank Draso.

Roscoe gripped her wrist, running a hooved finger over her wedding coil. "You okay, hun?"

"I'm fine," she said, though Draso knew that wasn't true. She focused her energy into her job, starting on the ankle first, feeling the damaged bone and knitting it back together. "Are you injured too, Darvin?"

"Just my pride," Darvin said, though he pawed at his left eye. "And I might have gotten another whiff of Lexi acid in the eye, but the pain hasn't really changed so I can't tell."

"I don't have an acid neutralization kit with me, so go get checked out as soon as you can," Izzy said.

"Will do," he snorted. "Cloaking someone as powerful as Lance takes a lot out of you."

"Give yourself some credit," Roscoe said. "You were cloaking three of us at once and we were all over the battlefield. Anyone would have trouble." He let out a sigh and twisted the now-healed ankle. "Thanks, love. That damn elemental got me good. It's lucky Darvin had enough sense to drag me out of its path."

"It's not an elemental," Izzy said, moving to the cuts now. "It's a summon."

Roscoe and Darvin perked their ears and exchanged a glance. "Really?" Darvin asked.

"How do you know?" Roscoe added.

"It spoke to me," Izzy said.

"Do you need assistance, GR Gildspine?" Kole asked, walking up to them, dragging long tail feathers through the dust. Sami, Cix, and Lance followed close behind. Lance's white fur was still stained red, but the wound had been properly healed.

52

Izzy stood. If these were summons, they needed to find the summoner. And until they did, Matt was in serious trouble. "Kole, do you know where Matt is?"

Kole nodded. "Kiara met him by the booths. He directed Defenders to get the civilians to the classrooms then went after the other elemental."

"Then we need to get to him," Izzy said. *"Now."*

SUMMONER

Matt dashed after the lightning kestrel, racking his brain.

Lightning bird. Elemental animal. Clearly not zyfaunos, but it spoke telepathically, using its element. Its magic. It was intelligent.

He gritted his teeth. This had to be a summon. All the clues pointed to it. A *summon*. And if this was a summon, that meant somewhere, there was a summoner. Lightning and air, when was the last time Zyearth saw a summoner?

The bird turned its head and stared Matt in the eye.

Matt flattened one ear. He knew who Zyearth's last summoner was. His grandfather, Tymon. He had died long before Matt was born, on a failed Golden Guardian mission on Erdoglyan. But he had summoned a pair of gryfons with fire and ice magic, not phoenixes. Not earth and electricity magic. This clearly wasn't his dead grandfather.

So, who was it?

The bird let out a rapid *klee klee klee*, blasted ahead of Matt, and dove among the covered booths. Electricity crackled around it.

Then the screams started.

Matt snarled. *Move!*

By the time he reached the booths, the crowd was in a panic. Uniformed Defenders ran about and tried herding them with little success.

Matt took charge. "Defenders, protect the civilians! Get them to the classrooms! Shields up!"

Defenders paused, staring at Matt, but quickly followed orders, rounding up civilians and herding them toward Defender classrooms. Several held hands out over the crowd. A high-pitched whining sound accompanied quick flashes of green and purple around the herd, before disappearing, casting everyone in shields. They wouldn't last long against magic that destructive, but it'd be better than nothing.

A secretary bird in a white and black uniform jogged up to him, clicking her beak in worry. She clenched a taloned fist and swept it across her chest in a salute, her long black flight feathers brushing along the ground. One of the senior healers. "Sir! Are you injured?"

"No, Kiara, but there are injured by the Arena," Matt said. "Gather up your healers and split them between the classrooms and the Arena." He paused. "GR Gildspine is there and she could use the help." Which was technically true, even if Izzy should be fighting, not healing.

Kiara rustled her head feathers and nodded, brightening slightly. "Yes, sir! My sister is near the Arena. I'll get her right on it." She jogged a few paces off, then took to the air, keening feral bird calls out to the healers. Several Defenders followed her on the ground.

Matt watched her. He flexed his fingers and twitched his short tail.

Okay. Defenders had orders. Civilians were protected. Time to get that bird.

Follow the destruction.

He flew through the booths, directing stray civilians and Defenders and trying to find signs of the odd summon. Follow the destruction.

But there was none.

The Meadow looked almost inviting. With devastating powers like this thing had, he expected more injuries, perhaps deaths, and at least more damage. But as he dashed between kiosks, he found everything still intact, just vacant. Even the imposing lightning was nowhere to be found.

Where was this thing?

"Get away from me!"

Matt whipped around. That was *Charlotte.*

He threw everything to the wind and ran for the source. His heart seized. Electricity exploded into the air near the back end of the line of booths.

Where Charlotte's shouts were coming from.

Not my sister! He pushed himself and whipped around a booth.

Charlotte was on the ground with her hands above her head, ears back and fur bristled. Her blue and white quills had been splashed with mud. A strong scent of an electric storm filled the open air, making his nose tingle. And the kestrel was hovering over her blasting electricity in every direction. Matt caught a bolt in his hand, which buzzed harmlessly against his skin.

I am looking for a white and blue Zyearthling, a voice in his head said. *The Prínkipas needs help!*

"I don't know what you're talking about!" Charlotte shrieked. "Get away from me!"

Enough. Matt rushed between his sister and the bird, spreading his arms out. Tiny twisters danced at his feet, but he dared not do more with Charlotte right there, unable to shield herself. *"Stay back!"*

The bird flapped backwards in surprise. It considered them a moment, then shot a tiny bolt at Matt's hand.

Which of you carries the dragon?

Matt frowned. "What?"

One of you carries the dragon, the kestrel said with a flash of lightning against Matt's shoulder. *Who is it? The Prínkipas needs help.*

Charlotte stood up, resting a hand on Matt's shoulder, pressing the chain of his Defender pendant into his fur.

His pendant.

His dragon pendant.

Matt reached into his shirt.

"Matt…"

"It's okay, Charlotte." He pulled the pendant out and let it rest against his chest.

The kestrel stared at it. Its eyes flashed, it raised its gaze to Matt, and with a jolt of lightning, spoke in a very different voice. *Help him. The Prínkipas… Ouranos… He cannot win this fight alone.* Then one more. *Seek the Black Cloak.*

That was odd. Matt pressed his lips together. Help the Prínkipas? What fight? Why had its voice changed? What was the Black Cloak? "Help him how?"

"That is enough, Jústi," a voice said. "I have this under control." The bird disappeared.

And a jet black quilar stood in its place.

But he wasn't like any quilar Matt had ever seen. Oddly shaped ears that bent backwards, thicker, longer quills on his head, some running down his back. Longer, tufted tail and longer snout… and he was tall. Matt was tall for his species, well over six feet, but this quilar stood at least seven feet. And his clothes. Pants with a long diamond shaped piece of fabric in brilliant red hanging from the belt and nothing else – no shirt, no shoes, nothing. Who dressed like that?

57

But the strangest thing was his eyes. Greenish-teal, matching the skin on his inner ears… and without pupils.

Matt's fur bristled. He wrapped an arm around his sister.

Around his eyes were tiny jewel shards, red and yellow. They looked like they had been implanted into the skin. Some kind of focus jewel? Very different from his own Lexi Gem. Though he had never heard of a focus jewel type so tiny before. What was that?

The quilar walked forward. "You are the white and blue Zyearthling who carries the dragon."

Matt narrowed his eyes. "You… are the Prínkipas."

The quilar raised an eyebrow, twitching his long tail. "Where did you hear that title?"

"The kestrel told me," Matt said. He perked up his ears, tried to look friendly, but it didn't work right.

The quilar's eyes widened now. "Jústi spoke to you?"

"Yes," Matt said. He slowly lowered his arm. He pressed his lips together. "Does that mean you're the summoner?"

"You know of summons!" the quilar exclaimed. "You are quite intriguing. But why would Jústi speak with you?"

Matt frowned. "He… he said you needed help." He licked his lips. "He called you Ouranos."

The quilar took a step back, bristling the fur on his shoulders. "I… Jústi… He gave you my name…" But then his body convulsed slightly and he took another step forward. His head twitched.

"You… will give me… what I need."

Matt twitched his ears. What was that? His voice changed. His mannerisms. Even the way he held himself. What the hell?

Ouranos moved forward again.

Matt wrapped an arm around Charlotte again. "Stay back."

"I… need… your power…to make my army."

Matt perked an ear. Army? What the hell did he mean by that? And… that voice change. That new voice, deep and angry. Almost… almost like it was a different zyfaunos.

The quilar, Ouranos, stepped forward again, as if straining against his own body. He tried taking another step, but snapped to the left instead, gripping his head.

"No more injury!" His original voice.

Then a snap to the right. "You will *obey!*" The angry voice.

Something was definitely off. A slight change in voice depending on which "side" of him was speaking. The first, cautious, curious, but not hostile. The second, clearly ready to rip someone's throat out. That voice did not belong to the Prínkipas that needed help. It belonged to… whatever demon plagued him. Almost like someone possessed him. Even the physical twitches seemed to suggest possession. Whatever sense that made. That only happened in movies and fairytales. Right?

Either way… trouble.

Matt stepped backwards, pushing Charlotte. "Go, go!"

"I'm not going to leave you!"

"Are you crazy?" Matt said. "Get out of here before you get hurt!"

Ouranos snapped again, this time standing straight and glaring at Matt. "You will give me the elixir!"

Elixir? What the hell was he talking about?

Ouranos held his hands out and the ground shook. Matt took another step back. Great, an earth manipulator.

But then a flash of embers gathered around one hand. A shock ran up Matt's spine. *Two* elements? But--

59

Then ice shards appeared around the other hand. A fierce wind blew around them. Lightning cracked from the sky. Stone spikes spat out from the ground. A ravaging rain pelted them.

Earth, fire, ice, wind, lightning, stone, water – every elemental magic Matt had ever encountered. Ouranos had *all of them.*

Then every element blasted them at once.

CHAPTER 08

ELIXIR

Matt threw up his strongest shield and shoved Charlotte aside. The pair of them barely rolled out of the way of the quilar's barrage of magic. Charlotte must have screamed, but Matt managed to squelch that reflex.

So many powers! Every element! How did he have that kind of magic? Gems granted at *most* two powers, a rarity in itself, and *never* two elements. And he had *all of them?* How was that even possible?

He pushed Charlotte behind a booth and squatted near her. "You have to get out of here. Go to the Defender classrooms with the other civilians."

"No." Charlotte said. "You're *not* going to leave me."

A blast of wind smashed into the booth, blowing merchandise, poles, and canvas by Matt and Charlotte's heads. Twin bolts of ice and fire followed. Matt herded them further down the row, shielding them both, keeping their heads out of the quilar's line of sight.

"You will not escape me!" Ouranos shouted in that dark, angry voice, blasting booth after booth with various elements. "Give me what I want or your companion *dies!*"

Matt's fur bristled. How could he give him what he wanted when he didn't even know what it was? And why would he do that anyway? What the hell could he do?

Charlotte gasped, her voice shaking. Matt gripped Charlotte's shoulder and pushed both of them into a run until they got a reasonable distance away. There was no way he could fight this stranger with Charlotte clinging to him. He met her gaze. "You *have* to go to the classrooms, Char."

"You're not leaving me to fight some unknown creature! That's what Dad did, and Mom and Aunt Solana and they all *died*, and I'm not going to lose you too!"

Matt paused. She wasn't wrong.

The booths in front of them exploded with electrified water. Matt raised a shield against the splintered plastic poles.

Nowhere to run.

No time.

"Stay behind this booth and *don't move* unless I tell you. Got it?"

Charlotte frowned. "But--"

"No buts," Matt said. "I can't fight him with you grabbing my tail and we won't outrun him. Stay here."

"You are running out of hiding places, Defender," Ouranos said. "Show yourself and give me the elixir or I will take it by force."

Matt shot a warning glare at Charlotte, then walked a few paces off, calling tornados to his fingertips. He peeked around one booth and caught sight of his enemy. His fur stood on end. The enemy who used his summons to ask for help. Who was clearly fighting something. Perhaps even someone.

But who was also threatening him, his home, and his sister. What was he supposed to do?

Fire and ice chunks floated around Ouranos' hands as he stood in the center of the carnage, but a second later, it all disappeared and he gripped his head, gritting his teeth. "Father, *stop.*" That higher pitched voice again.

Matt's quills bristled. Wait. Father?

His body twitched violently again, and the elements returned to his fingertips. "I am the Basileus and you *will* obey me, Prínkipas." The angry voice.

The elements vanished again with more twitching. "I will not let you do this! You cannot have my power!" Higher voice.

Matt didn't know what kind of demons this Prínkipas character was fighting, but now was his chance to fight back. He formed a twister behind Ouranos.

And stopped.

The kestrel -- Jústi, he had named it -- had asked for someone to help Ouranos. He had a name, a title, and apparently a father. And he clearly needed help, battling whatever was in his own head.

The Guardian Oath rang in Matt's mind. *I swear to support my fellow soldiers, protect the innocent, defend all creatures, and uphold the Defender Spirit.*

Defend all creatures... Damn it.

He silenced the twisters and stepped out, shielded, but unarmed. He held up his hands. "Ouranos."

Ouranos whipped his head up, ears back.

Matt took a deep breath. What the hell was he doing? *Being a Guardian.* He held a hand out. "Let me help you."

Charlotte hissed something, but he ignored it.

63

Ouranos shrank away, staring wide-eyed. "You would help me after all I have done."

Matt pressed his lips together and flattened both ears. "Yes. That's... that's my duty as a Guardian."

Charlotte gasped, but he once again ignored it.

"Guardian," Ouranos repeated. He met Matt's gaze, his fur on end, his tail between his legs and fear in his eyes. "I... I need--"

His fear flickered into rage and the angry voice took over. "--Your power!" He tackled Matt.

Matt yelped at the impact. He tucked his chin and knees and rolled backwards, trying to protect vital organs, but for some reason Ouranos didn't use magic this time. He rolled with Matt, fingerclaws out, scratching at Matt's arms and chest.

Earth and stone, those claws were sharp! Matt pressed his feet to Ouranos' torso, memories of a similar fight with a high school bully flooding his mind. He kicked at the quilar, but his enemy stayed fast.

"I have presented enough danger. Threatened your home. Give me what I want and produce the Cast elixir!" the angry voice shouted.

Matt hissed and called a twister and ripped Ouranos off him with it, then scrambled to his feet.

Ouranos fought back immediately with a twister of his own.

Matt could crush that twister... or use it. He added more power to it and aimed it at Ouranos.

His enemy waved a hand and it vanished.

Vanished. What kind of magic did he *have?* Just what kind of focus jewels *were* those?

Matt snarled, flattening his ears. The skin on his neck burned and his tail fur puffed up. No way was he going to get away with that. He held both hands out and drew every ounce of power he could from his Gem.

Ouranos fought back, and for every bit of speed and power Matt got with his twisters, Ouranos halved it.

Damn, he was strong! Wind manipulation was rare, and Matt had grown used to being the strongest wind elemental in the Defenders. This quilar's power threw him for a loop. But he wouldn't win. Matt had trained too long and too hard to admit defeat. He pushed beyond his limits.

A thin film of black liquid formed on the tips of his fingers and snaked its way up his hands, soaking his fur, making his skin buzz. He chanced a quick glance at it, grimacing. Damn it, not *now*. Why *now?*

A voice echoed in his head, accompanied by a tiny, jangly bell. *We need to get to him now!* Matt faltered. That sounded like Izzy. But not out loud. Only in his head.

Shit, shit, *shit,* this was not the time!

Ouranos' eyes widened, his gaze landing on Matt's hands. "There it is."

Matt frowned, the thoughts and bell blown from his mind. "What?"

Without another word, Ouranos wrenched control of the twister and shot it at Matt, knocking him down. He dove for him.

But a slab of rock shot up between them.

Larissa stood to Matt's left, her Gem lit up and whining, cane planted firmly into the ground. Her maroon and silver fur swayed in the leftover wind. She lowered her long badger snout to glare at Ouranos, ears flat against her skull. "Stay away from him." She spoke with practiced calm.

Ouranos stepped forward, still growling with that angry voice. "You meddle with affairs that are not your own, frail one."

Larissa narrowed her eyes, baring a single fang. She lifted the cane and slammed it down again, sending spider vein cracks through the slab of stone. "Stage one."

Matt hesitated. Stage one was a code phrase for combining their powers. It was meant as an attack. He glanced at Ouranos. Or… the angry thing possessing him.

Should he really attack him?

Larissa side-eyed him. "As we practiced, Matthew."

"But--"

"Stage one!" She slammed her cane and the rock shattered into pebbles. They started crumbling to the ground.

Matt gritted his teeth. He stood and obediently caught the pebbles in a tornado. No use in defying a superior officer.

"Stage two!"

Matt winced, but commanded the twister forward.

Ouranos flattened his ears and pulled back on the twister's power, stalling it. Matt pushed more power into it. The viscous black liquid on his hands crawled beyond his wrists now.

A heartbeat, not his own, pounded in his head, accompanied by huffing, worry, fear, words and a series of jingling bells. *Summon, summoner, Matt…*

That wasn't his voice. Not his heartbeat. It *was* Izzy's.

Damn it, this was the worst timing for this thought-sharing nonsense, especially with the strange bell sound drowning the sounds of the battle. He squelched his emotions and it faded slightly, but not completely.

Ouranos eyed the strange black liquid hungrily. He scowled and called fire and ice to his hands. "You cannot win this by yourselves."

Matt snarled. He kept the twister stalled, away from Ouranos, using the black quilar's powers as an excuse not to attack. There had to be a way out of this. If he could find a big enough stone in the debris, maybe he could knock Ouranos out without hurting him too much, giving them some time.

Ouranos formed a large ice spike.

Matt found a large stone in the tornado.

One clear shot--

A fireball blasted into Ouranos' side and he lost his magic grip on the twister. He cried out and rolled to the side, filling the air with the smell of singed fur. The tornado grew without his magic holding it back.

Cix, Izzy and the rest of their pack ran for them.

"Stage two, Matt!"

Too many commands. Too many options. Echoes in his head. Save Ouranos, fight Ouranos, follow Larissa, take the opening, *Is that the Prínkipas? Is he a summoner?* so many bells, just *do something--*

Ouranos growled, pushed aside Matt's tornado with a wave of his hand, and tackled him. He pinned Matt down and squeezed both hands around Matt's wrist. The strange black liquid on Matt's hands soaked into Ouranos' fur. Matt yelped, fighting to get his hand back. Ouranos grinned in triumph.

Matt's eyes widened. A moment of clarity. *Is that the elixir he was talking about?*

But before he could fight back, the electric elemental Jústi appeared above their heads. Ouranos snatched the end of the bird's tail and flew into the air, headed away from the campus. His face was a war of emotions – triumph battled with shame. The angry voice and… the Prínkipas seeking help.

Kiara and Kole took to the air after him, keening in anger, though he was far too fast for them.

Matt stared at his hands as the black liquid slowly vanished into his fur. What the hell was that all about? Was that what Ouranos… the angry voice… was after?

Charlotte ran up to Matt and threw her arms around his neck. She shook, but didn't say anything. Matt took a deep breath and held her back. At least Charlotte was safe.

Izzy jogged up to him, her golden-brown quills bristled and her ears flat. "Matt! Are you okay?"

Matt blinked, then looked up at her. "Physically, yeah."

Izzy bent an ear forward and frowned. "That was a summon."

Matt chewed his lip. That confirmed it. It was Izzy's voice in his head, talking about summons. Damn it all. Something had to be done about that. He pushed it aside for now. "And that quilar was the summoner," Matt said.

They exchanged a dark look.

Lance walked up to both of them, an air of calm on his face, but his white fur and wolf tail puffed up and bloody. Matt swallowed hard. Lance held a hand out. "Clearly we all have a lot to talk about."

CHAPTER 09

DEBRIEF

"Now," Lance said, leaning over the giant, polished stone table in the Defender Assembly Chamber. "Everyone, get something to drink and sit. Let's try to piece this together."

Matt glanced around the room, trying to organize his thoughts as he made his way to the center table. Tiny lights dotted the ceiling, spread out like Zyearth stars and constellations, bathing the polished cave in a gentle light. Four larger lights represented Zyearth's prime moon, Sepideh, and its three lesser moons, Badar, Pulan, and Aysu. The lights moved with the moons in the sky. Coffee and water had been placed on the back counters, but no one had had time to put together anything more.

He snatched up a bottle and sat on a large stone chair carved out of the cave that held the Assembly room. Everyone else awkwardly sat on identical chairs normally meant only for members of their governing Assembly, trying to find places for tails, hooves, antlers and paws. Cix, Sami, Darvin, Roscoe,

Izzy, and even Charlotte, a key witness, had been invited to this meeting, and no one was comfortable.

Only Larissa seemed relaxed, taking the seat to Lance's left, reserved for the Domini Defender. She sipped on coffee with all the elegance and earned arrogance of someone used to surviving anything. Though Matt noticed her badger ear twitching -- she was clearly unnerved, even if she didn't show it much.

A gleaming pewter Defender symbol had been etched into the seat above her head. It paired neatly with the black and gold Defender symbol on Lance's seat – the Master Guardian's seat. One of them, anyway. Master Guardians normally ruled in pairs, but Lance had lost his partner years before Matt was born. The other seat stood empty as he had never picked a replacement.

Matt's chair was just to the left of the chairs meant for the Golden Guardians. They sported identical golden Defender symbols, polished to a mirror sheen.

They had been vacant for a long time.

Izzy sat next to him, equally uncomfortable. Roscoe sat next to her, gently gripping her hand. The chairs didn't really allow them to sit close to one another, since they didn't move, but they still leaned toward each other anyway. Izzy rested a hand on her recovered hammer and squeezed her husband back.

After the battle, they had gone back for it and found that the feather she had pinned no longer held electricity. But when Matt picked the feather up, it definitely still held the air of magic about it.

They had dropped it off with two Defender specialists -- Aric Tesla, their magic specialist, and Jaymes Fogg, Matt and Izzy's own adoptive father, Lexi Gem specialist and biologist. Hopefully they'd have something to say about the feather and its magic after some time with it.

Matt pressed his lips together, his gaze resting on Lance. He had only been in this room twice before, when presenting to the Assembly. Lance reserved it only for Assembly meetings... and councils of war.

He didn't have to guess which it was today.

He chanced a quick look at his sister. She was uncomfortable enough with Defenders. Did she understand the significance of being in this room?

Lance flicked his tail and wrinkled his long wolf snout. "Anyone want to start?"

The group was oddly silent. Matt peeked at Izzy, who picked at a loose quill on her head, staring at the table, ears flat.

Lance sat down with a sigh. He adjusted his glasses on his snout. "Let's start with the elementals."

"They're not elementals," Izzy said immediately. "They're summons."

Everyone stared at her.

"I'm with Izzy," Matt said, before anyone could protest. He bent a blue-tipped ear. "And I believe the quilar we fought is the summoner. He practically confirmed it."

Lance perked his ears and widened his eyes. "Zyearth hasn't had a summoner since--"

"Since my grandfather, I know," Matt said. "But those birds spoke to Izzy and me, and even Charlotte, through their elements. They showed signs of intelligence. They had *names*. Elementals don't have that."

"They're also extremely powerful," Roscoe added. He shook his head, raining gray fur on the table, his antlers catching light. "I had a hell of a time keeping that owl from ripping the entire arena apart. Elementals don't do that."

"Some do," Cix said with a wolfish growl, twitching his black, blue-tipped ear. "Remember the ice lynx from last year?"

71

"But these things were also *organized,*" Roscoe countered. "The ice lynx just blasted through downtown Corinth and hit anything that moved. These things actually *strategized.*"

"I have to agree," Sami said, twitching her white fox tail. "It saw me as a threat. It calculated attacks. It recognized when Roscoe could counter its earthquakes and changed tactics. If that isn't a sign of intelligence, I don't know what is."

"And more than that, they lasted forever," Darvin said, leaning forward, glinting light off his silver antlers. "The ice lynx only had about fifteen minutes before the magic wore off. Most elementals only last two or three minutes. We were fighting this one for at least half an hour and it only disappeared after Cix finally hit it with a good fireball."

"And don't forget the smell too," Sami said. "They had strong smells associated with them. Musk and dirt for the owl, electric storms for the kestrel. Elementals don't have that."

The room fell quiet.

Lance raised an eyebrow, staring at Matt. "They have names?"

"Pax and Jústi," Izzy said.

"The electric one is Jústi," Matt added. "He told me so."

"She," Izzy corrected.

"She," Matt said. "And Ouranos confirmed it."

"Who?"

Matt shook his head. "The quilar we fought. His name is Ouranos."

Larissa frowned and pulled her data slate out, then began typing.

Lance's face grew dark. "You spoke with him."

Matt bent an ear back, the fur on his neck bristling. "Yes."

"And?"

72

Matt chewed his lip. How could he put all the complicated feelings and worries about that encounter into words? The strange voice change, the feeling like he was possessed, the mention of creating an army?

"Jústi called him Prínkipas," Charlotte said in a small voice.

Matt and Lance stared at her.

Charlotte shifted. "Jústi spoke to me. She said the Prínkipas needed help." She met Matt's gaze. "You said Ouranos was the Prínkipas and he responded to it."

"Pax also told us the Prínkipas needed help," Izzy said.

"I also heard Ouranos use the term 'Basileus,'" Matt said.

Izzy nodded. "Yeah, Pax used that too. He said the Basileus commanded them."

"You keep saying they spoke," Lance said. "But I didn't hear any words from the animals."

Sami shrugged, bending back a white ear. "When that bird hit me with a blast of sand, I... I thought I might have. In my head. But I don't know anymore."

"I didn't, and I got a face full of dirt," Darvin added.

"I didn't either, and I practically traded magic with the thing," Roscoe said.

Lance turned to Cix. "Cix?"

The blue and black wolf glanced at Matt a moment, then just shrugged.

Lance eyed Matt. "How did you hear them when no one else did?"

"I heard them in my head," Charlotte said quietly.

"Same here," Matt said. "I didn't 'hear' them so much as... felt them. They hit us with magic and I just... heard the words in my head." Izzy and Charlotte nodded.

Lance narrowed his eyes, swishing his tail.

73

"Prínkipas and Basileus are royal titles," Larissa said suddenly. Matt turned and saw her looking over the data slate. The screen's light illuminated the silver and maroon in her fur and reflected on her glasses. "Greek in origin, meaning 'prince' and 'king' respectively."

"*Greek* in origin?" Lance said. "As in an Earth language? Zyearth has no principalities. How did we find a *Greek prince* on Zyearth?"

"You are assuming this Ouranos is Zyearthling," Larissa said, staring pointedly at Lance.

Lance's ears perked. "That's honestly a good point. Maybe he's not."

Larissa turned to Matt. "You fought him before I got there, and he clearly matched you in strength." Matt's cheeks and ears burned with the notion, though she wasn't wrong, much as he wouldn't like to admit it. She glimpsed at him over her glasses. "What kind of powers did he have?"

Matt flicked one ear back. "Elemental."

"What element?"

Matt shifted. "All of them."

Lance's jaw dropped. "*All* of them?"

"Literally every element, though he favored fire, ice, and wind." Matt slumped back a little. Lightning and air, his command on wind was wild. Matt had never met any other magic user that had such strength with his magic specialty.

"Did he have a Gem?" Larissa asked.

Matt wrinkled his snout. "No. But I did notice he had tiny jewels around his eyes. Four of them, two around each eye, yellow and red. Looked like they were fused onto the skin or something. He wasn't wearing anything to keep them on."

"So he likely had focus jewels, but not a Lexi Gem," Larissa said. She turned to her data slate again for several seconds, then shook her head. "The focus jewel database doesn't have anything about the jewels Matt described.

74

And his name and title are Greek. Additionally, while he's clearly a quilar, he's unlike any quilar seen on Zyearth. Ears, snout, quills, feet, even his clothing are distinctly foreign." Larissa lowered her gaze. "I don't think Ouranos is from Zyearth."

"If that's true," Izzy said. "Then where is he from?"

"If his name and title are really Greek, maybe he came from Earth," Cix said. Matt shuddered at the thought.

"Earth hasn't developed deep space travel," Izzy said. "They haven't even been able to visit another planet in their solar system. He can't be from Earth. How would he get here?"

"Excellent questions," Larissa said. "I hoped that he might be registered in the summoner's database, but there's no one named Ouranos there. Nor are there summons named Pax or Jústi. Even searching for elemental owls and kestrels bears no results. Phoenix summons are outrageously powerful, making them extremely rare – almost nonexistent."

Matt narrowed his eyes, splaying his ears. "Those were definitely summons we fought, ma'am."

"I'm not saying they weren't," Larissa said, putting a hand up. "In yours and Izzy's defense, the summoner databases talk about summoners communicating with their charges, and elemental telepathy is the most common method. I'd have to do more research to see if they can communicate to others besides their summoners, however. Most summons have strong smells associated with them as well."

Lance bent an ear and wrinkled his snout, clearly unconvinced, but he said nothing.

Larissa lowered her gaze. "All I'm saying is this -- he's an alien invader. If he is a summoner, he is unregistered and in command of some very rare, very powerful creatures. He's an elemental magic user and he can clearly match any of our own elemental users in strengths and skill. Even you, Lance,

75

though I know you won't admit it. He has unfamiliar focus jewels. He attacked us, unprovoked, for no apparent reason, and injured a lot of people, including our own Master Guardian." She met Lance's gaze. "He clearly needs to be dealt with."

Matt frowned. Dealt with. Likely with brute force. No room to help him. He took a deep breath. If he was going to say something, this was the time to do it.

"He may have attacked for no reason, but he didn't come here without one," Matt said. "He came looking for help. His summons said so. I don't know what they mean by that, but he was clearly fighting a demon in his mind that he can't overcome. He kept stopping in the middle of an attack and shouting. It was like watching him fight himself, in his own head. He may not be entirely in control of his own actions."

Lance lowered his gaze. "You're saying this like he was somehow a puppet."

"That honestly might be accurate," Matt said. "I know it sounds impossible, but he's clearly fighting something. And I distinctly remembered Ouranos saying 'father.' His father may be involved in this, controlling him some way."

"Magic doesn't work like that," Lance said.

"Ours doesn't," Matt said. "But he's not using our magic, is he? Summons, every element, different focus jewels. For all we know, magical puppetry is something that can actually happen in his world." He sat up straight, hardening his features. "Something is clearly wrong with him. It was like Ouranos was fighting a separate, physical personality in his own mind, what with the odd body ticks and strange voice changes. I know it doesn't make sense, but how much sense does any of this make?"

Larissa lowered her gaze. "I can see your point. But he's powerful and dangerous. He injured a lot of Defenders, by himself, with nothing more than

76

his own magic and a pair of summons. If he is being used like that, I feel for him, but we cannot risk our resources and zyfaunos on a hunch."

"Larissa is right," Lance said. "I am sorry if that's the case, but we don't have definitive proof and we don't have the time or resources to confirm that theory. I don't know where he came from or what he's doing here, but we need to find him and stop him before he causes more damage."

Matt pressed his ears back, but didn't protest further. He did see Lance's point. Hell, he wasn't sure he should be willing to help Ouranos either. Except... the point of being a Guardian was to help others. Earth and stone, what was he supposed to do? He stared at his hand.

And stopped.

When he had pushed his powers beyond their limits, that strange black liquid had appeared again, as it had so many times in the past. And that excited Ouranos. He shook his head. No, the angry voice inside him. He had gone after it and maybe even gotten some of it before he flew off.

Why did he want it? He called it an "elixir" if Matt heard correctly. But an elixir for what? Should he say something about it? Assuming anyone would believe him. He had never mentioned the strange black liquid on his hands before. Why should he? He couldn't make it appear on purpose. Every time he had brought up something related to his Black Binding, he had been shot down, especially by the Master Guardian. He was already considered a freak for being Black Bound. No reason to bring up any more potential problems that would just be dismissed.

A rustle of feathers sounded at the entrance to the Assembly Room and Kole and Kiara walked in, crossing fists across their chests in a salute. Kole stepped forward. "Sir! We have something to report."

"Report please, then," Lance said. "Did you find where he went?"

Kole nodded. "We followed him to Corinth Woods, sir. We lost track of him after that."

"Where specifically in Corinth Woods?" Lance asked.

Kiara shifted. "The Dead Zone, sir."

ULTIMATUM

Matt shuddered, his fur bristling. Izzy drew her hand to her face. Darvin and Roscoe shook, and Sami snorted. Cix let out a low whine. Even Charlotte flattened her ears, sinking deeper into her chair.

The Dead Zone. That explained why they hadn't found him before he'd revealed himself, assuming had come from off-world. The Dead Zone was a strange pocket in Zyearth's magnetic field that made most electronics go haywire and made detection difficult. Cadets used to train there to learn how to survive without electronic aid, but they'd stopped the practice a couple of years ago after a catastrophic training session that left three trainee teams dead. The Defenders had declared it was strictly off limits.

Except now. Now they'd have to go.

Matt stood. "Sir, let me go after him."

Lance snarled, snapping his teeth in a rare sign of aggression. *"Absolutely not."* Izzy jumped and Larissa raised an eyebrow in surprise.

Matt splayed his ears, but stood his ground. "Sir--"

"No, Matt," Lance said. The aggression in his face faltered a moment in favor of deep worry, but he shook his head and it disappeared. "You're not qualified for something like this."

"How am I not?" Matt snapped. Lance's eyes widened and he took a step back at the defiance.

Izzy flattened her ears and furrowed her brow. "Matt--"

"Don't stop me, Izzy," Matt said. He crossed his arms. "Sir, with all due respect, I am a fully-fledged Defender and have been for decades. I completed extra years of training. I have been on more missions and in more battles than anyone of my year and many of my seniors. I have successfully completed every task that you have ever assigned me. I am one of only two Defenders even *eligible* to apply for Golden Guardianship based on your stringent rules. Rules, I might add, that you made stricter just before I was eligible to apply after my graduation. What disqualifies me for this mission?"

Lance narrowed his eyes, his black lips curling against white fur. He spoke in growls. "You're not a Guardian."

"Only because you have denied me over and over again!" Matt shouted. "It's always something, but today--" he ripped the rejection letter out of his pocket and threw it on the table. It smelled of electric magic. "--you didn't even have an excuse. You've run out of reasons to give it to me. Even the Assembly thinks I'm ready. Even DD Hobbes. But you still won't budge!"

"You're not *ready* for the Guardianship," Lance snarled through clenched teeth.

Matt smacked the table. "That's always your excuse! But if that's true, then tell me *why!"*

Lance shrank back, ears flat, brow furrowed. He wrinkled his snout, but he didn't speak.

Izzy gripped Matt's arm. *"Please,* Matt. *"* But he wrenched his arm away.

80

"I know why," he said. "Because of my father. My grandfather. Izzy's too. They all died as Guardians, under your watch, and you're afraid to lose another Guardian pair."

Izzy hissed. *"Matt."*

But Matt kept his gaze on Lance.

And Lance stayed silent, tucking his tail between his legs.

Larissa put a hand on Lance's arm, frowning, ears pinned back. "Lance..."

Lance ripped away with a snarl, then met Matt's gaze. "Fine. I concede. You're right."

Matt perked his ears and his jaw dropped.

Lance growled under his breath, turning aside. "Your fathers and grandfathers depended on me as their Master Guardian and I failed them. Then I spit on their graves by grooming you and Izzy to join the Guardianship as another pair of... of *livestock animals* for *slaughter*. And more than that, I watched you two grow up in these halls. I know you too well, too closely. I sent your fathers and grandfathers to their deaths, as their *friend.* I can't imagine doing that as your 'doting uncle,' as you've called me."

Larissa lowered her gaze. "Lance--"

"Let me finish, Larissa." Lance ground his teeth. "We're in a time of peace. We have enough senior soldiers to cover the Guardian tasks for now. We don't *need* to elevate you." He turned and stared Matt in the eye. "Or at least that's how I justified it. But you're right. We need the Guardians. This event is proof of that. Ouranos is powerful and unpredictable and I can't have him potentially crippling my military or taking intelligence to some invading planet. And you're right that you and Izzy are the only ones who are both trained and willing to try for the Guardianship. And I'm holding you back. That's unfair of me."

Matt pasted his ears back.

Larissa gripped Lance's hand, but he pulled away again. He pressed his lips together and took a deep breath.

"This is against my better judgement," he said. "But you can go after Ouranos."

Matt blinked. "Really?"

"Yes," Lance said. Matt slowly smiled, but Lance held out a hand. "But before you go celebrating, there are some conditions for you. You have some major issues to work through before you become a Guardian, and this is as good a time as any to test those."

"Anything," Matt said, unable to hide the grin.

"You bring a pack," Lance said. "I'll send whoever you want, regardless of rank, except myself and Larissa. We need to be here in case this fails and we need to rally the troops. But you will *not* go alone. You'll need the backup and frankly, you'll need some levelheaded partners to keep you from charging into things."

Matt nodded, glancing around the room. His pack was here already, and he was sure they'd all answer.

"You bring Izzy as a part of that pack," Lance said. "Don't think I didn't notice that all that Guardian stuff was all 'me, me, me' and not the two of you. She's your partner and if you aren't working together, you won't succeed. Do I make myself clear?"

"Crystal," Matt said, his ears and cheeks growing hot. He had forgotten mostly about Izzy in that rant, hadn't he... that was careless and rude. He'd have to apologize later.

"You will obey my *every order*," Lance said. "You have a tendency to ignore orders in favor of your own desires or what you think is best. While the Guardianship gives you more leeway with that, it doesn't give you free rein to ignore everything. More than that, *you are not a Guardian yet.* I am in charge, is that clear?"

Matt nodded. "Yes, sir."

Lance captured Matt's gaze. "And… think of this as a final test. This is your test to prove you're ready to be a Guardian. You follow my orders, you work with your pack, you be a proper partner to Izzy… and I'll grant you the Guardianship."

Matt's eyes widened. "You mean that?"

"I do," Lance said, flattening his ears. "But if you fail this… if you disobey orders, if you abandon your pack, if you ignore Izzy… then no Guardianship. Now or ever."

Matt's body buzzed with shock at Lance's words, setting his fur on end and sending a jolt up his spine. "What?" Everyone stared at him.

Lance's expression softened slightly. "The Guardianship is the most dangerous position in the Defender military, Matt. You know this, but I don't think you respect it. I need to know that you'll be prepared for what you will face. I sent your father and grandfather to their deaths. While I regret that, I also did it knowing that they were prepared. But I didn't want to lose them. They were dear to me." He lowered his eyes and met Matt's. "I don't want to lose you or Izzy."

Because we're dear to him, just like Dad and Grandpa. Matt didn't need the words to understand the implications.

How do you process that? He stared blankly at the table, willing his mind to work. Did… did he really not respect the danger of the Guardianship? He had watched his father die. He knew the price of the Guardianship. Right?

And he was dear to Lance.

Finally, this ultimatum. Either he took this mission and succeeded, earning the Guardianship… or he failed and lost it forever. Bid for it now, one final time… and either win his heart's desire or lose everything.

83

And how would that clash with the already conflicting thoughts about Ouranos? The Prínkipas had come here trying to find help, right? Shouldn't Matt be trying to help him?

But he had also attacked the campus. Injured a lot of zyfaunos, caused a ton of destruction, threatened Matt's family and fellow soldiers. But there was also some "Basileus" or his father or something he was fighting. Argh, why did this have to be so difficult?

What the hell was he supposed to do?

"Make your choice, Matt," Lance said.

"Fine," Matt said. "I'll do it." He had to. This was his chance. Maybe he could find a way to follow Lance's orders and succeed, but also help Ouranos. He could prove that he took the Guardianship seriously. There had to be a way. He just had to find it.

Charlotte winced, her face scrunching up with worry. Matt allowed himself one glance at her before turning away. He loved his sister and she meant the world to him, but this was his choice, not hers. He couldn't let her feelings get in the way of this now.

Lance crossed his arms. "Okay then. One more condition." He glanced at Izzy over his glasses. "Izzy, you're his partner. If these are the terms he agrees to, you have to agree to them as well, or no deal."

Izzy's ears perked, then flattened against her golden quills. Her gaze darted around the room before finally landing on Matt.

Oh, Draso's Palace, why did he have to drop that on Izzy? She hadn't even wanted to fight. She didn't think of herself as Guardian material, though Matt knew better. But now he was putting that on her too?

Roscoe tightened his grip on her wrist. "Your choice, Izzy. There's no shame one way or another."

And now Roscoe too. Damn it!

Izzy frowned. "I... uh..."

Come on, Iz, don't do this! Matt thought. *Agree to it! Just do it! We need to do this! Agree! Agree!*

"I agree," Izzy said abruptly. Her expression deadened for a moment, then she shook herself and gripped the side of her head, blinking, clearly confused. She met his gaze. Little bells jingled in his head.

Matt frowned. That... that had happened awfully fast. But why? His pleading? The ultimatum?

Or had she heard his thoughts in her head again?

During the height of battle earlier that day, he had heard Izzy's voice and heartbeat echoing in his head, along with the strange, ever-present bells that rang when they shared thoughts.

That... wasn't the first time either. While he could never definitively prove it, a lot of evidence suggested that he and Izzy's Gems had been magically bound together in a social bond – a long dead practice that had stopped because of the dangers it caused. Emotion sharing, thought sharing, and worse, though Matt couldn't recall what at the moment. The problem grew worse during periods of extreme stress though, and if this wasn't one of those periods, Matt didn't know what was.

So had she hear his thoughts in her head? Had she agreed because of that? His blood ran cold. Good Draso, he could not have that happening. Should he tell her? But every time he had tried to tell her in the past, she had dismissed the idea. Hell, Lance had too. Social binding can't happen by accident, everyone said. No one believed him.

But this was proof. Wasn't it? Damn it all, how could he fix this?

Lance raised an eyebrow and perked an ear, but didn't question it. "Okay then."

Damn it all, the damage had already been done. He buried his thoughts and emotions away, hoping he could keep it under wraps for this. Maybe he could try bringing it up again with Izzy while they prepared for this mission. She'd have to believe him after what had happened. Right?

Lance sat and waved for everyone else to sit too. "Your mission, then, is to capture Ouranos and bring him here, if that's possible."

"Okay. Okay good." He saluted Lance, keeping a tight grip on his thoughts. "We'll do that, sir."

"What if capture isn't possible?" Roscoe asked.

Matt shot him a look, but Roscoe studiously ignored him.

Lance adjusted the glasses on his snout. "Then you eliminate him. He cannot get away to do more damage or return to his home with potentially dangerous intelligence. Understood?"

Matt pressed his lips together. "Sir, he was calling for help."

Lance narrowed his eyes. "Are you already questioning my orders, soldier?"

Matt sunk into his seat. "No, sir."

"Good. Now, name your pack."

Matt glanced around the room. "Izzy, Cix, Darvin, Roscoe, and Sami."

"Any objections?" Lance asked.

"No, sir," everyone said, though Roscoe shifted uncomfortably in his seat. He wouldn't let go of Izzy's hand.

"Okay then," Lance said. "Prepare as you see fit and meet me in the hanger in one hour. I'll have a Delta-Z prepped for you. And Matt."

Matt looked at him.

Lance lowered his gaze. "Prove to me you're ready."

CHAPTER 11

DOUBT

"I can't believe you just stood up to the Master Guardian like that," Cix said. "You should have been roasted! Or at least iced."

Matt grinned. "Sometimes you just gotta push boundaries. Right Iz?"

Izzy managed a small smile, leaning on Roscoe. "Sure." But really, Lance shouldn't have caved. Matt would just pull the same stunt again.

Though Lance had told him that pushing it would mean losing the Guardianship. Hopefully he would actually *listen.*

Matt watched her a moment, slightly frowning, then he turned. "Let's go get outfitted. I wanna get going ASAP."

Izzy stepped away from Roscoe and trailed at the back of the pack as they headed toward the outfitters, one ear pinned against her scalp. Why had she agreed to this? She honestly couldn't comprehend it. One second she'd been thinking about how she could get out of it without hurting Matt's feelings and the next her brain bombarded her with *agree agree agree* so fast she'd practically gotten whiplash. It hadn't even sounded like her own voice either.

It was more like Matt's voice as he'd bored into her skull with his gaze, though her ears had started ringing the moment the words had entered her head making it hard to tell.

"Hey Izzy?" Matt said.

She looked up. "Yeah?"

"I didn't... I mean... I hope I didn't pressure you into agreeing to this," he said.

Izzy frowned. "I mean... you kind of did." She took a deep breath. "But it also wouldn't be fair to refuse when we promised to do this together."

Matt flicked both ears back. "I know. But you just agreed so fast. I wondered if you actually... if you, um..." He tapped his head and his jewel, as if he couldn't quite get the words out.

Izzy flicked both ears back and rolled her eyes. "You are not pushing this social bond thing on me again. We don't have one, okay? You can't make it happen by accident."

"But if you heard my voice in your head and agreed super quickly--"

"I didn't hear your voice in my head," she said. "Not really. It was just me feeling pressured because you want the Guardianship so badly."

Matt chewed his bottom lip. "'Not really'?"

Izzy looked away. She caught a glimpse of Roscoe, who stared at her, concerned. "I mean, maybe it kind of felt like it with you staring at me."

Matt lowered his gaze. "Izzy--"

"Please just drop it, Matt," Izzy said. "We don't have a social bond. It was just stress and me wanting to support you."

Matt wrinkled his snout and furrowed his brow, but he finally dropped it.

Izzy let out a short sigh. She was so sick of that argument. Social bonds didn't happen on accident. Hell, they didn't happen at all. They were too dangerous. She was just stressed.

And who wouldn't be? This Ouranos was a ridiculously powerful elemental user with two formidable summons. They needed a full team of elemental users and cloakers to even think about being able to tackle him. She didn't belong in that group. Not as a top member. Just… as support. Like always.

Hopefully she'd be enough support to get through this.

They entered the outfitters and started gathering equipment – hard, military grade Gem holsters for the hip to replace the cloth civilian one, ear COMS, basic first aid in case Izzy couldn't fulfill her duties as healer, field packs with a little food and water, and weapons. Izzy rested her hand on her hammer.

And what if they failed? Then they'd lose the Guardianship. She didn't know whether to be nervous at the prospect or relieved at this final test. Perhaps a bit of both.

At least they had finally gotten an answer from Lance about why he had denied them so many times. She shouldn't be surprised, considering the fact that she had suggested it just that morning, but still. Hearing it from Lance's mouth felt… odd. No wonder he had given them such an ultimatum, especially with such a difficult task. For all she knew, Lance had done it knowing they'd fail. Then he wouldn't have to give them the Guardianship.

Matt echoed Izzy's thoughts. *Lance gave me quite a task. But what if we do fail? What if I can't follow Lance's orders? What if I don't get the Guardianship?* A pause. *What if I can't help Ouranos? He's clearly suffering. What kind of Guardian would I be if I can't help him?*

"Matt, the best way you can try and help Ouranos is by listening to Lance and capturing him," Izzy said. "I don't know if I agree that he's suffering, either. He certainly didn't seem like it when he literally tried to kill you."

"What?" Roscoe said, kneeling near a weapons locker. "Where did that come from, Izzy?"

89

Izzy frowned. Everyone stared at her. She blinked. "What? We need to stay focused on Lance's orders if we want to do this."

"I get that, but that just came out of the blue," Sami said.

Izzy raised an eyebrow. "Why? Matt was talking about it."

Matt shifted uncomfortably, flattening his ears.

Darvin exchanged a glance with Sami. He eyed Matt. "You need to not mumble when you talk, Matt." Matt flicked an ear back. He moved to speak, but Darvin cut him off. "She is right though. You need to focus on capture and stick to Lance's orders. If you really think Ouranos needs help, that's the best you can do." He twisted a long ear back. "I really don't think he needs help though. Clearly he didn't need help to sic his summons on us."

But Matt wasn't paying attention. He stared at Izzy.

She frowned. He had to have muttered that under his breath, right? She had heard him whisper. She hadn't heard him in her head. She *hadn't*.

"Matt?" Darvin said, interrupting her thoughts. "Did you hear me?"

Matt shook his head. "Yeah, I heard you."

"And?"

Matt stared. "What, did you want a response for that?"

"At least an acknowledgement," Darvin said. "We all know you have a hard time following orders. Let's make sure that isn't a problem today, okay?"

Matt narrowed his eyes. "The Guardianship is on the line. I'm not going to jeopardize that."

"Good." Sami smiled at him. "Because we'd all like to call you Guardian Azure when this is done."

"And Guardian Gildspine," Roscoe said, gripping Izzy's shoulder. "You two deserve it."

"Speaking of that…" Matt turned to Izzy. "I'm sorry for earlier. Lance was right. I kept saying 'I' instead of 'we' when I yelled at Lance about the Guardianship. I wasn't being a good partner. That was bad of me."

90

Izzy perked both ears in surprise. "Uh, don't worry about it, Matt. It was in the heat of the moment. You're fine."

"Still," Matt said. "I need to include you more."

"I'll give you that," Izzy said. "Thanks."

Matt picked up a field pack and stuffed it with a blanket, some water, and mission rations. "Do you really think we'll get the Guardianship today?"

Izzy took a deep breath. Funny that she had asked him that this morning. Hell, had it really been just that morning? Felt like a lifetime. So much had changed today. "I hope so. That's the goal anyway."

"Is it?"

Izzy stared at him.

Matt shifted, flattening an ear. "I mean... you were pretty reluctant to rush into battle earlier today. And you admitted that the main reason why you agreed to this ultimatum was because of me."

"I know," Izzy said. "I just... wasn't prepared to fight at the Arena. Or have Lance give us this mission as a final test."

Matt gripped her shoulder. "I get that. I wasn't prepared to fight either."

"But you ran in without a thought," Izzy said.

"Yeah, but that's not always a good thing, right? It's what Lance was getting after me for. We both need to find a middle ground. And we will." He gave her a friendly squeeze. "I'm thrilled to have you on board. You're my best friend and partner. You deserve the Guardianship. We both do. And we'll prove that today."

She smiled. "Like I said. That's the goal."

"Good." Matt pulled a COM kit out of his weapons locker and began setting it up. Izzy went back to gathering supplies.

...Izzy's... powers... hold her back.

91

Izzy shot her head up. Had Matt really just said that? But he hadn't even been looking at her. He had his COM kit out and was talking about what to do if and when COMs stopped working in the Dead Zone.

So… what had she heard? That had absolutely been Matt's voice. But no one reacted or said anything. Certainly a claim like that would have at least gotten a scolding from Roscoe. Right? She hit the side of her head with the heel of her palm, trying to stop her ringing ears.

She really was just stressed. Tired. Worried. That couldn't have been Matt. It was just her own stupid insecurities. That was it. All those nagging voices were. They just sounded like Matt for some reason. Probably because he was always on her about her confidence. Matt was so confident in his own abilities, he couldn't imagine why Izzy didn't have the same confidence in hers.

He didn't understand the social stigmas of being a healer. And a Black Bound healer at that. She wished he try to understand more.

She shook her head. That was stupid. Healing or not, she did deserve the Guardianship, and Matt would be the first to tell her that. Why would he lift her up then immediately drag her down?

She formed a fist and pressed her lips together, twitching her short tail. It didn't matter anyway. So what if she had inferior powers, right? So what if she was just support and didn't have the element she wanted? She'd… she'd show him. She'd show everyone. She'd do this and win the Guardianship. She deserved it, no matter what magic she had. Plenty of Guardians had been healers. She'd… she'd do it.

She had to.

CLUTCHING AT CAST CHARMS

Ouranos adjusted his grip on Jústi's feet, dangling in the air, still clutching the black liquid he had harvested from the blue and white quilar's fur in his palm. There were only a few drops of it, but it was precious.

And dangerous.

The memory of the stranger who had bridged the gap to his soul played in his mind's eye. He remembered very little, beyond the great look of sadness on the stranger's face when Ouranos had achieved full clarity for the first time in years. And, now that he held the liquid in his hand, a reminder of sharp spikes of pain, though he could not recall if that was from the liquid or from some other injury he had acquired in his time in the war. Everything at that time was still so vague...

But one thing was certain. That stranger had produced the same black liquid on his fingertips, and it was that black liquid that had allowed Ouranos control over his mind again.

Granted, he had no idea how -- just that the stranger's had hands dripped with it, much like the Defender -- the Guardian's -- hands today. Ouranos had later found it in his own fur, black on black, near unnoticeable, save for the uncomfortable moisture against his skin.

He had been so distraught, and it had happened so long ago, he could not recall *where* on his body he had found it. He had tried to piece the image together so many times, but he could only summon up the image of black liquid on black fur and nothing more. A shame, as that would be helpful to employ it now. Though he doubted the few drops he held would be enough to achieve any kind of freedom from his father's puppetry. He would have to collect more.

But this small amount *could* serve his father's purposes -- for this liquid could create Shadow Cast. Or, at least, the Basileus believed it did. How his father had learned this, and how he had obtained the liquid and employed it without Ouranos' knowing, Ouranos did not know, but Theron had been practically shaking Ouranos' body with glee since he had grabbed it.

The one good side effect of his father's outrageous joy was that his control had slipped and Ouranos heard none of his thoughts, just felt his emotions. It would not last though, especially once they were in relative safety, but he relished the respite, however short it might be. It gave him some time to think...

What to do with his prize?

This then, was the conflict. Keep the liquid and fight with his father for its use, or release it and hold back his father's creation of Cast for a bit longer... at the expense of his own freedom and his ability to redouble the efforts against his father's destructive path.

After decades under his father's control, watching him destroy their home, their subjects, and even their neighbors for his own revenge... he could not bring himself to release the liquid.

Jústi keened and slowed her pace as she descended into the wooded canyon that held Ouranos' only home on this planet -- the space-faring plane his father had found and restored to get here in the first place.

From the air, the scar his crash had inflicted upon the forest was apparent, though once inside the canyon, the place became a maze. Hopefully that forest maze, along with the confusing halls in the plane itself, would give Ouranos the time he needed to prepare for the Defender's inevitable investigation.

Though, looking at the plane now was a sharp reminder that even if he got free, even if he stopped his father here, he was still an impossible distance from his own home. The ship that had brought him here would not take him home. He would need another way off the planet.

He alighted on the ground and dismissed Jústi with a thank you before entering the battered vehicle through a tear in the plane's body.

"You -*bzzt*- return!" a metallic voice echoed in the plane's tiny vestibule. A miniscule, blue-green, faerie-winged dragon simply named Pilot materialized above Ouranos's head, grinning at him, a homecoming as good as could be. The dragon was not real, or in the very least, not physical. The form was a "hologram avatar" for the artificial intelligence who governed this plane, though Ouranos was never clear on what that truly meant, any more than he understood what was artificial about the dragon.

The A.I. flickered in and out of view. His speech was often broken, damaged, perhaps even mad, and he had a habit of dropping and adding words irrelevant to the conversation. An aftereffect, the dragon had said, from many years and waning power wearing on his existence.

Ouranos simply saw it as illness. Athánatos Ei-Ei Jewels his people used protected against most illnesses, but that did not make them immune. He could still recall his great grandmother's awkward speech as she neared the end of her life, before she chose to separate from the jewels that made them immortal. This was much the same.

Pilot's image faded to black and white before popping back into full color. He tilted his head curiously at Ouranos. "Were you -bzzt- successful in--in achieving -bzzt- goals--*foals--coals*--?"

Ouranos chewed his bottom lip, still gripping the few drops of black liquid, waiting for the A.I. to fight through its damaged speech. Pilot was the only person Ouranos had been able to speak frankly to in many years, and though it often made conversations difficult he grew to find the dragon's speech patterns charming. "In a manner of speaking."

Pilot stared at him with pinpoint orange eyes, bright and round. He frowned, a comical sight on the long-snouted hologram. "You seem--*beam--gleam* disappointed -bzzt-."

"I am," Ouranos said. "I found my quarry and extracted the... tool I needed." He held his hand out, watching the shiny black liquid pool in his palm. "But I did not get enough. I will need more, which means I will need to confront him again." He took a deep breath. "I hurt people to get it. I will have to hurt more to get what I need. I am not sure this is worth it."

I never asked your opinion on the matter, Prínkipas, the Basileus spat in Ouranos' mind. Ouranos winced – his brief respite was over. *That elixir is mine, and I will gather it by any means necessary.* The Basileus pushed his will on Ouranos, reaching for his magic - his ice magic specifically.

He meant to freeze the liquid, permanently solidifying it, rendering it useless for Ouranos' purposes.

"No!" Ouranos snarled, pulling back on his father's control. "You will not take this from me!"

As if you have any choice, Prínkipas. He pressed his will deeper into Ouranos' mind.

Ouranos pushed back as hard as he dared. "I *do* have a choice, and I will not give in. You cannot hold me forever!"

A shooting pain ripped through Ouranos' body from the tips of his ears to the roots of his toeclaws. He screamed. His father laughed in his head.

You truly think you can escape me? The Basileus said. *You are mine to control. You will always be mine to control.* A heavy sigh. *You would be better off had you never regained awareness.* He snatched control of Ouranos' power. Ice formed at the tips of his fingers and worked its way down to his palm.

Ouranos tried to scream, tried to dispose of the liquid, tried anything to disrupt his father's will, but nothing worked. The ice grasped the edge of the black droplets.

And stopped. Ouranos pulled back his magic before the drops fully hardened, leaving them in a semi-solid state. Just solid enough for the Basileus to believe them fully frozen.

The Basileus could see everything through Ouranos' eyes and control his body as if it were his own, if Ouranos did not fight, but he could not feel what Ouranos felt. A shield the Basileus kept up for his own protection in case his puppet was seriously injured or... died. The Basileus was unwilling to experience death, even secondhand. Never mind that the precaution was purely selfish and he had no qualms about sacrificing his children to meet his goals.

This gave Ouranos little advantage normally, but provided the perfect deception now. It had ruined the liquid for his needs, but, hopefully, ruined it for his father's purposes as well.

Regardless of its effectiveness, he now held a possible means to create Shadow Cast. A Cast Charm. Assuming it worked. He was still unsure.

He cursed. Not... ideal. Draso's breath, he should have thrown this aside while he had the chance. He should have done anything to keep this from his father. His freedom was not worth the potential damage the Basileus could do. What was he thinking?

97

A rapid beeping echoed through the vestibule and Pilot flickered in and out of view. "Ouranos, I--I am detecting -*bzzt*- Defender troop--*scoop*--*droop* carrier--er plane -*bzzt*- heading this way. I cannot--not hope to Spook -*bzzt*- in- -in this state--*late*--*mate*. I don't have -*bzzt*- power."

While Ouranos did not understand it, Spooking was a technology that had allowed their plane to escape detection when they had landed on the planet. It took a tremendous amount of energy and the plane had been running low for days. It was no wonder that he did not have the means.

"Ouranos? Course of action -*bzzt*- please?"

Ouranos frowned. He needed to hide. Keep his father away from anyone who might come investigating. Even a semi-solid drop of the strange black liquid could be dangerous. Maybe he could at least shut and lock the doors--

His father burst through Ouranos' consciousness with a spike of pain through his head. "Open the doors, Pilot," the Basileus said aloud, preserving Ouranos' higher pitched voice. "Let us invite them in."

Pilot tilted his head. "Are you -*bzzt*- sure? This will -*bzzt*- put us--us in danger--*stranger*--*ranger*."

Ouranos fought back. *No!* But his father won out.

"Bring them to me," the Basileus said. "I could use some new… friends."

No, no, no!

Pilot stared a moment, lifted his wings in a simulation of a shrug, and vanished. The main hatch opened and landed into the dirt with a dull thud, flooding the vestibule with light.

"You cannot win, Prínkipas," the Basileus said in a mockery of Ouranos' own voice. "The victory will be mine."

Ouranos seethed in the recesses of his mind, fighting and failing to regain control of his body. What changed? He had fought and won numerous times since landing here, but now… He had lost. He could do nothing.

Unless one of their investigators was the blue and white quilar. Matthew, or Matt, his companions had called him. Unless he was the one coming and Ouranos could coax more liquid from him. Could he regain his freedom? Could he beat down his father? He did not know. But he had to try.

Draso, give me strength.

CHAPTER 13

THE DEAD ZONE

Matt gripped the controls of the Delta-Z troop carrier, headed for the Dead Zone in Corinth Woods. He double checked his Gem, tucked snuggly in the Gem Energy Converter, and readjusted course.

He tried finding any comfortable way to sit. It'd be at least a half hour flight so he might as well put this in on autopilot and kick back.

But nothing worked. All he got was leg cramps and a kinked tail.

Damn it all. Why couldn't he just calm down?

He peeked over his shoulder into the cabin where the rest of his pack were strapped in with their equipment. Roscoe and Darvin chatted excitedly about the mission, their antlers scrapping the ceiling, while Cix and Sami discussed strategies for fire wielding with enthusiastic tail swishing. The high tension made everyone's Gem glow slightly, showing off each jewel's colors. Everyone was anxious and thrilled. No one worried like him.

Well. Except his partner.

Izzy sat next to her husband, silent, fiddling with her hammer's strap, her golden-brown ears flicking about.

Matt took a deep breath. Izzy. She was why he couldn't calm down. She had heard him. In her head. Just like he had heard her during the fight with Ouranos. All those thoughts and worries about the Guardianship and Lance and Ouranos… that's why she responded like he said it out loud.

And damn it, she refused to admit that it was because of a social bond. If she could just accept it for what it was, maybe they could work on fixing the problem. There had to be ways to avoid hearing each other's thoughts.

But he really couldn't blame her. It was a ridiculous thought that they had created the bond by accident. He wouldn't have believed it himself if he hadn't researched it. And heard Izzy's voice in his head.

Or if she hadn't heard his.

Fire and ice, had she heard him thinking that he hoped Izzy wouldn't think her powers would hold her back? Actually, that one might not be so bad. She needed the confidence. Maybe hearing something that counter her own low opinion of herself would be helpful.

Maybe that made up a little for the fact that his thoughts influenced her to accept this mission when she clearly didn't want it.

He watched her closely, but she didn't look up at him or react at all. Good. He had shut down the connection for now. The last thing he needed was her hearing his thoughts all the time. She may not accept that they had a social bond, but he did and damn it, he was going to do everything possible to make sure it wasn't a problem.

The overhead holobulbs lit up and a tiny dragon with large leather wings, jagged curved horns, a spiked tail, and thick scales appeared in motes of blue and purple. He snorted rainbow smoke from his long snout. "Finally following in your father's footsteps, are you?"

Matt glared at the dragon A.I., Caesum. Lance wouldn't let them go without an A.I. to pilot their ship and record their mission, but of all the ones he picked, it had to be this jerk. Matt took on an air of authority. "I am in charge of this mission and I outrank you. I know you're old as dirt, but if you still have any shred of mental competency, you should recall that the appropriate form of address for the mission commander is *'sir.'*"

"I will refer to you as 'sir' when you prove yourself worthy of that honorific," Caesum said. "As of right now, you have failed to do so."

"Will you call me sir when I get the Guardianship today?"

Caesum snorted. "Of course. I'll even congratulate you. But I'm not halting my processors. You're not your father."

Matt ground his teeth. Caesum was a powerful A.I. who traditionally belonged to the Golden Guardians. He had particularly attached himself to Matt's father and was fiercely loyal to him. So much so that he had basically convinced himself that no one would be a good enough replacement. Not even his hero's own son. Yeah, Caesum was likely the most experienced A.I. for the job, but that didn't make him the best choice.

Caesum had grown extra bitter after the Sol Genocide, when his partner A.I., Solas, had been lost. While Matt felt for him, that didn't excuse the dragon's behavior.

"Shut it, Caesum," Matt snarled. "Like it or not, I am in charge and I don't have to listen to your backtalk. Fly the plane and don't come out unless I call you."

Caesum huffed rainbow smoke. "As you wish, 'sir.' I hope for your sister's sake you come back in one piece." The holobulbs dimmed and he vanished.

Matt chewed his lip. That was a reminder he didn't need.

Charlotte wouldn't even talk to him before he left. He had tried to say goodbye and she'd just waved him off. That... didn't feel great. He didn't know if Caesum somehow knew that had happened or if he was just trying to get under Matt's fur, but it stung nonetheless.

Was he really doing the right thing?

He shook his head. *No. I am not starting that. This is my choice and this is what I want.* He kept his gaze on the plane's instruments.

Time slowed to a crawl, but eventually they approached their destination. Matt turned to the group. "We're about to enter the Dead Zone, everyone. Gather your equipment. I'll be going manual soon."

"What are we looking for when we hit the ground?" Sami asked.

"Signs of life, food waste, fire pits," Cix said. "Though honestly, if he's really not from Zyearth like Larissa suggests, we should look for a space plane too."

Izzy coughed. "Do you really think he could fly a plane? He looked so archaic."

"Hey, the paleofaunos of Erdoglyan are tribal and wear *robes and cloaks* and their technology rivals ours," Roscoe said. "Looks can be deceiving."

"I was thinking about that, Matt," Darvin said, his voice growing serious. "If he really did come here from another planet, how did he escape detection when he entered atmosphere? Most planets don't have Spooking tech and we monitor everything."

Matt frowned. He had a good point. "I guess we'll find out." He nodded to Izzy. "Hey Iz, take the copilot's seat. I'd like a second pair of eyes. Not a lot of great landing zones here."

Izzy nodded and strapped herself to the copilot's seat. They cruised for a few minutes longer.

Izzy pointed. "Hey Matt, what's that?"

Matt craned his neck. A large groove a kilometer long and at least half as wide had been dug into the dirt and parted the trees. At the end of it... a massive space plane. Damaged, broken, unfamiliar, but a plane just the same. Clearly crash landed. That explained a lot.

"Suitable LZ 45 degrees starboard," Caesum said, poking his head out in the hologram readout. He managed a tiny sneer. *"'Sir.'"* Then he disappeared.

Izzy raised an eyebrow at Matt, but Matt didn't respond. He wouldn't give the A.I. that satisfaction. Instead, he took on the role of a leader. "Confirm LZ, GR Gildspine."

Izzy watched him a moment, but hardened her features and nodded. "Aye, GR Azure." She tapped some controls. "LZ confirmed. Descent authorized."

"Strap in, everyone. From this moment on, we're a pack on a mission. Normal chain of command. Understood?"

"Yes, sir," everyone said.

"Good. Let's make this count." Matt headed for the landing zone.

A few minutes later and Matt had successfully landed and Spooked the plane. If Ouranos' plane was unusable, there was no reason to make him a gift of this one. Delta-Zs weren't really designed for long, deep-space flight, but still, better to keep it hidden.

He also put Caesum on a data crystal and shoved it in his bag, then strapped the pack around his waist, effectively turning it into saddlebags. The A.I. might be a pain in the ass, but he could be useful if Ouranos' plane in the woods still had power. Depending on how deep in the power supply was, it might have escaped the electronic disruption of the Dead Zone. Plus, no good leaving Caesum for Ouranos to nab up if he found a way around the Spooking. Roscoe was right. They didn't know what kind of technology he had.

Matt led the pack out of the plane into the crisp autumn air. The evening had cooled considerably, but the evergreen sap had clearly warmed during the day and still permeated the air with its distinctive smell. Though it didn't mask the musky smell of stag from the Polttarit brothers. Thank Draso for Darvin's cloaking. Cloaking smells wasn't easy or perfect by any means, but it'd be better than nothing.

Sami pulled a data slate out of her backpack. "Our target is about half a kilometer away, sir," she said. But she frowned and tilted the slate. "Or... ten kilometers. The data slate can't tell."

"It's the Dead Zone," Matt said. "We're too near it. Stay close -- we'll likely lose COMs soon. Standard pack formation. Keep an eye out for trails and signs of life." Another chorus of "yes, sirs" and everyone spread out with a few meters between them. Matt took point.

The woods were oddly silent. No birds. No animals. Not even any wind, which was unusual in a canyon. With no wind, the pinesap smell hung deep in the air, though Darvin and Roscoe's smell faded as they walked behind him. Matt had never trained in the Dead Zone, so he had no idea if this was normal or not. He should have looked it up before they left. That was careless. Extra caution.

They walked about twenty minutes before they came to the gash in the dirt they had spotted from the air. Silently, he waved his pack to stick to the woods and out of sight. Another fifteen minutes and the plane came into view.

It really was unlike any plane he had ever seen. Huge, for one, about the size of a Delta-A, the much larger cousin to the Delta-Z, used for transporting large numbers of troops and civilians long distances, usually through space. The thing looked almost impossibly old... dented, rusted, mix-matched paint, haphazard repairs, outdated wing and fuselage design... and while he couldn't know for sure without deeper analysis, it looked to be made of inferior metals. Things they wouldn't even consider for space planes today.

And that was number two - its design clearly marked it as a space-faring plane, which practically confirmed that Ouranos wasn't from Zyearth. What was worse is Matt didn't recognize the design from any current space-capable planet. Knowing those planes was essential knowledge for Guardians because a lot of his missions would carry him off-world.

If he made the Guardianship.

But Matt didn't know this one. That meant one of two things. One, this was a new plane that some other planet had developed but hadn't registered with interplanetary authorities. Unlikely, considering the metal composition. Or two, considering its obvious age, it was from a planet that had discovered and repaired a damaged plane. Maybe even borrowed a plane. This was not the work of newly developed space flight. Also, considering Ouranos' unusual dress, his unfamiliar, not-quite-standard-quilar features, and his unregistered focus jewels and phoenix summons, this wasn't likely from a known planet.

Matt pressed his ears back and chewed his bottom lip. That might mean that Ouranos wasn't working alone. For all he knew, they could be facing an entire army in there. An entire army of element-wielding summoners with phoenixes so powerful that even the Master Guardian struggled with them. Hell, the main reason they'd been able to fight off the ones they had was because they honestly didn't seem that interested in destruction... they were too busy trying to find someone to help their Prínkipas.

But help him with what? There were too many unknowns.

Matt herded his pack out of view of the plane. Who knew who might be in there?

But Izzy stayed put, staring at the back fin, frowning. She waved to Matt. "Sir... Matt... you'll want to see this."

Matt's fur bristled, but he followed her gaze. And gasped.

On the tail of the plane, in faded black, was a Defender symbol.

THE PLANE

Everyone stared.

"What the hell?" Cix muttered. "A Defender symbol?"

"And a Yelar flag," Sami said, pointing out the flag for their continent under the faded Defender dragon. "But… not recent. See the colors? It's only representing eleven realms. It's been five or six generations since Yelar had so few."

Generations! Matt frowned. More than that, why would a Defender plane have the continent flag instead of their own country of Zedric? Yelar wasn't a unified continent. Each realm was its own independent country, albeit with an alliance. It hadn't been a single country since… since…

"Lightning and air," Izzy said. "It's a colony plane."

A colony plane. A *colony plane*. How could that even be? How had one survived? How had Ouranos gotten it working? Where had it even *come from?* It could be from *anywhere*.

Some of Zyearth's earliest treks to the stars had involved colonization of other planets -- zyfaunos desperate to escape a world war that had raged for decades. The planes took tens of thousands of zyfaunos in tight ship clusters headed anywhere but Zyearth. And the Defenders had led the charge. It was one of the major reasons they were created, even if their purpose had drastically changed over the generations.

But none had returned and almost nothing was known about where they went. The only real proof that they'd even made it anywhere safely came in the fact that there were zyfaunos on planets everywhere. Though most didn't know their origin.

That could explain why they hadn't detected the plane. These planes had primitive Spooking technology. Apparently this plane's Spook tech still worked.

"Matt," Roscoe said. "If this is a colony plane, then it must have cryotechnology on board."

Cryotechnology. This was why no one remembered they came from Zyearth. While cryotechnology effectively kept those who used it from dying on long space journeys, it also absolutely destroyed memory, even driving some zyfaunos insane. After the colonization crisis, they'd dropped cryotechnology completely and focused on speed in space travel instead of long-term preservation.

But… if this plane had cryotechnology… if Ouranos had used it… That could explain his erratic behavior. Maybe. But it did also give a lot more weight to the theory that he wasn't alone.

"This just got far more dangerous," Izzy said, clearly coming to the same conclusion. "Matt--"

"We're not going back," Matt said with more confidence than he actually felt. "We don't know anything for sure yet, and we can't go back without at least gathering intelligence."

"But someone back at base should know," Izzy said.

Matt's tail drooped. She had a point. He herded the pack back into the relative safety of the trees and checked his COM, though he knew it wouldn't work. No outside communication. That meant leaving the Dead Zone... wasting more time, giving Ouranos more opportunity to formulate a plan, weakening their chance to help him, making it more difficult to follow the Master Guardian's order...

That was another thing. If he retreated, that meant failing the Master Guardian's objectives, essentially -- capture or eliminate. So if he retreated... would he lose his chance at the Guardianship?

But Izzy had a point too. It could be dangerous to leave the Defenders in the dark. Damn it all.

Maybe he could get a volunteer.

"COMs don't work," he said. "If we do this, someone will need to leave the Dead Zone." He turned to his pack. "Any volunteers?"

No one said anything. Matt flattened one ear. Well, so much for that.

Izzy shifted. "Matt..."

"I think for now, we should just move on," Matt said. "We don't have time. We've got to do something before this gets out of hand and we've used a lot of time getting here already. We'll just have to be careful."

"But--"

"It's not up for discussion," Matt said. "I'm leading this mission and--"

"We *both* are, Matt," Izzy snarled. "And the Master Guardian was *very clear* that we needed to do this as partners. We're here to keep your hotheaded decisions from getting out of hand, and running headfirst into a potential army-filled plane without telling Lance is definitely that!"

Matt narrowed his eyes. "It's *not* a hotheaded decision. It's a calculated one. If we turn back now, we might lose our only window and give Ouranos

109

the chance to do more damage. Yes, I know it's dangerous, but we're going to be *Guardians*, damnit, and this is what we're *for."*

Izzy formed fists. *"Matt--"*

"I'll go."

Matt turned. Roscoe looked at him with a blank expression, his ears rigid.

Izzy stepped forward, fur bristled. "Roscoe."

"It's fine, Izzy," Roscoe said. "You both make good points. Someone should let the Master Guardian know how big this might be, but we also have a limited window. We don't want to bring the whole army here if it's just Ouranos, but we also don't want to waste a bunch more time with potentially useless reports."

Darvin flipped one ear back. "I suppose that's true. Maybe I should go."

Roscoe stretched his legs, testing his hooves grip on the dirt, then stood straight. He handed his field pack to Darvin, who strapped it to his leg. "I'm the fastest runner. I'll run out, send a message, then run right back. If I'm fast enough, I should be able to get back before you get too far into the plane. And if I do get back and you've run into trouble, then you'll have someone free who can go get help. Sir." He said the last word looking Matt in the eye and offering a short salute.

Matt chewed his lip and twitched an ear. "Permission granted."

Izzy gasped. *"Matt."*

"We have to do something, Izzy," Matt said. "And I asked for volunteers. Roscoe responded." He nodded to Roscoe. "Thank you." Roscoe nodded back, but stiffly.

Izzy shot a glare at Matt before turning to Roscoe. "Come back to me, okay?"

Roscoe snorted, but nodded. "In all fairness, you're the one with the more difficult mission. But you're a Guardian, that's your job."

"Not a Guardian yet."

"You will be." He trotted to Izzy and planted a kiss on her forehead. "I'll be back soon. Take care of yourself." He eyed Matt. "And take care of this idiot too. We need our Guardians." Before Izzy had a chance to protest further, he found a game trail and galloped silently back out of the Dead Zone.

Matt frowned, but shook his head of Roscoe's words. "Okay, Defenders, let's do this. Weapons out, Gems hot, but be cautious. Unless we get overwhelmed, we're treating this as an intelligence gathering mission until we find anything about Ouranos. No shooting first, asking questions later. Understood?"

"Yes, sir."

"I'll take point, Izzy, Sami, and Cix next, and Darvin last," Matt continued. "Feel up to cloaking all of us?"

Darvin gave a quick salute. "Yes, sir."

"Good." He unsheathed his sword and mentally reached for his magic. "Let's do this."

THE BRIDGE

Izzy followed behind Matt, a hand on his shoulder, as they searched the side of the plane for a door. Sami gripped Izzy's pack, and Cix grabbed hers behind her, all carefully concealed behind Darvin's cloak.

Darvin elected to stay in the woods, at least until Matt gave the all-clear, using the trees to hide himself. The shoulder gripping wasn't ideal, but in tight formation and with no electronic aids to mark allies, it was the only way they could navigate without smashing into each other.

Feeling Matt in front of her, without being able to see him or even her own hand, was more than a bit odd. Cloaking always unnerved her. And she already missed Roscoe. Hopefully he'd get his message to Lance and get back ASAP.

"There," Matt whispered. "I see an open hatch."

"It's open?" Sami said.

Izzy shrugged, though no one could see it. "They did crash land. For all we know they had to pry it open. This thing probably doesn't have power, considering where we are."

Matt tapped Izzy's hand for silence and they moved forward.

Sure enough, the large hatch lay open, the door resting against the scarred ground, creating a ramp into the belly of the plane. Matt let out a low whistle for Darvin to follow and led them inside.

The hatch led into an open vestibule with several large doorways leading down at least a dozen different dimly lit hallways. But not dark. Emergency lights lit up each pathway in a dull blue. The air had the musty smell of something old, and if outdated materials hadn't been proof enough of the plane's age, the rusted, peeling inner panels certainly were. Izzy was no mechanic, but even she was amazed this thing still flew. And it echoed wildly. Every shuffle, every footprint, amplified. It wasn't until they stood perfectly still that the echoing sounds stopped.

And that made things clear. No one was here. She had been on enough space planes to recognize the silence of an empty cabin. No shuffling, no talking, no footprints, no clinks or clangs of movement, not even any air from the air vents... just their own careful breathing and the near-silent hum of electronics.

But there were electronics.

"Matt, the plane has power," Izzy whispered. The whisper magnified against the metal walls.

Matt let out another low whistle and Darvin dropped the cloaking on everyone. "I see that. But it's also very quiet. I doubt there's anyone here, unless they're still in cryo." His tail twitched. "Maybe not even Ouranos."

"Wait." Sami jogged toward a glowing corner of the vestibule, her bare fox feet only slightly more muffled than Izzy's own boots. She kneeled and

113

the glow immediately died. Sami stood and jogged back to them, holding a long feather.

Izzy's eyes widened. She took the feather from Sami. "One of Jústi's feathers."

"I think so," Sami said.

Matt frowned. "If it just lost power, Ouranos probably isn't far behind. Jústi's feather only held power for a few minutes back at the Arena." He looked down at the corridors. "But this place is huge…"

"We should split up," Cix said. He pulled out two small pouches from his mission bag. "I've got pathmarkers here. They probably won't light up in the Dead Zone, but you can still stick 'em to the walls and find your way back and it'll keep us from taking the same path twice." He handed a bag to Matt.

"Good idea," Matt said. "Two teams. Izzy and I are Red Team. Darvin, Sami, Cix, you're Blue Team." He took one of the tiny round markers out of the bag and pressed it into the wall near the open hatch, with the red side facing out. "That way Roscoe knows we're in the plane. Darvin, you're senior here, so you lead Blue."

"Yes, sir," Darvin said with a salute.

"This place is too large to wander aimlessly for too long," Izzy said. "Let's make a plan to meet back here in an hour and regroup. The analogue watches should keep close enough time even in the Dead Zone."

"Good idea," Matt said. He saluted to Darvin. Izzy followed suit. "Good luck, soldiers."

"You as well." Darvin picked a corridor and started down it, cloaking Sami and Cix while they walked. He placed a marker at the entrance, blue side facing out. Izzy watched until his clip-clopping footfalls faded away.

Matt looked at the remaining corridors. "Pick one, Iz."

Izzy pointed to the far right. "That one, near where Sami found Jústi's feather."

114

"Then let's go." They headed down the corridor. Matt took point and handed Izzy the bag of pathmarkers.

The hall was tall, easily four meters to the ceiling, with the same peeling, rusted panels as they had seen in the vestibule. Emergency lights lined the floor in blue, though only about a third of them even worked. They found a few small automatic doors on each wall, but none of them opened. One of them had a handpad near it, but the activation lights underneath it were dead.

Strange that the plane didn't have Defender locks. Modern Defender planes locked everything with Defender pendants as IDs. Must have been before that technology existed. It really had to be a colony plane.

Everything smelled of rust and decay. Even the air had a metallic smell and taste to it, a sure sign the air scrubbers were saturated. There was also dust everywhere, and even some spiderwebs. How long had he been on the planet to get spiderwebs in the plane? The webs and dust caked on Izzy's boots, leaving behind little clouds. Maybe this wasn't the path to go down. It was clear it hadn't been used in a while. But they had already picked it. Might as well see where it led.

Izzy pressed a pathmarker to the wall every few meters, acutely aware of their loud footsteps in the dust. It finally threatened to drive her mad, so she stopped, pulled off her boots and stuffed them in her bag.

Matt smirked and did the same. Their padded footfalls echoed like felt against their ears with the occasional *click, click* of a long toeclaw that had escaped its sheath. She'd have to clip them soon, but at least it was better than the relative sonic booms from their boots. The dust didn't bother her as much as the sound, but she made a mental note to take a nice long shower when she was done.

A few more minutes and the corridor branched into four others. Three headed back the way they came, but the third went forward, and at the entrance, a large, oppressive, light filled the hall. Matt held up a fist and motioned Izzy

115

to stay behind. She pressed herself against the wall, watching him vanish into the harsh light. She stood there in uncomfortable silence, willing him to come back, when he popped his head back out. He motioned her inside.

"Izzy... You'll want to see this."

She entered the room and stopped.

They had found the bridge.

A central console sat in a half circle in the middle of the room, facing a massive, cracked window with two plump chairs secured to the floor in front of it. Five alcoves surrounded it with chairs and consoles of their own, and different, handwritten labels painted over each. NΛVIGΛΓION. WΞΔPΘNS. Δ.I. ΞNGINΞ. CΘMMUNICΛΓIΘNS. The words were faded, the letters, not quite modern. The oppressive outside light from the afternoon sun was blinding, even with the few scattered trees casting long shadows over the bridge. If there were any lights on in the consoles, it'd be hard to tell. Everything smelled of dust and rotting electronics and upholstery.

Except the captain's chairs. Both were dirty, but appeared to have been carelessly wiped free of at least the surface level of dust. They had cracks in the fabric, revealing faded yellow padding underneath.

"Well," Izzy said. "That was a stroke of luck."

"No kidding," Matt said. He pointed to the captain's chair. "I'd say someone's been here recently. Don't know if it's Ouranos or someone else. Either way, I'm going to see if I can pull up the captain's logs and see where this came from. Why don't you check out the other stations? If there's power, we might get some useful information."

Izzy nodded, hoisted her field pack higher on her back, and looked over the other stations, starting with Navigation. The tiny screen was dead, and, to her surprise, a lot of the buttons were simply missing. The chair didn't even look safe to sit in. How did they get here?

The other stations were similar. Engine was a bit better off. The screen even had a faded backlight, but she couldn't get it to activate. Communications was... shattered. Like someone had taken a big wrench and just smashed it to bits. Weapons was the same. Clearly someone had sabotaged these, though the rust and age of the leftover bits suggested it had happened long before the plane landed here. This probably wasn't something Ouranos or one of his allies did.

Then she got to A.I. Not surprisingly, there wasn't much in the way of controls here. Ancient holobulbs for A.I. display, some broken, a screen and keyboard for discreet communication, five dead A.I. crystal slots...

Wait. No... not dead.

In one of the slots, buried in a mild, pulsing green, was a live A.I. crystal.

CHAPTER 16

DISCOVERY

Izzy stared at the console. Did that mean there was an active A.I.? One of the *old* A.I.? A.I. were exceptionally powerful computers, even way back during their early conceptions, but they were also prone to code corruption and fragmenting, especially as they aged and if they didn't have sufficient power for their data crystals. Considering the ship's age and its lack of power, there was no way this A.I. could have avoided that. If it even had enough power to stay active. For all she knew, it was effectively "dead." It was amazing the crystal itself hadn't fallen apart, honestly. And it wasn't like it could be backed up – A.I. were bound to their crystals.

More than that, if the A.I. was live and its programming had gone haywire, that could pose all sorts of problems for the visitors on the ship.

"No good," Matt said, walking toward Izzy. "I can't get the plane's logs. Not enough power. It keeps giving me error messages. Any luck on your end?"

"There's a live A.I. crystal here," Izzy said.

"Really?" Matt looked over Izzy's shoulder. "Huh. Does that mean we have a live A.I.?"

"Possibly," Izzy said. "The NAV and COM stations are a bust. I can't imagine they could get here without an A.I. Assuming they were aiming for Zyearth." She waved at the console. "But if we do, it's probably corrupted. It's very unlikely it has enough power to hold itself together, if it's not dead already."

Matt reached into his bag and pulled out Caesum's data crystal. "Think Caesum could learn a little here?"

Izzy frowned. That could be a bad idea. "He could, but he also might get erased or pick up a virus. Or this other A.I. could attack and dismantle his code if they're viable. And that assumes that his data crystal will even fit in an A.I. slot this old."

Matt's tail drooped, but he shook his head. "If this A.I is alive, it's way too old to compete with Caesum. And A.I. storage hasn't changed much over the years. The crystals are different colors, but the shape's the same and we still use similar tech to attach them to ships."

"Maybe," Izzy said, though she wasn't really convinced. She shrugged. "It's your call."

Matt stared at the crystal in his hand. "I don't think Caesum would forgive me if he knew I got to this old ship and didn't let him poke around."

"I don't think Caesum deserves that level of respect, Matt." Izzy crossed her arms. "I heard him harassing you earlier."

Matt pasted an ear back, but didn't acknowledge Izzy's jab at Caesum. "I still think he'll be helpful."

"What about the power?"

"Eh, Caesum's crystal has enough power for him," Matt said. "He might even be able to reroute some of it to start some of the smaller systems onboard. Maybe get info on the inhabitants and access the data logs."

Izzy sighed. She wasn't going to get him to change his mind. "Fine, go for it."

Matt nodded. He gripped the handle of one of the A.I. chambers buried in the desk and pulled it up slowly until it locked in place. He pressed the button on the glass canister holding a dead crystal and the little door opened with a hiss of coolant steam. He slipped the dead crystal out, replaced it with Caesum's live one, then slid it back down into the console.

Immediately one of the holobulb clusters woke up and Caesum appeared. He shook his head and stretched his blue wings, sending flitters of blue and purple light motes to the edges of the hologram's reach. He paused, then looked up at Matt wide-eyed. "Lightning and air, I'm in a colony ship."

Matt smirked. "Well, you answered my first question."

Caesum flew in loop de loops. Tiny 1's and 0's flew off his body like so many drops of water. "The knowledge! The history! I didn't know any of them survived. How on Zyearth did you find one?"

"Ouranos came here on it," Izzy said. "But it crash-landed."

"Hmm, considering the weak power supply, I'm not surprised," Caesum said, rubbing his chin with his long-clawed fingers. "Didn't you say we were in the Dead Zone? I'm amazed it has power at all."

"I feel the same," Matt said. "Can you see deeper into the ship? Look for movement, let us know about any other important chambers? We're specifically looking for the cryochamber... I'd like to know if Ouranos is alone."

Caesum's eyes blanked a moment before he nodded. "I see the rest of your pack," he said. "They're pretty deep in, but they're just headed for an empty storage unit. Nothing important. Let's see... a mess hall, a library, a Gem chamber... all dead it seems. Needs more power." He paused. "Huh."

"What?" Matt asked.

120

"Medbay is active," the A.I. said. "Has a lot of power. Most of the equipment is still running."

"That's not really surprising," Izzy said. "If something went wrong then that's priority number one for power. You can't always count that you'll have a healer on hand. Even if they do, if the plane crash lands, they might end up with a lot of injuries and most healers can only work on one patient at a time."

"But how can it have active equipment?" Matt asked. "How can it have power at all in the Dead Zone?"

Caesum's image twitched and he nodded. "Ah, here's the power supply. Deep in the ship and magically insulated. That's probably why it escaped the effects."

Izzy perked an ear. "Magically insulated?"

Caesum nodded. "It draws on shielding magic to insulate the ship," he said. "Kind of like how we used cloaking magic to Spook our planes. Modern ships replicate the process electronically these days, like we do with Spooking now, but it probably means there's an unbound Gem integrated into the power supply."

Matt frowned. "Magic insulation doesn't work on our modern planes in the Dead Zone though."

"No, it draws too much power," Caesum said. "Even the electronic versions are poor replacements, though it works well enough if you happen to hit an electromagnetic pocket during space travel. Insulation this powerful really only worked when we used unbound Gems for fuel, but it literally burnt out the Gem after a few flights. Rendered them totally useless. Can't have that happening now since pilots use their own Gems to power planes."

Izzy shuddered at the thought.

"If it had more power, it'd possibly insulate the whole interior of the plane from the Dead Zone. But this plane is old and the Gem powering it is probably ready to give out. Considering where it came from, it's safe to assume it's had

121

at least two flights with the Gem. Unlikely they replaced it." He shook his head. "I'm struggling to see more. My reach is limited."

"No other movement?" Izzy asked.

"None beyond your own pack," Caesum said. "Wait... One of them is alone. Looks like PR Gildspine?"

"Oh good," Matt said. "Roscoe must have gotten our message out."

Caesum frowned. "He seems... loopy. Lost. I can't really see him well though, but I think he just fell. Wait, he's back up again."

Izzy frowned, her body buzzing with worry. "That's not good. I should go after him."

Caesum waved a clawed hand. "Don't bother, he's headed for the rest of the pack. They'll get to him quicker. He doesn't seem injured, just tired. He probably tripped. Not like there's good light in here."

Izzy pasted an ear back.

Matt frowned. "Caesum, he's a stag. The light shouldn't be a big problem for him. Where is he? I'll go after him myself."

Caesum turned to Matt. "Always gotta play the hero, don't you?"

"I'm *training* to be a *Guardian,*" Matt said with a snarl. "That's literally *my job.* Now tell me where the hell he is."

"Caesum, please," Izzy said.

Caesum sighed and pulled up a map of the ship in his hologram. A little blue light wandered a deep part of the ship. "He's here. But look at this." He pointed to three little green dots. "This is the rest of the pack. They're only a few meters apart. He'll get to them before you will."

Matt flicked an ear back. "Can you contact Darvin and his team?"

Caesum's hologram faded slightly, 0s and 1s flicking off his body. "Sure can. I'll send an alert to look out for PR Gildspine." He snorted at Matt. "Then you don't have to be the hero."

"It's not about being the *hero,*" Matt snapped. "It's about protecting my team."

"Sure it is."

Matt bared his teeth, but then shook his head. "Just get Darvin's team to Roscoe okay?" He tapped the edge of the console. "Steal a little power from the ship. We need to see if we can find Ouranos. I don't see any more dots on your little map here."

Izzy frowned. She should be going after Roscoe herself. "Matt--"

Caesum cut her off. "Give me a moment." His body glowed bright blue for a moment before fading. He froze a moment, his hologram distorting, then he stared down at the A.I. crystal chambers. "There's an active A.I. in here."

Izzy's ears flattened.

Matt leaned forward. "It's alive? Should I yank you?"

"No, no, not yet," Caesum said. "It's... fragmented. And... hiding." Caesum flickered in and out of view. "I'm going to chase it down."

Izzy raised an eyebrow. "Is that wise?"

"You want to know more about Ouranos and this plane, yes?" Caesum said. "What better way than to talk to the A.I.? Give me a minute--" He froze a moment, then his body flickered and fragmented before he vanished completely. The holobulbs died.

Matt cursed and reached for the A.I.'s data crystal, when Caesum reappeared. He stared Matt deep in the eye, his face a rare mask of complete seriousness.

"I found the cryochamber. And it has an active pod."

CRYOCHAMBER

Izzy chased Matt as he dashed through the ship, following the path Caesum had shown them on his antiquated digital map, her pack bouncing on her back. She tried moving quietly, but that wasn't easy while trying to keep up with her partner.

Matt clattered along, making no attempts to be quiet. His smaller field pack bounced on his hip.

In some sense, she understood. Caesum had found the cryochamber, their main goal besides finding Ouranos. It didn't hold an army, so he didn't feel the need to be so careful anymore. It was almost like he was broadcasting to Ouranos. *Come and find us.*

But it did have one active pod. And it was losing power.

And the occupant was dying.

They hadn't even talked about what to do with that information, but she felt the answer in her core. *Someone is dying. I need to save them.* It was almost like Matt's thoughts echoed in her own brain.

But that of course brought up all kinds of trouble. Was the occupant an ally of Ouranos'? Were they hostile? Would they attack? Assuming that Izzy and Matt could save them or that they'd even be in the right shape to attack.

Assuming they didn't immediately die.

But they were going to be Guardians. They were supposed to help others. Regardless of the consequences, they needed to do this. Which she only felt like she could do because Caesum had assured her that Roscoe wasn't acting erratically anymore and that Darvin's team had been alerted. Though she still worried.

Matt made another turn, then paused at the opening to a darkened room. He held up a fist, then pointed two fingers at the wall, a silent order to stay behind while he investigated.

Izzy pressed an ear back, but she nodded. Matt disappeared into the room. She stood there for several uncomfortable minutes before he returned and waved her in.

It was definitely the cryochamber.

Rows upon rows of cryopods in half-circle clumps, stretching out into the darkness, farther than she could see in any direction. Each group faced a center console covered in dark lights, switches, and a data slate charging port. Thick beams with clusters of dead holobulbs at the bottom and top connected each pod to the high ceiling. Paint peeled off most of the equipment, leaving rusted, damaged metal underneath.

There had to be *thousands* of pods. But dusty, dead, like the rest of the plane. So dusty the air tasted of it, and Izzy found herself swallowing to try and rid her mouth of it. All were closed and dim, and every console dormant.

Except one. Izzy padded to the nearest cryopod group. The center console had a single blinking green light and one of the pods had its side-hatch open. The empty gel bed still glistened under a layer of dust, as if it had been used recently. Izzy pasted one ear back. "Ouranos." Her voice echoed across the cavernous room, and she winced.

"I think so," Matt said.

"Draso's breath," Izzy said. "Real cryopods. I'm amazed they still work."

Matt looked over the cryopod, but didn't touch it. He frowned. "The other pods in this cluster are dark. I hate to say it, but with Caesum unable to see which of these pods is active, we might have to look at every one to find it."

"Every single one?" Izzy said. "There are *thousands.* That could take *days.*"

"And we apparently don't have days," Matt said. He wandered toward the left wall. "There's a console over here that looks like it might have some power. I'm gonna see what I can find. Maybe I can get Caesum in here. He'd be able to check these a lot faster than we can. In the meantime, will you try checking them manually? We might as well do something."

"True. I'll do that." Izzy headed right, checking each pod as she walked by. Despite being barefoot, her footsteps echoed against the walls, catching every tiny scratch from her untrimmed toeclaws. She'd definitely have to take care of that ASAP. Though her pack jiggled and sent little echoes throughout the room too, so the toeclaws probably didn't make much difference.

Draso's horns, the pods were unsettling. Massive things. Probably four meters wide and at least seven meters lengthwise, likely to accommodate any size zyfaunos possible, each with only a tiny window to the outside world. A few of them were even larger than the normal pods and almost square. Cryo for dragons, perhaps? She couldn't remember if any dragons had left Zyearth during the colonization. She'd have to look that up later.

All of them were caked with dirt, but she didn't dare touch it. The dead holobulbs, the dark windows, the smell of dirt, rust, and decaying gel... the whole thing had an air of death. The one comforting thought was that with Caesum's limited intelligence on the cryochamber, it probably meant there

126

were no other used pods besides the one active one. They weren't facing an army.

And, if all the empty pods said something, they weren't in a makeshift morgue either. Honestly, what would be worse? An army in pods waiting to invade, or a collection of zyfaunos who had died in cryo? She shivered.

Izzy got to the end of the front row and found nothing. This was going to take some time if she examined every pod individually, especially since she realized she had really only looked at half of the first row. There had to be a hundred rows at least. Probably more, considering the darkness prevented her from seeing very deep into the chamber. The whole thing made her feel very small. What would have it been like to come into this room, with untested technology, about ready to leave the only planet you knew to go who knew where? The war must have been absolutely terrible for them to be that desperate.

She scratched behind her ear. Ouranos' cluster still had a light on in the center console. Maybe an active pod would have the same thing. She glanced out deeper into the cavern, as far as her gaze allowed her in the dark.

Wait.

Four rows down… a blinking green light.

Izzy's fur stood on end. She glanced at Matt. He was engrossed in the console on the far wall. The holobulbs over his head flickered, so he looked like he might be close to getting Caesum in here. No reason to get him involved yet. Taking a deep breath, she padded over to the blinking light.

Unlike the pod cluster near the front, however, none of these pods were open, and a soft, almost unnoticeable beep accompanied the blinking light. She approached cautiously. This probably held their active pod.

She found her answer when one of the holobulbs near the base of a connecting pillar flickered. It displayed a medical readout for half a second in a tiny, one-inch square, then vanished. The flickering continued, trying to display readings, but it couldn't hold it long enough.

Izzy inched her way to the pod and glanced inside the window.

Sure enough, it was occupied. A quilar with black fur and quills lay on the gel bed, eyes closed. Cream-colored fur wrapped around their snout and eyes and they had purple skin on the insides of their ears. Very unusual.

But the most unusual thing were the jewels around the quilar's eyes. Yellow, red... and purple. One more set than Matt said Ouranos had. The purple jewel matched the color of the quilar's inner ear too.

The med-reader flickered again, catching Izzy's attention. This time, she made out an angry red phrase, though like with labels written on the bridge, some of the letters weren't quite right. It took some time, but eventually she understood its meaning.

EMERGENCY -- POWER SUPPLY LOW
CRYOPOD FAILURE IMMENENT
EMERGENCY REVIVAL INITIATED --
37% ESTIMATED CHANCE OF SUCCESS
PLEASE FOLLOW REVIVAL PROTOCOLS

Izzy took a step back. Failure. *Failure.* Just like Caesum had said. They had pumped the A.I. dragon full of questions, asking if the pod would kill the occupant if it failed, and Caesum didn't have an answer. Cryotechnology was dead on Zyearth, as was most of the knowledge around it. She had no idea what revival protocols there might be, or what she could do to try and fix this.

37%. That was not a high chance of success...

So... what should she do? What *could* she do? Should she try and get power to this thing? Open it now and try saving whoever was inside? Could she even open it? She might be able to smash it with her hammer, but she hated to think of what damage she could cause with that.

So should she do nothing and possibly let them die? Ouranos might have blood on his hands, but for all she knew, this quilar was completely innocent. Just the fact that they weren't in side-by-side pods made her question whether they were actually allies.

Even if she decided to try and help... could she even do anything? She didn't know anything about this ancient technology. And she wasn't even sure there was enough power to even attempt something. Her field pack had a medkit, but that only had basic bandages, painkillers, a CPR kit, and Lexi acid potions. None of that would do a damn thing for someone dying in cryo. And who knew if her healing power could do anything for the dying. She didn't even know what cryo did to its occupants, so she'd have no idea how to counter it.

Dear Draso, what should she do?

Then the holobulbs died completely. The green light vanished. The pod decompressed in a sharp hiss of frost and steaming gel.

And the hatch opened.

CHAPTER 18

FRIEND OR FOE

Izzy tried to get her body to move, but she stood, frozen, battling her fight or flight response, still warring with her inner conflict. What should she do?

Her fur stood on end at the sound of a cough and something -- someone? tumbled out of the cryomist onto the floor. The figure was tall -- at least two meters, if Izzy estimated correctly. Unlike Ouranos, who wore red, this quilar's clothes were purple and white and they wore a skirt and strapless top rather than the pants Ouranos wore. The same long diamond-shaped piece of fabric Ouranos had on his pants attached to their top instead of the skirt. The quills on the top of their head faced forward and they had long strips of quills running down their back, wrapped in purple and white ribbons.

The quilar turned over on their hands and knees, coughing harder and gagging.

Izzy's altruism won out and she fell to her knees to the fallen figure. "Keep coughing, you'll be fine."

The quilar hacked a long string of clear bile out of their mouth, then seemed to settle into a normal, if not harried, breathing pattern. They blinked, opened their eyes, and looked at Izzy. Very feminine. Her eyes had the same striking purple that was in her inner ears. She frowned.

"I... I am alive."

Izzy kept her ears perky, trying to look friendly. "You are. Can you stand?" She held out a hand, though she wasn't sure she'd be able to help the larger quilar.

But the quilar took Izzy's hand anyway and pulled herself up. She towered over her. "Where am I?"

Izzy couldn't help but flick her ears back. "You're on Zyearth."

The quilar's eyes widened and her mouth dropped. But before she could speak, Matt ran up to the pair of them, hardly even an outline in the dark, his field pack jingling as he ran. "Hey Izzy, Caesum was able to reroute some of his power to the ship and--" He stopped when he saw the figure in the darkness. "Ouranos!"

The quilar jumped. "How did you hear that name?"

Matt's eyes widened.

"Definitely not Ouranos," Izzy said, moving between them. "I found the active pod right before it died and she came out of it."

But the quilar moved closer to Matt. "You said Ouranos. Where is he...?" But she paused when she saw him close up. "You... you are the white and blue Zyearthling. With the dragon."

Matt took a step back, flattening his ears. A light breeze blew past them.

Izzy held out a hand. "Matt..."

But the quilar leapt forward and gripped Matt's shoulders. "Please. You said his name. You..." she paused, her voice trailing. "You must come to him. You are supposed to... to help him."

Matt frowned, twitching his snout, but he didn't move away from her. "I... I want to, but I don't know how."

Izzy fur stood on end. She should have worked harder to talk him out of this. "Matt... I know you want to help, but he's too powerful and he literally attacked the campus unprovoked. What could you even do?"

The quilar's strange ears perked. "What? He attacked you?"

Matt took a step back, forcing the quilar to remove her hands from his shoulders. "He did. With elemental magic and summons. Said something about 'elixir' and 'Prínkipas' and 'Basileus.'"

The quilar drew her hands to her snout, her ears flattening. "No... the Basileus... not here. I thought... the distance... he should be able to escape it..."

Izzy widened her eyes. She said Basileus. "Does that mean you know who this Basileus is?"

Matt lowered his gaze. "Is the Basileus Ouranos' father?"

The quilar's jaw dropped slightly and she furrowed her brow, but then shook her head and met Matt's gaze, ignoring their questions. "Where is Ouranos? Where is my brother?"

Izzy gasped. Brother?

"I... I don't know," Matt said. "We're trying to find him--"

"Kai's breath," the quilar swore. She shook her head. "No time." She turned and fled towards the exit.

"Wait!" Matt ran after her.

Izzy followed, her mind awash with questions. Ouranos was her brother? And she seemed so shocked that Ouranos had attacked them. Was that not their plan then? Was he seriously looking for help? More than that, she knew this Basileus. And she didn't seem to be happy that he was involved. Not good. *So* not good.

132

The quilar was fast too, easily out-striding even Matt. She vanished into the darkness, headed for the door leading out of the chamber.

Izzy almost reached it when Caesum's voice burst through the intercom.

"Matt, I found the other A.I.! He's trying to--" But he cut out.

Matt stopped in his tracks, shooting a look between the console and the retreating quilar's direction. He snarled. "Caesum, which way did the quilar go?"

A moment's hesitation. "She's--" the intercom buzzed. "--Headed for the exit. But Matt--" Cut out again.

"Damn it!" Matt turned to Izzy. "Talk with Caesum about the A.I. He's clearly got a problem. I'm going after her."

Izzy gawked. "You can't be serious. *Alone?*"

"No time, Izzy, just do it!" He ran after the quilar and vanished from sight.

Izzy snarled. Was he absolutely serious? So much for being a team.

Caesum appeared in a cluster of holobulbs at the exit to the cryochamber. "I've got the A.I. Go get -*bzzt*- Matt. He can't do this alone, no matter -*bzzt*- thinks."

Izzy frowned. "Are you okay?"

"I've -*bzzt*- got this. I'll try to -*bzzt*- get the rest of your pack."

Izzy nodded and rushed after them, tightening the straps of her field pack. *Damnit, Matt, why do you have to be such an idiot?*

PATHMARKER

Cix opened a metal locker in the storage room they had found. Empty, again, aside from the piles of dust. He twitched his white snout and his long wolf tail and held in a growl. What did Darvin expect them to find?

"Still empty," Sami said from her corner of the room. She hovered over a footlocker, also covered in dust. Her fluffy white fox tail swept more dust off the floor as she checked her watch. "Has it been an hour? We should probably head back."

Darvin frowned, poking his hooved finger at a wall-mounted data slate, though he got no reaction. "I don't want to go back empty-handed."

"I don't either, but I also don't want to miss our rendezvous," Cix said. He stood and adjusted his field pack on his hips. "Hopefully Red Team has had better luck. And Roscoe might be back now. He might be wondering where we are."

One of the holobulbs in the room warmed and a faint image of Caesum appeared over their heads. "Attention Blue Team. PR Gildspine has entered the ship and requires assistance." The image flickered while he rattled off directions to Roscoe. "This is an automated message and replies will not be recorded." The image died away.

Cix stared at the hologram. "How'd they get power to the ship to get Caesum in here?"

"Probably they're just running it off his own power supply," Sami said. She looked at Darvin, hopeful.

Darvin tilted his long black ears. "I don't like the fact that Caesum said Roscoe needed assistance. Especially when he didn't say why." He tightened the straps on his and Roscoe's field packs. "We're done here. Move out, Blue Team." He turned toward the halls, ducking under a cobweb to avoid it getting caught in his antlers.

Cix took up the rear, double checking the pathmarkers as they walked. Everything was so dusty, they might fall off. He was hoping that they might light up as they got deeper into the ship, because clearly something was protecting the power source in this thing, but no luck.

The one good thing was that it was pretty clear there wasn't anyone else around. It was likely that Ouranos was alone. They could at least take some comfort in that.

"I can't believe we found a real colony ship," Sami said quietly. "How did he even get this thing running? It's falling apart."

"Who knows?" Darvin said, quickening his pace. "I'll admit though, I'm curious about the power supply. How the hell did it escape the effects of the Dead Zone?"

"Maybe it has to do with its age," Sami said. "Different power supply or something. I wonder if this thing is even Gem-fueled. We've already established Ouranos doesn't have the same focus jewels that we do."

"I think old ships still used Gems, but they used unbound Gems," Darvin said. "Much more limited."

"Do you think he was aiming for Zyearth?" Sami said.

"I don't know what he was aiming for." Cix continued to check the pathmarkers. "But the fact that this is a Zyearth colony ship says he probably didn't get here by accident. I'm sure the NAV base has all kinds of maps."

"Assuming he used the NAV, or that the NAV was intact," Darvin said. "For all we know, he's using an A.I."

"Did they have A.I.s that far back?" Sami asked.

"We've had A.I.s since before space flight," Darvin said. "I bet this ship has an A.I. Possibly several."

"If it's not dead," Cix said. "A.I.s need a lot of power, which this clearly doesn't have."

Darvin shrugged. "Hopefully Matt and Izzy found something. In the meantime, our job is to see what assistance Roscoe needs." He slowed until he was walking in-step with Sami and slipped a hand into hers, gripping it nervously.

Cix stared at their hands a moment. "So I guess the rumors about you two are correct then?"

Darvin blinked, looked at Sami's hand and sighed. "Damn it, I slipped up."

Sami smiled at him. "It's not like we've been secretive about it."

"Horse spit," Cix said. "Every time I've asked Roscoe about it, he denied it. And hell, if Matt knew he'd tease you about it every chance he got. It's what he did with Roscoe and Izzy."

Darvin rolled his eyes. "Why do you think we've kept it from Matt? And Roscoe... he'll get used to the idea, but he's been trying to get me to date Jules for years and I don't want to sink his ship."

"You'll have to one of these days," Sami said. "I'd like to get married at some point, and I don't think he should find out about this on our wedding day."

Darvin laughed. "Okay, okay, you make a good point." He grinned. "Jules is great, but I always had a soft spot for Sami." He nudged Cix. "Besides, we all know you have a thing for Jules and I don't want to be stepping on any tails."

Cix's ears grew hot, and he turned away. Was it really that obvious? "Yeah, well, that won't happen because Dad wants me to marry a wolf. Preferably an Alpha or a Beta wolf, to raise our family's tier."

Darvin frowned. "I never understood that wolf tier nonsense. No one should be *ranked* based on their *birth*. And it's not like it really means anything for your potential. I mean, Lance is the freakin' *Master Guardian* and he's what, Theta tier?"

"Upsilon actually. Way low on the tier list."

"Exactly," Darvin said. "It's not like he let that get in the way of what he wanted. Tiers don't define you."

Cix shrugged. "I don't like it myself, to be honest, but Dad puts a lot of clout into it. A lot of wolves of his generation do. Hell, the only reason I even know Lance's tier is because Dad won't let me forget it, since our family is Lambda. He *accepts* that, but it bothers him that we're a higher tier and have to answer to Lance."

Sami frowned. "That's really messed up."

"I know," Cix said. "I wish he'd just drop it, like my generation is." Especially if he wanted a chance to date Jules. Or anyone who wasn't a wolf. But that felt like a dream.

Sami gripped Cix's shoulder. "It's difficult to teach an old wolf new tricks."

"But not impossible," Cix said. "Lance is in his final century and he's *famous* for his 'new tricks.' Dad just needs to get over himself."

Darvin paused. "Wait. Did anyone hear that?"

137

Cix slowed down and perked his ears, mentally cursing himself for letting his guard down on a mission. But he didn't hear anything.

Wait. A blue light on the wall. Was that the pathmarker? He jogged up to it, eyes wide. "The pathmarker is lit."

Darvin paused. "Wait. What?"

"Look," Cix said. He looked up and down the path, now littered with tiny blue lights on the wall. "All of them are."

Darvin ran a finger over the lit pathmarker. "It wasn't a second ago."

"Maybe Matt and Izzy got some extra power into the ship?" Sami asked.

"Not sure why that would light up the pathmarkers. We're still in the Dead Zone." Cix opened his bag and found they were all lit. "What the hell?"

"Wait." Sami pointed down the hall. "What's that?"

A cluster of holobulbs lit up on the ceiling down the hall, displaying a tiny cool-colored dragon.

Cix narrowed his eyes. "Was that Caesum?"

The dragon appeared again, for only a second, but it waved a hand and wing, beckoning them.

Darvin frowned. "That must be Caesum. He seems urgent."

Cix flattened his ears and whined. "Roscoe."

Darvin twitched his ears and tail and ran after the hologram.

"Darvin, wait!" Sami ran after him.

Cix cursed, lit his hands ablaze, and followed too. Draso protect them if this was going to end bad.

Catching Up

Matt sprinted, trying to catch up to fleeing quilar, his field pack beating against his hip. He caught her running down the tunnel he and Izzy had come down, but already she was too far ahead to follow anymore. Damn it all! Hopefully Caesum could find her and get that information to Izzy. He stopped a moment and leaned on a wall, huffing.

Shit.

Izzy.

He had just run off without her, hadn't he? *Damn* it all, he hadn't even found Ouranos and he was already breaking Lance's orders. So what should he do now? Go back and get her? Wait for her? See if he could get Caesum's attention? Continue after the quilar?

He gritted his teeth. No time. He continued down the hall.

And stopped.

The door with the hand pad lock was open.

What the hell? When did that happen? Come to think of it, all the emergency lights were on too. And... and Izzy's pathmarkers.

Caesum had mentioned getting more power to the ship. Did that mean he was also able to expand the magical electronic insulation?

He paused. If the insulation was on, that meant his COM might work. Should he send a message to Lance? Contact the rest of his team?

Go after the quilar?

He furrowed his brow, making a fist. He was going to be a Guardian. Now was the time to act, not beg for help.

He examined the hand pad and found a large handprint in the dust. That said everything. He headed into the room.

It was a gym. Ancient, dust-covered equipment and weights were strewn haphazardly all over the room, many on their sides, most broken. It smelled so strongly of rust that the room almost tasted of it. Footprints in the dust disappeared as they headed for the middle of the room. The emergency lights only lit up the outer edges of the massive area, leaving the center in complete darkness. A perfect place to hide.

Draso, he didn't want to fight her. He just wanted to understand. He wanted to help, damn it. Why did that keep biting him in the tail? He walked into the room, upright, ears perked forward, trying to look friendly, though he held a hand over his sword.

"Miss," he said. "I don't know who you are, but I don't want to hurt anyone. I want to help. Please come talk to me."

No answer.

"Please," Matt said again, walking deeper in. "I can't help if I don't know what's wrong. Please let me help you and Ouranos. I don't want to fight."

No answer.

Fire and ice. Maybe he could find the switch for the overhead lights, if the ship had enough power. He turned back toward the door.

A tall figure stood in his way, backlit by the emergency lights.

Matt took a step back. "Ouranos."

Ouranos stepped into the room, strained. Gritted teeth, glassy eyes, ears flat. But he didn't attack. He looked Matt right in the eye. "Did... did you mean what you said?"

Matt blinked. "What?"

"Please," Ouranos said. "I have... limited time... Do you... truly intend to help?"

Matt's heart beat against his chest and he held a hand out, ready to activate his Gem at any moment. But he was hesitant. That was the higher-pitched voice, not the angry voice. Actually Ouranos, not whatever possessed him. If that made sense. But could he actually trust him? Who knew.

But he was supposed to be here to help Ouranos. Capture, yes, but help. He couldn't do that if he didn't listen. He nodded. "Of-f course. What can I do?"

Ouranos leaned against a piece of equipment. "I... I need... the black liquid... you produce..."

Matt frowned, though he couldn't say he was surprised. But why? Ouranos had fought so hard to get some from him. He shook his head. No, whatever was possessing him wanted it. So what did Ouranos want with it? He lowered his gaze. "You... The Basileus called it an elixir."

Ouranos paused, frowning, but he pressed his lips together. "Yes..." He lowered his head and coughed. "It... it will help me."

Matt frowned. That was awfully vague. His body tensed. "How?"

Ouranos furrowed his brow, frowning, but just for a moment. "It... it..." He chewed his lip. "It suppresses my power. Keeps me safe." He looked up at Matt, hopeful.

Matt twitched an ear. Ouranos hesitated way too much. "That doesn't make sense."

141

Ouranos' face scrunched up, angry. And his voice changed. "Give it to me. I need it!" He stepped forward, fire building on the tips of his fingers.

Damn it, he'd lost him. Matt took a step back, lighting his Gem and calling two twisters.

But before Ouranos could do more, the fire extinguished and he fell to his knees, gripping his head. "You will not hold power over me!" he snarled, almost roaring. "You will not harm him, you will not get your Cast, and *you will not win.* My body is my own and *you will not have it!"*

But then he twitched right and writhed on the ground, almost in spasms. "You have no choice, Prínkipas." The angry voice again. The Basileus.

Matt couldn't take it. "Ouranos, *please,* how do I help you?"

Ouranos strained, twitching, sweating through his fur. He met Matt's eyes. "The... elixir... will sever his control of me... it will free me."

But the Basileus, or whatever it was possessing Ouranos, wanted it too. How could Matt trust this quilar? How did he know he wasn't just faking it? "I don't understand how."

Ouranos flattened his ears. "I... I do not either. But--" He shrieked and dropped his head. When he looked up, his expression hardened and the Basileus won out. "Too slow." He charged Matt. Matt shielded and braced.

But another large figure flew out of the darkness and smashed into Ouranos, knocking him aside. Matt rolled out of the way, leapt to his feet and stared at the newcomer.

The female quilar.

She kneeled on one knee, hands alight with fire and ice, though weak. Tiny flame tongues and ice crystals, not the powerhouse magic Ouranos had. Shock dominated her features -- eyes wide, jaw slack, as if she had never done such a thing before. She glanced between Matt and Ouranos, frozen.

Ouranos rolled over to his hands and knees and shook his head. He faced the female quilar.

142

For a brief moment, his eyes widened, and he gasped. "No--" But then his lips curled in a snarl, teeth bared. His fist blossomed with fire and the Basileus took over. *"Natassa."*

She bit her lip, the magic on her hands flickering in and out. "Father, please... let him go."

Father. *Father.* So it was his father possessing him! Of all the disgusting...

"You still think your pathetic begging will save him," he growled. "You have learned nothing. You should have died in the war, Prinkípissa." He charged Natassa.

Matt blasted him with wind, sending him reeling back into a pile of floor mats, then moved between him and Natassa.

Natassa stood, grabbing Matt's shoulder, frantic. "Please--"

"I didn't hurt him," Matt said, shrugging her hand off. Lightning and air, she actually stood taller than him. "But I need to know how to help him. What do I do?"

Natassa flattened her ears. "I... he..."

"Quick, Natassa!"

Too late. Ouranos regained his footing and ran toward them. Natassa squealed and held her hands out in defense.

Matt stood between them, knocking Ouranos aside. He turned to her. "Throw me a fireball."

She stared at him. "What?"

"If you can't use fire, give me some other element!" Matt said. "Ice, sand, rocks, anything!"

Ouranos stood and charged again.

"Natassa!"

She winced, but threw a tiny fireball at him.

143

He barely caught it, but he magnified it ten-fold and formed a fire tornado. Time to end this already.

Ouranos held his hands out.

Natassa stood and gasped. "No!" She threw her hands forward and a flurry of wind whipped up and blew dust through the room, blinding everyone. Matt used his own wind to calm the dust, but a purple-ish fire bloomed between them that he couldn't stop.

He stared. Purple?

In a flurry of feathers, a colossal raven bathed in violet flames appeared, spraying embers everywhere. It cawed loudly, the sound reverberating in Matt's bones as it bounced around the room. An egret in white flames appeared at the raven's side. It opened its beak and let out a dark, warbled croak that practically shook the air around it. The smell of fire wafted through the air. Multiple smells. One, clearly a forest fire, the other, more tame, perhaps a charcoal fire. One pleasant, one not, though Matt couldn't tell which smell belonged to which bird. Both had impossibly long tails, with colored peacock-like feathers among the black and white. They stared with intelligent eyes, wings bathed in their elements, just like Jústi and Pax.

Just like the summons. These were summons! Matt gawked. Were all these quilar summoners?

Natassa took a step back. "Excelsis. Deo."

Matt watched her, frowning, then turned back to the flaming birds.

The raven faced Natassa and blasted a puff of embers in her face before turning back toward Ouranos. Natassa shot a glance between the summons and Matt before running out the door. Matt caught a stray ember in his hand as she ran. It had only one word.

Run.

Ouranos shouted as Jústi and Pax appeared and tackled the black and white birds, the scents of dust and storms confusing the scents of fire. Matt dove out of their way as the summons vanished behind a wall of colored fire, lightning, and rocks.

And Ouranos evacuated the room.

Matt cursed and ran after him, dodging the elements as he went. He held up a shield, but one good bolt of electricity smashed it and sent him rolling. *Shit.* He righted himself and dove behind a broken piece of exercise equipment and shielded it, looking for another way out, all his fur and quills standing on end. Ouranos got lost in the fray.

Then all four birds vanished. And with them, Natassa and Ouranos. They had both escaped. Matt slammed a fist against the wall and ran for the door.

Izzy was just outside, eyes wide. She met Matt's gaze, her ears pale and her jaw slack. "What the hell was *that?*"

"Which way did they go?" Matt asked.

She blinked, thrown off by his question. "I… Ouranos… Ouranos was headed back toward the vestibule. The feminine quilar ran past me back toward the bridge."

"Shit," Matt snarled. He met Izzy's eyes. "The other quilar's name is Natassa and she just saved me from Ouranos. Go after her and I'll go after Ouranos."

Izzy frowned, baring a tooth. "You *left me* back there and now you're going to do it again? What happened to being a team?"

Matt flattened his ears. That stung, but what would have happened if he hadn't? He didn't have time to wait when someone was in danger. "I know, and I'm sorry, but we have more to deal with now. Please just go after her. I'll explain when we meet up." He turned and ran after Ouranos, not waiting for Izzy's response. She'd ream him later and he'd damn well deserve it, but now wasn't the time for regrets.

Now was the time for action.

CHAPTER 21

HELP

Ouranos dove into the recesses of his mind, not bothering to fight for control of his body as his father ran him through the plane. The Basileus' thoughts faded as he did, though Ouranos caught glimpses of his reasons for fleeing. Something about distance, regrouping, collecting, summons…

But how could Ouranos focus on that with all that had happened?

Natassa. His sister was *here*. How did she get here? She must have somehow snuck onto the plane before it took off. But when did she get on board? How had he not noticed? Why had she just now shown herself after all the time they had been on this planet?

What did she hope to accomplish?

His father pushed Ouranos' body forward, running for the exit.

Somewhere in his harried thoughts, Ouranos knew he had to regain control. But he could not convince himself to. Natassa was here. The Basileus had semi-formed Cast charms. He had the power and means to get more, despite Ouranos' best efforts to stop him. He had acted selfishly and clung to the black liquid, when he should have shoved it aside. He had lost. Why bother fighting?

But… if he did not fight, the Basileus would win. He would create his Cast, he would devastate this planet… their home… he would kill Natassa.

He would *kill Natassa.*

That was the push. Ouranos could not let that happen. He shoved his consciousness forward, driving away the Basileus' presence in his mind, fighting the blinding pain as his father fought back.

But he won. If only for a moment.

But a moment was all he needed.

He entered a junction in the hallways and glanced down the other tunnels. He needed to do something before his father regained control completely.

"Pilot…"

The faerie dragon appeared in the overhead holobulbs. "I'm -*bzzt*- here, Ouranos."

He stared at the dragon as it flickered in and out of existence. His only friend. Did he know about Natassa's presence on board?

"Were you aware my sister had followed me on the plane?"

The dragon lowered his head, his blue cheeks coloring slightly. His image grew distorted. "I… I was. She -*bzzt*- came aboard--*accord--adored* after you had entered cryo. She said--said she could help -*bzzt*- you, Ouranos. I… I just wanted to help--*kelp--yelp.*"

Just wanted to help. Oh, if only the A.I. knew the consequences of that help. "My father will kill her if he has the chance."

Pilot frowned. "I… I am -*bzzt*- sorry. I didn't know."

Pain shot through Ouranos' head, and his vision burst into stars as the Basileus fought once more for control. He pushed back on his father with everything he had, keeping his mind on Natassa. "I… need to hide. Protect her from him."

147

Pilot flapped his wings and circled around Ouranos' head. He flickered in and out of view. "That may be -*bzzt*- difficult. Matthew is headed this way--*slay--bay*, Isabelle has taken after your sister, out of my -*bzzt*- view, and I scattered the rest of--of their pack to try and keep -*bzzt*- them from you. But that means they are all--*ball--call* around you. Beyond that, they brought an A.I. with them and I -*bzzt*- am struggling to--to keep him off me. I don't--" He paused, flickering again. "Wait. There's something -*bzzt*- else. In the plane."

Ouranos frowned. That was not good. "What is it?"

Pilot froze in place, as if thinking, his face contorting into curiouser and curiouser expressions. Finally he tilted his head. "I -*bzzt*- don't know."

Ouranos raised an eyebrow. "What?"

"It... it looks like a -*bzzt*- puddle. It keeps forming and--and falling apart. But it's also moving on its own--*moan--loan*? A bulge in -*bzzt*- the center... Almost like a head. I swear I--I can detect a -*bzzt*- heartbeat..."

Ouranos' insides froze. No... How...? "Does it have three blue eyes?"

Pilot paused a moment. "If you could call those -*bzzt*- glowing blue orbs eyes -*bzzt*- I suppose."

Draso's breath... *a Cast.* An actual, true, living Shadow Cast.

But how did a Cast get here? Surely there had not been one on the ship. He would have known it. The Basileus would have known it. He would have—

Immediately the Basileus started pulling on Ouranos' mind, fighting for control, calling for the Cast. And Ouranos could sense the monster's response. The shriek of a stolen warrior, echoing in his skull, searching for its master...

No. He could not be allowed to have it. "Pilot, I need to be sedated. Put back in the sleeping chamber."

"Not -*bzzt*- possible," Pilot said. "We don't have -*bzzt*- enough power--*hour--cower*, and even if we did--did, I don't think the A.I. I'm fighting in--in our system would -*bzzt*- allow it."

"Then I need some other form of sedation," Ouranos said. "I need to keep my father from that--" The Basileus pounded in Ouranos' head, sending shocks of pain through his mind. He leaned down on one knee.

And heard footsteps. Lots of them. Matthew and his pack. Soon he would be overwhelmed. And with a Cast so near...

If he could just put himself out, he could sever the Cast's connection with the Basileus and the Cast would be harmless... for the time being.

"Pilot, *please.*"

"The medbay," Pilot said. The floor lights down one hallway turned from blue to purple. "Follow this -*bzzt*- path. I'll change the -*bzzt*- lights back as you run--run. Go. Hurry!"

Ouranos dashed down the hall, his legs aching with every step as his father fought him for control and called out to the Cast on board. Draso's mercy, how had a Cast gotten here? He could only hope that he could sedate himself before his father regained control enough to command the Cast and do serious damage.

Matthew had promised he wanted to help. His attacks had been more defensive than offensive, and it was clear he had been calculating every move, trying to determine how to help, not hurt.

He could only hope Matthew would keep his promise and protect Natassa should things go completely wrong.

CHAPTER 22

SHADOW CAST

Matt dashed down the hall, coughing, trying to process everything.

More summons. More magic. Natassa. And she'd told her father to let Ouranos go. But she hadn't been speaking to some other quilar Matt had missed in the dark. She had looked directly into Ouranos' eyes. She *knew.* That basically confirmed what Matt suspected.

Someone really was possessing Ouranos… and it was his own father. The Basileus. The king to Ouranos' prince as Larissa had put it.

His own damn father manipulating him like a puppet. Water above, that burned him.

But why? To what end? He'd said he wanted the strange black liquid Matt produced, but while Ouranos had said it would help him sever his father's bonds, whatever sense that made, the Basileus certainly wasn't sharing his own reasons for wanting it. That made things complicated.

He stopped at an intersection in the halls, frowning. No more pathmarkers. No sign of Ouranos. Where did he go? "Caesum, are you around? Can you tell me where Ouranos went?"

Caesum appeared in the holobulbs above Matt's head. He snorted rainbow smoke at Matt, though he seemed to be having a hard time keeping his image together.

Matt pasted both ears back. "Are you okay? Is that other A.I.--"

"You -*bzzt*- left Izzy."

Matt frowned, feeling his ears get hot. "This... this is not the time to talk about this."

"This is *exactly* the time to -*bzzt*- talk about this," Caesum snarled. "You *left* her. You *never* leave your partner. I don't think -*bzzt*- I have to remind you that Lance left -*bzzt*- Lovetta on the battlefield. That's what got her *killed.*" He narrowed his eyes. "It's what -*bzzt*- killed Izzy's father too."

Matt frowned. "I... I didn't..."

"What the hell happened to you, Matt?" Caesum said. "You used to -*bzzt*-go out of your way to make sure Izzy -*bzzt*- got the same respect, the same training, the same *everything* as you. You -*bzzt*- made it your *job* to ensure you had the right partner. But suddenly -*bzzt*- you've lost interest in that? What is *wrong* with you?"

Matt flattened his ears. "But... I didn't... I needed to get to Ouranos, and-_"

"You *needed* your *partner,*" Caesum spat. "And now you don't have her." He shrugged his wings, indignant. "I -*bzzt*- don't know where Ouranos went. His A.I. is -*bzzt*- blocking my view throughout -*bzzt*- most of the ship and as you can hear, I'm -*bzzt*- having a hard time staying active. He's fighting me. You'll have to find Ouranos -*bzzt*- on your own. And if I may, I recommend -*bzzt*- you go find your *partner* and work *together* on that -*bzzt*- while I do what I can in here." He vanished.

151

Matt stood there, stunned. Normally he'd just brush Caesum off, but this... this hit hard.

"Matt?" Darvin entered from one of the hallways with Cix and Sami behind him. "Damn, I thought we had gotten lost. Have you seen Roscoe anywhere?"

Matt stared at him, trying to refocus his thoughts. Roscoe. There was another place where he messed up. Where was he in all this mess? Was he even okay? He shook his head. He screwed up badly. "No, I haven't seen him. Did you happen to see Ouranos run your way?"

Darvin perked his ears. "No. Did you find him?" He paused and looked around. "Hey, where's Izzy?"

Matt's shame burned in his core, as he tried to find any excuse... but he didn't have any. What excuse did he have for abandoning his partner? What the hell was he thinking?

Lance's words echoed in his head about making the Guardianship about being *me, me, me*. He had promised he was going to include Izzy... that was part of the deal.

And he hadn't. He'd left her. No excuses.

Maybe... maybe he didn't deserve the Guardianship after all.

Not that he'd get it after what he'd pulled on Izzy. Separating himself from the pack, leaving Izzy behind, and putting aside Lance's orders to capture Ouranos to try and help him. And he'd failed at that, too. He'd taken Lance's three rules and broke every single one of them. He'd lost everything because of his own damn idiocy. His shoulders slumped.

He lost everything.

He frowned, trying to face his pack. He screwed up, but it was time to make this right. Refocus. Find the pack, regroup, protect them at all costs. Go after Ouranos as a team.

Like he should have been in the first place. "She's--"

"Whoa, whoa, *whoa,* what the hell is *that?*" Cix pointed down one of the halls.

Matt turned.

The emergency lights were completely out down one of the tunnels, turning it into a black void. But not completely. A set of three glowing blue orbs floated about in the dark, forming a strange triangle. For a brief moment, Matt thought they must be some of Cix's pathmarkers, but then they moved. They bobbed up and down, slithering about. A sickening wet, goopy sound accompanied the orbs' movements as they approached the group.

Matt took a step back. "What the hell?"

"I've got it," Sami said. She formed a fireball in her hand and sent it flying above the blue orbs. The fire magic briefly lit up the hallway.

A black, gloopy blob with a dripping bulge in the center flowed toward them. The three orbs shifted around in the bulge.

Darvin flipped his ears back. "What in Draso's name...?"

Matt frowned, but took a step toward it.

"What are you doing? Don't go near it!" Cix said.

Matt paused. Darvin was right. He projected a shield in front of his team, though he left it at purple level to save some energy. After all the summons and magic he had seen from Ouranos, there was no easy way to predict what this thing could do, but it didn't seem hostile. Better to approach it slowly and see what it did before assuming the worst.

Protect the team.

Though, that hadn't worked too well with Ouranos, had it? He strengthened the shield to invisible level.

The blob slithered toward them making a *squick squick squick* sound. It moved surprisingly swift, darting back and forth, before stopping in front of Matt. It lifted the blue-orbed bulge a meter and a half out of the viscous black puddle and listed to one side, affecting a curious side glance. It had a strange, musky smell, almost like a... a stag. Like Darvin or Roscoe.

Matt leaned down, squinting. "What are you?"

The blob "stared" a moment longer, but then the center of the bulge peeled back into a strange, jagged grin, complete with "teeth."

Then it let out a tremendous, high-pitched scream.

Matt leapt back, plastering his ears flat to his head. But before he could truly react, the dark blob dove on him, dragging him to the ground with surprising strength. It pinned his arms to his side and try as he might, he couldn't pull himself free. The creature squeezed him, crushing his ability to wiggle free, and snaked its way up his body toward his face.

Adrenaline burst through Matt's system, setting his ears ringing and his magic into overload as he desperately attempted to blow the monster off him. Somewhere beyond the ringing his pack shouted at him, but he couldn't make out a single word. All he could think was one thing.

Get it off, get it off, get it off!

As he fought the monster, his powers spun wildly out of control, drowning out every shred of sound besides his own frantic magic. Already his fingertips grew wet with the black liquid Ouranos so desperately wanted. Some still rational part of his mind fought it back -- he couldn't let Ouranos or the Basileus have it until he knew why they wanted it.

But as the monster engulfed his hands and slithered up around his mouth and nose, that rational part gave way to pure fear. The creature worked its way into his orifices, cutting off air, filling his mouth and nose with the taste and smell of iron. The thick slime melted into his fur, soaking his skin. The outside world faded behind his magic, his terror, his--

"Matt, shield!"

His Gem activated almost automatically, and he killed the wind magic to wrap himself in the strongest shield he could manage. Flames engulfed him in an instant, heating his fur and skin under the shield, causing the creature to shriek in terror and pull itself off him. He scrambled to his feet and pressed himself against the opposite wall, afraid to stop shielding. His heart threatened to burst with adrenaline.

The creature didn't move far. It bounced around, then with an otherworldly shriek, it threw itself at Cix. The wolf shrieked, lighting the air around him on fire, desperately trying to avoid the monster.

Not this time. Matt blasted it aside with wind, too much wind, fighting to regain his composure. This was a battle. Just a battle. He could handle himself in a battle, monster or not. He tried to speak, take control, direct his pack, but he opened his mouth and got only garbling, drowned in the rush of wind and fire.

Cix and Sami immediately doused the thing in flame, their own panic evident in the overuse of magic and their shrieks and shouts. The creature wailed behind the wall of fire, but it didn't seem injured by the flames as it held its ground. The metal walls creaked and glowed red with the fire's heat.

Matt took several deep breaths, trying to center himself. This was out of hand, and it was his job to get it back under control. He pushed a feral growl through his throat, searching for his voice, before finally grasping it. Protect the pack. Time to take charge *now*.

"Sami, Cix, pull back and give me a couple of fireballs! Stage two!" He nodded to Darvin. "Cloak them, Darvin! Make me the center of attention while we fight this thing!"

Sami and Cix pulled back their magic and they each threw a fireball at Matt. He caught them in a pair of twisters, spreading the flames into two well-controlled fire tornados.

Darvin seemed a little more hesitant to cloak Sami and Cix, but he did as he was told anyway, and the pair vanished. The black puddle tilted its three blue orbs -- eyes? -- confused, looking in Sami and Cix's directions, but then refocused on Matt. It broke into another jagged grin.

Matt snarled, baring his teeth. *Come at me, you disgusting monster.* He flung one of the flaming tornadoes at it.

But as the tornado approached it, it split its "body" apart and let the magic go right through it.

Matt's eyes widened. What the hell? He formed three more tornadoes. "Stage three! Shield yourselves!" More fireballs flew out of nowhere and set each tornado ablaze, doubling their size. Matt put up his own shield, then surrounded the creature with the twisters and pulled them all in at once, crashing the magic together in a flurry of sparks and embers. Metal groaned loudly through the halls. The creature's wails vanished behind the sounds of magic and metal.

When the flames died, the creature was nowhere to be seen. Matt heaved relief. Whatever that was, it had--

But then the floor gurgled and moved, and the three glowing orbs pulled themselves out of a dark shadow. The creature reformed, completely unharmed.

Matt's fur stood on end and his whole body buzzed with an adrenaline rush he didn't think was possible. What the hell?

"Matt, *the roof!*" Darvin called.

Matt looked up. The roof had four massive cracks in it, and metal, wires, and broken holobulbs hung down, swinging to and fro in the leftover wind magic.

The heat left Matt's face. "Out! Out now, *run!*" He pushed at Darvin, hoping Cix and Sami were right behind them. They dashed through one of the narrow halls just in time for the roof in the intersection to crash to the floor, blocking the entrance.

Matt huffed, shaking dirt off his quills. "Defenders, sound off."

156

"Captain Terrill reporting," Cix said, wheezing, now free of Darvin's cloak.

"GC Girsougon safe," Sami murmured. She shook her tail free of dust.

Darvin squatted down, pawing at one eye. "I'm safe. I mean, PR Polttarit reporting. But I've got another acid problem. Don't get too close."

"I think that might have gotten that monster, so there's that at least," Sami said.

"What the hell was that thing?" Cix asked.

But Matt didn't get a chance to respond. He stared at the debris blocking the door as a viscous black liquid oozed between the cracks in the rusted metals before reforming into a solid puddle, three blue eyes staring with a gleeful grin.

Matt's quills stood straight up. "Run. Out of the plane. Now!" He pushed Darvin and they ran for the vestibule.

His thoughts immediately dashed to Izzy. If she had to fight one of those things herself...

Draso, please let that be the only one, Matt thought. *I've lost the Guardianship, but I don't want to lose Izzy too!*

CHAPTER 23

IN EXCELSIS DEO

Izzy ran down the halls headed back for the bridge, holding her pack's straps to keep them from smacking too hard against her back. Her hammer's handle beat against her thigh.

Damn Matt. Damn him and his stupid need to be the hero, his stupid need to do everything himself, his stupid *need* to *rush into everything* without waiting for someone. She was his *partner,* damn it, and he'd *thrown that away.* If they actually got the Guardianship after this fiasco -- unlikely now that Matt had straight up broken every rule Lance had set for him -- there would be *words.* And maybe a punch to the gut.

He might get a punch to the gut anyway.

Caesum appeared above her head, flapping his purple wings, following along in the holobulbs lining the ceiling. "I found Matt and -*bzzt*- reamed him good."

Izzy snorted. "Thanks."

"Natassa has -*bzzt*- turned away from the bridge from what I can tell. She's -*bzzt*- headed toward the medbay. Make a left up here." He flickered in and out of view. "I'm barely able to -*bzzt*- fight off the other A.I. and for some reason, it's really protecting -*bzzt*- the medbay, so I can't see beyond this hallway. Hell, I really can't -*bzzt*- see anywhere in the ship anymore -*bzzt*- it's all blacked out. For all I know, Natassa or Ouranos -*bzzt*- could be around the corner. Be careful, okay?"

"I will. Thanks, Caesum."

"I'm going to slow down for a few -*bzzt*- cycles and see if I can't fight -*bzzt*- that A.I. back." Izzy nodded. She pulled out her hammer and made a left as Caesum wafted away into light motes.

Sure enough, Natassa was around the corner. Izzy paused. The cream-snouted quilar paced back and forth, muttering to herself. "How is Father able to manipulate him from so far away?"

Izzy took a step forward. "Natassa…" Natassa whipped her head up. Izzy held a hand out, wary. "We're here to help, so if you could just--"

Natassa gave a half-hearted snarl and shot twin bolts of electricity and fire Izzy's way, then dashed further down the hall.

Izzy shielded and dodged both, then took off after her.

Natassa threw blast after blast of various elemental magic at Izzy. But Izzy's lifetime of sparring, coupled with Natassa's clearly untrained magic ability, made it easy to avoid everything. And soon, she was catching up.

"Natassa, please!" Izzy called. "I just want to help!"

"You are not the one who will help Ouranos," Natassa called back. "Do not interfere!" She paused, waved a hand, and a blast of purple and white fire filled the hall.

Izzy halted. How had the fire suddenly changed color? But before she could act, the flames melted away, revealing a raven and a white egret,

159

hovering in place, both sporting unusually long tails. Summons. She stepped back and shielded.

The summons both stared a moment, still bathed in their respective bonfires, until the raven let out a high *caw caw caw* and spun about, twirling its purple fire until it vanished in the twister. Izzy took a step back.

Then the fire dissipated in a whirlwind of embers. The bird stood as tall, or perhaps even taller, than an avian zyfaunos, fully anthropomorphic. The egret disappeared behind its own white fire and reemerged anthropomorphic as well, standing gracefully next to its raven counterpart.

Izzy stared in awe. They both stood over two meters tall, draped in elegant feathers, their wings running down their arms, flight feathers scraping the floor. Just as they had in their earlier forms, they had impossibly long tails, made up not only of their own feathers, but also scattered peacock-like feathers, purple on the raven, blue on the egret, adding splashes of color to them. The tails seemed to magically wrap themselves loosely around their legs and float in place. Both of them had two long feathers cresting their heads, unnatural for their wild species counterparts. An unsettling smell of forest fire mixed with the more calming scent of charcoal fire.

The raven's deep blue eyes and the egret's flaming red ones stood out against their plumage as they turned and faced Izzy. They stared and while she knew it was stupid, they had this air of godlike omnipotence in their gazes. Like they saw beyond the constraints of time and she was somehow beneath them for just being mortal.

Good Draso, how could a simple gaze be that powerful? She must be imagining things. She took a step back, shielding, lifting her hammer, ready to dash away at a moment's notice. There was no way she could fight these things like this.

But they didn't attack. Instead, the raven lifted a wing and three tiny purple embers wafted toward her.

160

She watched the raven a moment then reached out and snagged an ember. It was pleasantly warm against her fur.

Do not interfere.

Izzy pasted an ear back. "You're not going to attack me?"

The birds exchanged glances. The egret waved white embers at her. *You are the blue and white Zyearthling's ally.*

Izzy relaxed a little, releasing a breath. Another ember floated her way.

He will be a willing sacrifice.

All of Izzy's fur stood up at once. Wait, *what? Sacrifice?* What the *hell?* "Did you say *sacrifice?"*

But the birds didn't respond. Instead they turned away and began fading into embers and sparks.

Izzy gasped. "Hey, wait, you can't just leave!" She reached for the raven's wing.

The raven suddenly seized up, closing in on himself, spitting embers in all directions. Izzy leapt back, shielding again. The egret watched with a tilted head, but didn't seem too disturbed.

The raven suddenly relaxed and turned to her, blinking, confused. He had a strange awareness in his eyes that hadn't been there before. Gone was the omnipotent gaze, and in its place, something very much in the present.

He stared at Izzy a moment and opened its beak. Two tiny embers shot out and smacked Izzy's forehead, burning slightly and lacking the control she had seen previously.

Lightning and air, it worked correctly this time.

Izzy frantically brushed the still-burning embers from her forehead. She frowned. The voice felt new, close, genderless, almost immature, compared to the omnipotent words from before. "What?"

The bird reached out and gripped Izzy's shoulders with taloned hands, his wingtips brushing her bare feet. Embers burst from the feathers. *Listen, I don't have much time--*

Izzy snarled and dropped her hammer on the bird's foot. He yelped and released her, but before he could respond further, she grappled his neck, and rolled back, kicking him off her and into a wall. He crashed in a heap as Izzy rolled back to her feet. The white egret lifted an eyebrow, amused. The raven's wings splayed out and it blinked several times as embers floated about him, staring at her upside down.

Ow.

"Don't touch me again."

Duly noted. Should have expected that. The raven slowly pulled himself to his feet and straightened his flight feathers. He stepped toward Izzy. *Now--*

Izzy picked up her hammer and brandished it. "What did I just say? Stay the hell *back!"*

The bird stepped forward, frowning, cautiously keeping its distance. *Guardian Gildspine, please! I have a message and I won't have Excelsis for much longer, so I need you to listen!*

She paused. Guardian? What the hell? She wasn't a Guardian. Probably never would be. And yet... "You... you said my name."

The bird's eyes widened, then he shut them, affecting a frown with his beak. He shook his head.

"How did you know my name?"

That's not important.

"You called me Guardian! What the hell was *that?"*

Izzy, it's not important--

"Yes it is! What--"

Izzy, you're speaking to the Black Cloak.

Izzy gasped. Pax's final words from this morning echoed through her head. *Seek the Black Cloak.* "I'm *what?*"

At the risk of being cliché, I don't have much time, so please just listen for a moment--

"Who's Excelsis?" Izzy blurted out.

The raven summon is Excelsis and the egret is Deo, the bird said. *But damn it, Izzy, please just listen a moment! I'm--*

A wave of purple embers blasted from the end of the bird's flight feathers, raining around Izzy's bare feet, though thankfully none of them set her fur on fire. The raven twitched a moment, closing in on itself. She stood back, lifting the hammer higher.

"Don't come any closer."

Excelsis frowned again. *I won't. Don't worry about that.*

"What the hell was *that?*"

Excelsis is fighting me, the embers said. *I won't have him much longer.* He met Izzy's gaze. *Look. Natassa has gone to the medbay. Ouranos is already there. You will get there before her.*

She leaned back. "How do you know that? She's way ahead of me now."

I just know. Now. He leaned in close. *You'll find a hiding place. You're going to hear them talk about Matt as a sacrifice, but don't let it derail you. You need to hear what they have to say.*

"Why?" she growled. "If they're going to talk about Matt being a literal sacrifice, I need to stop them before they get the chance! Don't tell me to just stand idle! To hell with what they say!" She lowered her gaze. "How do you know what they're going to talk about anyway?"

I just know! Please just--

"What are you, some kind of time traveler?"

Excelsis paused, his shoulders slowly drooping.

"Fire and ice, you better not be about to tell me you're a time traveler. Time travel isn't possible."

Just trust *me, Izzy. I can help you save Matt.*

"Then stop speaking in riddles and *tell me,* damn it!" Izzy snapped.

Excelsis lowered its gaze. *Natassa will talk about a white and blue Zyearthling as a sacrifice. But there's a reason for it.*

"I don't care what stupid reason they're trying to make up for killing Matt--"

Stop interrupting and listen! The bird said. *They're going to list reasons, but they're also going to talk about Ouranos. There's some important things you'll learn there. You need to hear it.*

"But *why?"* Izzy said. "Why can't *you* just tell me?"

Would you even believe me?

Izzy frowned, flattening her ears.

That's what I thought, the embers said. *Listen to them. Take that knowledge with you. Don't interfere, don't panic, and please trust me.* He paused, lifting a talon to his beak in a strange thinking pose. *And trust yourself.*

Izzy frowned. What the hell kind of patronizing statement was that? *Trust herself?* Good Draso, that was rude. She did trust herself! Right? ...Right? "How can I trust you when I don't even *know* you?"

You're just going to have faith.

Right. Have faith in the omnipotent summon trying to convince her that it's okay that her enemy wants to sacrifice her best friend and partner.

The bird winced again, sending embers in all directions. *I'm losing it--*

"One more thing," she said. "You called me Guardian."

Excelsis looked off. *...Yes.*

"And you're a time traveler."

Excelsis said nothing, but his expression gave it away.

Izzy pressed her lips together. "Does that mean I'll get to be a Guardian some day?"

That depends entirely on your own actions in the next few days.

She twitched her snout. "What the hell does *that* mean?"

But then Excelsis let out a deep *caw caw*, burst into purple embers and disappeared, leaving only a flaming feather behind. Deo, the egret, blinked a moment, then curled in on herself and vanished into white embers.

MEDBAY

Izzy pasted both ears back, the fur on her neck standing up. Trust this Black Cloak. Who had somehow managed to talk through a summon, telling her not to panic over the fact that Natassa literally wanted to sacrifice Matt. Because *that* made them trustworthy.

And... trust herself. Her face burned. She did trust herself. Most of the time. Sometimes.

Matt's words from the weapons room ran through her mind. *Izzy's powers hold her back.*

She chewed her lip. She'd made that up. It wasn't real. He didn't say that.

But if Matt didn't say that... who did? Why did she even think that? She tugged at a loose quill. Maybe she trusted herself. And... and maybe she didn't.

A single purple ember wafted down and landed on her head. *Go after Natassa.*

She shook her head. This was not the time for reflection. She hooked her hammer to her hip and headed down the hall. She eventually found signs directing her toward the medbay.

That Cloak character was far too confident that Ouranos would be there. That she'd beat Natassa there despite the huge delay Izzy had talking to them. Like they just *knew*. Unsettling. She'd have a good laugh when they turned out to be wrong.

The doors to the medbay were wide open, leading into a dark, silent room. Empty, Izzy thought. No Ouranos. No Natassa. She was right and the Black Cloak was wrong.

Something rattled in the medbay, metal on metal, before crashing to the floor. A male voice cursed.

Izzy's face grew hot and a shock ran down her spine to the tip of her tail. That was definitely Ouranos. Alone. How the hell…?

Who the hell was this Cloak?

Cautiously, she tiptoed her way into the dim room and let her eyes adjust.

Not surprisingly, the place was massive. Blue emergency lights ran along the walls, floors, and ceiling in intricate patterns. It hummed with the sounds of active equipment, slightly echoing against the metal. Beds held various machinery on them, drawers and cabinets lined the walls, clusters of holobulbs everywhere. Several data slate charging slots lined one wall and each bed had multiple mounting points for them as well. A handful of deployed, broken medi-arms hung loosely over beds. The air smelled of dust mixed with antiseptic, indiscernible medicines, and… latex, Izzy thought. It tasted of it too, which almost made her want to gag.

Ouranos stood near one of the large cabinets, ripping open drawers and digging through them, cursing, mumbling, hurried. Izzy ducked around one of the machines, likely designed to help move patients, hoping he hadn't heard. He paused a moment after she settled, but then went right back to the drawers.

167

She could get him right now. It wouldn't be difficult. He was secluded, alone, distracted… She could knock him out with a choke hold. She probably couldn't carry him out on her own, but the room had the right tools and the halls were wide enough that she could just load him up and get him out. She could capture him and bring him back to Lance without Matt's help. Without *anyone's* help. That'd be a kick in the face to Matt after all he'd done to her today.

A twinge of guilt ran through her head. That was the anger talking, and that wasn't fair.

But still… She could follow Lance's orders. Maybe he'd still give them the Guardianship. Or at least Izzy the Guardianship. If she even thought she could handle it.

No. She *did* trust herself. She *deserved* the Guardianship. Right?

But the Black Cloak had said Natassa would get here soon. They'd talk about Matt. She needed to hear what they said.

And the Cloak had said that her actions over the next few days would determine whether or not she got the Guardianship.

Did that mean she had to wait and listen like the Cloak said? Were they trying to direct Izzy in a way that would get her the Guardianship?

More to the point… What consequences would she face if she just listened instead of acting?

She chewed her lip.

Was it worth it to wait? See if she'd show up? Listen to them? How would this affect her Guardianship? Or Matt…?

"Pilot, I see no sedation equipment," Ouranos said suddenly.

Izzy dove further out of sight. Sedation equipment? What did Ouranos need with sedation equipment?

A broken hologram of a blue-green, faerie-winged dragon appeared above Ouranos' head. It fizzled in and out of view. "I am -*bzzt*- sorry, Ouranos,

168

but I'm -*bzzt*- limited here-*mere-peer*. I don't have the -*bzzt*- power to access the--the inventory."

So that was the A.I. that had gotten Ouranos and Natassa here. It was amazing the thing even functioned, what with its broken speech and difficulty holding a crisp image.

Ouranos frowned, meeting the dragon's eyes. "Pilot, please. I need to stop my father before he gains control of the Shadow Cast. I cannot do that while conscious."

Izzy perked her ears. Shadow Cast? And what did being conscious have to do with it? Did he intend to sedate himself?

Pilot's hologram shifted, looking aside. "I'm afraid he -*bzzt*- might have already."

Ouranos' eyes widened. "What did you see?"

Panic ripped through Izzy's chest, making her ears ring. A bombardment of thoughts practically blinded her. *What the hell is that? How is it so strong? It survived? Run, run! Cix, Sami, Stage two! Out, out now!*

She shook her head, feeling woozy. What the hell? That... that sounded like Matt... in her own head... what?

Pilot snorted, breaking her thoughts. "The blob I -*bzzt*- had identified earlier attacked the blue-*hue-queue* and white quilar and--and his pack. They fought it, but -*bzzt*- could not--not hold it at bay. They're running from -*bzzt*- it now, but they've moved beyond my--my range of sight."

Ouranos cursed. "Then it is more imperative that I find a method of sedation." He began digging through drawers again.

Izzy's fur bristled and she flipped her ears back. A... blob? And they couldn't fight it? What the hell was this Shadow Cast?

More to the point, what should she do now? Go find Matt and help? Offer to help sedate Ouranos? Stay hidden and wait for Natassa to arrive like the Black Cloak had told her to?

169

She hunkered down lower. If she stayed, was she staying of her own accord or because the Black Cloak had dictated her movements to her already? And was she doing this for Matt to stop this sacrifice... or for herself to get the Guardianship?

You need to hear what they have to say.

That depends entirely on your own actions in the next few days.

Damn it all!

She held in a sigh. She was stuck here. And she needed to get her act together. This was not how a Guardian would react. No more panicking.

Besides... Matt had his whole pack and she was just a healer with a hammer. What could she do anyway?

Trust yourself.

She shook her head. Matt didn't need her. He could handle himself.

No black blob could kill a Guardian in training.

She settled down and waited for Natassa.

CHAPTER 25

NATASSA

Natassa leaned against a wall, huffing, her long tail drooping to the floor. Perhaps all this activity right after her time in the cryopod was not the most intelligent course of action. And now she had lost her way.

She needed to find her brother.

Draso's horns... everything had gone wrong. Ouranos was supposed to come here free of their father's clutches, free of his puppetry, and finally able to get the help he needed. How could the Basileus hold so tightly to him from so far away?

How could he treat Ouranos like just an object to be used? Oh, why had the invaders visited her home so many years ago and drive her father insane?

There was a way to help him. A word from the Phonar summons had spoken of it. But Excelsis' prediction from so many years ago still puzzled her. *Seek the blue and white Zyearthling. They will be a willing sacrifice.*

Though it was forbidden, taboo, heartless, the only way to return the stolen soul of a Drifter was to trade another one for it. And Ouranos' soul had been stolen -- hidden away beyond the Twilight Gossamer to wherever souls go to await their final assent to Draso's Palace, used as a tool to puppet his body now. Ouranos, a prisoner. The thief… their father.

And the only way to free him was for someone else to willingly die for him.

So how could Natassa expect the blue and white quilar to be a willing sacrifice? She dearly loved her brother, but she could not bring herself to be such a thing… how could a complete stranger?

What had she been thinking, coming here?

And now Ouranos was missing. Again. Lost. Fighting her father. And she was once again powerless to do anything. *Draso, why are you testing me so?*

So many questions. No answers.

Excelsis and Deo were little help, too. She had hoped her protector summons would protect her against the brown quilar chasing her, but they had done no such thing. She was alone again.

Except… the dragon aboard this ship. Maybe he could help. "Dragon, can you hear me?"

The blue-green, faerie winged dragon appeared above her head. Fragmented. It was sickening to look at, but she needed his help and she shoved aside her discomfort. "Do you know where my brother is?"

The dragon looked off. "Ouranos asked me -*bzzt*- to keep you separate."

Natassa narrowed her eyes. "Why?"

"He believes you will die-*lie-eye* if you get -*bzzt*- too close to him."

Which was not an unreasonable line of thinking, considering her father's control over him. Still. "I have protection."

The dragon frowned.

"Please, dragon," she begged. "I need to help him."

The dragon blinked at her, sighed, then vanished. The lights on the floor turned from blue to purple, leading down one hallway. "He's in the -*bzzt*-medbay. Follow the -*bzzt*- purple lights."

She relaxed. "Thank you." She jogged down the hall.

The entrance to the medbay was dark, though thin blue lights lit the room. She snuck in quietly, letting her vision adjust.

"Pilot, you are sure none of this equipment can sedate me?"

Natassa shrunk in on herself. That was her brother.

"I am -*bzzt*- sorry, Ouranos, but even if such a--a device had enough power to-*hue-few* work, I fear the medicine -*bzzt*- would have expired. It... it might -*bzzt*- kill you."

Ouranos paused. "...That might be my only option then."

No. Natassa took a step forward, but accidentally kicked something on the ground, sending it flying against a metal table. The sound echoed in the room.

Ouranos whipped about, eyes wide. He saw Natassa and pressed himself against the counters. "Stay *back.*"

Natassa flipped her ears back. "Ouranos, please."

"Why did you come here?" Ouranos spat. "What do you hope to accomplish by putting yourself in the Basileus' reach?" He paused, hunched in on himself and screamed in agony.

Natassa reached for him. "Ouranos--"

"Stay back." Ouranos' dripped with sweat and he gritted his teeth. "He is trying to take me and if he wins, he will surely kill you. Keep your distance!"

Natassa made a fist. "You were not supposed to be in his reach this far from home! You were supposed to escape him and find the white and blue Zyearthling!"

Ouranos shook his head and stood straight again. He lowered his gaze, his tail twitching. "His name is Matthew."

"So?" Natassa said, though guilt bit at her. But she could not allow herself to know this quilar. If she knew his name, his history, his goals, how could she allow him to die for her brother? Better that he remain anonymous. "The only thing that matters is that he is supposed to be the willing sacrifice that Excelsis promised we would find here!"

Ouranos' eyes grew wide. "Sacrifice?"

Natassa covered her mouth. Oh no, had she let that slip? "I... I mean--"

"You did not tell me he was to be a sacrifice, Natassa!" Ouranos said. "Do you seriously intend to try and free my soul through sacrifice? Our people forbade that for a reason!"

"For *what reason?*" Natassa snarled back, tears building in her eyes. "If someone is willing to trade their life for another--"

"No one should have to make such a decision!" Ouranos shouted. "No one life is worth another's!"

"*Yours* is!" Natassa said. "Brother, we *need* you. Our people, those the Basileus hurt." She brought her hand to her chest. "Me. We need you *whole.*"

"So that justifies the death of another?" Ouranos said. "That justifies you *lying* to me? You told me he would help, not that he would die for me."

"Ouranos, it is the only way!" Her tears spilled over and wet her cheeks. "Do you not see? The only way you can be free is if someone sacrifices themselves for you, and Excelsis said the blue and white quilar would!"

"His *name* is *Matthew,* and I will not allow him to trade his life for my own," Ouranos snarled. "It is already too late as it is. Father has created Shadow Cast with the elixir Matthew's gem produces."

Natassa's whole body buzzed and her quills and fur stood on end. "Cast? Here?"

"They have already attacked Matthew and his pack, and I cannot stop it," Ouranos said.

Natassa shifted. "These Defenders... surely they can help."

"After what the Basileus has done to their people, using my hand to do it, their only goal will be to execute me," Ouranos said. He glanced off. "It would be welcome at this stage. I have failed everywhere else and now a Cast is loose. I would rather *die* than be his puppet a moment longer. If I were to--"

"That is *unacceptable,*" Natassa said, shock running through her system. Was he seriously considering ending his own life? "You need to be *free,* Ouranos, not *dead.*"

"If the only way I can be free is through another's death, then I would rather choose death for myself," Ouranos said.

Natassa balled her fists. "Unacceptable..." she muttered. "If... If you will not accept the blue and white quilar's sacrifice--"

"His name is *Matthew,* Natassa."

"--T-Then I will just have to accept it for you!" she spat.

Something behind Natassa crashed against the metal floor. She turned.

The golden brown quilar she had run into before stared, wide eyed, a handful of metal canisters on the floor in front of her. The three of them watched each other a moment, stunned, when the golden quilar furrowed her brow and snarled.

"You can't have Matt," the golden quilar spat. She ran out the door.

Panic ripped through Natassa. No! If she got to Matthew--

She shook her head. *No names.*

She took after the quilar. If she warned Mat—the blue and white quilar, how could Natassa hope to save her brother?

Ouranos called after her. "Natassa--!"

But she ignored him. He would thank her later. This would be all worth it. She had to believe that.

Ouranos followed behind, but Natassa paid no mind. Nothing would stop her from saving her brother.

Matthew would understand.

175

CHAPTER 26

BOUND

Matt fought back pure terror as he took up the rear of their fleeing pack.

That thing had survived. How was that even possible? He had literally dropped the roof of a space plane on it! Sami and Cix had set it on *fire!* What the hell was that thing?

It shrieked behind them, slithering along the wall.

"On your left!" Matt called. Cix tossed a fireball, far too large for the size of the tunnel, and it slammed into the puddle in a shower of sparks. Matt shielded, but the heat burned right through it.

The whole pack teetered on the edge of panic. Matt held on to one thought. *Protect the pack. Protect the pack. No matter what, protect the pack.*

The creature squawked, fell apart, but reformed and ran up the other side of the hall.

Matt blasted wind at it, despite knowing how ineffective it was. It might at least keep the thing from grabbing one of them again. The gust burst the puddle into so many black raindrops, scattering it, but it reformed almost instantly and was after them again.

Darvin and Sami looked back, but Matt just waved them ahead. "Go, go, go!" Draso, he would love to take advantage of Darvin's cloaking powers now, but they'd be no use in the tight tunnel. They'd just end up tripping over each other. They had to get to open ground.

Protect the pack.

Light flooded the end of the hall, and Matt held in a sigh of relief. The vestibule. The exit. Almost, almost, almost--

Someone crashed into his side just as they entered the vestibule, sending both of them flying against the far wall. He scrambled up and blasted wind magic at the intruder until he heard Izzy's voice, shouting at him to stop.

Matt frowned, pulling back his magic. "Izzy?"

Izzy got to her feet and gripped Matt's arms. "Matt, we have to get out of here now! Ouranos and Natassa--"

"Shields up!" Cix called, just as the shrieking monster dove for Matt and Izzy. Matt pulled his partner behind him and shielded, blasting wind at the creature, as Cix doused it in flame. But the fire died too quickly and Cix cried out, shaking his hands. Too much magic – he must have gotten Lexi acid on his hands.

Damn it all. Cix was injured, Sami and Darvin were worn out, Roscoe was nowhere to be found, and now Izzy was here. He couldn't protect them all at once.

The black monster screeched, pulling itself up and standing over two meters tall, glaring at all of them with leftover tongues of flame decorating its body.

Izzy shrank back. "What in Draso's name is *that?"*

"It cannot be," a feminine voice muttered.

Matt turned. Ouranos' sister, Natassa, if Matt remembered right, stood at the entrance to the tunnel Izzy had run down, staring at the black monster with wide eyes. Ouranos came up behind her, a shadow of fear on his features.

Natassa held a hand to her face. "A Shadow Cast."

The creature wailed… and Ouranos mimicked it. He leaned over, gripping his head, shrieking in pain. He managed four words among the shouts.

"Natassa, get them out!"

Natassa pasted her ears back, but she turned to the group. "Outside, now!"

Izzy gripped Matt's hand. "Matt, Natassa wants--"

"I don't *care* what she wants. Right now, we need to get out!" Matt said. "Everyone outside! Move, move, *move!*" He pushed Izzy toward the door and waved the rest of the pack out.

Izzy stopped when he didn't immediately follow. "Matt--"

"I'm right behind you." He made his way toward the door, concentrating twin tornadoes on the… Shadow Cast.

Protect the pack.

A hazy memory entered his mind. The Basileus had talked about making an army. Was this what he meant? Was this a… a "soldier" of his making?

The two black quilar still hovered in the hallway entrance. Ouranos had doubled over now, gripping his head and moaning. Natassa stood by his side, her gaze darting back and forth between Ouranos and the Shadow Cast monster, unsure of what to do.

She wants to kill you!

Matt stopped, his ears ringing. That was Izzy's voice in his head.

Natassa gripped Ouranos' shoulders. "Fight it, Ouranos, he cannot win!"

Matt frowned. Izzy had to be mistaken. Why would Natassa want him dead? He was trying to help Ouranos. She wanted that.

Natassa stared at the Cast as the monster's body contorted in the tornado, her ears and tail trembling in fear.

He had to do something. "Natassa, how do I stop this thing?"

Natassa whipped her head up, staring at Matt wide eyed. "I… I…."

"Natassa, please!"

"I… The Cast fear fire," she said. "It does not harm them, but it might keep it at bay."

Matt cursed. Of course it was fire. And his pack was already outside. Though that didn't make much sense to him, considering the one they fought hadn't shown any sign of fearing fire. But it wasn't like he had any other leads. "Help me fight it!"

Natassa flattened her ears. "My power is not strong enough."

Matt cursed. She had a point, considering the weak fireball she had used before. Only one option then. "Then throw me a fireball!"

She perked both ears. "After what happened before?"

"Just trust me!"

Natassa chewed her lip, but lobbed a tiny fireball his way.

It fizzled out before he could catch it in a tornado. "Try again!"

It took two more tries, but he finally caught one in a twister. *Alright, you monster.* He pushed more power into it, feeding it until it stood several meters tall, and whipped it around the Cast. The black puddle screamed and wailed, torn apart in the magic. But never for long. Never permanent. What did it take to kill one of these things?

He waved at Natassa. "Get Ouranos out of here!"

She frowned. "But--"

"We're no use to him in here, get him out! I'll hold this thing back. Go!" He added another tornado and stole fire from the first. He just needed a few moments…

Natassa snarled, but she grabbed Ouranos by the shoulders, forced him to his feet, and rushed him out of the plane. The moment they were free, Matt pushed one more hard blast of magic into the attack and followed behind.

179

He didn't notice the black liquid on his hands until Ouranos dove into him full-bodied, desperately grabbing at it. He dug a knee into Matt's torso, pinning him to the ground, reaching for his hands, manic.

"Give me the elixir!" The Basileus' voice.

"Ouranos!" Natassa shouted. "Fight him!

Matt practically roared at Ouranos – no, at the Basileus. He pushed him off his torso and kicked hard, sending the black quilar flying through the air. But before he could get to his feet, the Cast leapt out of the plane and dove at Matt, engulfing him.

"Matt!" Izzy shrieked, her voice muffled under the Cast's inky body.

"Shield!" someone shouted, but they sounded so distant, so muted, Matt couldn't tell who it was. He wrapped himself in his strongest shield, pushing on it, hoping to get the Cast off, but it tightened itself around him, cutting off his air.

Izzy's thoughts bombarded him making his ears sting with ringing. *Get it off, save him, get it off, get it OFF!*

The musk-smell engulfed him, the iron taste invaded his tongue, the slime made his flesh crawl right down to the bone, but the panic was so strong he couldn't tell what was even real. He caught a blast of heat and fire in his vision just as the monster wrapped itself around his head.

He wheezed, reaching for whatever air he had left behind his shield as the fire ate up the air outside of it. The monster clutched tighter, squeezing, shrieking wildly. Matt pushed, struggled, blasted wind at it, gasped for any dredges of air left and found none, his magic flew out of control, his hands dripped with black liquid, he was going to die, it was going to kill him, someone, please, *stop, stop, stop--*

The wild screeching died all at once and the Cast pulled itself off Matt and slithered away. Matt turned on his side, gagged, gulped air as if he would never breathe it again, threw up, then gulped more air.

Fire and ice.

He had to refocus. He stared at his black stained hands, covered in the strange liquid, trying to remember why it was important, why there was some fear there when he knew it was just a part of him when his powers went out of control. Right?

"Oh Draso, it can't be…" Izzy said.

Matt turned, coughing, suddenly acutely aware of the fact that there was no fighting. In fact, everyone stood a good few meters apart, staring at the Cast.

The Cast curled around something shining gold and red, catching the afternoon light. It gurgled and cooed quietly, almost sadly. Matt squinted and lifted his head. What was that?

The Cast swelled out of its center, the three "eyes" staring down at the golden, sparkling object. A bulge extended out of the center of the swollen part, almost… almost forming a snout. Long, jagged bits shot out of the top of its "head" like branches, spreading a few centimeters before cracking and breaking, falling back into its body. Long oval shapes formed under the branches…

No… Not branches. Antlers.

And then it registered. The object it encircled was Roscoe's wedding coil.

Dear Draso, was that--

"Matt!" Darvin shouted.

Too late.

Ouranos dove full force into Matt tumbling both of them beyond the plane's crash scar in the dirt and into the trees. Matt wheezed, still reaching for every scrap of air possible, animal instincts taking over completely. Ouranos snarled, reaching for the liquid on Matt's hands, his own charged with magic. Desperate, Matt gripped Ouranos' wrists, trying to push him away.

Light and pain exploded in his mind the moment their hands touched, sending blinding white stars bursting through his vision and drowning every sound in a rush of wind loud enough to burst eardrums. A hundred thoughts ran his mind, blurred words and images so melted together and yet so crystal clear and everything was coming apart at the seams--

Shadow Cast Natassa Athánatos Jústi Pax summon, Defenders, Guardian jewels Theron Basileus Black Bound Melaina war Gem mother Matt Izzy Lance Charlotte pack Pilot colony cryo damage death death death death--

Draso, make it stop--!

His body crashed to the ground, the stars vanished, the wind died, and the world stopped.

MISSING

Izzy fought panic and failed.

Roscoe. That nasty black monster was *Roscoe.* That familiar snout shape, the musky smell of stag, the way it slithered around his wedding coil... his wedding coil...

She gripped her snout. Lightning and air, his *wedding coil.* Was that thing really her husband? He was supposed to have the easier mission!

It's Roscoe... It really is Roscoe... I'm sorry.

She paused, listening to the thoughts, wishing her ears would stop ringing. She had no idea where they came from, but how could she deny them? And she should be sorry... It was her husband... Draso's mercy...

The black monster snaked a tentaclelike arm around the coil and lifted it in front of its "face." The swimming blue eyes slithered back and forth on the bulge, as if it were looking between the coil and Izzy. Slowly, it slipped along the dirt up to her and just stared.

She squatted down, carefully avoiding hitting her tail with her pack, and reached a hand out. The monster wrapped a tentacle around it and slipped the wedding coil to her. It tried to open its "mouth" along the snout, but it broke apart, dripping goop everywhere. The only sound it made was a soft, unrecognizable coo.

She stared. This couldn't be happening. This couldn't be her husband. This *wasn't* happening. This wasn't *real.* Tears ran down her face and stained her fur. She could hardly get her voice working. "Roscoe...?"

A nearly imperceptible nod.

Oh Draso, please end this nightmare. "Can you understand me?"

The blob gurgled and again, nodded.

"Draso's *mercy...* " She pressed a hand to the blob. Drops stuck to her fur. She sobbed.

"Izzy!" Darvin shouted. "Matt is *missing!"*

Izzy whipped her head up. "What?"

"He and Ouranos tumbled into the woods and we can't find them anywhere!"

Natassa ran up to them, shaking. "You are certain?"

Izzy moved between Natassa and Roscoe, for what little good it would even do. "Stay *back.* You want to kill Matt!"

Darvin's ears perked up. "What?"

Natassa took a step back. "I do not wish to kill him--"

"You called him a *sacrifice,"* Izzy snarled. "You said if Ouranos wouldn't take that sacrifice, you'd take it for him. Stay the hell *back!"*

"I--"

"None of this will matter if we can't *find him,* Izzy," Sami said, her tail shaking.

Izzy turned. Roscoe bobbed up and down excitedly, slithering under Izzy's legs and "standing" between her and Natassa.

184

Izzy's fur stood on end. "Roscoe, stay away from her!"

Darvin frowned. *"Roscoe? What?"*

"That monster is Roscoe!" Izzy said. "That's why he stopped fighting when he found his wedding coil." She pulled the coil close to her chest, her eyes welling up. "Water below, that's my husband..."

Cix frowned. "Izzy, that doesn't make sense."

"Roscoe is one of your companions?" Natassa said in a small voice.

Everyone turned. Darvin lowered his head, his white spotted eye looking particularly vicious while he stared Natassa down. "He's my brother."

Natassa rubbed her arm, staring at the black blob. "Then it is a possibility that the Cast is Roscoe."

Cix's black ears flattened. *"What?"*

Natassa lowered her head, tears welling up in her eyes. "The Cast are made from zyfaunos. I do not know how my father found the method for their creation on this planet, but it appears he has." She stared at the ground. "There is no known way to cure them."

"Like hell there isn't," Izzy said, gritting her teeth. Natassa winced.

Darvin stared, slack-jawed. "That... that's not real. That's a lie."

"I wish it were," Natassa mumbled.

"None of this matters if we don't find Matt!" Sami said. "Ouranos was ready to kill Matt and we have to find our packmate *now!"*

Izzy shook her head. Sami was right. Roscoe's condition notwithstanding... she was the senior officer here and it was time to take charge. And she needed to find Matt. Priority number one. She didn't hear any fighting, so that probably meant Matt had Ouranos under control and they could just be done with this stupid mission. Then she could figure out what to do with Roscoe. No known cure, her tail. She'd find one. She'd get her husband back. She *would*.

But she couldn't help him now. At least he was safe next to her.

185

But Matt wasn't. She wiped her face clean of tears and stood straight and tall, adopting a stoic look. "PR Polttarit, which way did he go?"

Darvin frowned, and blinked at her, still clearly shocked about Roscoe. But she held her expression. He took a deep breath and pointed to the woods. "That way."

"Roscoe should not come with us," Natassa said.

Izzy glared at her. "Just because your brother is out there somewhere does *not* mean you have joined my pack. You're in no position to tell us what to do."

Natassa lowered her gaze. "The Basileus controls the Cast through Ouranos. If we find Ouranos, the Basileus will regain control of Roscoe and he will be a danger again."

"He fought it off before," Izzy said with a snarl.

"Only when Ouranos had some semblance of control over the Basileus," Natassa said. "We have no way of knowing if and when he will lose control again, and you cannot rely on Roscoe being able to fight against it."

Izzy hissed. Roscoe was stronger than that. He'd fought it before. Did she really think he couldn't do it again? "I don't--"

"Izzy, she might have a point," Cix said.

Izzy turned her glare on him. "You better not be taking her side."

"I'm not," Cix said, holding up his hands. "But I also know the damage this… thing can do. It's better we don't risk it in case Roscoe can't hold it back."

Izzy turned down to her husband. Damn it all. He was probably right. She shook her head and leaned down to Roscoe. "What do you think?"

Cast-Roscoe lowered himself flat, almost in shame. He formed a small bulb and shook it side to side, whimpering.

Damn it all. "…Alright, I trust your judgement," Izzy said. "Go to the plane while we go look for Matt and I'll come back for you. Be safe, okay?"

186

Cast-Roscoe "nodded," and slithered away toward the plane. Izzy watched him with an aching heart.

Natassa rubbed her arm. "I am sorry."

Izzy scowled at her, a thousand angry words rushing through her mind. But she dismissed them. There was time for anger later. Now they needed to find Matt. She headed into the woods. Hopefully he'd just meet them with Ouranos already subdued.

The trail wasn't hard to find. Scorched trees, still smoking, patches of ice stuck to branches and rocks, leaves dripping water. The underbrush and fallen pine needles had been shoved aside in big gouges on the ground. Unnatural spikes of earth jutted out in all directions. Small stones littered the ground among the leaves. They followed the battle signs for a few meters when it just...stopped.

It just *stopped*. All the signs of fighting stopped.

No Matt. No Ouranos. No Gems, no packs, no swords, no bodies--

Izzy tried to calm her shaking as she leaned down and investigated. It couldn't just stop. There'd be evidence. A hidden path, some kind of clue. She stood and scanned the area.

The leaves and pine needles had been scattered in all directions in a wide circle, leaving a patch of visible dirt underneath. It was charred. Black. She ran her fingers over it. Hot.

A distant memory, faded and dull, raced through her mind. Her father, Dyne, fighting a red quilar, trying to save her, disappearing in a flash of light, leaving nothing behind but a charred patch of earth and his colorless, unbound Gem. Another red quilar fighting Matt's father, Jaden in the Sanctum, stabbing Jaden's Gem with an odd stone knife, breaking it. Another flash of light. Another charred floor. Jaden hadn't even left a Gem behind.

Her chest burned and her vision blurred. No. *No.* She refused to believe this was happening. Not again. Not Matt. There had to be something.

187

She looked around, desperate for any signs of the trail continuing --
footprints, gaps in the underbrush, flattened leaves... but there was nothing.
The trail ended here.

It *ended.*

Darvin walked up behind her, Natassa not far behind. Darvin flicked an
ear back. "Izzy?"

"You're sure they went this way?" Why had she even asked that? She
knew the answer. There were no other trails. No other signs of struggle. Where
else could they have gone?

Darvin snorted. "Yeah, of course."

Izzy stood and pointed to the black patch of dirt. "It ends here."

Cix looked at the patch, his tail drooping. "No. No, it doesn't. It can't."

"It does." Izzy stared. She... she should feel more. She should cry. Or
keep looking. Or call out for Matt. Or scream. Do anything. But she just stared.

"It *doesn't,* " Cix said. He walked out beyond the scorched earth, flicking
his wolf tail. "Matt! Matt, come out! We're here to help!"

Sami joined in, taking the other side. "Matt! Answer us, *please!* " Her fox
tail shook.

Darvin said nothing. He moved next to Izzy and put a hand on her
shoulder.

She should feel something, say something, do something. But she didn't.
She tried to picture his face, but she couldn't. Why couldn't she see him? Her
best friend, her partner, her brother whom she had known her whole life. And
she couldn't conjure his face in her mind. Couldn't imagine his laugh.
Everything was a blur. Her thoughts, her vision, her hearing. Her brain was
gone and, in its place, a down pillow. Soft, empty, meaningless. Nothing
worked. What was wrong with her?

Natassa walked up next to them and fell to her knees. She ran her hands over the charred ground, her tail limp and her ears back. "O-Ouranos…" Her voice shook.

Something snapped in Izzy.

She wrapped a hand around Natassa's arm and wrenched her to her feet. "You're under arrest."

Natassa gaped. "What do you mean?"

Darvin stepped forward. "Izzy, you don't--"

"Don't tell me what to do, Darvin." The tears finally found tracks down her cheeks. "She wanted Matt *dead* and now he *is*, and I don't even have a *body to bury* and Roscoe is some damn invincible, incurable *monster* and damn it, *don't tell me what to do!"*

"We don't know that Matt is dead," Darvin countered, his voice shaking. "The charred earth--"

"This is exactly *how our fathers died,* Darvin," Izzy said. "No remains, no shreds of clothing, and in Jaden's case, no Gem. They're *gone."*

Darvin frowned. "But that's somehow her fault?" Natassa winced, but didn't attempt to escape Izzy's grip.

Izzy took a deep breath, Darvin's words echoing in her head. It wasn't… she didn't… she shook her head. "I don't know. But we're going to find out."

CHAPTER 28

A GUARDIAN'S FEAR

"Those were definitely not elementals," Dr. Aric Tessla said, placing a box on the metal table.

Lance leaned over, swishing his white wolf tail, eyeing Aric as the black, orange-spotted cheetah began pulling things out of the box. He and Larissa had gone to the focus jewel and magic labs to see what Aric and his lab partner, Jaymes Fogg, could tell them about the elemental creatures. They were in a small side lab with little more than empty cabinets and a scattered few metal tables on wheels.

Lance still wasn't entirely certain the creatures his Defenders had fought were summons. Summoners were, frankly, the rarest magic users in the universe. They weren't born or created or earned. They were *chosen*. Someone had to be lucky enough for a summon to approach them and swear an oath of service. And summons were in short supply. A trawl through the databases suggested there were perhaps only three or four hundred registered summons in the known universe. All of them had current partners, and almost all summons swore their oaths in pairs. Two summons to a summoner. None of them were phoenixes.

Not that phoenix summons didn't exist -- plenty of history books talked about them, especially after the zyfaunos species of phoenixes had been long wiped out. But they hadn't been seen in millennia. No modern society had recorded one. Perhaps he'd have to do more research about why that might be later, but the fact of the matter was that he needed true proof before he believed it. "And you can prove that."

Aric grinned. "Absolutely. Sir," he added quickly, bending an ear back. "It's simple logic if you follow the signs."

Jaymes nodded from the corner, his fiery quills rustling. He pushed his glasses up higher on his snout. "Quite simple, Lance," he said in his broken, accented words. "Is easy."

Lance flicked an ear back. Jaymes was... tense. Normally he was all smiles and he frequently took control in these demonstrations. But not today. Today he was distant

And how could Lance blame him? Izzy and Matt, his two adoptive children, were out on a dangerous mission. Too many unknowns. Jaymes must be feeling that. Lance sighed. He adjusted the glasses on his muzzle. "Then walk me through it."

"Certainly," Aric said. "To put it simply, elementals are formed when naturally occurring magic temporarily attaches itself to a living creature, usually an animal without natural magic tendencies. Elementals are very temporary, lasting only a few minutes, and they usually aren't very powerful." He laid out pictures of the phoenixes they fought, caught on surveillance cameras. "These creatures were massively powerful, and the entire attack took almost half an hour."

191

"Strong elementals exist, Aric," Lance said. "Cix brought up the ice lynx from last year."

"That is only one of the signs," Aric continued. "The other is this." He put a scraggly piece of mineralized rock on the table. "Fulgurite."

Larissa looked it over, bending a silver badger ear back. She rubbed the silver and maroon fur on her chin. "I've seen this before. This is what lightning makes when it hits the ground."

"Precisely," Aric said. "Because an elemental uses naturally occurring magic, the lightning behaves like naturally occurring lightning. This means any fulgurite created by an elemental will look like this.

"Now," he pulled out a box of soil and placed it on the table. "If a focus jewel user's lightning hits the ground, it can also create fulgurite." He held a hand out over the soil box and zapped it with his own electric powers. The box shuddered and the soil broke apart, sending tiny chunks into the air. Aric put on a thick rubber glove, shielded it and dove through the soil, pulling out a dense chunk. He ran some water over it, revealing an almost perfectly smooth tube of solid minerals and placed it near the fulgurite. "This is the fulgurite created by a magic user. Someone in control of magic gifted to them through means other than temporary, wild magic."

Lance frowned at it. A smooth, almost manufactured-looking tube next to a rough, natural looking tube, jutting out in all directions.

Aric reached into his box and placed another piece of fulgurite on the table. A smooth tube. "This is a piece of fulgurite retrieved from the Arena. Clearly created by a magic user instead of wild magic. An elemental could not have made this." He looked from Lance to Larissa. "But a summon could."

"Draso's breath," Lance swore.

"Is more than just that," Jaymes said. He shook his fiery quills and pulled out two long feathers, which Lance recognized to be the ones recovered from the battle this morning. "Feathers still carry magic properties. Observe." He

192

passed Jústi's to Aric, who pumped a little electricity through it. The feather immediately lit up with magic, lightning swirling around it as it had when it had been attached to the creature. "Is same with Pax's. They still channel magic. Elementals do not do this." He stared at the feather, his gaze distant. Lance flicked an ear back.

"The final piece of the puzzle is the smells," Aric said. "Multiple Defenders said in interviews that there were really distinctive smells when they got near the summons. A bit of research shows that most summons have individual scents associated with them. It's one of the ways they communicate."

Lance pinched the fur between his eyes. "A real summoner. We haven't had a summoner on Zyearth since--"

"Since Tymon," Larissa said.

Lance pasted both ears back. He didn't need that reminder. Tymon, who died doing what should have been a simple mission, right before he was due to retire, right before Matt's father Jaden was supposed to take his place. Then Jaden, who also died before his time, fighting some bloodthirsty tribe on a different planet, leaving Matt an orphan at age six. And now Matt so desperate to be a Guardian himself. And so very not ready. He still had the hotheadedness of his father and grandfather.

And it was all Lance's fault. The grooming, the lack of training, the pushing too hard, and letting him go off now.

Damn it all to hell.

Larissa rested a hand on Lance's elbow. He frowned at her.

She frowned back. "Their deaths aren't your fault."

He looked off but said nothing. It wasn't like he hadn't been told that before. At least a dozen different therapists had said the same thing over the years. Tymon, Vyse, Jaden, Dyne, his Golden Guardians. Lovetta… his wife and Master Guardian partner. Maybe if he had been told that sooner, he'd

193

believe them, but no one had contradicted him. Lovetta's parents had completely disowned him. And while Jaymes had never once said it out loud and likely never would, Lance suspected he felt it was his fault too. Hell, if Matt and Izzy got hurt now…

If they weren't his fault, then whose was it?

Jaymes looked over his glasses at Lance. "You really deny Matt and Izzy Guardianship?"

Lance kept his gaze trained on the fulgurite. "Yes." He didn't explain why.

Jaymes nodded. "I see why."

Lance looked up, raising an eyebrow. "You do?"

"Yes," Jaymes said. His ears flattened and he lowered his gaze. "You worry for them."

Lance flipped an ear back. "Matt thinks I'm worried about losing another Guardian pair."

"You are," Jaymes said. "Because you love them all."

Lance's tail stopped its slow swish. He'd really hit the nail on the head, hadn't he? And that was probably not a good thing. How could he send them into battle if he actually *cared?* He should never have allowed himself to be the "doting uncle" if he was planning on granting them the Guardianship.

Jaymes felt it too, Lance knew. He had been close friends with all of them. It was why he took Izzy and Matt in when they were orphaned. Really, he was the only father Matt and Izzy knew. How did he feel about sending his children into the Guardianship? Knowing their fathers' and grandfathers' histories? Lance should have asked before, but shame kept his mouth shut. He really should gather the courage and ask.

Fire and ice, he should never have agreed to this stupid challenge with capturing Ouranos. That was dangerous. Too dangerous, especially when they weren't Guardians yet. He prayed a quiet prayer that they were okay.

"Larissa?"

Lance turned. Larissa's wife Viriandia walked into the room, her floppy, silver-gray ears droopier than normal. As the head of the weapons department in the Defenders, she normally had an air of confidence about her at all times, but now she stood timidly in the doorway, staring at her wife with glassy eyes.

Larissa walked forward. "Viri? Is something wrong?"

"The... the team is back," she said. "From the Dead Zone."

Dread curled up in Lance's core, making him feel sick. "What happened?"

"I... I think you need to come see for yourself," Viri said. She met Jaymes' gaze. "Jaymes should come too."

The fur on Lance's neck stood up. That definitely wasn't good. "Meeting in the Assembly room now."

Viri looked up at him as a tear escaped one eye. "You... you might want s-something more private."

Jaymes made a strange, pained noise.

Lance's face burned and fear shocked his core. "My office." Jaymes was out the door instantly. Lance followed. If they were safe... if they had survived... He'd never be able to grant them the Guardianship. He knew that now. He should have kept them closer.

Oh, Draso, please let them be safe.

CHΛPTEᴙ 29

THE ATHÁNATOS

Natassa sat on one of the plush red chairs in the massive office belonging to the white wolf currently sitting behind a heavily polished desk in the middle of the room. Floor-to-ceiling bookshelves lined the walls, filled with tomes, knick-knacks and pictures. Everything smelled of fresh polish and some kind of cleaner, Natassa suspected. Something with lemon. Very odd. The low evening light from the windows had been enhanced with some electric light bulbs, making the natural shadows fade. Her experience with such artificial light was limited, and admittedly ugly, considering her reasons for visiting the mainland, and this experience did nothing to change her opinion of that.

A small statuette of the dragon god Draso sat on his desk, with Draso's child Kai next to him, bearing the elements of his three forms -- the bighorned sheep, the mighty lion, and the heavenly dragon. Kai's mortal mother, Mona, sat next to it, a bighorned sheep draped in the traditional billowing fabrics, gold and purple, laying at the foot of the double-beamed cross. To find the symbols of her religion so far from home surprised her.

But despite the homey, inviting atmosphere of the place, the room stood in still silence, save for the people occupying it. It allowed her to hear every breath and every heartbeat in the room. That, paired with more than a few sniffles.

Isabelle, the golden brown quilar, sat in a chair next to her. She stared at the ruddy carpet, fiddling with her hands, her ears pressed flat against her quills.

Natassa watched her with a deep pressure in her chest, and a heavy weight on her shoulders. She regretted ever considering trading another's life to save her brother. If she had been planning on taking that route, she should have been willing to die herself. What a selfish, horrible person she had been.

But... she could not accept that Ouranos was dead. There was no body. No jewels, no clothing scraps, no blood, nothing. The jewels did not sing for her, as they should have if Ouranos had died. And more than that, she had not heard from Jústi or Pax. If her brother was gone, the summons would have approached her, the eldest, according to their oath, to protect the remains of the royal family. She had no children, nor did she have nieces or nephews to lay claim to the two phoenixes.

The fact that she did not carry all their family's summons gave her hope that her sisters Alexina and Melaina were still alive as well, despite having not seen Alexina in years and despite Melaina's current state as a half-formed Cast. If the summons still deemed them needing protection, then Natassa must be able to save them... once she saved her brother.

But for now, she had to do what these Defenders wanted her to. They were in mourning. She would respect that. Then when she could escape, she would find Ouranos. They would fight back her father.

They *would* win.

"So," the white wolf said. Lance, she had heard him called. "You say Roscoe has become a puddle monster."

Ah yes, their companion who had been turned into a Shadow Cast. He had behaved so strangely. She had never heard of a Cast taking the shape of the zyfaunos they had once been, or stop attacking when seeing something of value from their waking life. Perhaps he would be the missing link that could help find a cure.

Izzy nodded slowly. "I wouldn't have believed it if I hadn't seen it myself."

"But you said he communicated with you, in some way," he continued. "If that's the case, why didn't you bring him back with you?"

Izzy shifted. "We... we couldn't find him." She wiped her snout free of tears. "I told him to go back to the plane while we looked for... while we continued the mission, but when we went back for him, we couldn't find him anywhere. He didn't respond to calls. We searched the ship high and low. Even Caesum couldn't find him." She shook her head. "Caesum offered to stay behind and keep looking while we came back with Natassa. I didn't tell him about... Matt." She could hardly get his name out.

"You seem so certain, Izzy," Lance said.

Izzy nodded. "There weren't any trails leading away from the black patch of earth," she said. "I don't see how he... could have escaped whatever did that."

"Mmm." Lance stared at the desk a moment, then pulled up a small flat rectangle of metal. He pressed on it, making soft padding sounds. "For now..." He paused and shook his head. "For now, I'll list him as MIA."

Izzy snapped her head up. "Sir--"

"A patch of scorched dirt isn't... really the proof I'd want," Lance said, clearly choosing his words carefully. He put the metal slab down. "He's MIA. We'll search for him when we send a pack back there."

Izzy tilted her head. "You're sending another pack."

"Several, I think," Lance said. "We need to get Roscoe."

Izzy flipped an ear back, opening and closing her mouth like she wanted to speak, but nothing came out.

Lance turned his gaze on Natassa instead. She stiffened in her chair.

"If you don't mind," Lance said. "I would like to ask you some questions."

Natassa placed her hands in her lap and took a deep breath. Lance leaned back, his face stiff, his gaze, distant. Like he was detaching himself from reality while he mourned. She had done that herself more than once.

She had to keep that in mind while she answered questions for him. He deserved answers. "What would you like to know?"

"Let's start with your name," Lance said.

Natassa nodded. "I am Prinkípissa Natassa of the Athánatos."

"And Ouranos?"

"Prínkipas Ouranos of the Athánatos," Natassa said. "He is my brother." She twitched her nose. "I believe our titles are 'princess' and 'prince' in common English. We are royalty to the tribe of Athánatos."

The silver and maroon badger, Larissa, shifted from one foot to another, twitching her ear. "Athánatos... sounds familiar. Greek, I think."

Natassa tilted her head. "I am unsure of the word's origin, but I believe it means 'immortal.' It references the state of our people."

Lance raised an eyebrow and perked an ear. "Like... the state of your tribe? Metaphorically?"

"The state of our people, literally," Natassa repeated. "Our focus jewels make us immortal."

The room grew uncomfortably silent.

The red quilar with the yellow and orange tipped quills stepped forward, tense. Jaymes, Izzy had called him. Her father. The moment he had seen Izzy,

199

he had drawn her into a tight hug. Izzy could only mutter "dad" over and over while he had rubbed her back.

Jaymes did not cry, though his expression betrayed a deep level of mourning hidden behind a professional, though cracked, mask. One that threatened to shatter. Was he also somehow related to Matthew? She had not wanted to know Matthew's history, but seeing it now only heightened her disgust for her previous actions.

Jaymes crossed his arms, almost angry. He spoke with a heavy, unrecognizable accent. "Immortality is impossible."

"For your focus jewels, perhaps," Natassa said, attempting to be delicate in her counter to his claim. "But we have been immortal since the discovery of the Ei-Ei jewels."

"You live forever," Jaymes continued.

"Most choose not to," Natassa said. "We are protected from deterioration of the body and mind, but we are not protected from the burden of living. Most grow cynical with the world as they age and find living to be too taxing. But our immortality means we can choose when we die. And some fall to injury or illness. We are immortal, but not invincible."

Jaymes lifted an eyebrow. "Then you are how old?"

Natassa rubbed her chin. "I cannot be certain as we typically do not keep track after we are bound to the Jewels, though I know I am well into my second century of life. My father is in his fifth century."

Lance raised an eyebrow. "Quite an age difference between him and his children."

"The Ei-Ei Jewels significantly slow our reproductive processes," Natassa said. "Children are rare on Athánatos."

"Hmm," Jaymes said, frowning. "Is the same with us." Jaymes pinched his snout between the eyes and shook his head. "But immortal... how?"

"The Ei-Ei Jewels protect us mind, body, and soul," Natassa said. She pointed to her jewels -- a yellow diamond, a red jagged shape, and a purple triangle. "The yellow Mind Jewel protects the mind. The red Body Jewel protects the body. The Soul Jewel keeps the soul bound to the body. They also grant the Athánatos royalty control over all magical elements, though it is quite limited for most of us. The head family controls all magical elements, while each Archon and their family control only one element."

Izzy frowned. "Ouranos doesn't have a Soul Jewel set."

Natassa shifted. "No, he does not. Not anymore."

"Why?" Jaymes asked.

"The... the Basileus has stolen them."

Lance raised an eyebrow and perked one ear. "Matt mentioned that term. Who is the Basileus?"

Natassa shifted in her chair. "The Basileus is... is my father. The ruler of the Athánatos."

The white fox twitched her tail. "And he's here too?"

"Not in a physical sense." She leaned back.

Lance lowered his gaze. "What does that mean?"

"Matt seemed to think Ouranos was possessed or something," Izzy said. "And he kind of acted like it when we met him in the woods."

"Possessed is perhaps a good word," Natassa said. "The Basileus can control Ouranos' physical body because he forcefully removed Ouranos' Soul Jewels from his Ei-Ei Jewel set and controls him through his magic. This means his soul no longer possesses his body. We call the soulless Drifters."

"You have a specific name for it?" Larissa said. "Does that mean you have a lot of soulless individuals?"

"It is a rare occurrence, but it does happen sometimes," Natassa said. "Usually when an Ei-Ei jewel user is grievously injured. The soul cannot live in a damaged body and will leave if injury is too much. Sometimes the soul can be coaxed back if the body is healed."

The black and white wolf with the blue in his fur shifted slightly. "Are his final set of jewels purple as well?"

"The Soul Jewels are the color of the user's eyes," Natassa explained. "Eyes are the window to the soul. When a user chooses to die, the Soul Jewels will lose their color until they are bound to a new user." She shifted. "Ouranos is essentially soulless, as are all Drifters, though his means of soul separation are different than normal. But as long as the Basileus possesses Ouranos' soul and his magic, he can use him as a puppet and Ouranos has very little control over it." She frowned. "I had hoped that leaving our home would have put enough distance between them to sever that connection, but that does not seem to be the case."

The gray stag crossed his arms. "You seemed to think that killing Matt would somehow fix that problem."

Everyone stared.

Natassa winced. "I... I apologize for that, though I know that means very little to you. But the only way to restore a stolen soul to a Drifter is to trade a living soul for it. Excelsis had promised me that Matthew would be a willing sacrifice. The Phonar summons are somewhat out of time, though they speak in riddles and their glimpses into the future are often difficult to interpret. I likely misunderstood his words." Her eyes burned and her vision blurred. "Believe me, I did not intend to hurt him. I only... I only want my brother back. He has been in this state for nearly seventy years. Our father has used him to destroy our people, destroy the villages neighboring ours, and attempt to destroy me and my sisters because we dare to stand against him. I am getting desperate."

Izzy scoffed, though her face was softer than Natassa expected. Lance merely shook his head.

Jaymes would not even meet her gaze.

Lance pasted both ears back. "But why would the Basileus do that to his own son?"

Natassa frowned. "The Basileus desires to create an army of Shadow Cast. His destruction of our people and the nearby villages were failed attempts at this creation. I do not know how, but he learned that this place may hold the secret to creating them. He used Ouranos to come here in search of that method and... it seems he has succeeded. I am sorry to say that one of your warriors fell victim to the horrors of the Cast."

"And that's what happened to Roscoe," Izzy said.

Natassa took a deep breath. "Yes, unfortunately."

"How?" Lance said. "How are they created?"

Natassa shook her head. "I am unsure. The original method for creating Cast has been lost to us. My father... the Basileus... he has found some other way." She leaned deeper into the chair. "I believe he had been using Matthew to do this, with some black liquid his focus jewel produced."

Izzy furrowed her brow. "I heard him say that, but Matt's Gem didn't make any kind of liquid. Hell, I don't think I ever saw him make Lexi acid, and he had lots of instances where he should have."

Natassa shrugged. "I do not know what Ouranos meant by that."

"What is a Shadow Cast?" Lance said.

"We call them stolen warriors," Natassa said. "They are invincible beings created from zyfaunos who have had their souls suppressed. The Cast is what is left when all reason, intelligence, and personality have been stripped of them. They are merely a shadow of their former selves, cast from some alternative reality." Natassa folded her hands in her lap. "An Athánatos queen of generations past created them in an attempt to conquer the world. History tells us that those who opposed her struggled and suffered much, though all our history is very vague. The Shadow Cast are mindless, dangerous, and

203

impossible to destroy. This is why our people banned their creation generations before mine and destroyed all records of their creation or cure, leaving only a vague record of the intense suffering as a reminder."

Izzy lowered her gaze. "If the Cast have no reason, intelligence or personality, why did Roscoe communicate with me? He clearly recognized me and followed directions."

Natassa shook her head. "He is… unusual. There is no record of any Shadow Cast reacting the way that he did." She shifted. "I hope that his unusual state is a reason to hope for a cure. Perhaps he is the missing link."

"You said there was no cure," the black and white wolf muttered. Izzy winced at his words.

Natassa shook her head. "Even if we had records of the old Shadow Cast, the Basileus has found a new method of creation, so a new method of restoration must be found as well." She stared at the ground.

Her sister Melaina had been the first of their father's victims. Half-formed, lacking some of the Cast's key features, unable to speak or communicate in any way. It was a nightmare she had lived for over a century. And Natassa could do nothing to fix it.

"I… I have researched my father's creation methods since he began this outrageous path, hoping to discover a cure, but I have been unsuccessful at every turn."

Lance pasted an ear back. "Why is your father trying to create them again?"

Natassa formed a fist. This, perhaps, was something to be vague about. "Put simply, my father has taken leave of his senses. He has recreated Cast and destroyed his children and our home in the process."

"That doesn't answer the question, Natassa," Lance said, his voice firm, almost angry. "Why is your father creating Cast?"

204

Natassa pressed her lips together, then forced herself to relax and appear neutral. "I am unsure."

Lance narrowed his eyes. "I don't believe that for a minute."

"I am sorry you feel that way," Natassa said, retaining her neutral expression. "But that is the only answer I have."

Lance eyed her, then threw up a hand and looked off.

"And that's why he's using Ouranos," Darvin said, looking back and forth between Lance and Natassa. "To make Cast."

"Ouranos is the most powerful magic user of us all," Natassa said. "And while I have an oath with the most powerful of the Phonar summons, Jústi and Pax are still formidable."

"Do all of you have phoenix summons?" the silver and maroon badger asked. "We couldn't even find any phoenix summons in the databases."

"The Phonar have a unique oath with the Athánatos royalty. The Order consists of eight elemental phoenixes and they protect the royal family. If any of us have children, the Phonar will redistribute to them. If one of us dies, the phoenixes attached to that zyfaunos will attach themselves to others in our family. This is how it has always been with us."

Lance lowered his gaze. "From what little we know about you, we've surmised that you aren't from Zyearth. The colony ship you came here in is proof of that."

Natassa shifted. She knew this was coming. How would they react? "That is true."

"Our colony ships traveled to the farthest known habitable planets in their time," Lance said. "That doesn't make it easy to decide where you came from. Perhaps you could enlighten us."

Natassa took a deep breath. "Ouranos and I are from Earth."

CHAPTER 30

SECOND CHANCES

The words fell like a blow to the chest, and the shock it sent through Izzy's already shattered system threatened to tear her to pieces. Everything blanked – her vision, her hearing, her sense of presence. It was all she could do to just stare at the carpet. Her thoughts focused on one word.

Earth. Earth. *Earth.*

Hers and Matt's fathers had died there, fighting genocidal red quilar bent on killing everyone on Matt's home island of Sol. Her mind traveled back in time, reliving everything.

The stink of blood. Smoke and fire burning her eyes. Her father literally exploding in front of her from a power overload.

Like… like what had probably happened to Matt.

Matt's entire family, his entire island, murdered in cold blood, leaving her, Matt, and Charlotte behind, alone, orphaned, starving…

The sudden pain of starvation burst through her stomach at the memory, dragging her back to reality. She shook her head and forced her eyes to focus.

Everyone stared at her.

She flattened her ears, but worked to keep her face neutral. That was a long time ago. She had been only four. Even the memories, sharp as they were now, didn't usually affect her. She had enough distance there. She didn't have to let them affect her.

"Where on Earth?" Lance said. Izzy clung to his words and let them bring her back to the present.

Natassa breathed deeply, her violet eyes shimmering. The Athánatos princess was clearly struggling to keep her composure with all these questions. A pang of guilt broiled in Izzy's stomach, now that she knew Natassa's reasons for what she had tried to do. Maybe she should have tried to understand rather than react as she had. Maybe they could be allies instead of enemies.

Maybe Matt would still be alive.

Though... maybe Natassa was the enemy. How much of this could they really believe? How did some ancient tribe on a backwater planet like Earth have the ability to fix up a colony ship and get it all the way to Zyearth? It boggled the mind.

Natassa glanced at Izzy a moment before continuing. "We are on a large island off the mainland not far from a city called El Dorado. We call our home Athánatos, though I believe the mainlanders call it the Vanishing Island. There are two other islands near us, and together they are called the Trinity Islands."

Izzy's insides went cold. It would be Trinity Islands. One of those was Sol, where Matt was born... and where her father had died. Another was Omnir, where their attackers had come from. She couldn't remember much about the third island, but considering the trauma she'd gone through while down there, that wasn't surprising. Of all the places on the entire planet... all the outrageous coincidences... how had this happened?

But she had to know. "How did you find a working colony plane? They're centuries old. Millennia even."

Natassa rubbed her arm. "Admittedly, I know very little of how that transpired. My father found it and worked with the dragon on board to restore it. But I was unaware of what he was doing, so how he restored it, I know not."

Lance glanced at Izzy. "Dragon?"

"The A.I.," Izzy said. "We found an active one on the bridge. That was one of the reasons why Matt put Caesum in the ship, actually. He wanted to see if we could learn something from the A.I. But the dragon on board was hostile. Caesum fought him, but wasn't having the easiest time. Because of that, Caesum struggled to search the ship. But when we left him, he was pretty sure he was wearing down the other A.I."

"I doubt this ancient A.I. could do anything to Caesum," Lance said. "He'll be fine until we get to him." He stood, looking over everyone gathered there. "Which brings me to my next point. I think for now, we've learned all we can from Natassa. Our next task is to decide how to help Roscoe. And to do that, we need to go find him."

Izzy immediately stood. "Permission to lead the expedition, sir."

Lance flicked both ears back and wrinkled his snout, clearly reluctant. And really, she couldn't blame him. They'd lost their target. They'd lost Matt. For all they knew, they'd lost Roscoe as well. And though Izzy wasn't ready to believe it would affect her, like it or not, she was tied up emotionally in this whole endeavor.

But before Lance could respond, Larissa spoke. "Permission granted."

Lance eyed her.

Larissa hardened her features. "You could send no better leader to retrieve Roscoe than his own wife. And don't you dare tell me otherwise, Guardian."

Lance sighed. "Alright. I concede." He turned to Izzy. "Then your pack's objective is to find and recover Roscoe. And Caesum, if that's possible."

"Yes, sir," Izzy said.

"If we're going to form packs based on emotional investment, then take Darvin and Sami with you too."

Cix frowned. "Sir? Not me as well?"

"No, because you will lead the pack looking for Matt," Lance said. Izzy flattened both ears and recoiled. Jaymes made a dark, choked sound. Lance shook his head. "Look, I know what the evidence points to, but until I find more concrete proof that Matt somehow... disintegrated while fighting Ouranos, I will treat him as MIA."

"There may not *be* any proof, Lance," Larissa said, her long whiskers shaking. "When Dyne and Jaden died--"

"They *left behind evidence,*" Lance said, growling the words. "Dyne's Gem. Jaden's blood. Both left quills and fur too, and lots of it. We may have lost their bodies, but there was evidence of their deaths. There will be evidence in the woods, too."

Larissa lowered her gaze like she wanted to protest further, but she didn't say anything. Lance lifted his head and snorted before turning back to the black and white wolf. "Cix, you and your pack will either find Matt alive, or find solid, definitive proof of his death. I want nothing less, understood? We don't leave our own behind."

Cix stood and saluted, a fist across the chest. "Yes, sir!"

Natassa stood now. "I am going with this wolf to look for my brother."

Lance narrowed his eyes, baring a fang. "You will do no such thing."

Natassa stepped back. "But--"

"Make no mistake, Natassa," Lance said. "I can't trust you to join my pack. You have shown up, unannounced, bringing a dangerous individual to my planet, knowing his condition is a problem. If your brother is alive, I can only expect you to prioritize him over my Defenders, and considering how dangerous he was, I can't allow that to happen."

Natassa sat back down, frowning.

209

His face softened slightly. "Since your story about Ouranos' condition seems to coincide with what my Defenders are telling me, I accept that he is in trouble. If he is alive, and we can help him at all, we will. But my Defenders, my home, and my planet come first. I can't have him and the Basileus running around turning everyone into these Shadow Cast monsters, especially when we have no way of fighting them or fixing them." Lance took a deep breath. "I will ask you to stay here, but if you refuse, I will keep you here by force. That's not my first choice, but I will do what I have to in order to protect those under my care. I am the leader of a realm and my realm is my responsibility. As royalty, I hope you'll understand."

Natassa flipped an ear back. "I... I understand. But I do not like it."

"I don't expect you to," Lance said. "But thank you for understanding. Now." He sat down. "The question is where to put you."

Izzy glanced at Natassa. She looked so broken. In all the rush of emotion, Izzy had forgotten that she had also lost someone... lost several someones, if she could be believed. It sounded like she had spent a lot of her life mourning. And if she really was immortal, that was a lot of time. She needed someone who could just listen. She looked up at Lance.

"Maybe we could ask Charlotte to stay with her," she said.

Lance raised an eyebrow.

Izzy took a deep breath. "Until we know for sure that Matt is actually gone, we probably should keep his... possible death a secret from Charlotte. But her brother is missing. Natassa's brother is missing. And Charlotte is a good listener. They'll have something in common. I'm sure Charlotte wouldn't mind."

Jaymes nodded. "Is good idea. They stay with me in my suite, yeah?"

Lance sighed. He turned to Natassa. "Are you okay with that?"

Natassa wrung her hands together. "I suppose so."

"Okay then," Lance said. "Jaymes, please contact Charlotte and get everything set up. The rest of you, you have your orders."

The Defenders in the room stood as one and saluted. "Sir!"

"One more thing," Lance said. "Matt's MIA status is top secret until we know more. Consider it Vaulted -- no one else should know. Is that clear?"

Everyone nodded with another "sir!" and they filed out of the room.

Izzy pressed her lips together as she led Natassa to Jaymes' suite. MIA. She didn't know whether to cling to that in hope or dismiss it and save her feelings later. Remembering that patch of scorched dirt, she didn't see a reason to hope. Especially after seeing that same patch of charred earth after her father's death. She pushed the images out of her mind. Lance should know better than to cling to that. He shouldn't be giving everyone false hope. Matt was gone.

Matt was *gone* and that was the end of it. Time to learn to live with that. No time like the present.

Though a tiny seed of hope buried itself in her heart anyway.

CHAPTER 31

REPRIEVE

Wake up.

No. Everything hurt. Every muscle ached. Breathing hurt. Thinking hurt. Better to just shut his eyes and--

Wake UP.

But *why?* He had lost the Guardianship. He had disgraced himself with his idiotic determination to do everything himself. His tendency to disregard orders based on what he thought was right. His selfish need to play the hero, even at others' expense. Fat lot of good that did. He couldn't even do that. He couldn't even save the one zyfaunos who came to him for help. He was *done.* Why continue?

WAKE UP.

Someone shook him. He fought consciousness, determined to just shove it away, but whoever was shaking him wouldn't give up. He groaned. Damn it all. He rolled over and opened his eyes.

Darkness flooded his vision, though his eyes adjusted quickly. He blinked. He was still in the woods, though it must be late into the night. Sepideh, the prime moon, shone brightly through the trees, hiding the presence of the lesser moons. He stared at it, trying to will himself to move, but he found he was more content to just lay on the forest floor and wait for the pain to stop.

"Matthew."

He sighed. That was Ouranos. He fought every aching muscle and sat up.

The Prínkipas was nearly invisible in the dark with his black fur. He kneeled over Matt on a patch of clean dirt, surrounded by pine needles and leaves from the forest floor. His face relaxed, as if he released a held breath, then he sat back on his knees. The quilar's pupilless blue-green eyes glowed eerily in the moonlight.

Matt blinked at him, trying to process everything. He should do something. He should capture him. Get him while his guard was down. Take him to the Master Guardian and finally be done with this stupid mission. Accept the fact that he'd lost the Guardianship and figure out something new to do with his life. If anything, they should be fighting. Ouranos had attacked him, attacked his pack. He was the enemy.

But he needed help. The more Matt interacted with him, the more he realized that. And if he had already lost the Guardianship, nothing was stopping him from helping Ouranos the way he wanted to.

More than that, Ouranos seemed in control, for once. Not gripping his head in pain, not attacking unprovoked. If he was in control, now was the time to listen. If Ouranos was willing to talk.

Ouranos pressed his lips together. "You are alive."

Matt stared at him for several uncomfortable seconds. He drew his knees up and leaned on them. "So are you."

Ouranos flipped an ear back. "Only because the Basileus has relinquished his control over me."

Matt raised an eyebrow. "He did? Why?"

Ouranos shrugged. "I do not know, but I cannot pretend that this will be permanent."

Several more uncomfortable seconds. Matt glanced around. "Are we alone?"

"I… have not seen any of your pack. Nor my sister." Ouranos shifted. "Nor the Cast."

The Cast is mine, I will have it, it will obey me, let me free, let me go, FREE ME--

Matt gripped his head, gritting his teeth. What the hell was *that?* Some foreign, angry, hateful voice, ripping through his mind, sending sharp pains spiking in his head, drowning everything in darkness. He glanced up at Ouranos.

The black quilar also gripped his head, his eyes shut tight. "He is… he is trying to push through. But he is apparently held at bay. For now."

Matt stared wide eyed. "Wait. You heard that too?"

Ouranos whipped his head up. "What?"

"*The Cast is mine, I will have it,* all of that?"

Ouranos's jaw dropped. "Do not tell me you also heard that."

Oh. *Hell.* Matt stared at the forest floor, trying to remember everything that had led up to this moment. He and Ouranos… the Basileus… had been fighting. Ouranos' hands had been charged with magic. Matt's had been covered in that strange black liquid and they connected. Their magic connected.

Had their focus jewels connected too? Had he bound his Lexi Gem with Ouranos' focus jewels? The way he had bound with Izzy?

Draso's *holy breath.*

Matt stared at Ouranos. He could test it. Maybe. He had never tried just thinking at Izzy on purpose. That would mean they were bound without a doubt

214

and he really wasn't ready to face that. For that matter, Izzy still probably wouldn't believe him. How many times had he suggested that to her and she had dismissed it? Even that morning... Draso, was it really that morning?

But if he could connect with her, if he could send her thoughts on purpose and she could hear them, that would actually confirm things. It would be the same with Ouranos. He concentrated all his energy and stress and worry into the words.

Ouranos, can you hear me?

Ouranos gasped. "Did I just hear you in my head? How is that possible?"

No. It can't be. Matt shut his eyes. How could this have happened? They had totally different focus jewels. He hadn't tried to bind them on purpose.

And more than that, what would happen now? Was he just bound to Ouranos forever like he was with Izzy? What did that mean when their jewels were so different? How would it affect them?

...And would anyone believe that they were bound? When Matt had first learned that he and Izzy were possibly bound way back in his Young Defender days, he had brought it up with Lance. But Lance had completely dismissed it. Said that binds between two Gems had to be done deliberately and no one even knew how to do that anymore. There was no way Matt could have done it by accident.

Despite all the evidence that he had.

And again, Izzy consistently denied it too, despite the fact that she had literally experienced the side effects firsthand. No one believed him.

Matt had ignored the bind since then. What was the point of worrying if no one believed him? And he still hadn't convinced himself to try and strengthen the bond so Izzy would actually believe him. Especially considering what he had done to her during his botched attempts to keep his wild Gem under control. He'd never forget seeing her horrid weakness while his Gem suppressor had stolen power from her Gem to power itself and keep his magic safe. He was lucky he hadn't killed her.

So what happened now if the Defenders... executed Ouranos? Would that affect Matt? Would he die too...?

He will be a willing sacrifice.

Matt snapped his head up. That was in Ouranos' voice. His inner voice, if that made sense. Though it felt like a memory, not a thought. The memory sounded almost genderless. Certainly not Ouranos' natural voice. Or the Basileus.

Ouranos stared at him.

Matt ran a hand down his face. This was going to take some doing, and he didn't even know where to start. "How long do you think you'll have control of yourself?"

Give me control now, you are MINE you WILL NOT WIN GIVE ME--

Both Matt and Ouranos winced. Ouranos snorted in pain. "Not long."

"Then while we have a reprieve, maybe you could help me understand your situation."

Ouranos sighed. "We may not have the time."

"Then be quick."

Ouranos pasted an ear back, then shook his head. "Fine."

Matt listened patiently while Ouranos explained everything -- his tribe, his war with his father, the Cast, the Basileus, his state as a Drifter... Matt struggled with the idea that the Basileus had Ouranos' soul and that's how he controlled him, but it wasn't like any other explanation would make his possession any more believable.

As Ouranos spoke, bits and pieces of his thoughts floated through Matt's mind. Scattered words - Athánatos, Melaina, Alexina, mother, Prinkípissa - followed by images that Matt took to be Ouranos' memories. A young Ouranos playing with three siblings. Inky black monsters, similar to the Shadow Cast,

216

though not quite the same, with floating eyeballs in them. Fragmented segments of wars -- plural, because one was fought with farm implements, magic, the phoenix summons, and strictly quilar similar to Ouranos, and the other with guns, tanks, planes, and zyfaunos of all species. Perhaps even some humans, if the images could be believed, though that didn't really narrow down what planet Ouranos might be from. Humans were almost as common as zyfaunos in the universe.

The image that bothered him the most though, was a massive island off some coast that Matt took to be Ouranos' home. It looked ridiculously familiar, but whatever familiarity Matt might have had with it wasn't pleasant if the pain in his gut said anything. He didn't ask further.

There was also the occasional flash of some red zyfaunos... possibly even a red quilar... but the memories were so repressed, Matt couldn't make them out. Considering it had been a pack of red quilar that killed his father, he wasn't sure he wanted to.

When Ouranos was done, the images and words faded slightly. The Athánatos prince sat cross-legged and rested his hands in his lap.

Matt took a deep breath. "So Cast are made from zyfaunos then."

Ouranos nodded.

Matt eyed him. "But you're sure you don't know how?"

Images of some dark room housing a black puddle with floating golden-brown eyes flashed in Matt's mind.

Ouranos chewed his lip. "That image you see is the result of my father's early experiments with the Cast. A half-formed monstrosity that lacks the strength and invincibility of a true Cast. We believe it retains the awareness of a living zyfaunos, based on their reactions to the world around them, albeit without being able to communicate. But I only saw the result, not the execution."

"And the Cast we saw today?"

217

"That is more akin to a normal Cast, from what little I understand of their history," Ouranos said. "Though I have never heard of one taking the shape of a zyfaunos before. They struggle to retain any shape at all. Though again, I did not see the execution. I am honestly at a loss as to how my father could have turned it using anyone here, since I have no memory of it and he would obviously need me to do it."

Matt leaned back. "Do you have any memory gaps?"

"Besides the gap between our last fight and now, no," Ouranos said.

Matt cleared his mind, looking for any of Ouranos' thoughts that countered his claim. The only thing he got was the image of a quilar in the dark, staring at him, at Ouranos, with sad, green eyes, though the blurred image, foreign smells, and sounds of gunfire in the background suggested that had happened years ago, not recently. Ouranos seemed to be telling the truth. Matt pressed his lips together. "Is it possible the Cast had followed you onto the ship?"

Ouranos rubbed his chin. "I had considered that possibility. I do not know of any other."

"Hmm." Maybe that thing wasn't Roscoe after all. Maybe it just liked shiny things. Maybe it was just mimicking Darvin or something. Who knew? But at least it was some hope to cling to. The thought of Roscoe being trapped in that shape forever haunted him, especially since it had been Matt's orders that had put him in a vulnerable position in the first place. "And you don't know how to fix them."

"If we did, I would have fixed the few Cast my father has created the moment I learned of the cure."

"Fair, I suppose," Matt said. He lowered his gaze. "So what's the deal with your sister? Izzy seemed to think she wanted to kill me."

Ouranos winced, and Matt got images of him arguing with Natassa inside the plane. "She... does not want to kill you."

218

"But she apparently sees me as a sacrifice?" Matt said. "I'm seeing the memories, Ouranos."

Ouranos stared at the ground. "Matthew, I am a Drifter."

"So you said."

"There are only two ways to return a Drifter to their natural state," Ouranos said. "If someone became a Drifter because physical injury forced the soul from the body, then the body can be healed, and the soul coaxed back on its own. But if the soul was forcibly removed, as mine was, the only known way to retrieve it is to trade a willing, living soul for it."

Matt's eyes widened. "So Natassa..."

"She has been led to believe that you will be that sacrifice, willing to trade your soul -- your life -- for mine."

Matt sat back, stunned. He opened his mouth, but nothing came out.

"Matthew, please know that I would never consider such a trade," Ouranos said. "My escape from my father is not worth the life of another. Especially a stranger."

Matt frowned. "Your sister thinks it is."

"My sister has lost everyone dear to her and is desperate," Ouranos said. "But despite her desperation, her arguments lacked a bite to them. She only wants me back and is willing to do whatever is necessary to do that. But our people banned this method of return for a reason. Most Drifters in my state are simply led to their final resting place when possible."

"Are most Drifters as aware as you are though? You described them to be more like zombies."

Ouranos shifted. "Drifters do not retain memories, intelligence, or even speech in most cases. I am the only Drifter I have ever known to regain these abilities without regaining my soul, and I still do not fully understand how I was able to do so. I suppose I am unique."

Matt frowned. "I can see why your sister is willing to do anything to save you then. You're still alive to her." He lowered his gaze. "Can I--"

"I will not allow it," Ouranos said. "It is not done, and it is not worth it."

But a seed worked its way into Matt's heart. Wasn't his whole purpose of becoming a Guardian to save others in the face of impossible odds? If this didn't fit, then what did?

"Matthew."

Matt met his gaze.

"I *will not* allow it. It is not negotiable."

Matt just shrugged, as if it didn't matter.

"More to the point," Ouranos said. "There may be other, less destructive methods."

"Sure," Matt said, and stuffed the idea in the corner of his mind, away from Ouranos' presence.

Ouranos sat back. "May I ask you a few questions? While we still have the reprieve."

Matt twitched his snout. "Uh. Sure."

"Who is Jaden?"

CHAPTER 32

HOPE

Matt's fur stood on end and he straightened, his eyes widening.

Ouranos winced. "Your reaction physically hurt. Did I bring up a sore subject?"

"I mean, kind of?" Matt said. Did he say it physically hurt? He'd have to be more careful with that. "Did you hear that name in your head?"

"Repeatedly."

Matt leaned back. "That's my father. He was our previous Golden Guardian. Probably one of the best in our history – completed numerous missions, built tons of allies and communication avenues with far-off planets. Won more medals than almost every Guardian before him, including two Silver Wreaths and a Golden Orchid, which is just unheard of." He rubbed his arm. "He died on the job when I was only six. My mom too." He pressed his eyes shut a moment. "Kind of on the job. He wasn't supposed to be. He had taken a leave of absence to start a family and was dragged into a battle he couldn't hope to win."

Ouranos lowered his gaze. "My apologies."

"It's not your fault," Matt said. "If I'm honest, I don't even remember hardly anything about him. He was an ice fabricator. He had white fur and green eyes. He liked to paint. But that's all I remember. Not his voice, his scent, his touch, his laugh... And honestly that assumes those facts are things I actually 'remember' and not that I read it in class while learning about Guardian history." He took a deep breath. "But I want to be a Guardian because he was."

Ouranos lifted a brow. "You are not a Guardian then as you had claimed to be?"

"Not... not yet," Matt said. "And now I probably never will be."

Ouranos pasted both ears back now.

"I just... I want to help others. That was the whole point of being a Guardian. I'll have to find another way to do it." It wouldn't be as effective, he knew, but he couldn't just sit on his ass and do nothing. That'd be a waste.

"Mmm," Ouranos said. "I am sorry I brought up your father."

"It's fine. You didn't know."

His father, the white quilar, the Guardian of Sol...

Shock ran through his system. Did he just hear someone say Sol?

"How is it that we can hear each other's thoughts?" Ouranos asked.

Matt blinked a moment then shook his head. He must be hearing things. "It's kind of complicated. But I think when our magic combined earlier, we accidentally created a social bond between our focus jewels."

"A social bond?"

"Zyearthlings used to do them all the time," Matt said. "It was essentially binding the force of two Gems together in a show of solidarity. For romantic partners it was supposed to increase their affection for each other. For battle partners, it was supposed to make each other more powerful."

Ouranos frowned. "You repeatedly said it was 'supposed to.'"

"Yeah, turns out it didn't work the way they expected, which is why we don't do it anymore," Matt said. "What it really does is cause problems. Bound users hear each other's thoughts, feel each other's feelings, steal power from each other. It gets quite dangerous..." his voice trailed.

"You sound as if you speak from experience."

Matt shrugged as if it didn't mean anything, but held tightly to the memories of Izzy's near death because of their stupid social bind. He didn't need Ouranos seeing that. "I've done my research on it."

Ouranos eyed Matt, like he expected more, but he didn't say anything else. His gaze wandered to Matt's Gem holster. "If I can ask, what is Black Bound?"

Matt flipped an ear back. "Damn, picking all the doozies aren't you?"

"Do not feel obligated to answer."

"Eh, might as well," Matt said. "Being Black Bound means I've bound myself to my own focus jewel. Izzy is the same way. That's very unusual in our culture. Some people think it makes me extra powerful, possibly even dangerous. It's kind of a stigma. Zyearthlings fear Black Bound individuals. When I was younger I used to brush it off. Izzy and I took forever to get our powers and we really hadn't shown a tendency to be extra powerful. But the more I explore my magic, the more I think there's some truth to that. Being Black Bound does make me different."

"Such as the black liquid forming on your hands?"

Matt pressed his lips together. Both Ouranos and the Basileus wanted that black liquid. He didn't really understand either of their motives -- partially because he didn't really understand the black liquid on his hands at all. And he was reluctant to talk about it. Yeah, Ouranos was in control now, but the Basileus could take over at any time, and he really didn't want him having any information about that elixir. And for all he knew, the Basileus could still hear Ouranos' thoughts.

223

Though he hadn't heard the Basileus' voice in his head in a while. Maybe it was okay, as long as he was careful with his words. "I suppose."

"What is the elixir, if I might ask?"

"I… don't know," Matt said, which was technically true. "But it only seems to appear when I'm overloading on power. Which is unusual, because for most Gem users, overloading on power creates Lexi acid vapors, not this strange black liquid."

Ouranos shifted. "I am aware that it only appears when you are straining your magic. It is why the Basileus felt the need to attack you as he did."

Matt looked down at his hand a moment. "You said that you needed this elixir for something."

Ouranos looked down, but nodded. "I believe I do, yes."

"You don't sound too sure of yourself."

"It is… complicated," Ouranos said. "But I believe the elixir is what granted me partial control over my body again, and what allowed me to regain my ability to speak, think, and form memories. Somehow it suppressed the Basileus' control and gave it back to me. Though only to a degree. My hope is that I will be able to use more of it to rid myself of his control completely, if I have the courage to employ it. It is not, perhaps, the same as having my soul returned, but it would have the same effect, and then no one would need to die for me. Then once I had completed my task of stopping my father, I could live my life and choose my death as all our people do."

Matt looked at his hand, twisting it slightly. That made some sense, if he thought about it. The liquid only appeared when Matt's powers went out of control. As if it was trying to suppress them. And it appeared instead of Lexi acid. Come to think of it, Matt had never produced Lexi acid… ever. Only that black elixir. And he could think of dozens of times when he had overloaded on power. Times he should have created Lexi acid, and he hadn't. Maybe it neutralized the Lexi acid even, or the two substances canceled each other out. It made sense that it might suppress the Basileus too. He looked up at Ouranos.

"You said you needed the courage. Why courage?"

Ouranos chewed his lip, and Matt felt a strange searing pain through his gut. He gripped his stomach and groaned.

Ouranos sighed. "I apologize. But that is one of the reasons. I do not remember much about my return to the waking world, but I do remember abject pain. It took days to recover from, and all I could do is lay down, out of sight, and endure it. I could not eat, I could not sleep. It was the most miserable experience I have ever had, despite everything I have been through in life."

Matt frowned. As Ouranos spoke, more images entered his mind. A dark forest, the smell of gunpowder, planes and bombs in the distance. A feeling of intense hunger, the insanity of a lack of sleep, nearly unbearable pain wracking his body. Matt curled up on himself.

But it all vanished in a moment. *I apologize.*

Matt shook his head. "It's… it's fine. I see your worries though. Did that happen because of the elixir?"

"Because of my mental state, I am unsure if the pain was from the employment of the elixir or from some previous injury I was unaware of. Regardless, I worry what this elixir may do to me. But I am so very ready to be rid of my father's control, no matter the cost."

"Hmm." Matt stood. "I think if I try hard enough, I can probably create the elixir on purpose. But I don't like the idea of using it on you if it's going to hurt you." He rubbed his chin. "I'd like to suggest that we go to the Defender campus and try this in the hospital wing in case something goes wrong, but after the Basileus' attack of the campus, I don't think Lance would even be willing to try."

Ouranos' face fell.

"But," Matt continued. "The medbay in your ship is still active."

"Pilot has told me that he does not believe the equipment is still viable," Ouranos said.

"Your A.I. is old," Matt said. "But I left Caesum in there. Since he's an A.I. designed as a companion for the Golden Guardians, he has all the programing for deep-space flight A.I.s and that includes ship-bound medical equipment. He might be able to make it work if something went wrong."

Ouranos wrung his hands together. "I do not suppose you could do anything to fix Pilot's deterioration? He is the only friend I have in this world right now and I do not like to see him suffer so."

Matt rubbed his chin. "Maybe. I might be able to transfer his consciousness to a new A.I. crystal and rebuild the cracks in his programming. But we have to fix your problem first or the Defenders won't even let you near them."

Ouranos stood now too. "Perhaps you're right. But are you really willing to help me after everything I have done?"

Matt took a deep breath. "You didn't do anything. Your father did, using you like a puppet. And I meant what I said. I want to be a Guardian so I can help others. You need help. That's enough for me."

"Even after losing your chance at Guardianship?"

"Especially so," Matt said. He brushed the leaves and pine needles from his pants and tightened his field pack around his waist. "If I'm going to do this, I might as well do it now before the rest of the pack finds me. You've been in this area a while, from what I've gathered. Is there a place deeper in the woods where we won't be detected? I can try getting some elixir there, then we can head to your medbay."

Ouranos took a deep breath. "I will lead the way."

CHAPTER 33

A ROSY-FINGERED DAWN

Ouranos led the way through the woods, his heart and mind aching.

Matt's strength, his determination, and his thoughts, now singularly focused on their task, pounded at the edge of his mind, ever present, powerful, blinding almost. Like a bright light in his peripheral at all times.

One would think that after decades of having his father occupy him body and mind, he would be inured to someone else's presence in his head. But Matt's noble determination to help him for no other reason than to help someone in danger was so drastically different than the constant poison his father had been feeding him for so long. It was like a loving embrace after a day in the storm, a speckle of sunrise after a long, cold night.

It reminded Ouranos of what it meant to be himself again.

It was not without its drawbacks, however. Yes, he felt Matt's powerful positive outlook, but his fears bled into that outlook. At the edge of Matt's consciousness was a deep, present, though rather vague worry. Matt had not put that worry to words yet, but Ouranos already could. His fear over the

Guardianship. His concerns about his pack. His knowledge that he was, in all truth, helping the enemy.

"You have me pegged that well, huh?" Matt said behind him.

Ouranos frowned. He slowed his pace and matched it with Matt's. "I am sorry. Were my thoughts projecting then?"

"A little," Matt said. "You're right, though. You got it down pat."

Ouranos' tail drooped. "That was not my intention."

"I'm sure it wasn't," Matt said. "But I think we'll have a lot of these back-and-forth things for a while, until we get used to this."

"Mmm."

A moment of silence.

"I don't see you as the enemy, Ouranos."

Ouranos took a deep breath. "I know. But your people do."

A pause. "They don't understand."

"They see an unknown and powerful threat attacking them unprovoked, with no reason to believe that I am in danger as you claim," Ouranos said. "They understand perfectly well."

Matt furrowed his brow. "That doesn't make them right."

"And you will set them right?"

Matt rubbed his arm. "I want to be a Guardian. Part of that means analyzing situations based on my own understanding and making judgment calls outside of what my superiors see. It gives me the ability to act as I see fit, even if it's not how *they* see fit. You're not a threat."

"Matthew," Ouranos said, facing him. "I *am* a threat. I make no excuses for that, nor do I pretend it is not true. Until I can be free of my father's imposed will, I *am* the enemy. I say so with great shame, but without hesitation. They are trying to protect your people. They are not wrong to do so. You should acknowledge your superior's attempts to protect the people under his care, even if you choose to disobey him. One person's wellbeing is not worth sacrificing others."

A wave of pink surged through Ouranos' mind, which he took to be Matt's shame. It quickly melted into the ever-present golden dawn, however. Shame into understanding.

More silence.

"You're right," Matt said finally. "I should keep that in mind. I guess I let that blind me sometimes."

"We all have things that blind us to the consequences and reason for our actions," Ouranos said. "I fully admit that mine is my sisters. I have made foolish decisions with their wellbeing in mind, which I frequently regret."

"Hmm," Matt said. "I can see what you mean. I'd do anything for my sister, and I could see myself being really stupid about that."

Images of Matt's sister, named Charlotte, if he read Matt's memories correctly, wafted in Ouranos' mind. Smiling, laughing, painting, filled mostly with joy, aside from a few pictures he took to be rather recent, if the crispness of the image could be believed. The pictures accompanied a deep pink in his mind, a feeling of joy, which blended perfectly into the golden dawn.

"You have some pretty vibrant descriptions for my presence in your mind," Matt said. "Do you actually see it?"

Ouranos rubbed his chin. "I suppose I do in a sense, though not as vivid as I describe. They are more like colors rather than images."

"Oh?"

"Yours is like the first rays of sun against a blue sky," Ouranos said. "A rosy-fingered dawn. Though the edges are colored purple with your worry. Your shame appeared as pink, though so did your joy."

Matt flipped an ear back. "Sorry."

"Do not be," Ouranos said. "It is welcome after the drowning black of my father's poison. It is like I am finally able to see where this ends."

229

"The light at the end of the tunnel," Matt said. "I hear you." He paused a moment. "Do you see your father the same way?"

"I must, though I had no point of reference to understand until now. He is like a looming black cloud over my consciousness. Just anger and hate and deception. I feel it more than I see it."

Matt frowned. "That's got to be awful."

"It is easier now."

Matt rubbed his hands together. "You know... I haven't heard your father in my head in a while."

Ouranos pressed his lips together. "Nor have I."

They walked several more yards in silence.

Ouranos wrinkled his snout. Now that Matt had brought it to his attention, his father's absence unnerved him. Those first few pushes had held the same anger and vigor that it had always had, but then he had retreated. He had left. But why? Were Matt's rays of light in his mind too much for his father's darkness? That would be a thing to hope for.

"We should have a plan," Matt said.

Ouranos glanced at him. "For?"

"When your father takes back over," Matt said. "Something I can do to stop him, or some way you can signal me that isn't just grabbing your head and screaming."

Ouranos winced, but he nodded. "I am unsure of how to stop him should he take over again, though I will be sure to let you know if I feel his presence."

"We need a code phrase or something," Matt said. "Something only you and I would understand."

"Hmm," Ouranos said. He met Matt's gaze and just... thought at him. *Perhaps if I spoke to you like this?*

Matt's eyes widened, but he gave a slight smirk. "Sure. And you're right. I understand what you mean about colors. I think that'd make it pretty clear when it's you speaking and not the Basileus."

Ouranos perked an ear. "Oh? Then what are my colors, if I might ask?"

"A dark blue, lined with a lighter blue and a thin layer of white," Matt said. "Dark blue for resignation, light blue for curiosity, and white... for hope."

Ouranos perked both ears. "Hope." He glanced up at the sky, the faintest blue light fighting back the night. "What a luxury to have hope again."

They continued on for another twenty minutes before entering a large clearing. Brittle green and golden grass still clinging to the edge of summer found holes in the leaves and pine needles of the forest carpet and reached for the first light of the sun. The canopy parted above them, revealing the few stubborn stars still dotting the sky. In the far distance, a lake, which had spilled a gentle, thin mist over the grass, giving everything a pleasant, clean smell.

But Matt's mind went dark for half a moment and he stopped in his tracks. Ouranos frowned. "Are you okay?"

Matt looked at him with a spike of shock on his face, before shaking it free. The rosy dawn returned to Ouranos' mind. "Just... memories. This is Solek's Clearing. I did my initial training here when my Gem broke."

Images of massive ice spikes and damaged tree branches accompanied a deep, deep fear. Ouranos pasted an ear back.

But Matt waved his hand. "When my powers first broke, they were outrageously powerful and completely out of control. I learned control here, but it was absolutely terrifying. But that's done now, and I have perfect control of my powers." He unhooked his field pack from his waist, dropped it on a pile of pine needles, and kneeled next to it. "You're quite good at waxing poetics, you know that?" He rummaged through the pack.

"A product of my upbringing," Ouranos said. "My mother wrote poetry."

Matt froze a moment. A faded memory of a white, golden tipped quilar entered his mind, though the quilar had no visible face. Matt coughed and the image blew away. "My mother. I can't remember her face, really."

Ouranos took a deep breath and, carefully, shared an image of his own mother with Matt. Sleek black fur with gentle blue eyes and quills streaked with Natassa's soft cream color. "I too, know what it is like to lose a mother."

Matt frowned. "Guess we have more in common than we thought."

"Indeed."

Matt closed his eyes a moment, then pulled a water bottle out of his pack. He drank half, then passed it to Ouranos. "You must be thirsty. Drain this, then we can use it to collect the elixir." He cracked his knuckles and did some stretches. "I'm going to need your help to do this if I wanna keep this under control. Give me a minute and let's get started."

Ouranos nodded and sipped at the water while Matt stretched. After years of battling for control, fighting against all odds, doing unspeakable things against his will... this seemed too easy. Yes, he had helped repair a ship, survived the voyage, fought the Defenders, and managed to, somehow, win Matt's unwavering trust, which was an incredible journey thus far. But to be this close to freedom and to not feel his father's imposing presence...

Something was wrong.

He took another sip, and the thought hit him like a boulder to the face.

The Cast charms. Could the Basileus be waiting to get a hold of the elixir and create more? And what had happened to the ones he had? Had he lost them somehow?

I must have... lost them.

Ouranos shook his head. But he did not remember losing them.

It was quite a battle. Of course I would not remember losing them. But they are gone.

232

But... but were they? How could the Basileus lose something so precious?

They fell when I fought him, when I won. They are gone.

Ouranos paused. Did he see black creeping in his mind around Matt's rosy dawn?

It must be my blue. My curiosity. Give it time and it will be hope. Oh, to hope again.

He stopped. Waited. Poked in his mind at the colors. But they faded back to Matt's colors in his peripheral. Back to normal.

"Ouranos?" Matt drew Ouranos out of his thoughts. "You finished with that water?"

Ouranos blinked and stared down at his water. He waited a moment longer, trying to coax the thoughts back.

Ouranos? Matt's voice in his head, spreading the sunlight through his mind. *You still there?*

Ouranos met Matt's gaze. "Yes, I... yes. Yes, I am here." He drained the rest of the water and passed Matt the bottle. "I am ready to assist."

Matt watched him a moment, then smiled. "Okay, then. Just keep my magic under control." He blew a powerful wind through the meadow, forming a tall tornado in the center.

As Ouranos called on his own powers to keep the wind steady, he tried to grasp back at the thoughts about the Cast charms. But they were gone. He pressed his lips together. If... if he truly thought he had dropped them, then it must be true.

That is correct. They are gone. We are safe.

Ouranos brushed aside his worries and focused on Matt's powers instead. Soon... soon he would be free.

Soon this nightmare would end.

He thought he heard a laugh echo in the back of his mind.

233

But that was probably just his imagination.

CHAPTER 34

SISTERS

Natassa folded her hands in her lap, sitting in the sunken living room of the suite Izzy had brought her to. Jaymes, who she had since confirmed was Izzy and Matt's adoptive father, was in the kitchen making coffee, if the smell was any indication. Izzy sat next to her, though Natassa noticed she kept a calculated distance.

And across from them, on the opposite sofa, was Matthew's sister, Charlotte, wearing a dull gray shirt and black pants. Her blue streaked, white quills reminded Natassa far too strongly of Matthew, missing because of her actions, though Charlotte's rich pink eyes were more reminiscent of the vibrant colors of Athánatos eyes. She had her lips pressed firmly together, hands digging into the fabric of her pants.

"So," Charlotte said, her voice firm, her ears perked straight up, and her face stoic. "You're telling me that you and Matt fought Ouranos, and somehow both of them got lost in Corinth Woods."

Izzy shifted. "Yes."

"And you came back to get help finding him."

"That's right."

"No, Izzy, that's *horse spit,*" Charlotte said, anger bubbling in her voice, causing both Natassa and Izzy to jump. "You're his best friend and in some ways more of his sister than even I am, and his Draso-damned *Guardian partner*, even if you aren't Guardians yet. You didn't leave him behind. You wouldn't have given up without a damned good reason. Now tell me what really happened. Where's my brother?"

Izzy sat back, shocked. "I... Char..."

"Izzy," Jaymes said from the kitchen. "Speak the truth."

Izzy looked at Jaymes a minute, then frowned. "Okay, fine. I think... I think Matt's... dead."

Charlotte's expression did not change. "You *think* he's dead."

"He and Ouranos fought each other in the woods," Izzy said, her voice cracking. "The trail ended in a clearing with a bunch of lingering magic and we can't find them anywhere. There was no trace of them, just like with my father. And yours. Lance won't take that for an answer though, so he's sending a search party." She stared at the floor. "But I think he's... dead."

"I do not," Natassa said.

Izzy shot her an angry look. "The ground was *charred black*, Natassa. They were nowhere to be found, and there were no other trails. They didn't just get up and walk away from that and not leave any evidence. What else could that mean?"

Charlotte finally broke and let out a tiny, choked sound.

Natassa remained firm. Izzy might have given up, but she had not, and she had reasons not to. "There was no physical evidence of death. No blood, no charred remains, no jewels. The Ei-Ei jewels are indestructible. Even if Ouranos' entire body had been destroyed, I would have been able to hear the

236

jewel's song and find them. I heard no such song." She took a deep breath. "More than that, Jústi and Pax have not come to me. Their oath with our family would have brought them to me after Ouranos' death."

"But that doesn't say anything about Matt," Izzy snarled.

"Matthew also left behind no evidence," Natassa said. "Surely his Gem…"

"Matt's father's Gem was never recovered after he *literally exploded.*"

Charlotte finally broke. She let out a sob and brought a hand to her snout.

Izzy frowned. "Char, I'm sorry, I didn't… I'm sorry."

Natassa's heart ached for Matthew's sister. But still, she stood firm. "I am still on the side of your Master Guardian. Further evidence is needed to prove Matt's death, and until I see it, I believe he is alive."

Silence pierced them all like the quick sting of a bee. Finally, Charlotte stirred. "…Thank you for your confidence." She met Natassa's gaze. "Jaymes said that Lance asked you to stay here while they looked for them."

Natassa bent an ear back. "If you will have me."

"He won't let you go looking for your brother?"

"No," Natassa said. "He believes I may be a hindrance if we find him, since I will choose my brother's well-being over the well-being of his Defenders." She pressed her lips together. "In fairness, he is not wrong. It was either put me up here or hold me somewhere by force. I chose the easier option. I have been held hostage by force enough in my lifetime to know I do not want it."

Charlotte chewed on her lip. She glanced at Izzy, but Izzy turned away. Charlotte threw up a hand. "Sure. Stay here. We'll play chess or something."

Izzy sighed relief. "Thank you." She turned to Natassa. "If it comes to it, you can have my old bedroom to sleep. Dad never took them down when we moved out."

"You visit a lot," Jaymes said.

237

Izzy eyed him. "We live across the hall."

Jaymes sipped his coffee. "I miss my full nest."

Izzy pressed her ears back, but shook her head. "I'm going to head out. I'll be back soon."

"Izzy," Jaymes said.

She met his gaze.

"Don't lose hope."

She stared at him a moment, frowning, then left without a word.

Jaymes flicked an ear. He sipped his coffee, smiled sadly at Charlotte, then disappeared down the hallway.

Natassa stared at the door Izzy had vanished behind. *Draso, be with her while she searches for Matt.* She flattened her ears. *And bring my brother back to me.*

"I'm sorry," Charlotte whispered.

Natassa looked at the white and blue quilar. She hung her head, real tears appearing now. She would not look Natassa in the eye.

Natassa twitched her snout. "For what?"

"Lance asked me to keep you company and all I can do is argue with Izzy and turn into a blubbery mess," Charlotte said. "I'm sorry."

"You are a woman who may have lost your brother, your only family," Natassa said. "I am the same. I see no reason to be sorry."

Charlotte let out a dark chuckle. "A woman, huh? You sound like an Earthling."

Natassa shifted. "I am from Earth actually. Do you not use the term woman on this planet?"

Charlotte shot her gaze up. "Wait, really?"

Natassa nodded. "Ouranos and I both."

"Huh." Charlotte sat back on the couch. "Larissa was right then." She picked at a loose quill. "'Woman' and 'man' are human words. We just use

238

male and female, or the species name for those who identify as neither. Same thing with 'people' or 'person.' We just say 'zyfaunos.'"

"That is… interesting," Natassa said. "I had not realized how much of human culture had bled into our own lexicon."

Charlotte twitched an ear. She got up and came back with a folding table and a chess set. "Do you play chess?"

Natassa nodded. "My mother was quite skilled at the game."

Charlotte set up the folding table and began setting up the chessboard. "Then let's play a few games and I can talk to you more about Zyearth culture. I'm an amateur historian, so feel free to ask questions."

Natassa smiled. It was, if anything, a distraction for Charlotte while she processed everything. Besides… Matt was alive.

She knew it.

"Thank you. I will play black."

CHAPTER 35

CUT TO THE QUICK

Izzy stood in the entrance to the outfitter's room, trying to make her brain work.

It had been a long, sleepless night. Lance had insisted that everyone rest, saying they'd go after Roscoe the next day. Natassa had assured him Roscoe wouldn't go far, and he wouldn't be in any danger, nor would he be dangerous himself without the Basileus controlling him. And they needed the respite, Lance said.

Like she could get any rest after everything that had happened today.

Sleeping in her bed was impossible. She needed Roscoe. His scent, his warmth, his light snoring, his precarious, yet oddly charming, nightly routine of finding a comfortable position to sleep in with antlers...

She eventually opted to sleep on the couch. She probably got two, maybe three hours of sleep before she finally admitted to herself that she would never find rest. Maybe never again.

The nightmares were too much.

Black quilar, black blobs, black dirt, black night--

She shook her head, trying to chase the images away. That didn't do anyone any good.

Since she couldn't sleep, she got an early start on prepping for the mission. A very early start, considering Lance intended to send them that afternoon after he spent more time pumping Natassa full of questions. He was determined to find out why the Basileus was making an army.

He wasn't going to get anywhere though, and Izzy knew it.

But it also gave Cix time to get a team together, as discretely as possible, since Lance had Vaulted Matt's MIA status until he knew more. Top secret, hush-hush, no one is to know.

Izzy chewed her lip. It didn't escape her notice that Lance still pretended Matt was MIA, but had no qualms admitting Ouranos was dead. She hadn't heard Lance say his name once since Izzy had gotten home.

Though he had said Matt's name a lot. Maybe he thought that if he said it enough, it would mean Matt wasn't dead. Maybe it would bring him back to life.

Grief made zyfaunos behave strangely.

And of course, she had her own strange coping mechanisms. If those could really be called "coping."

Which is why she was in the outfitters, at 0600, prepping for a mission that started at 1400.

Matt would normally be out running down the beach at this time. Barefoot, like always, tossing wind at the waves, dreaming of when he got to be a Guardian--

Damn it all, *not now.* She needed to focus.

What did she need to find to… to pack up her husband and carry him home? She couldn't just expect him to follow if Natassa could be believed.

A net...? No, he'd just get right through it, and it wouldn't seal well enough. A bag? Would he just break through it? Would he be able to breathe in a bag? Do Shadow Cast breathe?

She shook. Water around her, why did she have to ask questions like this? What the hell was even going on? She'd lost Matt. She'd lost Roscoe. She'd lost the Guardianship. She was going to lose more. She was going to lose *everything*. She just... she...

No. She couldn't give into that. She had to *focus*.

She walked into the room.

And her toeclaws clinked against the floor.

She looked down. Had she not put on shoes that morning? How had she not noticed that? Come to think of it, she wasn't even sure where she'd left the field pack that held her boots from yesterday. Probably on the troop carrier. She'd have to get another one. She took another step.

Her toeclaws clinked again.

She snarled. Take care of that first. She dug through one of the portable grooming kits, found a set of claw clippers, sat down on a green weapons locker, and began clipping. And clipping. And clipping. And--

"Ow!" She pulled her foot away from the clippers. A single drop of blood formed on the tip of one of her claws. Damn it, she'd cut it to the quick. She reached for a first aid kit and wrapped the tip of her toe.

"Izzy? You okay in here?" Darvin walked in. "I heard you shout."

What the hell was he doing up this early? She didn't look at him. "It's fine. Just trimmed the claw too short."

Darvin tapped his hoof. "Why are you trimming your claws in the outfitters room?"

"Too long," Izzy said. "Kept making noise."

"You could have trimmed them at home."

"Didn't remember until now." She clipped another claw.

242

"You don't normally go barefoot."

"Boots too loud." She clipped another one, too close.

"Izzy."

"I'm fine," Izzy said. "Just let me--ow!" She'd clipped another one at the quick. *"Damn it!"* She reached for the bandages again.

Darvin rested a hand on hers, his hooved fingertip clinking against the nail clippers. "It's okay to admit you're not fine."

She glared at him, ready to rip into him, when she noticed his eyes. Dark and bloodshot, probably like hers. Just... dead. Lifeless. Gone. The white spots in his left eye looked bigger than ever behind the wall of tears.

He furrowed his brow, frowning. "I didn't sleep either."

She blinked and her vision grew blurry, her cheeks, wet. She didn't stop him when he closed his arms around her in a hug.

She didn't know how long she fought the sobbing. She was supposed to be a *Guardian,* damn it. A *soldier*. She was bound to lose her fellow soldiers. She *knew* that. She should be stronger than this...

But she eventually gave in and cried in her brother-in-law's arms for Draso knew how long.

To Darvin's credit, he said nothing. He could have said a lot, filling the air with meaningless platitudes and empty words, but he was smart enough to know nothing would fix this. He just held her. And while Darvin's musk wasn't the same as Roscoe's, it was comforting just the same.

She eventually pulled away from him and wiped at her eyes. "...Thanks."

"It's what family's for," Darvin said. "You know you can always come to me, no judgment."

"I know," Izzy said. "I'm sorry."

"Don't be. It's not like any of us are clearheaded right now."

Izzy fiddled with her hands. "I don't know what I'll do if we can't get Roscoe back."

"I don't either," Darvin said. "But we have to try."

Izzy pressed her lips together, grateful Darvin hadn't insisted they were going to get him back. Because for all they knew, he was gone forever. "Yeah." She looked around. "We… should prepare."

But they both just sat there. Izzy tried pushing herself, to move, to stand, to speak, to do anything, and she just couldn't. She was done.

Darvin frowned, but he eventually stood up. "What are we going to use to transport Roscoe?"

Izzy shrugged. "I dunno."

"No ideas?"

Izzy blinked back tears. "I was thinking a bag or something."

Darvin picked up a portable weapons locker. The thing was painted in funky rainbow colors with cutesy unicorn stickers from a popular cub's show all over it, a frequent prop used when teasing new trainees at boot camp. "We could always sick him inside Rainbow Barf. He was one of the few zyfaunos who actually got himself out of it when Chief Hawthorne locked him in it during boot."

Izzy actually snickered. "I think he'd find that ironic, honestly. Maybe he'd even be drawn to it."

"That settles it. Rainbow Barf it is." He hoisted the thing up. "Wanna help me get this to the plane? Then we can stop by the hospital wing and find a healer get those claws fixed up. Don't wanna be tackling this mission while in pain, no matter how mild it might be. And let's get some sparring in. We've got time and we might need it." He held a hand out to her. His white-spotted eye still glistened.

Izzy shifted. Darvin was good at this. Give her a list of tasks… something to focus on. Something to strive for. Something to work towards. "Okay…. Okay. Yeah." She took his hand and the pair of them walked out and headed toward the hangar.

True to his word, Darvin kept her busy far into the afternoon. By the time the teams were lining up in the hanger at 1400, she was able to keep her composure. At least enough that Lance didn't seem to notice.

Cix had been in charge of putting together his own pack, and he'd managed to find over thirty volunteers to go looking. Wolves, a few common felines, one tiger, quite a few stags and doe, one snowy owl/leopard gryfon, and a couple of hawks. A good mix of species. They could search by air, scent, stealth… Cix had done a good job. Almost all of them were elementals too, though there were two healers and one cloaker as well.

The extra packmates would make for a tight trip over, but it would be worth it. Izzy might even be able to pilfer a few of them to help with Roscoe.

Darvin gave Izzy's shoulder a squeeze before jogging over to Sami. The pair took their places behind Cix and his team.

Lance stood over all of them, his stoic mask of composure making his face rigid and strained. No one seemed to notice the hairline cracks in that mask.

But Izzy did.

It suddenly got harder to keep her own mask from breaking.

"Defenders," Lance said. "I know this isn't going to be an easy mission. Words can't express that. But I know it's a mission you will all succeed in. Bring our packmates home." He glanced at Izzy. "GR Gildspine is in charge and her word is law. Understood?"

"Yes, sir!"

"Good. Go with Draso's blessing." He waved at them and the packs began piling on the Delta plane.

As Izzy stepped toward the plane, Lance gripped her shoulder and pulled her aside. "Izzy. I just wanted to say one more thing before I send you off today."

Izzy frowned. "What's that?"

Lance looked deep into Izzy's eyes, his own gaze firm. "What happened to Roscoe and Matt isn't your fault."

Her ears and cheeks burned at his words. Had she ever thought it was? She didn't think she had, but now that he said it, her brain started throwing every possible reason why it *was* her fault.

She shouldn't have let Roscoe go.

She should have stuck with Matt.

She should have tackled Ouranos in the medbay.

She should have stopped Natassa.

She should have insisted they go back for reinforcements.

She should have taken charge when Matt stopped following orders.

She shouldn't have listened to the Black Cloak, that bastard.

Damn. Damn, damn, *damn.* Lance couldn't have said anything worse if he had flat out blamed her for it.

"Izzy?" Lance whined quietly.

"Yes, sir, I understand," Izzy said, but she didn't wait for an answer.

Earth and stone, it was going to be a long flight to the Dead Zone.

CHAPTER 36

CHANGE

Matt leaned over, huffing, letting the sweat drip down his face and quills. He lifted a hand, literally oozing with the black elixir from his fingertips to his wrist, and squeezed it with his other hand onto the tarp they had laid on the ground. While autumn was in full swing, the clearing provided no shade and he was starting to overheat.

It was mid-afternoon, nearly 1400, if he could really trust his wristwatch. The face had broken in the scuffle with Ouranos, and while he had wound it the moment he'd remembered to, who knew how far off it was. What he wouldn't give for a digital clock. He had tried looking up the time on his Defender pendant, but the hologram had immediately fizzled out when he'd brought it up. Still too close to the Dead Zone. Had it been that way when he had trained here with Lance all those years ago? He couldn't remember if either of them had ever used their pendants at that time.

It had taken hours of trial and error to figure out a system for collecting the liquid. It was relatively easy to produce it, but the moment they paused to collect it, his body started absorbing it, and by the time it was safe enough for Ouranos to get near him with the water bottle, most of it was gone.

Also, it never really produced much, at least at the levels Matt was pushing. Just a little on the fingertips, and on the center of the palms, and almost never enough to actually drip off his fur.

He'd resorted to pushing even further, blasting wind in all directions, ripping up grasses and tearing down tree branches. Ouranos was exceptionally powerful, but even he had a hard time keeping Matt's wind under control during these sessions, and it drained both of them after only a few minutes. And still no luck trying to collect it.

Matt finally pulled out a small tarp from his mission bag and spread it out. The moment he got enough liquid on his hands, he reached over the tarp and squeezed it onto it, then shielded it to keep the wind from blowing it away. Ouranos could come collect it at his leisure.

Not that any of this had any sense of "leisure" to it.

It only took about five to ten minutes to get enough liquid on his hands, but it was so draining he needed an hour or more before he could attempt it again. And even their ideas of "enough" really weren't enough. They had been at this for at least ten hours and had barely filled the bottle halfway.

On top of that, he had been awake since at least 5:30 yesterday morning and hadn't slept at all beyond whatever few hours he had gotten after his and Ouranos' jewels had bound together and knocked them both out. And that probably didn't count for much. It's not like it was actually restful.

He needed to get this done and get him and Ouranos back. Get some rest, figure out what to do next.

There was a lot to figure out.

Matt squeezed off the last drop he could get before the rest absorbed into his body. He wiped his brow and flicked the sweat on to the grass to avoid getting it all over the elixir.

248

And what had happened to his team? He hadn't seen or heard them in the whole time they were doing this. One would think that all the wild wind whipping about would attract them. But there was no sign of them.

That made him nervous. Were they even in the woods anymore? Should he go look for them?

Ouranos calmed Matt's latest tornado with a flick of his hand, sweat soaking his fur. Matt frowned. If he found his team, they'd never let him help Ouranos. But if they were in trouble and he didn't help them, what kind of Defender did that make him?

Damn it all. He'd have to look for them before he got started helping Ouranos or he'd never forgive himself. Protect the pack.

He shook his head. Finding them didn't mean he had to engage them. As long as he knew they were safe, he could keep away from them and help the Athánatos prince. He glanced down at the elixir still left on the tarp. "Did we do it? Is this enough?"

Ouranos leaned down and collected the last of the elixir. He sat on the forest floor, closed up the bottle, then wiped sweat off his face. "I do not know. But if we try this much longer, I fear I will perish from the energy expenditure."

"Same," Matt said, wheezing. "We'll have to make do." He carefully rolled up the tarp and stuffed it in his mission bag. "We're gonna take it real slow getting back to the ship. I need the rest. And I should be looking for the rest of the pack. It's weird that they haven't come looking for us yet."

"You make a fair point." Ouranos stood and handed Matt the bottle full of elixir. "Take this. I do not trust myself with it."

"Fair enough." Matt took the bottle, then frowned. "Has the bottle always been this warm?"

"It has gotten warmer with every new addition."

"Hmm," Matt said. "Something for Dad to check out at home, perhaps. Gem and magic maladies are his specialties. I think he'll like the new project." He took a deep breath, pausing a second to recharge. "Right now, I think I'll just hold on to the bottle. I don't want it to get too warm in my pack. Who knows what kind of reaction that'll create."

"A good plan."

Matt frowned at the massive disaster his magic had left behind. He hated doing that, but at least he could trust that the forest's fae dragons would take care of the leftover magic and resulting mess. Sure enough, tiny motes of light flittered into the clearing as they walked toward the ship. Matt nodded at them and whispered good luck, though the fae rarely acknowledged species outside their own.

"Your magic is impressive," Ouranos said. "Do all Zyearthlings possess such power?"

"Oh, no, definitely not," Matt said. "Most Zyearth Gems only grant long life. Only about twenty to twenty-five percent of the planet actually has magic like mine."

"There seems to be a higher concentration among your Defenders."

"There is," Matt said. "It's one of the main places to get training and one of the few places where magic is useful for employment, at least on the continent of Yelar."

"The badger who fought me on your campus," Ouranos said. "She had said something about 'stage one' and 'stage two' as you battled."

"Stage magic," Matt said. "It's kind of a contract between two magic users where they combine their powers for greater strength. It usually takes a lot of time and practice to decide how each stage works and to learn control. Some hit it off instinctually though." Matt rubbed the back of his head. "DD Hobbes and I spent almost a year working on things before we were comfortable with our level of control, but Cix and I connected immediately. It just depends."

"I see," Ouranos said. "It is very unlike our own use of magic. Perhaps I could employ some of these methods should I get free from my father. It would be useful to fight back against him."

"Ouranos," Matt said. "If I can get you free of your father, I'll help you fight him. Hell, we'll talk to Lance about getting you a whole army. You shouldn't have to face him alone."

Ouranos perked his ears. "I... thank you. That is very kind of you."

"I'm a Defender. It's my duty."

The pair trudged slowly back toward the plane. Matt gripped the bottle tightly, going over the plan in his head.

First, they'd make sure his pack was okay, then get to the plane. He'd activate Caesum, maybe even bring his crystal directly into the medbay, and they'd get whatever equipment they might need to help Ouranos if necessary. Then they'd try the elixir. How, they weren't sure. should he drink it? Smear it on parts of his body? Who knew. They'd just have to experiment and see what worked. And if things went south... well, hopefully between him and Caesum they'd be able to prevent the worst damage.

But how did they use it? They could use up all this elixir just trying to figure it out and the thought of having to do that all over again just to get more was murder.

"You really have no idea how we're supposed to use this?"

Ouranos shrugged. "I have so little memory of the event."

"Let's talk through it," Matt said. "You said that the Basileus has control over you because he has your Soul Jewels."

"That is correct."

"How does that give him control over you?"

Ouranos rubbed his chin. "A good question. In order to control an Athánatos, one must control the magic bound to our life forces. That requires controlling one of the jewel sets that gives them that magic."

Matt winced. "I hate to think about what he did to figure that out."

"It is not a pretty memory, certainly," Ouranos said. "Removing the Body Jewels causes immediate deterioration of the body. Removing the Mind Jewels distorts the mind, possibly to the point where it could not even provide the basic functions to keep the body alive. Removing the Soul Jewels only removes emotional functions – memory creation, logical thought, critical thinking, emotional response, compassion, and so on."

Matt furrowed his brow. "You say 'only' as if those aren't necessary in life."

"A puppeteer would not consider those necessary if the Drifter's only purpose was to be a lifeless puppet," Ouranos said. "In fact, it is the only option if one wants the resulting puppet to be physically useful."

"So does he physically have your Soul Jewels?"

"He does," Ouranos said. "Young Athánatos hold their Ei-Ei Jewels in a woven bracelet before they are bound, and the Basileus holds my Soul Jewels in a similar manner."

"Hmm," Matt said. "So he holds you because he holds an important part of your magic." He lifted the bottle. "If this elixir really does suppress things like we think, it'll suppress your father's hold on your magic."

"It may also simply suppress my connection to the Jewels," Ouranos said. "Which may have the same effect as if we removed all of them."

Matt flicked an ear back. "And what would that do?"

"At my age, the only thing keeping me alive is my Jewels," Ouranos said. "If I were to lose my connection with them, I would die."

Matt flicked the other ear back now.

Ouranos lifted his head. "It is a solution either way."

252

"Death isn't a solution."

"Death may be the *only* solution," Ouranos said. "I accept that. Employing this elixir will either suppress my father enough that I can escape his grasp, or it will finally end the nightmare living as his puppet. I am prepared either way."

Matt stared at him. "That's very brave of you."

"It is very selfish of me," Ouranos said. "If I had been brave, I would have ended my life years ago, the moment I had regained a connection to my soul and remembered myself, instead of allowing my father to continue using me to do harm."

"Ouranos, you're not selfish," Matt said. "It's natural to want to try and save yourself. No one gives up their life easily."

"You were willing to give your life for mine almost immediately, once I had explained the means to free my soul," Ouranos said. "Do not think I cannot see that thought still lingers in your head."

Matt's ears grew hot, but he stood firm. "That's not the same thing. It's one thing to be willing to give your life for a suffering individual, especially when you see that suffering first-hand. It's another to convince yourself that you need to die for a sea of unnamed, unfamiliar creatures."

"I see no difference," Ouranos said. "I have seen the suffering of the unnamed, and I still cling to life. Sometimes it is necessary to sacrifice oneself for the sake of the masses."

Matt stopped. "Ouranos."

Ouranos looked at him.

"Don't be so hard on yourself. No one can be expected to willingly give their life. It goes against every instinct we have."

Ouranos flipped both ears back, but he said nothing. The white hope still clung to the edges of Matt's mind, but a soft pink invaded as well, a mark of shame.

253

Matt started up again. "So, if we need to suppress your father's hold on your magic, we would need to go for the source of your magic."

Ouranos frowned. "That is logical."

"Which means we'd likely have to coat your Ei-Ei Jewels in the elixir."

Ouranos paused. All the color in Matt's mind vanished.

Matt turned and frowned at him. "You okay?"

The colors slowly bled back into Matt's mind. "I… suppose. But this is akin to how an Athánatos chooses to end their life."

Matt lowered his gaze. "Are you sure you're okay with this?"

"We have no other choice," Ouranos said. "I can only hope the pain will be minimal."

Matt pressed his ears back. He had a point. No matter what the outcome, this was bound to be painful. And there was no way to know if the medical equipment in the plane could help with that at all. Draso, what he wouldn't give for Izzy right now.

Assuming Izzy would be willing to help, Ouranos' thoughts bled into his.

Matt frowned. "Sorry, I was projecting again."

"It is fine," Ouranos said. "We are both exhausted and cannot be held accountable for our thoughts and worries."

"Hmm." He pressed his lips together.

They continued on.

Draso, what was Izzy doing right now? They still hadn't found any sign of his pack. Were they looking for them? Not likely. Izzy would have found them while they were conked out, or while they were in the clearing blasting everything to bits. Fighting the Cast? But it had stopped fighting after seeing Roscoe's wedding coil, and Ouranos had assured him that he would be harmless without the Basileus pulling the strings.

That still shook him.

Maybe she had gone went home. Got reinforcements. Took Natassa out of the equation. Maybe that's why they couldn't find them.

That would be likely, except for the fact that she hadn't taken Matt and Ouranos with her. Just the fact that they'd found themselves alone in the woods and that no one had found them in the clearing made the whole idea suspect.

Maybe Lance had called her home. Maybe they'd just abandoned him because he'd broken all of Lance's rules. But that was ridiculous. Even if he'd broken all those rules, and even if he couldn't get the Guardianship, he was still a Defender. That hadn't changed. And Lance wouldn't abandon him, Defender or not.

He pressed his lips together. Now that he thought about it... how would life change back home? He wouldn't be striving for Guardianship anymore. He had lost that goal. So how would his role change? What would he strive for now? Where would his life lead him?

His shoulders drooped. Nothing would be good enough. He knew that. Nothing would be the Guardianship he had wanted his whole life.

What was he supposed to do now?

"There are other ways to help those in need," Ouranos said.

Matt looked over at him.

Ouranos glanced back. "You were projecting again."

Matt pressed an ear back.

"I meant what I said," Ouranos continued. "You have led yourself to believe that the only good you can do in this world is possible with the title of Guardian. And yet, you are here, doing good for me, and by extension my sister and my people, at great personal risk. Is that not your ultimate goal?"

Matt wrinkled his snout. "I haven't done anything yet."

"You have brought life back to my mind after decades of drowning in my father's poison," Ouranos said. "You have given me hope when I have had none for decades. You have shown me kindness and understanding when I

255

attacked your people. You have no idea, the good you have done, whether or not we free me from my father's prison."

Matt frowned. Ouranos' colors in his mind swelled, the curious light blue transforming into a deep purple, which Matt took to be admiration. Perhaps even a budding friendship. And the white hope... it completely drowned out that dank resignation blue from before.

Ouranos smiled at him. It was the first time Matt had seen him smile. "You have given my life purpose again, Matthew."

"I... I'm glad," Matt said, trying to process Ouranos' words.

The pair walked for at least half an hour in silence. Matt reveled in the colors Ouranos left in his mind. It was comforting. Soothing. Maybe he was doing him some good.

It made him wonder. If he really allowed this connection with Izzy to grow, would they also see colors like this?

Then a pulse of black beat against Ouranos' white hope. He frowned and stared at the black quilar.

Ouranos frowned. "I... I fear that is my father."

Matt twitched an ear. "We haven't heard from him in a while, have we?"

"No," Ouranos said. "But he is certainly still here."

"Then we better be quick."

Soon the silhouette of Ouranos' plane appeared above the trees against the afternoon sun. Matt let out a sigh and picked up speed.

Then stopped. There were mumblings. Footsteps – definitely a biped, not one of the animals running around the forest. Matt held a hand up. *Stop. I hear something.*

Ouranos frowned. *Your packmates?*

Probably, Matt said. So Izzy hadn't abandoned them. Maybe they'd just gotten lost somehow and missed Ouranos and Matt in the woods. She had probably spent all day and night looking for him. How she had missed their escapade in the woods was beyond him, but at least they seemed to be safe. He chewed his lip, stewing in guilt. Maybe he should have looked for her sooner.

He shook his head. No, she never would have helped them. He still questioned whether he should be helping, in all honesty. But too late now. He'd make up for it later.

Ouranos met his gaze. *Should we engage them? We would be more likely to succeed with help.*

No one will be willing to help, Matt said. *We need to do this on our own. I'm just glad to know they're safe. We'll wait for them to go by and head for the plane.*

The crack of a twig.

Matt squatted behind a bush, pulling Ouranos down with him, and stared out. A figure, a zyfaunos, moved in the forest shadows. But just one. Silent. Who was it? Why just one? Were they split up looking for them? Matt squinted.

And gasped.

The zyfaunos was Roscoe.

257

CREATION

No.

That couldn't be right.

That couldn't be Roscoe.

Something was wrong.

But here he was, sprinting through the woods. Gray fur contrasting his teal uniform, copper antlers catching bits of sunlight, cloven hooves plodding along as he jogged. He stared forward, communicator in his hand, singularly focused, as if--

Matthew! The Basileus--

Matt whipped around, but too late. Ouranos smashed into him, sending him flying, skidding along the forest floor. Matt rolled and recovered, shaking his white and blue quills free of leaves.

Ouranos dashed straight for Roscoe.

Matt gasped. "Roscoe, *watch out!*"

Roscoe turned, confused. "Matt?" But Ouranos tackled him to the ground with a loud thud. Roscoe let out a shout as he fell. *"Get off!"* He struggled under Ouranos' strength, kicking at him, pushing against Ouranos' chest, but the Athánatos prince had the upper hand. The ground shook under them, likely Roscoe's magic.

Matthew, I am powerless! Stop him!

Matt growled and pulled himself to his feet. *Ouranos, fight him!*

I cannot! He-- The voice cut off completely. Matt's eyes widened. How could the Basileus cut Ouranos off like that? He dug his toeclaws into the ground and--

You will not win-I alone control him-You are powerless-You are no Guardian-Ouranos is mine-STAY BACK-HE IS MINE-I WILL HAVE MY CAST--

Matt cried out, falling to his knees. Pain shot through his skull and jolted down his spine to the tips of his toeclaws. He gripped his head and shut his eyes against the bombardment of thoughts and agony. The Basileus' vicious blackness engulfed huge chunks Ouranos' white and blue in Matt's mind, practically blinding him. He pushed back, roaring. *Get out of my head!*

"Stop! Get back! Get *back!*" Roscoe gagged. The ground shook harder.

Matt pushed through the throbbing pain, opened his eyes, and forced himself to move. He managed to get to one knee.

Ouranos had Roscoe pinned to the ground, a knee in his torso and an arm pressed against his neck. Roscoe gagged, pushing, struggling. Slabs of earth jutted out all around him, trying to knock Ouranos off, but the Prínkipas--the Basileus--countered every attack, reaching out his free fist and blasting the earth slabs into dust with his own magic the moment they appeared. The dirt cloaked the pair in a grimy haze.

Matt dashed forward, building his wind magic, for what little good it might do, when the Basileus lifted his hand. He had his finger and thumb

259

pinched slightly, like he was holding something. Matt squinted, trying to see what it was.

Matthew, stop him now! We will lose him, stop him!

HE IS MINE-I NEED MY CAST-YOU WILL NOT WIN

Matt winced. *I can't fight him off!* The Basileus' black drowned out Ouranos' colors in his mind completely.

But somewhere in the darkness, a bright white pushed through. *Reach for me!*

Matt did, clinging to Ouranos' hope, forcing his eyes open.

Ouranos twitched over Roscoe, straining against the invisible force of his father. Roscoe stared, confused, still pinned.

Now was his chance. Matt charged a tornado--

I. WILL. WIN!

A stab of pain ripped through Matt's head. He shrieked.

The Basileus slammed his hand directly into Roscoe's eye, his overwhelming blackness in Matt's mind vanished completely.

And Roscoe screamed.

Matt clapped his hands over his ears and squeezed his eyes shut. Water below, it was unlike any scream he had ever heard! Wildly high pitched and vicious and gurgling--

Gurgling?

Matt flashed his eyes open.

The Basileus had stepped off Roscoe, but the stag still lay on the ground, writhing around, pawing frantically at his eye.

But then his hand collapsed into an inky black mess.

Matt gasped. *No.*

Roscoe continued shrieking as his other hand also collapsed. Then a foot. A leg. His arm. Then a viscous black ink oozed out of his mouth and ears, dissolving his body into a dark puddle, gurgling, shapeless, deadly.

No. No, this can't be right. This can't be *happening.*

The Basileus cheered, pressing the darkness into Matt's mind again.

"Finally… my Shadow Cast."

Eventually the puddle settled down and stopped moving. A single object floated at the top of it.

Roscoe's wedding coil.

But… but how? How was it here? How had this happened? What the *hell was going on?* He couldn't tear away. That puddle had been Roscoe? But that was yesterday! How had it… what on Draso's Zyearth…?

The dark blob bulged and three small blue orbs – no, eyes - formed in the center. It bobbed around, darting those creepy blue eyes left and right, no awareness, no intelligence, no Roscoe--

Matthew, run! Run!

Matt snapped his head up. The Basileus turned to him, a vicious grin on his face. "Take him."

CHAPTER 38

COMPASSION

Cast-Roscoe opened his mouth in a jagged grin. With a vicious shriek, it leapt after Matt.

Matt dashed left, narrowly escaping, blasting several frantic gusts of wind at him, but he couldn't kill him. That was his brother-in-law. That was Roscoe.

Holy hell, that thing is Rosco!

Roscoe dove again. Matt dodged, but Roscoe anticipated it this time and brushed his leg, snaking a tentacle around his ankle and dragging him to the dirt.

Matt tugged, shot tornadoes, shielded, everything, but Roscoe held tight and fought his way up Matt's body.

He didn't know what to do, how to fight. Everything blurred. His memories fighting the previous Cast flashed by. But how could that be Roscoe? That was yesterday! This was so wrong, so, so wrong, this wasn't even *real--*

A burst of fire slammed into Roscoe, chasing him off. Matt glanced up.

Ouranos stood a few meters away, holding out one hand, gritting his teeth. "Matthew, *run!*"

Matt stood. But Ouranos' face changed. The lines grew sharper, his eyes narrowed, he held his ears at a crisper tilt, and he stared.

The Basileus. Matt followed his gaze.

He stared at the water bottle that held the elixir.

Holy hell. When had he dropped that? Matt dove for it.

"Cast!" The Basileus shouted. Roscoe sprung after Matt.

But Matt spied Roscoe's wedding coil. He snatched it up and threw it full force at the Cast, slamming it into his makeshift face. *Please work this time too, please!*

Roscoe stopped the attack and sunk into a shallow puddle. He stared at the coil with the three strange eyes.

Matt squinted. Had it worked?

Then Roscoe wailed, his black body rising up and up and up until it reached Roscoe's natural height. And it grew arms... and legs... a snout... antlers...

"Draso's mercy," Ouranos spoke in the Basileus' deep voice.

Roscoe stared at both of them, his face hardly distinguishable. He paused a moment, frozen, the obsidian veneer of a Cast dripping off his body, then he turned and dashed back toward the plane, spewing black everywhere.

"Cast, return to me *at once!*" The Basileus' shouted. But Roscoe didn't stop.

Now was his chance. Matt dove for the bottle of elixir.

A slab of earth shot up between him and the bottle, followed by a deep *hoot, hoot.* Pax, the burrowing owl phoenix, hovered in place a meter above the earth slab, his long tail flowing down, sand dripping everywhere. His musky, earthy smell overwhelmed Matt's senses. Matt skidded to a halt and turned to Ouranos.

263

The Basileus glared at him, gritting his teeth. "That is *mine.*"

"Like *hell it is.*" Matt threw sharp wind gusts at the slab of earth, breaking it apart.

Pax rebuilt it immediately.

Matt snarled and aimed a tornado at Pax instead. But the owl brushed it off with a wave of a wing. Matt huffed and leaned over, wheezing. Damn, he was still so low on power…

The Basileus smirked. "You and my son are so naïve. Did you truly believe he had control?"

Matt turned his anger on the Basileus instead, building two massive tornadoes… then stopped. The Basileus may be in control, but that was Ouranos' body. He was still in there.

The Basileus smirked. "The Prínkipas believes he has found an ally in you. He truly believes you two can defeat me. Pathetic."

Ouranos' white hope vanished completely, replaced with his resignation blue. He didn't speak, but Matt got the message anyway.

He was giving up.

Matt snarled. *Don't you dare give up, Ouranos. He won't win, I promise you!*

No response.

Pax lunged for the bottle of elixir.

Matt cursed, threw a twister at it and dove for the bottle again. Pax flew off, hooting indignantly. The Basileus charged full strength at him, but Matt dodged left, rolled, and snatched up the bottle.

A spike of earth shot up and sliced Matt's hand, sending the bottle rolling into the underbrush. He gripped his hand, hissing, catching blood in his white fur. He took a cursory glance at the wound. Shallow, thankfully.

Pax opened his mouth and let out a raspy hoot.

Matthew!

Matt whipped about. The Basileus made another attempt at the bottle.

They battled for what felt like hours, back and forth with magic and summons, pausing to breathe, attacking again, shouting at each other in their minds, rolling around, ripping up the forest floor, desperate for the upper hand, desperate for the bottle of elixir. Damn, if only he could have a moment to bind his hand. Every movement hurt.

Matt paused, leaning down to catch his breath, while the Basileus leaned on his knees several meters away. He caught a quick glimpse of his watch. It had only been twenty minutes. This couldn't continue. They'd kill each other through exhaustion alone.

The Basileus lifted his head, breathing hard. But then he smirked slightly and dashed forward. Matt couldn't see the bottle in the undergrowth anymore, but clearly something had drawn the Basileus' attention. And he couldn't let that happen.

He formed several small twisters, acutely aware of the elixir once again forming on his hands. It didn't take much now to get that effect – he had used up so much energy and the elixir was more likely to appear when he was at his limit.

These wouldn't take the Basileus down. He couldn't fight both Pax and the Basileus. He couldn't beat them.

But he could hide the bottle.

He guided the twisters around frantically, stirring up the ground cover, filling the air with leaves and pine needles and dirt, dragging a few tree branches down for good measure. The Basileus stopped in his tracks, holding his arms up. Pax got caught in a tornado and fell to the forest floor.

Matt smirked. *Find it now, you heartless monster!*

The Basileus turned, growling, and blasted a lightning bolt at Matt.

Matt shielded and dodged. The shield stayed purple, too weak, and shattered immediately when the bolt hit it. Matt tumbled out of the way, trying to drag up another shield. Earth and stone, he was nearing the end of his rope.

"Fight me, *Defender.*"

And hurt Ouranos? Give you more elixir? Hell, no! He dashed for the safety of a tree. All he needed to do was stay back and keep that bottle away from the Basileus.

The Basileus shot a fireball at the tree, blowing up the trunk and sending bits of flame into the air. Matt shielded, but the fire fizzled out almost immediately. It lacked bite. Was Ouranos still fighting? Matt couldn't tell.

"You have given Ouranos false hope," the Basileus said. "You promised him freedom, but your own compassion stays your hand. You could never free him. He is mine and will always be."

Ouranos' colors retreated completely now, his presence in Matt's mind gone.

Matt snarled. *Ouranos, don't give in, don't stop fighting!* But the colors didn't return. He fired another tornado at the Basileus, trying to distract him from the elixir. Too weak. He huffed. Damn it all, he was right. He couldn't beat him.

The Basileus waved Matt's magic away with a hand. "You wish to save a stranger," he said. "To give everything for one life. One life that you know nothing about. But how can you when you cannot even save yourself? Ouranos misplaced his faith in you." He eyed Matt. "Compassion never won wars."

Matt gritted his teeth. That did it. He whipped up two more tornadoes, the black elixir forming on his fingertips and running up his wrists. He aimed one at the Basileus. The Basileus waved a hand and pulled the tornado apart, but while he did, Matt aimed the other tornado at a tree behind him, ripping it out of the ground.

266

The Basileus yelped and leapt aside, as Matt formed a third twister and dragged another tree down, and another, and another, trapping him. *Sorry for this, Ouranos.* He darted forward, vaulted over the tree trunk, and kneed the Basileus in the stomach, pinning him to the ground. He glared.

"Compassion isn't a weakness," he snarled. "It's what separates those who use others for their own gains and those use their power to *help*. It's the difference between *you* and *me.*"

The Basileus smirked. "You think we are so different."

Matt growled. *"Don't* give me that cliché villain talk."

"Your compassion holds you back," the Basileus continued. "It keeps you from besting me, because you have found some reason to care for the quilar attacking your academy and turning your soldiers into monsters. It puts you at risk to help a zyfaunos who deserves no more than death."

Ouranos's colors pulsed red and black – anger and hate, aimed at himself. Matt caught one quick phrase before the colors faded again. *I deserve death.*

Hell no! "How can Ouranos be held responsible for anything he's done when you're pulling all the strings?" he snapped. "Compassion isn't stopping me from destroying someone who deserves death, it's pointing me to the true villain. You really think I can't see through that? The only one who deserves death is *you!*"

Ouranos' cool blue slowly returned, lined with white hope. But small, oh so small.

But it was something.

The Basileus furrowed his brow and snorted. "Then deal the punishment if you see yourself so righteous."

Before Matt could speak, the suffocating smell of a thunderstorm assailed his nose and talons grabbed his shoulders, ripping him off Ouranos in a flurry of electricity. Matt shielded and glanced up. Jústi held him by the shoulders, her wings wide and crackling with lightning. Matt shot a sharp gust of wind at the bird's midsection, forcing her to let him go. Jústi squawked and released him. He hit the dirt and rolled.

Pax emerged from the forest ground cover, shaking his body free of leaves and sticks. He hooted again and spread his wings. Sharp barbs of earth formed over his flight feathers, and he dove on Matt.

Matt shielded and fired wind at him, just barely chasing him off. There was no way he could fight both summons on a good day, but when he was this drained, he didn't stand a chance in hell. And with the Basileus too, he--.

Matthew, watch yourself!

Matt dashed to the side again, shielding. He tried reaching out. *Ouranos?* But he was gone again.

Damn, how could the Basileus have as much power as he did when Ouranos was just as drained as he was? He ran away from the fallen trees, snatching a glimpse behind him.

The Basileus scrambled up one of the tree trunks, but he didn't go after Matt. He turned left instead, headed for a dark patch on the ground.

All the heat left Matt's face. *No.* The elixir bottle! How? Matt dashed after him, but he'd never get there in time. *Ouranos, fight him!*

A silent ping of white echoed through Matt's mind and the Basileus paused, gripping his head. "You will not win, Prínkipas!"

Take it, Matthew!

Yes! Ouranos hadn't given in completely! Matt sprinted forward. His ears rang.

She wants to kill you!

Matt stopped so fast he almost fell over. "Izzy?" What? That was Izzy's voice in his head. Was that the ringing? Who did she mean? ...wait. Natassa? Hadn't she said that same thing yesterday?

Ouranos paused too, looking around, confused. A rush of wind magic, not Matt's or Ouranos', blew around the forest near the ship.

Then, shrieking in the distance. Shouting. Someone screaming to shield. Then another thought, with more ringing bells in his ear.

Get it off, save him, get it off, get it OFF!

What the hell...?

Ouranos got it first. *The Shadow Cast.*

Matt's eyes widened. Roscoe. And he was attacking Izzy's pack. He turned toward the ship.

Roscoe's wedding coil lay in plain view.

Matt chewed his lip. Get the bottle and stop the Basileus, or get the coil and stop Roscoe?

The Basileus turned to Matt, then rushed after the elixir.

Izzy screamed, distinctively this time.

Matt gritted his teeth and dashed for the coil. He had to save his partner. *Ouranos, I'll be back for you. Hold on!*

Save your pack! was Ouranos' reply as Matt dashed through the woods toward the screams.

TRAVELER

Matt gripped the coil tightly and ran as if his life depended on it. Which was partially true. Izzy was his life. She was his partner, his sister, his best friend. Fire and ice, he should have been better when they'd been fighting yesterday. He'd make that up to her. He'd fix it.

But he'd have to save her first.

He found the tail end of the plane and followed it along in the forest, chasing the sound of screams and shouts. *Damn it all, just let me get there in time!*

Darvin shouted. "Damn it, it's got him too tightly! Hang on, we're fighting it!"

"Cix, get that thing off him!" Izzy shouted.

"I can't!" Cix screamed. "It's not moving!" A pause. "Please, shield, we're trying, hold on!"

Matt pushed himself harder. He didn't know who Roscoe had, but he knew the suffocating feeling of a Cast attack. If he didn't get there in time--

270

Izzy let out a sob. "Oh Draso, he's *dying.*"

No! Matt's legs burned and he couldn't hardly draw a breath, but damnit, he was not going to let Roscoe kill someone! He was almost there. The plane's door was in sight through the trees. Almost, almost--

His foot caught on a tree root and he crashed to the forest floor, getting a mouthful of plant debris. He pulled himself to his knees and spit it out, trying to get his bearings.

The whole pack was gathered in front of the plane, staring at someone wriggling and fighting under the Cast. Cix and Sami threw fireballs at it, Izzy screamed at it to stop, Darvin kept shouting "Shield, shield!" and Natassa held on to Ouranos as he--

Wait, *what?* How did...? Ouranos...? There was no way he had beaten him here. He hadn't even been running for the pack. He'd still been fighting the Basileus back in the woods.

And that was his whole pack. Izzy, Cix, Darvin, Sami... So who was that other zyfaunos under the Cast?

"Please, *hold on!*" Cix screamed again, throwing another fireball at the Cast.

Matt coughed, spitting out the last of the forest debris. No time. He lifted the coil and tossed it into the fray, hoping Roscoe would notice. The coil rolled across the dirt and bumped into the Cast. Matt coughed again, leaning on his knees, trying to catch his breath. He just needed a minute. Hopefully the coil would work.

Roscoe lifted his head out of the puddle and the three eyes stared at the wedding coil. Carefully he slid off the zyfaunos on the ground.

Matt heaved a sigh of relief. Thank Draso. It worked. He glanced at the victim.

And his heart stopped.

Lightning and air. That... this... what... This couldn't be.

The zyfaunos who had been fighting the Cast was... him.

Matt sat on the forest floor. That couldn't be real. This was a nightmare or something. He was asleep. Knocked out. In a hospital or something somewhere. Ouranos had hit him too hard and he was unconscious. This was just him imagining things. This wasn't real.

The Matt in front of the plane turned over, coughed, gagged, and threw up. He wiped his face clean and stared at the ground, clearly disoriented.

Matt felt like throwing up himself. What the hell was going on? How could he be looking at himself? What the hell had *happened?*

One phrase ran through his mind.

Time travel.

Which he immediately rejected. Horse spit. Time travel couldn't happen. No magic did that.

Well. No magic he knew of. But Ouranos had magic no one had ever encountered before. Unfamiliar focus jewels, summons, command of every magical element...

Could he time travel?

Past-Matt stared at his hands, covered in the elixir, looking confused.

"Oh Draso, it can't be..." Izzy said.

Matt turned, as did his counterpart, and everyone stared at Roscoe. The Cast snaked a tentacle around his wedding coil and cooed.

Just like he had yesterday. But today was yesterday. Good Draso, this made no sense.

Roscoe's center bulged out and formed a vague representation of his head. Matt stared, mesmerized.

"Matt!" Darvin's scream ripped him out of his trance and he watched as Ouranos barreled full-force into Past-Matt. They rolled toward the tree line, magic flying in all directions, Past-Matt's hands dripping with elixir.

Matt yipped and hid behind a tree as his double and Ouranos rolled passed him in a flurry of elements. He watched them continue fighting until Past-Matt grabbed Ouranos' magic-charged hands with his elixir-charged ones.

Then came the explosion. But it was unlike any Matt had ever seen. Or heard, really, since he heard nothing at all.

A flash of magic, light, and elements of all kinds. Charred ground and magic-scarred trees. Ice spikes buried in the branches. Stones and spears of earth.

And his past self and Ouranos vanished.

But there was absolutely no sound to speak of.

There it was. Matt and Ouranos' charged magic had, in fact, forced a social bond on them.

And they'd time traveled.

Roscoe's cooing caught his attention and he turned.

Izzy had kneeled near the Cast that was once her husband, in utter shock, like she didn't know how to respond. A thought wafted through his mind in her voice.

Is this thing really my husband?

Matt chewed his lip. *It's Roscoe... It really is Roscoe... I'm sorry.*

Water below, he should have done more to protect Roscoe. At least he could try to make things right now. He stepped toward the group.

A sudden, piercing white exploded in Matt's mind.

Matthew, watch out!

Ouranos' voice.

Matt turned, but too late. The smell of a storm exploded around him and a pair of taloned feet grabbed his shoulders, whipping him up into the air at surprising speed, dragging him away from his packmates. Jústi. He blasted wind at the bird. "Let me go!"

Jústi shocked the top of his head with a little bolt. *Calm down, you're in good hands.*

Matt snarled, trying to pull at the bird's talons. "You're working for the Basileus!"

The Phonar work for no one, the bird said with a flash of lightning. *Especially now.*

"You *literally attacked* me just a few--"

I am not Jústi, the bird said.

Matt stopped struggling. "What, there's more than one of you?"

Jústi has been pushed aside so I can control her.

That made no sense at all. "Then why the hell are you taking me away from Izzy? Bring me back right now! She's in danger and she needs to know I'm safe, damn it!"

But Jústi wouldn't respond. She continued deeper into the woods.

Matt snarled, and fought, but his powers were weak, and he couldn't manage more than a few short gusts. He was stuck.

Unless Ouranos could help. He reached for the Prínkipas, hoping he had some control back. *Ouranos, can you hear me?*

A soft blue bled into Matt's mind. Back to the dank resignation. *Thank Draso, you are safe. Did you save your packmates?*

Ouranos, Jústi has me in her talons and she's taking me away from the ship! Can you make her turn back?

A pause, and a new color, a strange, churning yellow, swirled with the blue, which Matt took to be Ouranos thinking. The yellow faded after a moment.

I am sorry, Matthew, but I cannot make her turn back.

Matt's blood ran cold. *Why not?*

Another controls Jústi, Ouranos said. *I know you have no reason to, but please trust the one controlling her.*

274

Matt snarled and fought the bird's grip, throwing a blast of air at it. The wind brushed harmlessly off its feathers. *Fire* and *ice*, he couldn't do anything! All the strength of a Black Bound, and of course *now* it was totally useless. *But she's taking me away from Izzy!*

The one possessing Jústi uses "he." Ouranos said quietly. *And he would not pull you away without good reason.*

What reason--

Guardian Azure, Jústi said with a zap to Matt's shoulder. *Trust me.*

Matt paused. "Did you just call me Guardian?"

But the phoenix didn't answer. She continued flying over the treetops, far away from the ship and his pack.

Matthew, Ouranos said. *I understand why you would struggle to trust the person possessing Jústi. But if you do not trust him, then please, trust me.*

Matt chewed his lip. The summon called him Guardian. He shook his head. The one possessing Jústi did. Called him Guardian. *Guardian.* That wasn't a word to be thrown around lightly. And Ouranos trusted whoever possessed the bird. Considering Ouranos' own experience with possession, that was a big deal.

Matt stared up at Jústi. The bird kept her beak forward. Something about the way she held herself... she was different. This wasn't the bird Matt had fought before.

Matt swallowed hard. He needed to know where this was going. *Okay... Okay. I trust you.*

Good, Jústi said with a zap to Matt's forehead. *Hold on, we're in for a trip.*

CHAPTER 40

REFLECTIONS

The sun had just disappeared behind the mountains when Júsi finally lowered Matt into a deep part of the forest, long out of sight of the plane. Matt had so many questions, so many things he wanted to say. To Júsi, or whoever was controlling him. To Ouranos...

To Izzy.

After seeing that charred crater he and Ouranos had left behind, Izzy probably thought they were dead. Damn it all.

But after over 48 hours without any real rest or sleep, with one energy draining event after another, it was all he could do not to fall asleep while Júsi carried him. The only thing keeping him semi-awake was the awareness that the ground was very, very far down and he had really no idea who was whisking him away.

He just had to trust Ouranos.

And this bird who called him Guardian.

The Athánatos prince was surprisingly quiet, though Matt wasn't surprised. He had been awake nearly as long as Matt, if not longer, and he was definitely as drained. He probably needed rest too. Just the fact that Ouranos hadn't woken Matt up from his semi-slumber with frantic messages about the Basileus attacking was already proof of that.

Matt hit the ground gently, surprised to find his legs were practically jelly. He shook himself, trying to get feeling back into his limbs. There were tall trees everywhere and ankle-deep underbrush, as it was in the forest by the plane.

Jústi engulfed herself in a flurry of lightning before emerging as an anthropomorphized version of herself. Long limbs, wings on the arms, floating tail, and deep, penetrating eyes. The storm smell was stronger than ever. She stared at Matt.

I'll leave you here for now, she said with a zap. He? She? The bird was apparently female, but the one controlling it was male. And yet the voice was completely genderless. Matt shook his head. Jústi softened her gaze. *Get some rest.*

"Wait, wait, wait," Matt said. "I have questions."

Jústi curled in on herself, sending lighting flying in all directions. A bolt caught Matt in the stomach, the shock running through his system.

I can't stay. Jústi is fighting me and it's getting dangerous. Seek me out tomorrow.

Matt formed a fist. "But you called me Guardian!"

Jústi lowered her gaze. *Seek me out tomorrow.*

Matt took a step back. "But who *are* you?"

I'm the Black Cloak. Jústi exploded in electricity and vanished.

Matt gawked. A memory from what seemed like ages ago wafted through his mind. Jústi, staring, serious, telling him to seek the Black Cloak. But who was this Cloak? Why had he dropped Matt off here? Why did he keep saying to go seek him out?

Why the hell had he called Matt *Guardian?*

Water around him, this was too much. Especially for his sleep-deprived brain. He needed rest. He picked a tree and started climbing. No way was he going to try and sleep on the ground with all the wild animals. He picked a branch about five meters up. Careful of his injured palm, he climbed up, settled in close to the trunk, then fished a rope and a camping blanket out of his field pack and tied himself to the branch.

He looked through his pack and cursed. His boots were missing. Who knew how he'd lost them, though he'd miss them tonight in the crisp air. Quilar fur wasn't exactly meant for cold weather. Oh well. He took out some bandages and treated his wounds as best he could. Not great. He'd have to find Izzy tomorrow. His heart ached, missing her. Draso's wings, he really screwed up there. If he had just treated her like the partner she was, he wouldn't be in this situation now. He flattened his ears. He didn't know how he'd be able to make it up to her.

He snacked on a pack of field crackers and some water, counting the emerging stars.

He had just closed his eyes when Ouranos spoke to him. *Matthew?* A soft blue poked at Matt's mind. Back to resignation. Gone was the hope.

Matt took a deep breath. *I'm here, Ouranos. Are you safe?*

I am, as safe as can be, Ouranos said. *Are you?*

Decently. Stuck in a tree. Trying to rest. He paused. *Did the Basileus get the elixir?*

...I believe so, Ouranos said. *Though I am unsure. I do not have it on my person, though I blacked out after you left our fight. My body finally gave out. I believe the only reason I am awake and in control now is because my father*

has retreated temporarily. Though I cannot sense him, I suspect he is sleeping. Even my father has his limits.

Hmm. Matt stared up at the sky through the tree branches. *You should sleep too.*

It is my intention, Ouranos said. *Are your companions safe? You did not answer me before.*

I'm not entirely sure, Matt said. He paused. *Can I ask you something about your magic?*

Of course.

Can you time travel?

A pause. *Pardon?*

Time travel, Matt said. *Travel forward or backward in time. Like, visit yesterday or tomorrow instead of today.*

Ouranos was silent for several minutes, the same churning yellow swirling through his mind. *I have never heard the term before, admittedly.*

So that's a no, then.

I believe not, no. Ouranos said. *Why do you ask?*

I ah... I think we time traveled, Matt said. *We somehow traveled to the past. When I got to the pack, I literally found myself fighting with the Cast like I had yesterday. You were there, with Natassa. I watched everything happen, right before the Basileus tackled me and we formed that weird social bond.*

Ouranos paused again. *That does not make sense.*

No, it doesn't, Matt said. *But either we have doubles or we time traveled. And that would explain why we never ran into them in the woods when we were gathering elixir. We left a huge crater when we fought. They probably thought we died.*

Ouranos' colors shivered in Matt's mind. *You are right. I hope Natassa is coping.*

I hope Izzy is too, and the rest of my pack, Matt said. *That had to be quite a blow... Either way, we need to be very careful about our powers when we're near each other. I don't want that to happen again.*

A long pause, as if Ouranos was trying to come to terms with Matt's declaration. Matt couldn't blame him. He really couldn't believe it himself.

Fair, Ouranos said finally.

Ouranos, Matt said. *The thing the Basileus used to... to turn Roscoe into a Cast. What was that?*

Ouranos was silent for quite some time. Matt frowned. *Ouranos?*

It was a Cast charm, Ouranos said.

Matt's eyes grew wide. *What? What the hell is that?*

It... it is a solidified version of your elixir.

Matt sat back against the tree. *Made from the elixir you got when we first fought.*

Yes.

Matt flicked an ear back. *So that's why the Basileus wants the elixir. That... explains a lot.*

Ouranos grew silent. *I am sorry, Matthew. I meant it when I said I was unsure of how my father created Cast, but... I admit I had some notion that he used the elixir. I just was unsure how.* A faint hint of his white hope entered Matt's mind. *Do we still intend to try to employ the elixir for our own purposes? Despite the Basileus' use of it?*

Matt frowned. Should they? Honestly, if he had known that it created Cast... actually, if he had known, he probably still would have tried to help Ouranos. He shook his head. *That's my hope,* Matt said. Ouranos's colors pulsed, as if surprised. *Look, either we use it and try to save you, or he uses it and creates a bunch of Cast. We've already created it. We can't let it go to waste or leave it to be used for the wrong reasons.*

I am sorry, Matthew.

Don't be, Matt said. *What's done is done. What we really ought to do is just sleep a few hours, find the bottle, and meet up in the plane again, before your father has a chance to regain control. I'll see if I can set an alarm and wake you up in, say, four hours?*

As good a plan as any, Ouranos said. *We shall try it.*

Good, Matt said. *Get some sleep.*

Matthew? One more question.

Yeah, sure.

Ouranos' hope grew a little. *Do you truly believe compassion to be a strength?*

Now there was a question. Matt had never seen compassion as a weakness, though the Basileus wasn't wrong when he'd pointed out that Matt had never beaten him. Not really. But he couldn't imagine going into battle without compassion. Compassion is what separated zyfaunos from monsters.

I do, Matt said. *Compassion is what led me to help you and the lack of it is what led your father to just use you.*

Helping me has not reaped any great rewards.

If you're helping someone only for your own personal benefit, you're doing it wrong, Matt said. *I'm not trying to help you because I expect some kind of reward. I'm helping you because you're a zyfaunos who needs help. Simple as that. Yes, sometimes that means I lose, and yeah, your father is right that I technically haven't beaten him. But if I have to trade "winning" for compassion, I would. Your father has a different definition of winning anyway. If beating him means killing an innocent zyfaunos, then count me out. That's not winning in my book.*

Even though I deserve death?

Ouranos, we've been over this, Matt said. *You don't deserve death. How can you be responsible when your father is using you the way he is? That's not your fault.*

281

Hmm. Ouranos' white hope expanded deeper into his mind. *Thank you for your honesty.*

Of course, Matt said. *Get some rest, okay? I'll see you in four hours.*

Certainly. Ouranos' colors faded from his mind.

It took some time, but Matt was finally able to set an alarm on his damaged wristwatch. He could only hope it would actually go off and they'd be okay. He settled into the tree and closed his eyes, hoping for a restful sleep.

CHAPTER 41

NOT ACCORDING TO PLAN

Izzy guided the Delta-Z to the same landing zone she and Matt had used yesterday.

Just yesterday. Yesterday they were going to be Guardians. They were going to stop a threat, earn their titles, and find their place in the world.

Yesterday Matt had been alive.

She closed her eyes and leaned on her hands. Draso, how was she supposed to do this?

"GR Gildspine?" Darvin said. "Orders, ma'am?"

She shook her head. She couldn't let this get to her. She was made of stronger stuff. She needed to get her husband. She'd finally get the proof of Matt's death and she could start the mourning process.

She wasn't helpless.

Izzy stood and faced her packs. "Defenders. From what Prinkípissa Natassa has told us, Roscoe... the Cast, should be harmless without her father pulling the strings. The Master Guardian is under the impression that Ouranos is dead, though until we have proof to the contrary, we will treat him as if he is alive and that he and the Basileus are still threats. Roscoe may have been harmless in our last encounter, but he may not be when we approach him." She stood straight. "I know a majority of you came with Cix to look for Matt, but I'd like at least one or two volunteers to join Darvin, Sami, and me in looking for Roscoe. And more importantly, looking for Ouranos."

Two stood, a water deer wearing a healer's uniform, and a doe wearing an elemental uniform, and saluted to her.

She nodded to them. "Thank you. Now, let's move out. COMs will go out very quickly in the Dead Zone, so let's make sure we stick close to each other and watch each other's tails."

A chorus of "yes, ma'am!" answered her and everyone started filing out of the plane. Darvin squeezed her shoulder and grabbed the weapon's locker, Rainbow Barf, before heading out with them. Sami stood stoically by her side as well. Izzy would have to thank them both for the support later.

The two packs walked to the plane in silence. Izzy led the pack, not just because she needed to keep the air of leadership around her, but also because she wanted to look for any new signs of life. Footprints, scars on the ground, signs of a battle. Anything that might indicate Matt was still alive.

She found nothing.

She halted everyone when they got to the plane's entrance. "Cix, this is where we split. Take your pack and see what you can find. We don't have COMs, so every half hour, send someone to meet here and we'll do the same."

Cix nodded.

Izzy chewed her lip. "Honestly… you have the harder mission. If you need a break, don't be afraid to take it. Your mental health is just as important as your physical health. Understood?"

Cix responded with a half-hearted salute across the chest. "…Yes ma'am."

"Good."

"If I may speak out of turn, ma'am," Cix said. "The same goes for you."

Izzy pasted both ears back and frowned. But he was right. "I'll concede that. Thanks."

Cix managed a short smile and headed for the charred ground in the woods.

Izzy turned to their new packmates. "Can I get your names?"

"Cayde," the water deer said.

"Astora," said the doe.

"What's your specialty, Astora?"

"Fire."

"Good," Izzy said. Supposedly the Cast feared fire. Supposedly. She hadn't seen much evidence of that during their fights. Regardless. She waved to her pack. "Let's move out." She led the pack into the plane.

It was dark and echoey, just as it had been when they had first entered, though at least her toe claws weren't clinking anymore. Her pathmarkers were still there, and in fact, were still lit. Hopefully that meant that Caesum had enough power too. She pulled out two more bags of pathmarkers and passed them to Darvin and Astora.

"Let's make sure we're keeping track of where we've been."

"Yes, ma'am," Darvin said.

She took them down the path that led to the bridge. Might as well start somewhere familiar. Caesum hadn't contacted them yet, but that could be for a number of reasons. "Caesum? Can you hear me?" No answer. He could be in sleep mode. She lifted her head and spoke firm and clear, hoping the sound system picked her up well enough. "Caesum, exit sleep mode. Defender Override Code: Zenith Alpha Two."

The holobulbs above their heads warmed and Caesum appeared, though he struggled to keep a solid image. "I'm -bzzt- here."

Izzy frowned. "How are your power levels?"

"Decent," Caesum said. "I've got -*bzzt*- maybe two hours -*bzzt*- left before I'll have no choice but to -*bzzt*- shut down."

Izzy flattened her ears. Not a lot of time. Hopefully they'd find Roscoe soon. "Any sign of the other A.I.?"

"I think he -*bzzt*- powered down immediately after you left the plane," Caesum said. "I didn't see -*bzzt*- anymore of him before I went to sleep, and -*bzzt*- I'm not seeing anything now. But he's sneaky. I'll -*bzzt*- keep an eye out."

"Hmm. Do that," Izzy said. "Were you able to find Ros-- the black monster in our absence?"

"No, unfortunately."

"Keep looking for it," Izzy said. "We're here to capture it."

Caesum paused. He looked over the two new pack members. "How long -*bzzt*- have I been out? And where's -*bzzt*- the rest of your pack?"

"Nearly 22 hours," Izzy said. "The rest of them are in the woods."

"Why?"

"Sorry, Caesum," Izzy said. "That's been Vaulted."

Caesum blinked at her. *"Vaulted?* What the -*bzzt*- hell happened when I was asleep?"

"It's classified, Caesum."

"Even -*bzzt*- from me?"

"From everyone who isn't directly involved," Izzy said. "Sorry."

Caesum tilted his head, but didn't question her. "I'll go look for that -*bzzt*- monster." He vanished.

Darvin flipped an ear back. "You probably could have told him."

"And have him offer pointless condolences?" Izzy snarled. "Or worse, make fun of Matt? You heard him harassing him yesterday. I can't trust

Caesum to be kind or serious about it and the last thing I need right now is to blow up at him while we're trying to find Roscoe."

Darvin lowered his gaze. His white-spotted eye gleamed in the low light. "Okay, fair enough."

Izzy continued down the hall. "Besides that, it's--"

"Hey, is that the Cast?" Cayde pointed.

A small, gurgling puddle lay across the entrance to the bridge. Three glowing blue "eyes" bobbed around on the surface.

Izzy sighed relief. It was Roscoe. She nodded to Darvin to open the weapon's locker and walked toward the Cast. "Roscoe? We're here to take you home."

Cast-Roscoe formed a bulge in the center of the puddle and tilted it, curious, but he didn't move.

Izzy had planned for this. She pulled out his wedding coil. "Come on, let's get you home."

The bulge collapsed and splashed ink droplets everywhere, and the puddle slowly moved toward Izzy. He snaked a tentacle around the coil.

Darvin moved forward with the weapon's locker. "Come on, bro, hop in."

Cast-Roscoe lifted his "head" and peered into the locker.

Then he let out an otherworldly shriek.

Izzy dropped the coil and pressed her ears to her head, trying to drown out the sound. She took a step back. "Astora, Sami, fire!"

"On it!" Sami hit it with a rolling wave of flame. Astora let loose a barrage of tiny fireballs. Cast-Roscoe shrieked, but he didn't seem too perturbed. He lifted his body out of the puddle and spun about wildly, sending fire flying in all directions.

Izzy shielded and reached for the coil. "Darvin, cloak us all! Let's see if we can herd him into the locker!"

But before Darvin could cloak anyone, Cast-Roscoe dove on Cayde and knocked him to the ground, engulfing him immediately. Cayde didn't even get a chance to scream.

Izzy gasped. "More fire, *now!*"

Astora and Sami drowned Roscoe in fire as Cayde wriggled and fought to escape. Roscoe shrieked under the flame bath, but he wouldn't let Cayde go.

In seconds, Cayde stopped moving. But Roscoe still wouldn't let go.

"Cut the fire, *cut the fire!*" Izzy shouted. Sami waved a hand, dousing all the fire immediately, and Izzy reached her hands into Cast-Roscoe's body, trying to pull him off. The Cast body wasn't even warm. But her hands sank into the ink and she couldn't grip him. "Roscoe, let him go, please! Let him *go!*" She grabbed his wedding coil and shoved it in his eyes, but he still wouldn't move, still singularly focused on Cayde.

Without warning, Roscoe squeezed Cayde's body with a loud and sickening crunch. He slithered off, leaving Cayde's body behind. Limbs jutting out in all direction, head crushed, torso a pulpy mess. Blood pooled under him rapidly.

Izzy fought not to be sick, her heart aching for her dead packmate. There was no saving him. He was gone. Draso, he was *gone.*

Was that the power of the Cast? What the hell happened to Roscoe? Why wasn't he *listening?* Could she ever get her husband back?

Even worse… would he even want to come back after this?

Cast-Roscoe turned on Astora next.

"Run!" Izzy shouted. "Everyone run, now! Out of the ship!"

But Roscoe blocked the path leading to the entrance. Izzy stood in front of her team, hammer drawn, knowing she couldn't do a thing to protect them.

The blue lights down one path turned purple and a flickering dragon appeared above Izzy's head in the holobulbs. "Follow the -*bzzt*- path. Go, hurry!"

What choice did they have? "Follow Caesum! Now!" She shoved everyone down the hall. Roscoe following, wailing.

Izzy turned down one hall and recognized her pathmarkers. They were headed to the cryochamber. A perfect place to lose Roscoe and get free. "Follow the signs for the cryochamber!" she called. The group called out acknowledgements and they ran for it.

Natassa's words flew through her head. He should be harmless when no one pulled the strings.

But if he wasn't harmless, then he was being controlled. And if he was being controlled, that meant the Basileus was still around. Which meant Ouranos was still alive.

Which meant Matt might be as well.

Despite everything… maybe there was a silver lining here.

But they had to escape the Cast first.

Draso, just let this plan work!

CHAPTER 42

CHOICES

Natassa picked her way through the Defender campus, looking for an open area to escape.

Lance had spent nearly the entire morning and much of the afternoon questioning her about everything -- the Cast, Ouranos, the Basileus, his motivation for creating the Shadow Cast, the Athánatos, her home. All the things he had already asked her about when they had first returned to the base. He had focused mainly on her father's purpose creating the Cast, but she had managed to elegantly dodge the Basileus' real motive with every question. It was not necessary for Lance to know.

She had little more to tell him, but she hoped her answers satisfied him. At least long enough for her to escape.

Isabelle had long gone to the colony plane in search of Matt and Roscoe.

And Natassa would not be left behind.

Lance may be right that she would prioritize her brother over these Defenders. But she also refused to stand idle while angry strangers went looking for him. She needed to save Ouranos.

She ducked behind a line of trees near a large amphitheater and made it to the edge of the campus. Strangely, few students and Defenders were about this time of day, but at least that made it easy for her to escape unnoticed. Under a clump of trees, she summoned Excelsis, hoping his black plumage would be harder to notice against her dark fur. She took in his soothing scent of fire, letting it ground her, and they took off toward the plane. No one followed or raised an alarm, as far as she could see.

It was not ideal. She had promised the Master Guardian she would stay. Breaking his trust would make it difficult to return home later. How could he trust her if she had already broken that trust once?

But what choice did she have? She would just have to find a way to make up for it later.

Isabelle's transport came into view as Natassa approached the colony plane, though the Defenders were not visible from the air. She could only hope they had not yet found Ouranos and she could find him unhindered.

If she found him and subdued him, perhaps the Defenders would be willing to imprison him until she could find a solution to the problem. Perhaps they would even help her find a means to save the Cast.

Though that was probably too much to hope for.

It would be a miracle if they chose to let him live at all.

She shivered. She would have to cross these bridges when she approached them. For now, finding her brother was top priority. She had Excelsis drop her by the tail of the plane and she quietly walked toward the entrance where she had last seen Ouranos.

As she neared the doors, a chorus of people calling for Matt echoed through the woods, with as many loud footsteps in the underbrush. She frowned. The woods would not be safe to search. Though it was unlikely Ouranos would be in the forest after all this time. She expected him to be in the plane.

Isabelle likely would be too, probably with packmates. After all, it was where she had told Roscoe to go. Natassa entered the plane.

Calling for Ouranos would be folly. Doing so would attract Izzy's attention and get Natassa arrested again. Instead, she found a small alcove down one hallway. "Dragon? Are you there?"

A dragon did appear... but it was not the dragon she knew. This one was blue and purple, with large leather wings and a spiked tail. It hovered over her head among motes of light, eyes wide and frantic.

"Natassa!" the dragon called. "Quick, how do we fight off the Cast?"

She took a step back. "Who are you? Where is my dragon?"

"Hiding," the dragon said. "That doesn't matter. The Cast is attacking Izzy and her pack and I don't know how to fight it off! Please, you have to help!"

The Cast was fighting? "Did she use Roscoe's wedding coil?"

The dragon frowned. "I don't know and I don't care! It killed Praeses Cayde and it's going to kill the rest of them if we don't stop it!"

Natassa's jaw dropped. No... the killing had begun.

But had the coil not worked? And it was attacking. It should have been harmless without the Basileus. There was only one logical answer for that.

Ouranos was alive and her father once again controlled the monster through him.

She... should go look for her brother. She had no hope of helping Izzy and her pack. "I... I must find my brother."

"You have to help Izzy or she could *die!*"

She winced. The dragon was right. But... that was not her responsibility. Ouranos was. Right?

But then Lance's words ran through her head. *You have shown up, unannounced, bringing a dangerous individual to my planet, knowing his condition is a problem.* She pinned both ears back. His words were true. She had, in some sense, brought him here. Did that not make this her problem?

And then... Ouranos. *If the only way I can be free is through another's death, then I would rather choose death for myself. No one life is worth another.* Should she choose to save Izzy over finding her brother? Is that what Ouranos would want? She could not help Ouranos fight the Basileus. That much was certain. Was this the only way?

"Natassa, *please!*"

"I..." she shook her head. Ouranos had asked her once to get the Zyearthlings to safety. This is what he would want. To make up for her past mistakes. She nodded to the dragon. "Take me to her.

CHAPTER 43

LOST

Matthew!

Matt woke with a start, so disoriented that he jerked left and pitched himself halfway down the branch before the rope caught him. Thank Draso he had had enough sense to buckle himself in. He fought, but eventually got himself back on top of the branch.

Then he noticed the sun high above his head. Oh *hell.* He checked his watch. Nearly 1500. The damn alarm hadn't gone off! Why the hell had he trusted this broken thing? How had he slept so long? Yesterday had taken too big a toll.

Matthew! Ouranos' blue invaded his mind, a deep purple creeping along the edge. Worry, Matt thought.

I'm here, Ouranos, Matt replied, fighting to free himself from the ropes. *I'm sorry, I slept all day and--*

The Basileus is after Isabelle!

A shock ran through Matt's spine. *What?*

He has come back with a renewed vigor, Ouranos said, his colors pulsing purple with worry. *He had somehow found a way to suppress our ability to communicate, and regained control of the Cast. I have been fighting for hours to contact you. It was only after his attentions were split that I could slip past his defenses.*

Matt stuffed the rope and blanket in his pack and slid off the branch to the ground, landing in a roll. His ankle twisted a little, but he brushed it off. *Why are his attentions split?*

Cix has appeared with several dozen Defenders looking for you, Ouranos said. *The Basileus plans to confront them while also commanding the Cast after Isabelle. I am trying to keep him at bay, I truly am, but--*

How do I get to the plane from here?

Ouranos paused. *I am sending Jústi toward you. I cannot guarantee she will have her wits about her by the time she gets to you, but you can at least see the direction she came from. Please hurry!*

Matt took a deep breath and started running, hoping he was actually headed toward the plane. *Fight him, Ouranos. I know you can. I'll get to you soon!*

Please-- Then Ouranos was cut off.

Matt cursed and pushed himself harder, stifling a shout as the ankle injury shot pain through his leg. *Push it aside, worry about it later, right now Izzy needs you!* But damn it was hard to ignore. Why the hell had he jumped out of that tree?

Five minutes of hard running later, he caught a glimpse of Jústi through the trees. He frowned. That was awfully fast. They had flown for ages last night. Maybe he was closer than he thought--

Jústi spotted him, shrieked, lit her body with electricity, and dive bombed him.

Matt shielded and rolled. Oh, *hell* no. Not now. He formed a massive tornado aimed at the bird. It connected, sending Jústi flying through the trees with a screech. He continued off on the same route. "Thanks for the directions," he muttered.

Another five minutes and he got to the plane. He paused to catch his breath and curse out the Black Cloak. If he'd been so close last night, that damn cryptic could have told him. He could have spent the night in the plane instead of in the uncomfortable tree and found a proper alarm to wake him up. He could have already been here to protect Izzy. *Ouranos? I'm here.*

The plane! Ouranos said. *I have the Basileus distracted, but I can do nothing for Isabelle!*

On it! Matt ran inside.

I cannot guarantee how much longer we can communicate.

Just keep him back, Matt said. *I'll get Izzy then we'll all come find you. We'll get through this, Ouranos, I promise. Just hold on!*

No response. *Just a few minutes,* Matt prayed. *Just a few minutes, and I can get to him.* He lifted his head. "Caesum? You still here?"

The holobulbs in front of an unfamiliar hallway lit up and a dragon appeared in them. But not Caesum. This one had faerie wings. Matt frowned. "Pilot?"

The dragon opened its mouth, then the image jerked about and flickered and Caesum appeared in its place. "Matt! Izzy is--"

But it flickered again, and Pilot appeared. "The Cast is--"

Pilot vanished in a flicker and Caesum appeared. "Don't take this from me--"

Pilot emerged again and he waved a wing. "Come--!"

Caesum again. "--This way!"

The lights at the entrance turned purple and the dragons' fought for control of the holobulbs as they made their way down the hall.

Matt cursed and followed. What other choice did he have?

As he ran, Caesum and Pilot continued fighting for control of the holobulbs, appearing over doors and down corridors.

"This way-way!"

"No, this -bzzt- way!"

"Down here!"

"Turn left-left!"

Their voices and images were so distorted, it was impossible to determine who was who. Fire and ice, what a *mess.*

"Caesum, shut him down and tell me where to go!"

"You think -bzzt- I haven't tried that already?" Caesum shot.

"What do you think -bzzt- I've been trying to do?" Pilot retorted.

Damn it all, he'd never get them to shut up. Why had he followed them in the first place?

Soon he was completely lost. Purple lights flickered against the blue ones down every corridor, Caesum and Pilot jumped around every doorway. Nothing looked familiar, and he saw no pathmarkers.

No sign of Izzy or her pack anywhere.

Matt stopped and leaned on his knees. Despite all his rest, he still felt drained. "Caesum, where--"

Someone screamed down a dim hallway.

Matt didn't recognize the scream, but he immediately ran down the hall, hoping it would lead to Izzy.

The hall led to a digital library that was somehow still lit -- barely. Digital shelves and rotating carousels with holographic books lined the walls and dotted the floors. The shelves managed to stay visible, though the books flickered in and out of view, changing shape, size, and color, obscuring titles. Several holobulbs above them were shattered, and glass littered the floor. With no physical shelves to speak of, the dust had gathered in piles on the floor along with the glass.

But that also meant that there were thick, visible footprints in the dust.

Matt picked his way through the room, careful to avoid broken glass, wishing he hadn't lost his boots.

Something glinted in the dim light. The footprints headed that way. And somewhere, another scream.

Screw it. He threw caution to the wind and ran through the dust and glass toward wherever that glint had come from. He managed to miss most of the glass, but some crunched under his feet, lodging itself in skin and fur, forcing him to slow down.

But he couldn't stop. Izzy needed him now.

The outline of a figure appeared almost the bookshelves. "Izzy, I'm coming!"

But he stopped.

It wasn't Izzy. It wasn't any of his packmates.

It was a tall figure draped in a black cloak.

THE BLACK CLOAK

Matt gawked. No way. No way was this happening. "You…!"

The figure turned, holding a digital book in his hands. He wore a thick, silver mask that covered his entire face, not including the eyes. No recognizable snout shape. Just a solid bulge with tiny ornate carvings in it that shrouded any distinguishable features. If he had external ears, Matt couldn't tell, and even the little bit of visible fur around his eyes was an unnatural jet black, suggesting he had masked that too.

The one thing that stood out were his eyes. Icy blue, almost abnormal, shining even in the dim light. They practically pierced Matt's heart with that gaze.

The Black Cloak turned and faced Matt. His eyes crinkled, like they were smiling, and he put the "book" back on the "shelf." It vanished in a flicker. "About time."

Matt made note of everything. Deep voice, masculine, unrecognizable, calm, amused.

Amused. "What, you think this is *funny?* Leading me on while Izzy is facing some damn invincible monster? Forcing me to sleep in the damn *woods* last night? Sending cryptic messages through the summons, but never enough information to actually be *useful? And why the hell did you call me Guardian?* What the hell is *wrong* with you?" He waved his hands. "You know what? No. I'm not dealing with your crap. I don't know who the hell you are, but Izzy's in trouble. I'm out of here." He turned.

"Do you still *want* to be a Guardian?"

That made Matt pause. He glanced back.

The Black Cloak lifted his head. "I know you do. It's your life's ambition."

"What's it to you?" Matt said. "You can't make me a Guardian by just calling me one."

"No," the Black Cloak said. "But I have a warning for you."

"A warning," Matt said. He shook his head. "I don't have time for your riddles."

"It's about the Guardianship."

Matt flipped an ear back and frowned. He would say that. Damn it all, why was he letting this cryptic moron get to him? He didn't know anything about the Guardianship.

And damn it, Izzy was in trouble! "I *don't care.* I'm going after my partner." He turned his back on the Cloak.

The Black Cloak whipped around Matt and met his eyes, his "If you choose to help Ouranos, you will succeed and Lance Tox will grant you the Guardianship."

Matt paused, his eyes widening. "What? Why would Lance do that after everything I've--"

"...But if you earn the Guardianship, someone close to you will die."

Shock rushed through Matt's blood like lightning. *"What?"*

300

The Cloak held his gaze. "This is the price you will pay."

Matt took a step back, crunching glass under his heel. "But... how do you even *know?*"

Someone screamed again. This time it was unmistakably Izzy. Matt turned.

The Cloak tilted his head. "Better hurry."

The shock in Matt's body doubled. He turned and bolted out of the library.

Someone close to you will die.

Izzy.

He meant *Izzy.*

That wasn't acceptable. Not Izzy. Nothing was worth that. Not even the Guardianship. Forget Ouranos. Forget the Basileus. Forget the Cast and the Guardianship and Natassa and the Defenders and forget *everything.*

He was not going to lose his best friend.

He turned down the hall and chased the screams.

Draso, just let me get to her in time. I don't want the Guardianship.

I only want my partner!

CHAPTER 45

STAGE ONE

Izzy dashed behind a cluster of cryopods, gasping for air and trying to keep quiet all at once. She suppressed a cough.

Darvin and Sami hid behind the cluster next to her, both panting. Sami leaned on Darvin, trying to keep her breathing under control and Darvin tilted his head back, gulping air. Sami flickered in and out of view as they sat there. Darvin had tried cloaking them as they ran, but the energy expenditure was too much and all he'd managed was some flashes and Lexi acid clouds. He pawed constantly at his spotted eye now, extra irritated by the acid.

Astora had volunteered to stay behind and fight Cast-Roscoe. She hadn't come in yet and the sounds of scuffle and fire magic had died completely.

She was probably dead.

Damn it all! Why the hell had Izzy allowed that? What was she thinking? What kind of Guardian was she trying to be if she just left a packmate like that?

She knew the answer. A frightened one. And who wouldn't be after that?

302

Cast-Roscoe was far faster and stronger than she'd realized. He had chased them down the hall with lightning speed and thwarted every attempt to fight him back. Sami and Astora had exhausted themselves trying to drown him in fire. He'd eventually caught Astora's leg and snapped a bone. Astora had bathed him in fire and demanded everyone leave her to fight him off.

Nothing worked. Nothing stopped him.

And Astora was probably *dead. Damn it all!*

Even the safe haven of the cryochamber was only temporary and Izzy knew it.

Though... so far so good. He hadn't followed them. Yet.

But what now? Going back into the main ship just invited him to chase them again. Staying here wasn't a permanent solution. And they were in the Dead Zone. No communication. She tried her pendant, hoping that the magic insulation protecting the ship's power might give her pendant power.

No such luck. Damn it!

Darvin snuck up next to Izzy. Despite everything, he had managed to hang on to the massive weapons locker. "So now what?"

"I'm still thinking," she said. She frowned at the weapon's locker. "You kept Rainbow Barf?"

Darvin shifted. "If we can just get him in it..."

Izzy flipped an ear back. He didn't want to give up. And she got it. She didn't want to either.

After all, that murderous monster was her husband.

"Shh!" Sami hissed. "Something's coming!"

Izzy hunkered down, listening. The uneven clip-clop of deer hooves sounded down the hall and soon Astora hobbled into the room, panting, panicked, dragging her broken leg behind her.

Cast-Roscoe rounded the corner and nipped at her heels. She screamed.

Izzy turned. "Sami, do something!"

Sami held out a hand, but the fire fizzled at the tips of her fingers and a cloud of Lexi acid surged forth. She shook her head. "I can't!"

Cast-Roscoe shrieked and leapt for Astora.

Izzy cursed. "Darvin, *cloak me!*" She ran out from behind the cryopods, hammer in hand, hoping Darvin had the energy to cloak her.

Cast-Roscoe ignored her.

Izzy muttered a silent apology and slammed her hammer in the middle of Cast-Roscoe's bulge, sending him flying across the room, raining black droplets everywhere. Roscoe shrieked so loud it echoed in Izzy's bones. Astora gasped and hopped away to Darvin. Izzy brandished the hammer, waiting.

Two things. Take care of Roscoe. Heal Astora's leg. Then they could escape. She could do this.

Roscoe snarled and dove for her.

She swung her hammer again and connected, but the Cast was ready this time. He wrapped a tendril around the hammer's head and yanked it from her, throwing it across the room. The back spike stuck fast into the metal wall. Before Izzy could run, he leapt on her, dragging her to the ground.

The Cast engulfed her immediately, cutting off her voice, cutting off her air, crushing her. She shielded, shrunk in on herself, gulping any air she could, forcing herself not to scream, images of Cayde's broken body overwhelming all her senses, she was going to die, just like Cayde, just like Matt--

Then Roscoe shrieked viciously and slithered off her. Izzy scrambled to her feet and ran for her hammer.

And stopped.

Natassa stood in the doorway leading out of the cryochamber, hands forward, palms out, little embers floating around her fingers.

Izzy stood there, slack-jawed. "Natassa?"

"Watch out!" She shot a thin ribbon of fire through the air. Izzy dove out of the way.

The fire connected with Roscoe, but it did little to stop him. Izzy ran to the wall, ripped her hammer free, and whipped about to face the Cast.

Natassa growled and waved a hand again. This time twin plumes of purple and white fire appeared, swirled about, and Excelsis and Deo emerged from the flames. "Excelsis, distract the Cast! Deo, get the others out of here!"

Excelsis leapt into the air, circled around to pick up speed, and dive bombed the Cast in a flurry of purple flames. Deo winged its way to Darvin, Sami, and Astora.

Izzy hesitated. "Astora's leg is broken."

"Deo can carry her. She has the strength," Natassa said, lighting her fingers aflame again. The flames were hardly bigger than candle lights. Nothing like the walls of fire from Sami or Astora. "Leave while you are able. I will handle the Cast."

Deo gently plucked Astora in her long talons and led the pack past Izzy and Natassa, out of the cryochamber. "Izzy, come on!" Darvin called.

Izzy gripped her hammer tighter. "I'm right behind you. Get out of the plane and find Cix!"

Darvin flicked his ears back.

"Superiors orders!" Izzy snarled. "Get Astora to one of the healers, *now!*"

Darvin cursed, but left, still pulling the weapons locker with him.

Natassa's tail flicked in irritation. "What are you doing? Leave with the others!"

Izzy spun the hammer in her hands. Natassa could never handle this on her own. Like it or not, they were a team now. "I'm not leaving you to do this alone."

Excelsis lit itself ablaze and dove on the Cast again. But the Cast rose up like a wave and practically ate the raven summon. He dragged Excelsis to the ground wrapping around it completely. Feathers stuck out like reeds in the mud. He squeezed. Excelsis squeaked, then the feathers vanished in a puff of violet flames.

Izzy flattened her ears, her eyes wide. "Did he just *kill* your summon?"

Natassa swirled fire around her hands. "No, the summons cannot die. But Excelsis will need time to recover. He will be no use to us. We are on our own."

"Then let's make it count," Izzy said. "Cover me!" She rushed forward with her hammer. Natassa shot a string of fire forward.

But rather than hitting Roscoe, the fire hit Izzy's hammer, lighting the head ablaze. Izzy brought it down on the Cast with intense force, sending sparks and embers everywhere. The Cast wailed and broke apart.

Izzy leapt back. "Whoa, what was that?"

Natassa frowned. "Does your weapon always do that?"

"I don't know!" Izzy said. She stared at her hammer, then turned to Roscoe. It seemed to take the Cast far longer to pull himself back together with that last strike. She narrowed her eyes. "Natassa. That was stage one. Let's take it further. Light up the hammer! Everything you've got! Stage two!"

Natassa nodded, formed two fireballs, and lit the hammer ablaze. Izzy shielded and smashed the Cast. He broke into a thousand flaming droplets, sailing in all directions.

The flames died slowly. The ink droplets inched their way across the floor, trying to reform. He moved at an absolutely sluggish pace, unlike before.

Izzy faltered, her heart aching. Natassa said Cast couldn't die but the way he responded…

This might actually kill him.

But it might be what he'd want after what he'd done as a Cast. She fought a sob.

Natassa grabbed Izzy's arm, breaking her thoughts. "Now is our chance. Hurry!"

Izzy shook her head, snatched up Roscoe's wedding coil, and ran after her, not looking back. *Goodbye, my love.*

"What are you doing here?" Izzy said, tearing her focus away from her husband. "You were supposed to stay with Charlotte!"

"I came looking for my brother," Natassa said, running hard. "Your dragon found me and said you needed help."

Izzy flicked an ear back. "You gave up looking for your brother to help me?"

Natassa nodded. "It is what Ouranos would have wanted." She met Izzy's gaze as they ran. "And Matthew."

Izzy pressed her lips together, but managed a small smile. "Thanks."

"Think nothing of it," Natassa said. "I am paying back a debt."

"If you say so."

A shriek echoed down the hall. Izzy winced. Not dead. Her heart warred with elation and fear. "Keep running. Don't look back!"

They ran for the front of the plane.

CHAPTER 46

THE BASILEUS' ARMY

Cix stood near the strange, blackened crater where Matt and Ouranos had apparently died.

He shook his head. Not died. Vanished. They weren't dead. Matt wasn't, anyway. There was no way some odd quilar being puppeted by his father could have killed Matt. Matt was going to be a Guardian. He was made of tougher stuff than that.

Matt wasn't dead.

Or at least that's what Cix kept telling himself. But the longer his pack of thirty-plus Defenders scoured the woods, calling for Matt, looking for evidence, and coming up with nothing, the harder that was to believe.

They had been here almost half an hour and had probably covered close to a three-kilometer radius and had seen no sign of Matt or Ouranos.

Cix kneeled by the strange magic crater, his black and white wolf tail brushing the leaves on the forest floor. He pressed his hand to the charred ground.

It was still hot. Not just mildly warm, but burning. He pulled his hand back. How could it be so hot after all this time? More than that, it felt strongly of magic -- a constant, pulsing feeling in his bones and skin, smelling slightly of apples and burning leaves, that made his Gem glow. He tilted one blue-tipped ear back. That was really unusual. The magic should have dispersed pretty quickly in a space this wide, or at least latched on to some of the wildlife and dissipated that way. But it still felt powerful and robust. Weird.

He chewed his bottom lip. A scar this bad in the woods would normally attract the fae dragons who lived in the area, too. They were practically compelled to keep the forest healthy and they would have been the first at the scene to gather up this wild magic. But he hadn't seen a single sign of them. No light motes, no wild magic, no scar clean up, nothing.

Maybe they were just as freaked out by the magic left behind as he was. He wished one would show up so he could try to talk to them and get some insight to this problem.

A flap of wings sounded in his ear and he stood just as the snowy owl gryfon landed next to him. She shook her feathered leopard tail free of leaves and saluted to Cix. Her teal uniform was wrinkled and wind-swept. "Praeses Ruuna reporting, sir."

"At ease," Cix said. "Find anything?"

Ruuna flexed her paws, catching leaves between her toes and on her claws. "Negative, sir."

Damnit. "I think it's time to send someone to the ship to meet up with GR Gildspine's representative. Do that for me."

"Yes, sir!" She saluted one more time and took into the air.

Cix kneeled back down. Something was wrong with this magic. It felt damaged. Corrupted almost, if that made any sense. But way too present for the time it had sat here. It should feel distant, or at least faded.

Hmm... maybe...

He pumped a low-level pulse of fire magic into the charred earth.

The earth instantly exploded with a blinding, sparkling blue light that grew from the center scar in the ground and expanded out, running through the forest floor and up tree trunks, dispersing through the leaves and into the air.

Everyone in Cix's pack stopped and looked up. "What the hell was *that?*" a tiger asked.

Cix frowned, watching as the magic slowly faded. "I don't know."

"I do."

Cix turned. A figure emerged from between the trees. Tall, dark, vicious teal eyes, no pupils.

Ouranos.

No. Not with that angry, hateful look in his eyes. This was not the zyfaunos who had begged his sister to save strangers from a monster. This is the one who had *created* that monster.

The Basileus.

"It is a beacon," the Basileus said, walking toward the blackened ground. He held a water bottle filled about halfway with some thick black sludge. He poured a small pool of it into his hand, froze it with a flurry of ice crystals, and crushed it in his palm, creating tiny black shards. "It has led me, at last, to my army."

"We're not your army, Basileus," Cix said, lighting his hands on fire. Several Defenders followed suit, calling forth nearly every element the Gems had to offer. Cix subtly waved a hand, directing his packmates to circle their prey.

The Basileus lifted a brow. "Basileus, am I? It seems my son's narrative has pierced through your ranks. Very well. No sense in keeping up appearances. Not that it matters."

Cix let out a howl.

Star, one of the golden doe, rushed the Basileus, her hoof-tipped hands alight with electricity. But the Basileus stepped to the side, slammed his knee into her back, and pinned her to the ground. He flipped her around, and before the nearest Defender could stop him, he slammed one of the black shards into her eye.

Cix gaped. What the hell? It was so damn fast!

Star shrieked and slithered out from under the Basileus, but as she moved, ebony ink poured out of her orifices -- eyes, nose, mouth, ears, covering her entire body in darkness, drowning out her shriek in favor of deep gurgles. Her arms, legs, and torso popped like rotten eggs, spewing black liquid everywhere. It bubbled and bulged like toxic sludge. On the front of a large bulge, three blue "eyes" emerged, "blinking," one after the other.

In an instant, Star was gone. In her place, a Cast.

Cix could only stare, his whole body buzzing as he fought to keep himself from vomiting. He didn't. He *couldn't*. How?

The Basileus smirked and nodded to the newly formed Cast. "My new army awaits."

Cix's Defenders scattered in all directions, many screaming.

Cix snarled. He had to regain control. "The bottle! Get the bottle! Fire users, on that Cast, *now!*" He shot a ribbon of fire at the Cast. The monster slid to the side and avoided it, diving on a stag next to it, pinning him. The Basileus gripped the stag's snout and shoved another shard in his eye and the process started all over again.

Two Cast. *Two.* He had to get this under control *now.* "Defenders--"

But the two Cast chased down two more Defenders and the Basileus snatched two more Cast.

The remaining Defenders ran into the woods, Cast at their heels. The felines and panthera climbed trees, but the Cast ascended the trunks just as quickly, dragging them down, holding them for the Basileus. Two hawks took flight, but one of the Cast bounced into the air after them, trapping one and dragging her to the floor, and the Basileus pounced.

Cix backed up against a tree, shooting fire after every Cast, but the black monsters were fast -- far faster than the Shadow Cast he had previously encountered. Even if the Cast were affected by his magic, he couldn't move fast enough to hit one.

His mind warred.

He should run.

But he shouldn't abandon his pack.

But he should save himself.

But first he had to save the others.

Shit, shit, *shit!* How had this gotten so out of control so fast?

The Basileus chuckled darkly as the last of Cix's pack vanished into the woods being chased by Cast. "Abandoned by your own people. I know your pain." He poured more black liquid into his hands. "Fear not, the pain will end soon."

Cix snarled. *No.* He lit the air around him ablaze and charged the Basileus.

The Basileus leapt back, shock on his face, but he was too slow and Cix connected, knocking the bottle out of the quilar's hands and dragging both of them to the ground in a fiery ball. The smell of singed fur stung Cix's nose

The bottle bounced against a tree trunk and splashed black liquid all over Cix's hip and Gem holster.

Then everything went white. Cix's whole world disappeared and vicious pins-and-needles pain shocked every inch of his skin, draining his energy, draining his magic, draining his life, Draso, did he scream? he must have screamed, what on Zyearth was happening, end this *please--*

Interesting, a voice echoed in his head, accompanied by blackness, more, more black more-- *To enter the mind of another... I did not believe it would be this easy.*

312

Get out of my head, get out of my head, give me my magic, give me my life, get OUT OF MY HEAD--

Find the golden brown quilar, the voice said. It sounded so familiar. Why did it sound so familiar? But it wasn't his. Was it? It wasn't. It wasn't. Lightning and air, what was in his head? *Calm yourself. Find the golden brown quilar. She will save you. Hurry, before it is too late.*

His vision returned, though blurry, painful. Everything was in black and white with splashes of color. Random greens. Fiery reds. Pain. *Pain, pain, pain.*

Ouranos lay on the ground not far from him, gripping his head with one hand, whimpering. He held several of those black shards in his hand, which shook as he did.

Cix stared, trying to make sense of the image. Ouranos was in pain. It was Ouranos then, yes? Not the Basileus. Ouranos. He should put him out of his misery.

I am too weak, a distant voice said. *I need help.*

Then... then he should take the shards. Destroy them so they couldn't cause more damage. But as he reached for them, his vision darkened and pain shot through his head.

A distant voice... *Obey me and find the golden brown quilar.*

...What the hell was that in his head? He shook it, trying to clear his vision.

Find the golden brown quilar NOW. His eyes stung.

He stood, shaking, trying to make sense of the words. That's... that's right. He needed help. He needed Izzy.

Then he spied the bottle, still a third full of black liquid. He should spill it out. Get it away from Ouranos. Hide it. Destroy it. Burn it.

I should take it, the voice said again. *It might be useful. We can learn from it.*

313

Cix blinked, trying to will away the pain. That didn't feel right. He needed to get rid of it.

I need to save it.

Lose it.

Save it.

Destroy it.

SAVE IT.

The pain redoubled and he saw stars again. Okay… okay. Save it. He capped the bottle and hobbled back toward the plane. Izzy would save him. She *would.* Ouranos… Ouranos could fight his own battle.

One thought. Find Izzy.

CHAPTER 47

DARVIN

Izzy and Natassa dashed through the plane, leaving Roscoe far behind. The damage their last attack had done had left him in little pieces, and as far as Izzy knew, he hadn't pulled himself together enough to follow.

But her heart was heavy. Yes, she'd escaped, but had she just killed her husband? She clung to Natassa's claim that they couldn't be killed, but he was in *pieces*. He might not be able to pull himself together. He might just be a mess of black drops. Natassa might not see that as "dead" but what the hell else would it be?

After everything he'd done as a Cast, that might be for the best. He would want that. He wouldn't want to think about the lives he took.

The lives he had taken... Would Roscoe think of himself as a murderer? Even when he wasn't in control of his own actions?

Water below, that thought was terrifying.

It kept her running.

Natassa leapt out into the open air at the front of the plane and fell to the dirt, breathing hard. Izzy followed behind, leaning on her knees, trying to fill her burning lungs. They were out. They were free.

But they hadn't gotten Roscoe. And for all she knew, they never would. Her heart ached.

Darvin and Sami stood near Deo, now in anthropomorphic form and holding Astora in her winged arms. Astora looked upset, but she seemed to be keeping her pain under control. Next to them was the snowy owl gryfon. Ruuna, if Izzy remember correctly. Ears back, tail twitching anxiously, gaze darting about.

That was not good.

Darvin looked up, frowning. "Izzy? Natassa? You okay?"

Izzy coughed and stood straight. She had to hold her composure, no matter what had happened to Roscoe. She didn't know if he was dead, but she did know she had packmates to protect. That was priority number one. Natassa took one last big breath and pushed herself up. "We're shaken, but okay," Izzy said. She met Ruuna's eyes. "Praeses Ruuna, I assume you have a report, and based on your expression, I imagine it's not good."

"I'm honestly unsure, ma'am," Ruuna said. "Captain Terrill sent me here for check in, but the moment I landed, I heard screaming in the woods. I thought it'd be better to tell you before going after them."

"Oh, *no,*" Natassa said, drawing her hands to her face.

Darvin and Sami both pasted their ears back. Astora shivered in Deo's arms.

Izzy's ears and cheeks grew cold. Definitely not good. "You did the right thing." She moved to Astora and began work on her leg. "How did you escape?"

Astora's face relaxed with the healing magic. "I don't know. For whatever reason the Cast kept stopping, pausing like he was thinking, or he had some new awareness, if that even makes sense. He didn't go wild again until we got to the cryochamber."

Hmm. Odd. "We'll keep that in mind for our reports. For now, we need to help Cix." She met Natassa's gaze while she worked. "Come with us?"

Natassa nodded. "Of course."

"Izzy," Darvin said, lowering his head. "Can we trust her to actually help us?"

Izzy narrowed her eyes and bared a tooth. "This isn't up for discussion, Darvin. She saved my life. She saved your ass too, in case you forgot. She's clearly willing to fight on our side." She finished with Astora, and Deo helped her to her feet. The doe tested her leg then moved closer to the woods, away from the entrance to the plane.

"Against the Cast," Darvin said, crossing his arms and tapping a hooved finger. "Not against her brother."

Natassa formed a fist and furrowed her brow. "I came here to help."

"You came here to find *Ouranos,*" Darvin snarled. "And if you find him, you'll *abandon us.*"

Natassa pasted her ears back, her face still scrunched in anger, but she said nothing.

"Izzy…"

Izzy turned.

It was Cix. The black and white wolf stumbled out of the woods, his eyes half lidded, panting, gripping his hip. He fell to the ground.

Izzy gasped. She ran for him. "Darvin, help me!" Darvin dashed over and together they pushed him on his side. She poked and prodded his hip, looking for the injury. But there was no blood. She checked for bruises, broken bones, sprains, but there was nothing. "What happened?"

"Gem…" Cix muttered.

Oh, *no.* She pressed the emergency release on his Gem's hip holster and pulled the jewel free. A thick black sludge covered it. She pulled her hand back, gagging, trying to shake her hand free of the substance. What the hell? "Is this from a Cast?" Draso, the implication that there was more than one...

But Cix said nothing. He closed his eyes and his breathing grew shallow.

Shit. She had no idea what this was, but she needed to clean his Gem *now.* "Natassa, we need water!"

Darvin looked like he wanted to protest, but before he could speak, Natassa dashed over and doused the Gem. The sludge sloughed off and hit the dirt before quickly vanishing. Izzy checked it for cracks and leftover sludge, then put it back in the holster for safekeeping.

Cix groaned.

Izzy and Darvin helped him to his knees. He coughed. Izzy frowned. "Are you okay?"

"I... I think so." Cix shook his head, fur flying. The blue streaks in his fur and on his ears caught little bits of light. "Fire and ice, that was the worst thing I have ever felt. Like I was losing connection with the Gem. I thought I was going to die."

"What *was* that stuff?" Izzy asked.

"I don't know," Cix said. He blinked rapidly. "I don't... I don't know."

Izzy looked over his body once more for any sign of injury. Nothing. But she did find a water bottle half full of a similar black sludge. "Is this what you got on your Gem?" She reached for it.

Cix pulled it back immediately and shoved it in his pack. "Don't touch it!"

Izzy flipped an ear back. "Cix, if I can just see the bottle, I might--"

"Don't!" Cix said. "It's... it's fragile. We'll take it to Jaymes. He'll know. He'll know."

Izzy leaned back a little. "What does Dad have to do with it?"

318

"He'll know," Cix said. He rubbed his head and groaned again. "I don't know what happened. I can't think. Everything is just black. Need to get home. Gotta get home. Everyone is gone. Gone, gone, gone…"

Izzy flipped an ear back. He was in shock. They needed to get him back before it got too bad. She'd have to split her team and go find the rest of his pack. "We'll get you home. Rest for now." She turned to Natassa. "Thank you."

"Of course," Natassa said. She looked over at Darvin. "I am here to help."

Darvin snorted. "Until Ouranos shows up."

Izzy glared. "Darvin, *shut it*. Natassa *saved my life*. She saved Cix's life. She isn't going to just abandon us!"

"Hmm," a voice said. "Shall we test that?"

Izzy turned. Ouranos stood in the entrance to the woods, a sly smirk on his face.

Ouranos. Ouranos. *Ouranos.*

Izzy immediately stood and brandished her hammer, her mind racing. Ouranos was alive. He was *alive*. That meant Matt was alive. He had to be. He *had* to. "Where's Matt?"

"A good question," Ouranos said. No. The Basileus. He narrowed his eyes then lit his hand on fire and blasted a fireball at Izzy.

Izzy shielded, but the fire didn't connect. Deo dove between them and blocked his fire with her own. Izzy stepped back.

The Basileus raised an eyebrow. "You have betrayed me, Deo?"

"The Phonar are not yours to control, Basileus," Natassa said. She pasted her ears back and lit her hands ablaze, her tail twitching.

The Basileus eyed her. "Perhaps not. But I have others to command." He held out a hand.

And an enormous black mass burst through the woods, covered in dozens of glowing blue orb clusters.

319

Izzy leapt back, hammer lifted, panic rising in her chest. Were all those Shadow Cast? There had to be *dozens!* How had he gotten so many?

Natassa's interview from yesterday flashed in her mind. *Shadow Cast are made from zyfaunos.* Izzy's insides froze.

These had been made from Cix's pack. How the hell were they going to fight them all? *"Fire, fire, fire! Natassa, stage one, now!"*

Sami and Astora blasted a wall of fire over the Cast, though four Cast slithered under it and dove on Astora, engulfing her completely, then crushing her. The same sickening crunch of bones and flesh sounded from under the Cast, a large pool of blood forming under them. Astora was gone. Izzy's chest ached.

Ruuna screamed and leapt into the air, but the Cast leapt up after her and dragged her to the ground. The Basileus pounced on her and shoved something tiny and black into her eye.

Her body burst in a flood of black ink and gurgling screams. Izzy fought back a gag as three blue orbs formed on the surface of the ink.

A Cast. *Another Cast.* How had he done that?

The Cast turned on Izzy. She wielded the hammer. "Natassa, forget stage one, give me stage two! Everything you've got!"

Natassa shrieked, and blasted Izzy's hammer with flame. Izzy swung the hammer through a wave of Cast, breaking them up into flaming droplets.

But these reformed much faster than Roscoe had. What the hell? "Sami, Cix, Natassa, fire on my hammer, *now!"* Sami and Natassa lit the hammer aflame and she swung through the Cast again, scattering more.

But Cix didn't help. He held his head between his legs, moaning, mumbling. He turned and threw up, letting out a long groan.

Izzy pasted her ears back. They needed to get him out of there. They couldn't face this many Cast, especially with the Basileus making more and with two of their packmates down.

Four Cast separated from the pack and dove for Sami. She blasted them with fire, but the fire fizzled out in a cloud of vapors -- too much magic. She vanished under the wall of black.

Izzy snarled. This was *not going to happen. "Natassa!"* The Athánatos princess blasted her hammer with flames and Izzy glided the hammer and fire over the top of the Cast covering Sami. The Cast popped and screamed, slithering off her in all directions. One turned on Izzy. She roared and slammed her fire-bathed hammer into it, breaking it into flaming pieces, then glanced around, daring the others to come after her.

Sami sat up, hands ablaze, breathing harried. The white fox darted her head left and right, panic in her eyes. Izzy gripped her hand and pulled her up.

"Izzy, Sami, *watch out!"* Darvin shouted. Izzy turned just as the Basileus pounced.

Darvin shoved Izzy and Sami aside and the Basileus connected with him instead. They rolled about, until the Basileus pinned Darvin to the ground, his arm pressed under Darvin's chin. He snarled and shoved one of those black shards in Darvin's white-spotted eye.

Sami screamed. *"Darvin!"*

Izzy's insides went cold. *No.* Not Darvin!

Darvin wailed and black ink spilled out of his nose and mouth, drowning his body until there was nothing left. The three blue "eyes" formed slowly as his Cast form slumped around on the ground.

The Basileus turned on Izzy, gritting his teeth. She held up her hammer, snarling, ears back, rage building in her belly. *That disgusting bastard!* He would *die* for this! That *horrible, nasty, ghastly--*

"Ouranos, fight back!" Natassa said. "Do not let him win, *please!"*

The Basileus paused and gripped his head. He moaned. "Let... me... go!"

Ouranos. Not the Basileus. *Ouranos.*

That made Izzy stop.

Ouranos was just a puppet. Matt and Natassa both said so. She could kill him right now, but damn it, wasn't Matt trying to save him? Wouldn't Matt try to help? Damn this *whole situation!*

Ouranos fell to one knee, still gripping his head. His body jolted left and right, then settled. He stood, staring at Izzy, harsh, angry lines on his face.

Ouranos was gone.

The Basileus was back.

He furrowed his brow and flattened his ears against his head, his tail twitching in anger. "You wish to know of Matthew's fate?" he said through clenched teeth. "I shall whisper it as I make you one of my own."

Izzy shielded, her heart pounding boiling blood through her. Draso, what the hell was she supposed to *do?*

Then one of the Cast leapt up between them and tackled the Basileus to the ground.

Izzy stared, wide eyed. The hell was *that?*

The Basileus ripped the Cast apart with a blast of fire, but it reformed and bowed out from the center, standing nearly five feet tall. A bulge formed on top, with a short snout, ears, antlers… two arms formed at its side, which it held out in a protective stance, though the arms kept breaking off and crashing into the black pool below.

For a heart-wrenching second, Izzy dared to believe the Cast was Roscoe. But then it spoke.

It *spoke.*

"Izzy, get everyone out of here!" Obviously Darvin's voice, though gurgling and muffled.

"Draso's mercy, how is this possible?" Natassa whispered.

The Basileus stood back.

"Izzy, *go!"* Darvin dove after the Basileus. He stepped aside, but Darvin whipped about and dove on him again.

Izzy didn't wait another minute. She pulled Cix to his feet and waved to Natassa and Sami to follow. Sami paused a moment and snatched something off the ground before following. As they ran, Izzy chanced a backwards glance.

The Basileus' army of Cast piled on Darvin just as Izzy's pack entered the woods and she lost sight of them.

THE ULTIMATE DECISION

Matt dashed frantically through the ship, darting down every echoing hallway, desperate to find Izzy.

But the screaming kept sounding farther and farther away. He couldn't follow it. Pilot and Caesum hadn't reappeared. No sign of his pack. No sign of the Cast. No sign of the Black Cloak.

No sign of Izzy.

He fought panic with every spare scrap of energy that he hadn't put into finding his partner. The Black Cloak's words echoed in his head.

If you choose to help Ouranos, someone close to you will die.

He pushed the thought out of his mind, though the words bounced around anyway.

He could spend hours, days even, combing the halls and rooms of the ship. He'd never find her in time.

What if he was too late?

Should he reach out to her mentally? Like he had with Ouranos? Could he do it on purpose for Izzy? How would she respond? How would he even do it? He closed his eyes. He had to try. He reached for Izzy. *Izzy, can you hear me? Where are you?*

A slight ringing in his ears. The feeling of panic rose in his chest. Two words screamed at him. *Not Darvin!*

His insides froze. *Izzy, where are you? Answer me!*

Then the ringing died.

Matt's whole body buzzed, his heart racing. *No.* Had he lost her?

Something gurgled in the hall.

Matt threw himself in a room. That sounded like the Cast.

Sure enough, Cast-Roscoe came slithering down the hallway. Sluggish. Little tongues of fire clung to his "body." He didn't seem to be in any rush, but he still moved with a singular purpose, crawling along, barely faster than a slug.

Matt pressed his lips together. Fire. If Roscoe had fire on him, he had to have been battling a fire user, likely Sami or Cix. That meant Roscoe was following them. If he followed Roscoe, he'd find them. Izzy would be with them. He stepped out into the hall.

His toeclaw clinked against the metal floor. Roscoe whipped around, staring with those three dead eyes.

Matt shielded and whipped wind around his ankles. So much for that idea.

But Roscoe didn't attack. He lifted a bulge out of the center of his body and tilted it curiously. Then he lowered himself back into his body, bubbling.

Matt blinked. Why didn't he attack? He almost looked... shamed. Matt licked his lips. "Roscoe?"

The Cast gurgled back. The last of the embers on his body faded away.

Matt took a step forward. If Roscoe wasn't attacking... if he had some control over himself... then something was wrong with Ouranos. Mentally, he reached out to him. *Ouranos, can you hear me?*

No answer.

Matt tried again. *Ouranos, please answer me. What's going on?*

No answer.

Ouranos, please. I want to help... But was that really true? Maybe not anymore. How could he, if helping Ouranos would mean the death of someone he cared about? But how could he leave Ouranos to his father's puppetry either? He cursed. Why was this so complicated? *Please, Ouranos.*

No answer. Not even any colors, now that he thought about it. Had they faded before? Had Matt not noticed? That wasn't good.

Definitely something wrong. "Roscoe. Can you take me to Izzy?"

Roscoe twisted around, and headed down the hallway, picking up speed. Matt dashed after him. They headed for the exit.

Then he heard the screaming. But it wasn't Izzy.

It was Ouranos.

Matt ran harder and burst out of the plane into the sunlight.

He gasped. A huge mass of swirling black ink spun wildly around the dirt, its walls standing several meters tall. Ouranos was on his knees in the center, holding his head, screaming, shaking back and forth, cringing, gritting his teeth, eyes held tightly shut. Matt caught dozens of blue eye clusters in the churning mess.

Dozens. Dozens of Cast! He'd created *more!* Damn it, he should never have left the elixir in the Basileus' possession.

Matt's heart practically stopped. Oh Draso, what if one of those was Izzy? What if that was why she'd stopped screaming? Why she'd stopped responding? He'd never forgive himself.

326

Roscoe suddenly shrieked and dove into the mess, disappearing in the darkness, leaving Matt alone.

Earth and stone, what should he do? He couldn't fight all those Cast. And what if one of those *was* Izzy? Did Cast feel pain? He knew they couldn't die, but what if every attack hurt? Damnit, why hadn't he asked Ouranos when he'd had the chance?

Ouranos screamed again. "Let him *go!*" Then he doubled over in pain.

Matt frowned. Let who go? Was there someone *in* that horrible mess? He mentally reached for Ouranos, but the moment he did, a wall of black shot up in his mind with a sharp pain.

YOU CANNOT HAVE HIM.

Matt gripped his head. Shit! He tried pushing against the blackness in his mind, but it wouldn't budge. Damn it all, he couldn't just let Ouranos sit there and suffer!

If he couldn't reach him mentally, he'd just have to reach him physically. But there was no way he could get through the mess of Cast.

He'd have to get rid of them.

Growling and drawing on every crumb of strength from his Gem, he snaked wind around the rolling mess of Cast. The monsters shrieked, breaking apart into tiny droplets, their blue eyes blinking out of existence.

Black elixir formed on Matt's palms and up his wrists, but Matt ignored it. *Just push the Cast away. Give me an opening...*

Then a Cast slipped out of his tornado.

Shit. Matt reached for more power, trying to grab the escaping Cast, but before he could, the Cast turned around and bolted into the woods.

Two more slipped out and did the same thing. Then three more. Then five.

Lightning and air, how many of these things *were* there?

Another slipped out and dripped its way to a weapons locker. Matt frowned. Rainbow Barf. How had he missed that before? What the hell was that doing here? The Cast slithered under the locker and took off into the woods with it.

Strange.

But if they weren't going to attack, let them leave. He'd go after them later. Right now, he had to stop Ouranos' screaming.

Another minute and the final Cast slipped out of his whirling tornado and disappeared into the woods. Matt had counted thirty-two. How the hell were they going to fight thirty-two Cast? He could barely hold his own against *one*. Hell, with how easily they'd slipped out, he couldn't even believe he really had any control over this situation.

He'd need the entire Defender army to take care of this mess.

Ouranos continued screaming.

Matt cringed and took a step towards him… but stopped.

If you choose to help Ouranos, someone close to you will die.

Matt gritted his teeth. Screw the Black Cloak. What did he know anyway? Ouranos needed *help*. And Izzy would never forgive him if he let someone die from pain like that because some weird cryptic dropped vague fortune telling on him. None of his friends or family would. He was a Defender, damn it!

Matt looked at his hands, still covered in elixir. Time to do this. He took a step forward, thinking back to their conversation about ways to fix this.

Just get some on the Ei-Ei jewels. It'll suppress his father's hold.

But it would also suppress Ouranos' connection with his magic. Ouranos had said this was akin to how his tribe chose to end their lives. And they were nowhere near the medbay. If something went wrong…

But if this broke his connection with the jewels, nothing in the medbay could save him anyway, any more than it could save Matt if his Gem bond broke.

Ouranos would die.

Matt had promised Ouranos that he was going to get him out of this, alive. But maybe he couldn't. Damn it all, what should he do?

Matt pressed both ears back and shut his eyes. He could feel the elixir sinking back into his fur and skin. Running out of time.

Ouranos cried out. He gritted his teeth, pressed his eyes shut, and held his body, leaning almost to the ground. The tears soaked deep into his fur. "Just end me, *please.* "

A memory wafted through his head. Not his. Ouranos'.

I would rather die than be his puppet a moment longer.

Matt furrowed his brow. He had promised Ouranos he'd get him out alive. But if he couldn't, he would at least get him out of it.

I'm sorry if this doesn't work Ouranos. He reached into Ouranos' mind and pushed against the Basileus' black. The Basileus fought hard, and pain shot down Matt's spine, but he pressed forward anyway and blew apart the wall of darkness. With a will, he shoved as much hope as he could through their connection.

Ouranos lifted his head, eyes finally open, staring at Matt with tears streaking down his face. But he calmed, just a little.

Matt offered him a sad smile. He kneeled next to Ouranos and showed him the elixir on his hands. Ouranos didn't speak, couldn't speak, but he nodded through the tears and leaned his head down slightly. Matt pressed his elixir-covered hands to Ouranos' Ei-Ei jewels.

ALIVE

Izzy jogged through the woods, her slung hammer's handle beating against her thigh. Sami and Natassa followed behind, neither daring to look back. Izzy still held Cix up, his arm around her neck, him leaning nearly his entire body weight on her as they jogged. Cix was pretty much incoherent now, mumbling to himself, clutching his pack where he had stuffed the bottle of black liquid.

She didn't know what that was, but it was clearly bad news.

They neared the Delta-Z, huffing. Izzy chanced a glance behind her. No Cast.

No Darvin.

"I think we can slow down now," Izzy said.

Sami stopped, leaned on her knees, and let out a sob. She held something in one hand, gripping it like a lifeline.

Darvin's Gem.

Izzy flipped both ears back and stared down the path.

They'd lost him. They'd seriously lost Darvin. Her packmate, her brother-in-law, her close friend. How much was she going to lose before this was over? It felt like they had lost everything. Water above, she wanted to let go of these tears.

But she had to be the leader here. She fought the tears back.

"Your packmate spoke," Natassa said.

Izzy looked up.

Natassa fixed her gaze toward the crashed colony ship, her brow furrowed as if she was deep in thought. "He spoke," she said again. "He spoke and he retained everything about himself. More so than Roscoe. The only thing that changed was his body."

Izzy frowned. "Your point?"

"Perhaps he is the key to recovering the Shadow Cast."

Izzy's bones buzzed. Maybe he was. Maybe she could save him.

Maybe she could save her husband.

Something rustled in the woods.

Izzy instantly shielded, and Natassa lit her hands on fire. Izzy waved to her pack. "Get in the plane, everyone, go, go, go!"

"Wait!" a gurgling voice said. The rainbow painted weapons locker squeezed itself between some bushes, with a thick black puddle under it. "Please, don't leave without me."

Sami shot her head up. "Darvin?"

"Yeah," Darvin muttered. His muffled voice didn't come from any particular place on his Cast body, which unnerved Izzy. He dropped Rainbow Barf to the side and bulged a little out of the center of his puddle. He had a difficult time forming antlers, but he managed to keep his snout and at least one arm in place. The three blue "eyes" floated in the center of his "face" in a slow circle.

Sami drew her hands to her snout.

Natassa stepped forward. "How have you retained yourself?"

"I was hoping you could tell me that," Darvin said.

"If only I could," Natassa said. "Do you hear the Basileus in your head?"

"Is that that strange echoing?" Darvin tapped the side of his head with the heel of his "hand," shooting black gunk out of one "ear." "It's so muted. Like, I can hear it, and it clearly wants me to do something, but somehow I can ignore it? I don't know if that's really him, but if it is, it's not affecting me."

The relief in Izzy's bones was like a soothing balm. Maybe this was it. They could save Darvin and Roscoe and everyone else lost to the Cast. They just had to get home. "We need to get you to the labs," Izzy said. "If we do, maybe they can figure out why you reacted differently and we can fix you... and everyone else."

Darvin turned slightly and faced Natassa. "Do you think I'm safe?"

Natassa flicked an ear back. "I do not know."

"Hmm," Darvin said. "Then we should act like I'm not." He slithered over to Rainbow Barf and started fiddling with the latches, but his tentacles couldn't seem to grip it properly. "Shit."

Sami walked over and opened them herself. "Inside. We'll get you home."

Darvin reached out to her with a long inky arm, but then pulled back and leapt into the weapons locker instead. Sami looked at Natassa. "He'll be okay in here, right?"

Natassa nodded.

Sami took a deep breath and shut the locker. Natassa padded over and lifted it herself. Sami led her into the Delta-Z.

Cix said nothing. He just stared at the ground, mumbling quietly. It was like he hadn't even noticed Darvin was there.

Izzy adjusted her grip on him and headed into the plane.

332

Natassa placed the weapons locker on the floor and Sami secured it to the wall. Izzy helped settle Cix into one of the seats and strapped him in before showing Natassa how to strap in herself. She took the pilot's seat and invited Sami to take the co-pilot's chair. Sami nodded and took a seat. Izzy dropped her Gem into the energy converter slot and started launch procedures.

Her mind wandered.

The Basileus had made a cryptic reference to Matt's "fate." What did that mean? Did... did that mean Matt was a Cast? Injured and lost in the woods?

Dead?

Assuming the Basileus was even telling the truth. And that was a big assumption.

She gritted her teeth. Dead. Why else would he go this long without showing himself? He loved playing the hero. He would have dived in there to save the day if he still had the ability to.

He was dead.

She needed to let go of the dead.

As the plane started toward the Defender campus, she turned to Sami. "Did I see you had Darvin's Gem?"

Sami nodded.

"May I see it?"

Sami flicked an ear back, but handed her the Gem. Izzy looked it over.

It still held its color and the high-polished sheen of a bound Gem. That boded well. If the Gem had lost color and polish, it'd be a sure sign that the bond had broken and there'd be no saving him. He had had the Gem far too long to live without it.

"Izzy," Sami said quietly. "Ouranos is alive."

Izzy turned, flattening her ears.

"That means Matt is probably alive."

Izzy sat back. "Maybe."

"Likely," Sami said. "Very likely. Because we still couldn't find him."

"Then why didn't he come running to help us?" Izzy said.

"There's a million answers for that," Sami said. "Maybe he was in the plane, or the forest. Both of them are mazes. He could have been fighting Cast. He could be injured. But I'm sure he was trying to get to us. We just missed each other. I'm sure of it." She looked Izzy in the eye. "He's *alive,* Izzy."

Izzy handed Darvin's Gem back to her and turned her gaze forward. Her hope warmed her chest. Sami had a point then. Matt probably was alive. He *had* to be. She couldn't imagine Ouranos overpowering him. Not Matt.

But why hadn't she seen him? Where was he during this whole mess? Why hadn't he come back to them?

But… he might be alive. The hope was almost painful.

She chewed her lip. If he was alive, that meant she was abandoning him. Leaving him probably injured and confused when he needed her the most. Damn it all. She should turn back.

Cix let out a low wolf whine. Natassa spoke soothingly to him, but the whimpering continued.

And the light from Darvin's Gem caught her eye.

Izzy's fur bristled. She couldn't turn back. Right now, she needed to take care of Cix and Darvin. Keep her team together. Take charge. Once she knew Darvin was okay, that they could do something… she'd come back.

I'll come back for you, Matt, she thought. *I promise.*

A LITTLE LIGHT

"Hmm," Aric said, flicking his cheetah tail. "This is unlike anything I have ever seen before."

Izzy leaned against a metal countertop in one of the large magic labs on the Defender campus. The moment they had touched ground, they'd contacted Lance and quickly got Cix into the hospital wing for treatment. Last Izzy had heard, he was in deep shock. Healing magic couldn't touch shock, so they had to do things the slow way. No one could get a word out of him about what had happened. He just rocked on the bed, muttering about the Cast. He refused to let anyone touch the bottle of black liquid.

That honestly scared her. Hopefully they'd be able to get it from him once they calmed him down. Apparently the sedatives weren't working the way they were supposed to, so they definitely had a long process ahead of them.

After they'd gotten Cix settled in, Natassa carried the weapons locker that held Darvin to one of the vast chamber labs, at Lance's insistence. The labs were designed for testing magic strength, so it would hold him if he started behaving like the other Cast. Lance and DD Larissa met them in the lab. Aric and Jaymes had Darvin in a massive, reinforced glass room, and ran every scan possible.

Jaymes frowned, looking over the readings. His fire-colored quills rustled as he moved. "Is like... he is empty. Not here. Lacking everything."

Lance flipped a white ear back and flicked his wolf tail. He pushed his glasses up on his snout. "What does that mean?"

Aric pointed to the screen. "See this image? This reading measures magic. Zyearthlings, especially those bound to Gems, have innate magic that this should pick up. But he doesn't show up at all. He's just a black void."

Sami shuddered and held Darvin's Gem close to her. She flattened her ears and tucked her tail in. Izzy squeezed her shoulder. Natassa turned away.

Lance twitched his tail. "You sure the machines are working?"

"We can test that," Aric said. He spoke into a microphone. "Darvin, would you mind moving to the wall? I'm going to drop a ball of magic in there to recalibrate the equipment."

Darvin formed a head out of the center of his puddle. "Yeah, sure." He moved aside.

Good Draso, the way he "spoke." Just random sound coming out of nowhere, gurgling, echoing, like it was some thrown voice from a puppeteer rather than his own.

Aric formed a cage of electricity around his hand and opened up a chute leading into the room. But before he could get the magic in the chute, it fizzled out. He shook his hand. "Damnit. I can't hold it. I never was that great with this."

"I will use mine," Jaymes said. He formed a small fireball and dropped it in the chute. The fireball landed harmlessly in the center of the room.

Aric pointed to the readings. "See how the magic shows up here? Darvin should be doing the same thing. But he's not. It's like he's just... missing. Or worse, acting as a black hole and sucking up whatever innate magic he had."

"Hmm," Lance said, rubbing his chin.

Izzy flicked an ear. She turned to Natassa. "Do you know why that is?"

Lance eyed her.

Natassa shrunk down, avoiding Lance's gaze. "No."

"Of course not," Lance said with a growl. "I shouldn't even let you be here. You took off after you gave me your word you'd stay."

Larissa snorted, her silver and maroon badger fur blowing in the AC. "Lance--"

But Izzy beat her to it. "If Natassa hadn't shown up in the Dead Zone, we would all be *dead*. She literally saved our *lives.*"

Lance's tail flicked in annoyance, but he shook his head. "Okay, you're right, but I'm still not happy with the running off. Natassa, we'll have to talk about this later."

Natassa took a step away from Lance, looking off. Izzy shot a glare at the Master Guardian, but he had already turned back to the windows. Larissa gave him a not-so-subtle push with her cane, but he ignored it.

Darvin pressed himself against the wall. "Can you please get rid of this fireball? It's making me extremely uncomfortable."

"It is?" Aric said. "Why so?"

"I... I don't know," Darvin said. He curled into a small black ball. "It just is. Make it go away."

Izzy lifted a brow. "Natassa did say they fear fire, though it doesn't hurt them."

Aric and Jaymes looked at her. Natassa shifted. "They do, though I do not understand why. It has never been clear."

Larissa flattened an ear. "Did you use fire on the Cast before?"

337

"We did, yeah," Izzy said.

Larissa wrinkled her snout. "And what did that do?"

"It certainly made them run," Izzy said. "The ones we fought just now anyway. Roscoe didn't seem quite as affected by it. I don't know why."

"Is anyone actually listening?" Darvin said. "This thing is freaking me out. Get rid of it already!"

Jaymes looked to Lance, who nodded. Jaymes waved his hand and the fire disappeared. Darvin visibly relaxed.

"He doesn't show up on the thermal cameras either." Aric frowned. "I think we're going to be here a while."

Lance took a deep breath. "In that case, we'll leave you to it." He turned to Izzy and Sami. "Dismissed, Defenders."

Izzy stood her ground. "Darvin is my packmate and he's my responsibility. I want to stay."

"And I said dismissed," Lance said, tail twitching. "Take what little time you can to rest because as soon as I can get a team together, we're going to have to go after the Cast in the woods. They can't be allowed to stay."

Izzy's fur and quills bristled.

Larissa sighed. "I think he has a point, Izzy. We'll contact you as soon as we have a team together. You need rest."

Izzy formed a fist, but didn't question it.

"Sami, you're on medical leave," Lance said. "You've had quite a shock and you need the break. Get checked in at the hospital wing."

Sami blinked, then gave Lance a weak salute. "Yes, sir." She turned to Izzy. "Ah, thanks for saving me. If you hadn't fought the Cast off, I probably would have…"

"It's fine," Izzy said, pushing the deaths of the companions out of her mind. The last thing she needed was to dwell on what she couldn't change.

338

"I'm glad you're safe." She wanted to smile, but couldn't. Sami patted her shoulder and left the room.

Lance risked a look at Natassa, then turned away. "Izzy, keep Natassa with you and be ready for when we've got a team together to tackle the Cast." He took a deep breath. "Natassa, you've clearly proven yourself valuable to this team, so I'll let you go with Izzy. But we will still need to have that talk, okay?"

Natassa said nothing, though she nodded.

"Dismissed," Lance said. "Don't question it this time."

Izzy sighed and gave Lance a salute. She gently tugged on Natassa and pulled her out of the room.

"I am sorry," Natassa said the moment they were out of earshot.

"No, don't apologize," Izzy said. "I meant it when I said we'd be dead without you. Lance doesn't appreciate what happened back there."

Natassa rubbed the black fur on her arm. "But I could not save your other companion."

"You're one zyfaunos," Izzy said, though a twinge of guilt ran through her body. Images of Cayde and Astora's broken bodies crept through her mind. She tried to shove them aside, but they lingered. "You can't be expected to save everyone."

Natassa lowered her gaze. "You hold yourself to that expectation."

Izzy stopped. She pressed her lips together and flattened her ears. Did she? "I, ah... I want to be a Guardian." She shrugged "Guardians are expected to defend all creatures. Put those they're protecting above themselves. It's literally a part of the oath. I guess I responded that way because of that."

She continued toward her suite with Natassa beside her. "But I'll never be a Guardian now. Matt and I have been denied over and over again, and this last mission was an ultimatum. Succeed and win the Guardianship, or fail and lose it. And we failed spectacularly." She rubbed the fur on her arms, trying to fight back the emotions. Damn it. It was sinking in now. "Even if it wasn't for that, I don't have the right magic to be a Guardian. I'd never support Matt well enough as a healer… and now I'll never support Matt again…" A sob caught in her throat.

Lightning and air… it really was the end of her dreams, wasn't it? She had lost the Guardianship. She had lost Roscoe.

She had lost Matt.

How had it come to this so fast? Weren't they just running on the beach and goofing off two days ago? The future was uncertain but at least it wasn't bleak.

Now the light was gone.

"Isabelle," Natassa said quietly. Izzy turned. Natassa flattened one ear. "I understand if you wish to stop pursuing the Guardianship without Matthew. Though I firmly believe he is alive."

Damn it, why did everyone keep insisting that when he was clearly dead?

"But… to think yourself incapable simply because of your magic does you a disservice."

Izzy stared, blinking back tears. "What?"

"You speak as if your magic holds you back," Natassa said. "As if the ability to heal is a detriment and the ability to harm is a benefit. As if the fact that you are a healer means you are not a warrior." She managed a smile now. "I have seen evidence against all of this. You have saved lives with your healing and with your prowess as a warrior. You have made the effort to understand mine and Ouranos' plight and turn me from enemy to ally, which shows compassion beyond measure. You have consistently put others before yourself, even if that put you in significant danger." She gently gripped Izzy's shoulder. "You are a healer and a warrior. In my eyes, you are already a Guardian."

Izzy paused again, trying to process Natassa's words. Her vision blurred as she thought back on the last few days. Natassa had a point. She had saved people with her magic. She'd held her own in every battle. Yeah, they hadn't won, but how could you against invincible monsters?

But there were others she hadn't been able to save. Astora and Cayde. The Defenders turned into Cast. Roscoe... Darvin...

Matt.

But what had she told Natassa? *You're one zyfaunos. You can't be expected to save everyone.* She took a deep breath. Maybe she should listen to her own words.

And Natassa's big claim... *As if the ability to heal is a detriment and the ability to harm is a benefit.*

Water above, is that how she was seeing it? That the ability to harm others was the only way to be a Guardian? Damn, she was doing this all wrong... what was she thinking?

Natassa gave Izzy a small smile. "Regardless of what happens next, you gave me hope that I have not had in decades. You reminded me there is still good in the universe. For that, I thank you."

"I... you're welcome," Izzy said. "And uh... thanks. I think I needed to hear that. The part about healing as a bad thing and harming as a good thing. You're right. I shouldn't see it that way."

"I am glad to be of service," Natassa said. "Perhaps we should retire to your home until Lance calls on us again."

"Yeah." Izzy turned toward the resident campus.

But someone ran for them from the hospital. Izzy squinted.

It was Sami.

She dashed forward, eyes wide, panting, trailing fire. She waved a hand, screaming something, but Izzy couldn't make it out.

Then a wave of inky mess with scattered blue orbs splashed toward her in a horrific wall of shrieks and screams.

And Cix rode the top of the wave, holding the bottle of black liquid. Smiling.

HE RETURNS

Every bone in Izzy's body buzzed at the sight before her.

Cix. Riding a wave of Cast. *Smiling.*

What the hell was even happening? What was *wrong* with him?

Natassa shook her, and every emotion flooded her at once, focusing on one thing.

Sami.

"Sami, *run!*" Izzy screamed. She whipped out her hammer. "Natassa, give me fire, *now!*"

Natassa wasted no time and doused the hammer in flames. Izzy ran for the wave of Cast even as Sami ran from it. No matter what Cix's problem was, Izzy would not lose Sami too. She had already lost too much.

But she'd never win against so many Cast. This could be her last fight.

But she didn't care.

She had to save Sami.

343

A wave of ice shards appeared over Sami's head and sliced through the wall of Cast, breaking them apart. Cix fell among them and vanished in the ink. Izzy turned.

Lance stood behind them, his Gem whining, wearing a wolfy snarl. Jaymes stood next to him, his hands ablaze, determined, but shaking. Larissa stood at his side, fist-sized stones floating about her.

Izzy flicked her ears back. "Lance--"

"Got a call from the hospital wing," Lance said. "Cix killed five nurses and a doctor in charge of his care, then fled. I've already rallied the troops. We need to get him *now.* "

Izzy gaped. "But why would he *do* that?"

"I don't know," Lance said. "But he wasn't himself. His mannerisms and speech changed like he was--"

"Like he was possessed..." Izzy muttered.

Lance frowned.

"The Basileus," Natassa whispered. "He... he has..."

"He's possessed Cix," Izzy finished. "Just like he did Ouranos."

Lance's eyes grew wide. "Draso's mercy." They turned back to the mess of Cast.

Cix stood slowly, brushing Cast ink off his black and white fur. The blue streaks on his face and ears lacked their normal luster. The dragon Defender pendant looked like a curse around his neck. He stared at the group of them, baring fangs.

"It seems you have the way of it," he spoke. Izzy took a step back. Lightning and air, that really was the Basileus. "I suppose I can drop any attempts at playing the victim."

"Father, *let him go!* " Natassa screamed. "He has done *nothing,* he--"

"He makes a perfect vessel, daughter," Cix said. No, the Basileus. "Young, strong, and not so ruined as your brother."

Natassa flattened her ears and took a step back. "What did you do to Ouranos?"

"Me?" The Basileus said. The Cast formed around his feet, their blue eyes blinking back into existence. "No, daughter, *you. You* are the one who left him behind. *You* fled when the Cast surrounded him. His ruination is *your* doing."

Natassa took another step back. "I--"

"Don't give into that horse spit, Natassa," Izzy said. "This was all the Basileus. *All* of this is. Ouranos, Roscoe, Matt, Cayde, Astora, Darvin, Cix, the whole pack. It's *his fault."* She lifted her hammer, baring fangs. "And he'll damn well *pay for it!"*

The Basileus smirked. The Cast rose up around him, breaking into jagged grins. There had to be at least double the amount that Izzy had left in the woods. Damn it all, how had he made them? Where had he gotten those damn black shards? "You will have to catch me first." He threw out his hand, and the Cast attacked.

Lance shot the monsters with a barrage of ice spikes, breaking them apart. "Natassa, Sami, Jaymes, help me separate the Cast and keep them busy! Larissa, let's see if we can cage them with our magic! Izzy, go after Cix!"

Izzy froze and stared at him, wide eyed. "What?"

"Natassa said that the Cast are only dangerous with the Basileus pulling the strings," Lance said, shooting more ice spikes. Jaymes shot ribbons of embers at the monsters, and Sami fired bolt after bolt of fire. Natassa seemed torn, but in a flurry of fire and burning, she summoned Excelsis and Deo. Lance frosted a wave of Cast with diamond dust as Larissa built a stone wall to corner them. "We need to sever those strings!"

Izzy's blood ran cold. "Are you asking me to *kill him?"*

345

"Whatever you have to do!" Lance said. "If we don't stop this now, the whole peninsula will be overrun in no time!" He charged a swarm of Cast, hands and tail frozen with ice crystals.

Earth and stone, how the hell had it come to this? Killing an ally? A *friend?* She'd never be able to do it. She'd... just have to knock him out. Get close enough for a sleeper hold. Sever the strings didn't mean sever the lifeforce. She brandished her hammer, still alight with Natassa's flames, and batted Cast out of the way, headed for Cix.

The black and white wolf seemed quite preoccupied with the others fighting the Cast and didn't even acknowledge Izzy as she slowly approached him. The blue strips on his ears were still stained with the remnants of Cast – that unnerved her. What the hell was even happening?

Somehow she managed to get behind him without being noticed. She drudged up spars she and Cix had over the years, trying to remember his weaknesses. He tended to leave his right side and his legs open... But would that matter if it wasn't Cix controlling his body? She had no idea, but it was better than nothing.

Just a quick movement. An arm around the neck. Hold him in place. She had the strength. Just incapacitate him, hold him for fifteen seconds, and it'd all be over. She could do this.

But dammit, she shouldn't have to!

Dammit all!

She leapt up toward Cix and got her arm around his neck.

But Cix grabbed her. He eyed her with a smirk that could only belong to the Basileus. "You should have killed him when you had the opportunity." He flipped her over his head, sending her flying into a mess of Cast. She slammed into them and sunk into the ink of at least a dozen monsters, catching Lance calling her name before drowning in a world of muffled silence. The Cast crushed around her.

She was going to die. She couldn't breathe, couldn't see, couldn't hear, couldn't fight, couldn't heal, couldn't shield, she was going to *die* and she deserved it, she--

A wave of hot flame ran over her, chasing the Cast off in wails, singeing her fur, though thankfully not the skin. She turned over and coughed. A scent of musky dirt rushed over her as someone walked between her and the retreating Cast.

She looked up.

Standing between her and the monsters, with Pax hovering overhead, hand up and ablaze, teeth gritted and brow furrowed, seemingly more in control than she had ever seen him, was Ouranos.

CHAPTER 52

FREEDOM

Ouranos called wave after wave of fire to his hands, drowning the Cast in flames, chasing them away from Isabelle.

So long as he drew breath, he would not let his father hurt anyone else.

It had been a miracle that he had survived Matt's attempts to sever the shackles his father held on him for so long. The moment Matt touched the elixir to Ouranos' Ei-Ei Jewels, a blinding pain ripped through his body, relieving him of all other senses, causing everything to shut down and pass out.

But Matt called to him, his rosy dawn a beacon of light in the darkness of his mind, finally chasing his doubt, his fears, his worry, and most certainly his father, away. Matt told him it took almost two hours to coax him back to full consciousness, but it was a consciousness as clear as day to night.

Finally, that dawn had chased away his father's darkness. Finally, he was free.

And he would use his newfound freedom to finally end his father's destruction.

"Pax, to the left!" Ouranos called. "Herd them this way, keep them away from the Defenders!"

Pax let out an angry hoot and sailed off to the left, trailing dust along his tail, filling the air with his dusty scent. He crusted his wings with sharp stones and dropped them like bombs, adding to the silver and maroon badger's barrier of rock and separating the Cast from the ice-wielding white wolf and the others.

Ouranos called more fire to his hands and waved it over the Cast with a fury he had not felt in an age.

The Basileus *would not win.*

A hand gripped his arm and he turned. Izzy, her eyes frantic. "Ouranos!"

"I am in my right mind, if that was your question," Ouranos said, staying focused on the task at hand. "The Basileus controls me no longer."

Natassa was there now, wrapping herself around Ouranos' other arm. She moved like she wanted to speak, but no words came out.

Ouranos gripped her hand. "I am here, Natassa." She let out a sob, and buried her face in his shoulder.

"But how?" Izzy said.

Jústi appeared to Ouranos' right, filling the air with her metallic scent, flashing lightning bolts all around, dropping the zyfaunos responsible for Ouranos' freedom. Matt landed on his feet, tornadoes swirling about him, his face a mask of determination. His rosy dawn filled Ouranos' mind with light and confidence.

Ouranos nodded. "Matthew saved me."

Izzy stared, her mouth open and eyes glassy. "Matt...?"

"Later," Matt said. "Cast first." He turned to Ouranos. "Remember what we practiced on the flight here."

349

Ouranos nodded. "Name it."

"Stage three, fire," Matt said. "Give me everything you've got!"

Ouranos wound ribbons of fire through Matt's tornados, forming tall twisters of flame. Matt broke the twisters in twain and sent them hurling through the Cast, separating them into blazing bits and sending them screaming into the void. They scattered, fleeing with shrieks and wails. Jústi and Pax chased after them, keeping the Cast busy while the monsters tried to pull themselves back together.

Izzy walked up to Matt, her eyes shining. She drew her hands to her face. "You're alive..."

Matt gave her a sad smile, his ears flat, and pulled her into a deep hug. "I'm sorry."

Izzy hugged him back, shaking. "Don't apologize. I'm glad you're safe." She pulled back. "But how? What the hell *happened?"*

"Long story," Matt said. "Very long story. We'll have to explain after we fix this mess."

The white wolf and maroon badger walked up to them now, Lance and Larissa, Ouranos thought, plucking the information from Matt's head. Sami and a fire-colored quilar, whom Matt identified as Jaymes, stood next to him. The red of Jaymes' fur pulled at Ouranos. Matt gave him a look. Ouranos' thoughts must have bled into his, but he pulled back. There would be time to tend that wound later.

Lance stared at Matt, jaw loose.

Matt drew a fist across his chest, a serious look on his face. A salute, if Ouranos read Matt's thoughts correctly. "GR Azure reporting for duty, sir." He nodded to Larissa. "Ma'am."

Lance stared, working his jaw like he wanted to speak, but could not find the words. He finally turned to Ouranos.

"He's safe," Matt said. "Don't ask me to prove how, because we don't have time. You'll just have to trust me."

Lance blinked. "His father isn't in his head anymore, is he." It was a statement, not a question.

Matt raised one eyebrow and pressed an ear back. "No. But I thought you didn't even believe he was in the first place?"

"I wasn't sure I did," Lance said. "Until now."

Ouranos flattened his ears and flicked his tail.

Matt twitched an ear. "What changed?"

The wails of the Cast demanded their attention and they turned. The Cast had formed a slow swirling pool of black, like the very gate to hell itself. If Ouranos could guess, their numbers had doubled, at least.

At its center, stood Cix. Ears back, teeth bared, fists formed, he held himself awkwardly, repositioning constantly, like he was uncomfortable in his own body. He glared at Ouranos and Matt.

"You were supposed to *die* when I left you," he snarled. "Alone, out of sight, out of mind. I had no intention of wasting my time *watching.*" He lit both hands ablaze, scattering the Cast. The monsters hovered about him, jagged, angry grins on their faces. "But now I will relish every scream as you *burn to ash.*"

Ouranos took a step back. That was not Cix.

That was the Basileus.

Lance frosted his fingers with ice, forming a shield in front of him. "That changed."

FALTER

Matt stared at Cix, jaw hanging.

No.

Cix. His sword partner, his dear friend, his fellow Defender. Gone. And in his place, the Basileus. Creating the Cast, murdering left and right, controlling Cix as he had controlled Ouranos.

The Black Cloak's words pierced his heart.

If you help Ouranos, someone close to you will die.

Cix took a step forward, his fur dripping with sweat, his hands and tail blazing with fire, his gaze not his own.

Matt formed fists.

No.

"Cast!" The monsters flooded forward as Cix -- the Basileus -- shot a ribbon of fire at Ouranos and Matt.

Matt threw up a shield in front of him and Ouranos and whipped up four tornados. *"Ouranos, stage three!"*

Ouranos nodded and filled the funnels with flames. They directed the fire through the Cast, spreading them out. Sami and Jaymes followed suit, and Lance frosted his fingers, shooting dozens of tiny ice spikes into the approaching wave. Larissa broke them apart with stone spikes, but they didn't stay broken for long.

Lance took a step forward. "Rise up, Defenders! Jaymes, go protect the labs! Anyone else with fire, herd the Cast to me!" He held a hand out and built a wall of solid ice. "Let's see if we can trap them!"

Jaymes nodded. "Matt, you have explaining to do! Protect yourself!"

Matt nodded. "Take care of yourself too!" Jaymes called out an affirmation then continued toward the labs.

The Basileus snarled again, but rather than attack, he turned to the residential campus. A flood of Defenders ran for them, many with elemental magic lighting the air.

Matt pasted his ears back. Reinforcements. Or victims.

Lance perked his ears and gasped. He waved at them. "Defenders--"

But he was too late. The mess of Cast split cleanly in two, with half following Cix after the advancing Defenders and half turning on their pack, pounding on Lance's ice wall. Larissa pummeled them with stone spikes, but they vanished into the Cast with no effect.

Natassa leapt back, her fire fizzling out, but Sami stood near her, bearing down on them with flame. Natassa furrowed her brow and set Izzy's hammer ablaze, which Izzy brandished against the advancing monsters. The Athánatos Princess called out to her two summons and they flew over the Cast, spewing flames.

But nothing worked. Nothing stopped them.

The soldiers caught on to the Cast problem, but fled too late, falling to the wall of monsters. The Basileus still carried the bottle of elixir. He poured some into his hand, froze it in a flurry of diamond dust, then threw it into the eyes of the trapped Defenders.

Instantly more Cast were born.

"This ends now!" Lance shouted. "Defenders, herd those Cast! Those who can, turn back!" He turned. "Matt."

Matt faced him.

"Take him out," Lance said. "No matter the cost." He flipped an ear back. "Cix would want it to be you."

Matt chewed his lip, but didn't question it. Not now. "Yes, sir." He nodded to Ouranos and they rushed after Cix.

But he wouldn't kill him. Cix hadn't done anything to deserve that. Matt could stop this without killing him.

Someone close to you will die.

No, he won't! I won't let him!

Ouranos' blue inked its way into his mind. Not the same resignation from before. It was different. Adrenaline, jitters, determination.

Worry.

Can he truly be saved? He is not Athánatos nor is he soulless. He is not me.

There has to be another way, Matt said. *There has to be! I saved you. I can save Cix.*

Ouranos met his gaze, his brows furrowed. *I am with you, whatever your decision.*

Cix turned as they approached, a deep snarl on his black lips. "You think you have won, when you have not once beaten me."

Matt edged to the right. *Take his left, Ouranos.* Ouranos acknowledged him with a blink of white in his mind. Matt glared at Cix. "Let him go, Basileus."

The Basileus narrowed his eyes. "You think your pathetic squabbling will free your companion? He is mine to command and makes a far better puppet than my son. Helpless against the fight, easily commanded." He smirked. "There is nothing left in here for you to save, Defender."

Matt gritted his teeth. He formed two thin twisters. "We'll see about that!" *Ouranos, help me knock him out! Stage one, stones!*

Granted! Ouranos threw several fist-sized stones into Matt's twisters.

The Basileus took a step back and formed a shield, though it remained purple, the weakest strength. Cix had much better shields than that. Clearly the Basileus didn't have as much control as he thought.

Matt guided the tornado toward the Basileus, swirling the stones about, picking up speed. It might do some significant damage, but he could avoid killing him. Damage could be fixed. Death couldn't. "Ouranos!"

"Here!" Ouranos waved a hand and together they flew three stones toward Cix. One bounced off the shield, a second shattered it.

But a Cast rose up and caught the third.

The Basileus smirked. "Did you forget I am not fighting alone?"

Damn it all! Ouranos, split focus! Fire on those Cast, herd them toward Lance and I'll get to Cix.

Protect yourself! Ouranos concentrated fire on the Cast.

Matt ran forward and threw himself on Cix, knocking him to the ground. The pair of them rolled through the mess of Cast. The Basileus clawed and bit at Matt, blasting the air about him with fire, but Matt wrapped himself in a shield and blocked most of the attacks. *I just need to immobilize him then I can--*

Cix flopped to the ground, landing hard on his back. Matt moved to pin him, but he held his hands up, his eyes wide and glistening. "Matt, *wait!"*

Matt paused. "Cix?"

Cix stared at him, shaking. "What the hell happened? Where am I?" He gripped his head and whined. "Who the *hell is in my head?"*

Matt chewed his lip. "It's the Basileus, Cix, he's--"

"He's *killing me,* Matt," Cix said, squeezing his head and shutting his eyes. "He's breaking my Gem bond, he's stripping my magic, he's--"

Matt gripped Cix's shoulders. "I'm going to get him out of there, Cix, I promise, just please--"

"You can't," Cix snarled, staring at Matt now. "He's *rooted in there.* He *won't leave.* He--"

"Cix, you have to trust me--"

Cix grabbed Matt's shirt. "Just *end me now* before he takes over completely! Stop him, stop the Cast, please, I'm begging you--*Ahh!"* He gripped his head again and curled into a ball, baring his teeth.

Matt flattened his ears. He was *losing him.* "Cix, *hold on--"*

Cix whipped about and slammed Matt with a wave of flames to the face, shoving him off of him. Matt rolled aside, grateful he'd thought to keep up his shield. He turned.

Cix stood, the fear gone and anger in its place. He snarled and wiped his snout. "Pathetic wolf, you were supposed to beg for your life, not give it up!" The Basileus again. He turned toward the fleeing Defenders and rushed after them, leaving Matt and Ouranos behind.

Ouranos came up to Matt. "Matthew."

Matt stared. The effects of battle raged around him – screaming, death, Cast, elements, the smell of burning flesh, the taste of electricity in the air, the ever-present fear that he would lose someone he cared for...

Izzy, Lance, Jaymes, Charlotte, Natassa... all of them were at risk. They had already lost so much.

Roscoe... Darvin...

Cix.

Someone close to you will die.

But Cix was still in there. He was still worth fighting for. He could save him. He *had* to save him.

Someone close to you will die.

Ouranos gripped Matt's shoulder. "We need to end this before everything is lost."

Matt formed a fist. *Damn it all.* "…Then let's do it as painlessly as possible." He and Ouranos ran for Cix.

GUARDIAN

Izzy rushed a mess of Cast, chasing them with a flaming hammer toward Lance's ever-growing ice prison. They wailed and screeched, but hardly followed Izzy's shepherding, leaping about in black waves, taking off all over the place, grinning all the while. Izzy gritted her teeth.

They were losing and she knew it.

The moment the Cast turned on the advancing Defenders, the air filled with the monster's shrieks, zyfaunos death screams, the iron smell of blood, and the violent, shaking air of wild elements flying all about them.

And still the Cast kept coming.

Two days ago this area had been a carnival. Now it was a warzone.

Some monsters pounced on Defenders and in an instant turned them into a Cast, which meant the Cast had to be carrying the black shards the Basileus was using to turn zyfaunos. Those who weren't turned were killed, mostly by crushing, leaving broken, mangled bodies everywhere. Natassa had already thrown up once seeing one of the barely recognizable victims.

Many Defenders had fought back and escaped, thankfully. While fire seemed to have the most strength, the Cast also fell apart with every other element, though never permanently. Izzy counted her blessings as they ran. Imagine if this had happened in a civilian city... they'd be powerless.

The elements flying about wildly created a second hazard though, and Izzy's constant shields around her and Natassa wore her down.

Lance rallied Defenders around him as he built the ice walls to try and keep the Cast in place, but if he let up on his ice magic even a moment, the Cast threw themselves violently into the walls and broke them apart. Even the other ice users around him had no chance of keeping the wall intact. With Lance fully occupied, the Defenders lacked direction.

The only thing keeping them slightly together was Larissa barking orders, but her leg injury prevented her from moving fast enough to direct the way they needed. She used her stone magic to help herd the Cast, but it wasn't long before she had to stop. Lexi acid clouds floated about her from overuse.

And more fell to the Cast.

"Izzy," Sami stood by Izzy's back. She blasted a wave of Cast, but her fire lacked its normal strength. "We can't keep this up."

"I know," Izzy said, slamming another Cast.

"Izzy, *watch yourself!*" Lance called.

Izzy turned just as a Cast pounced. She shielded.

But another Cast slammed into it and sent it flying. It stopped in front of Izzy and Sami, standing tall, forming a snout and antlers.

"Darvin!" Sami said.

"I'll keep them busy," he said.

Izzy stepped forward. "Darvin, none of this will matter if we don't contain the Cast! Help me herd them to Lance's ice walls!" Darvin nodded and dove onto an escaping Cast, forcing it back. With Darvin and his invincibility as a

Cast, they might have a chance. "Natassa, take a step back and give me stage two!"

Natassa nodded and lit Izzy's hammer on fire before leaping back away from the Cast toward a protective group of Defenders. "Stay safe!"

Izzy shielded herself and Sami then slammed the Cast with flames. Sami directed her fire over them and Darvin smashed into them, pushing them toward the ice wall. It worked, slowly. The Cast were finally being herded. But more than anything, it gave other Defenders a chance to either escape or fight back. If they could just move a little faster.

As they fought, another Cast showed up and followed Darvin's direction, blowing Cast after Cast against the ice wall. Izzy caught a glimpse of gold in the Cast's body. A wedding coil.

Roscoe's wedding coil.

Roscoe. He was using his wedding coil to keep his mind and help fight back. Her heart swelled. That was the extra help they needed! They might actually have a shot at this. If they could just get the Cast under control, and Matt could get Cix, then--

"Natassa, *watch out!"* Sami shrieked.

Izzy turned just as Natassa screamed and disappeared under a Cast. The monster dragged her to the ground crushing her. Blood shot out from under the Cast and the sound of Natassa's bones snapping threatened to break Izzy.

No! Not Natassa too! Izzy flipped her flaming hammer about and grazed it over the Cast, screeching at it. *Not Natassa!*

The Cast wailed and slithered off her in a flurry of embers, but the damage was already done. Blood pooled under Natassa, her legs and one arm bent in awkward, unnatural directions, and tears streamed down her face and she gasped desperately for air, blood bubbling in her mouth.

But she gasped for air. She wasn't gone yet.

Izzy was by her side in a second. "Hold on!" She *would not lose Natassa!* She pulled every scrap of healing magic from her golden Gem and pressed her hands to Natassa's chest. "Just keep breathing, *keep breathing!*"

Natassa's condition railed against Izzy's mind the moment she touched her. Broken ribs, collapsed lungs, crushed flesh. It was a miracle she could get a single breath in.

And Izzy couldn't heal her fast enough.

"Sami, get me another healer, *now!*" Izzy shouted, tears soaking her fur. "Please, I need help!"

Sami bit her lip, then ran for a pack of Defenders.

But it wouldn't be fast enough. Izzy already knew that.

Fire and ice, it *wouldn't be fast enough.*

She pushed even harder. Her Gem whined and glowed, actually growing hot at her hip. Natassa's rips knit back together, her flesh slowly repaired itself, but her lungs wouldn't refill. Too much crush damage. Too much broken flesh in the way. Too much, too much.

Natassa gagged as more blood pooled in her mouth.

She was going to die.

No! Izzy pulled harder on her power and buried her hands in Natassa's broken body.

The moment she did, her Gem flashed and a thick black liquid formed on the tips of her fingers. Light exploded through Izzy's palms, blinding her, but still she pressed. And in her mind's eye, she saw Natassa's healing. Her lungs filled with air and cleared themselves of fluid. Her body reabsorbed the blood and her flesh filled and repaired itself. Bruises disappeared, bones knitted, lacerations mended... And in almost an instant, Natassa was fully healed and well. The light faded and Izzy's Gem cooled immediately.

Natassa sat up and coughed, spitting out blood, but she breathed easily. She stared at Izzy, panting.

361

"You saved me."

Izzy stared at her hands, now covered in viscous black liquid almost to her wrists. How did she do that? Natassa should have died!

But she didn't. Izzy saved her. Fire and ice, she *saved her*. How did she do that?

You see your healing as a detriment.

Damn. She shouldn't do that. It had saved Natassa. She had been literally dying and Izzy practically brought her back to life.

Was this because she was Black Bound? Matt had always denied that his powers were stronger because of being Black Bound, though Izzy knew better. But she had never shown anything of those strengths herself.

Until now. Until it mattered the most.

She stared at her hands. Despite the war going on around her, one thought crystalized in her mind.

Maybe she could still be a Golden Guardian.

She stared at the thick black liquid.

"It is like the liquid Ouranos mentioned Matthew produces," Natassa said, staring.

The heat left Izzy's face. "Like the liquid used to make Cast." She wiped her fingers on the grass, though the liquid absorbed into her body before she got much off.

"Izzy," Natassa said. "I was dying. I know it. But you saved me. How?"

Izzy blinked. "I... I think it's because I'm Black Bound."

Natassa smiled sadly. "Regardless of how... thank you. I thought myself dead for certain."

"Izzy!" Sami ran up to them with Kole at her heels, her long feathered tail catching leaves on the grass. "I found a—wait, what?"

Izzy stood and helped Natassa up. "Don't ask because I can't put it to words."

"Izzy!" Darvin called. "Need help!"

She turned to the mess of Cast. She might be capable of being a Guardian, but they needed to stop this onslaught of monsters before she even entertained the idea of Guardianship.

But now she knew she could. She turned to Natassa and Sami.

"Let's do this."

CHAPTER 55

BROKEN

I can't do this.

Matt and Ouranos fought their way through waves of Cast, trying to chase down the Basileus. Their enemy moved with surprising speed and with the Cast slowing them down, he was getting away.

But Matt's heart wasn't in the chase. Catching him meant killing him.

Damn it all.

Have you thought of no alternative? Ouranos spoke telepathically, blue worry and white hope swirling through his mind.

Matt blasted a Cast back with a powerful wind gust. *I don't know! I don't know how to fix it!*

Ouranos seared a path through the Cast. *We can try again to render him unconscious.*

I think he has too many Cast protecting him, Matt said, leaping away from one. *And that doesn't fix the big problem. How do we get rid of your father? What happens when he wakes up again?*

364

"Shield up!" Ouranos shouted.

Matt threw up a shield and Ouranos filled the area with fire. *If we are to separate the Basileus from Cix, we need to discover the equivalent to what worked with me.*

Matt paused. "His Gem." They needed his Gem. If he could coat his Gem in the elixir, that could sever his bond with the Basileus like they did with Ouranos.

Right?

But that also meant separating his bond with his magic, at least temporarily. That had nearly killed Ouranos. And it would do the same to Cix, if it broke his bond with his Gem. Which, considering what the elixir did to everything else it touched, it could do exactly that.

Matt had fought frantically to bring Ouranos back, and it likely only worked because of the social bond between their jewels. Something Matt didn't have with Cix. And even if he had the time to attempt to make one, he had no idea how to do it on purpose. No one did anymore.

He was stuck.

But what else could they do? He had to try.

Ouranos, we need to get close enough to Cix to get his Gem from him, Matt said. *If I can coat the Gem in the elixir like we did with your Ei-Ei jewels...*

Ouranos' eyes grew wide. *You are right. He may have a chance then.*

Matt pointed to his Gem holster. *He has a holster like this, and there's an emergency release button near the top. If we can hit that, we can get the Gem. I'm going to shroud us in wind and get that elixir going. Be careful!*

Shield me. I will distract him. Get the Gem! He rushed for Cix, firing every element he could in his general direction. The Basileus slowed and faced him, countering with shields and fire.

365

Matt shielded himself and Ouranos and swirled a massive tornado around them all, encasing them in the pulsing wind and debris, pushing the Cast back. They wailed, but slowly fell back to the power of Matt's magic at its limit.

Elixir formed on his fingers almost instantly.

He ran for Cix's right, hoping to catch him off guard. If he could just get that Gem, he'd be okay. And Cix tended to keep his right side open.

Only that wasn't Cix in there. Damn it all! He'd just have to hope he got the right opening or that the Basileus got stuck with some of Cix's quirks.

The Basileus turned on Ouranos, growling. "So, do you think that by fighting me, you can redeem yourself?" he snarled, barely able to be heard over the vicious wind. "You think this one act of goodwill absolves you of a lifetime of wrongdoing?"

"Those were your actions, not mine!" Ouranos shouted. He shot a spike of earth at Cix, though, thankfully, cleanly missed.

"It was your hand that did the deeds," The Basileus said. "Your actions that destroyed."

Ouranos' colors wavered in Matt's mind, just slightly. Matt snarled. *Don't believe him, Ouranos!*

Ouranos stopped, glaring. "I will not fall for your mind tricks again, Basileus."

The Basileus narrowed his eyes. "You will always carry your sins, Ouranos."

"No," Ouranos said. He swirled fire around himself, lining the inside of Matt's tornado with flames. "Because Matthew has shown me that I no longer have to feel guilt over destruction I did not create."

The Basileus glared, but then faltered. His eyes grew wide and glanced around, as if suddenly remembering Ouranos wasn't alone. "Wait--"

That was Matt's opening. He dove for Cix's Gem holster and smashed the emergency release button. The holster opened and his Gem tumbled out, rolling along the grass. Ouranos tackled Cix and they both fell to the ground. He held Cix in place. "Matthew, get the Gem!"

Matt dashed for it. Just one shot. One try. He just needed the Gem.

But he stopped the moment he saw it.

The Gem should have been Cix's characteristic black with the streaks of white along its cut edges, carrying the reflective sheen of magic.

But instead, it was colorless and dull. The gleaming shades of a bound Gem were gone.

Matt fell to a knee. No. How could that be? What happened to it? He dropped his rushing wind, leaving Ouranos' fire wall to keep the Cast at bay. The monsters wailed behind the wall. He let the elixir absorb back into him, and picked up the Gem.

It wasn't broken or chipped, but it was... dead. Lifeless.

Unbound. Matt shook.

The Gem was no longer bound to Cix. Which made him as good as dead.

Matthew, quick! Ouranos said. *I cannot hold him much longer!*

Matt stared at the unbound Gem, trying to process everything. How the hell had that happened? How had a Gem bond broken that easily? How did the Basileus even have the *ability* to break a Gem bond? It defied the imagination.

But no matter how it had happened, it meant only one thing. Cix was dead. Even if his body moved and even if he spoke, and even if Matt got the Basileus out of him, without the Gem bond, he'd instantly die. And there was no way to bind him again -- once a Gem bond broke, there was no fixing it, no rebinding it. He was *dead.*

Someone close to you will die.

Matt didn't even know how to react. He lost. He couldn't save him.

Cix was gone.

"Matthew!"

Matt blinked, staring at the dull Gem. *It doesn't matter.*

What do you mean? Ouranos said. *I--*

The Basileus smashed Ouranos, knocking him off and sending him sailing toward Matt. Matt gasped and shielded, catching Ouranos.

The Basileus stood, eyes bugging out and angry, his teeth gritted so hard he drew blood. *"You will not take this from me!"*

Ouranos stared at Matt. "We *had* him!"

"We don't," Matt said. He lifted Cix's Gem. "He's somehow unbound from the Gem. He's as good as dead, Ouranos. Even if we got the Basileus out of him, he would die instantly. Painfully, without the magic. He's had the Gem too long to live without it."

Ouranos stared wide-eyed. "Then--"

"Give me my *revenge!"* The Basileus charged them.

Matt snarled. This ended *now!* He leapt up and tackled the Basileus, pinning him to the grass again. "We are *done with this!"*

Immediately the Basileus retreated, taking his hate and fury with him. Cix bubbled to the surface and his face softened to the face Matt knew so well. He stared at Matt, panting, frantic, with tears streaking down his face. "Matt...?"

Matt's face softened. Damn it all. *Damn it all!* He was right there, and he couldn't save him, damn it! "Cix... Your Gem bond... I--"

Cix flattened his ears. "I-I already know. I felt it... when..."

Matt furrowed his brow. "I'm sorry."

"Just... make it quick," Cix said, his voice shaking. "And look after Robert for me."

Matt frowned, but fought back tears. He wouldn't give the Basileus the satisfaction. "I will."

Ouranos kneeled by Cix's head and gently placed his hands on his scalp. Cix darted his gaze to Ouranos, shaking frantically, but calmed when he saw who it was. Ouranos offered him a reassuring glance. "This will be painless."

368

Cix watched him a moment, tears pooling over. But he calmed. The shaking stopped. "T-thank you," he muttered. "I'm sorry."

"All is forgiven in Draso's Palace," Ouranos said. "Rest now. You have friends here."

Cix shut his eyes. He gripped Matt's hands and held tight. Matt squeezed back.

Ouranos pressed gently.

Cix shuddered once, then immediately stopped breathing, settling onto the grass. He released his grip on Matt's hands.

The wild shrieks of the Cast ended at once. Things grew quiet and calm. Ouranos' fire faded and the monsters sunk down and stopped attacking.

Matt shut his eyes, letting the tears burn. He placed Cix's hands on his chest. *I'm sorry, Cix.* He wiped his eyes and gazed up at Ouranos. "…What did you do?"

"Froze his brain," Ouranos said. "A standard procedure for Drifters who cannot be saved. I am saddened to say I am well-practiced in the ritual as an Athánatos royal. It must be done in close proximity to the dying. It is instant and painless, the greatest mercy for those who have no future."

"Why did the Basileus give him up so easily?" Matt said. "Why didn't he fight?"

"I can only assume he realized he had lost, so he gave Cix up," Ouranos said. "The Basileus fears death. He would rather flee and give up his connection here than feel death."

"Matt…"

Matt turned. Izzy walked up to him with Sami and Natassa by her side. Two Cast followed them, one forming the shape of a stag. They stared at Cix's lifeless body.

Matt frowned. "I couldn't save him." His voice cracked.

Izzy dropped to her knees next to Matt and threw her arms around his neck. "You can't be expected to save everyone." Matt choked on a sob and hugged her back.

Lance walked up now, limping and gripping his arm, one lens in his glasses broken. Larissa followed behind, clutching a crushed arm. A handful of other Defenders followed them. Lance looked over Matt and Ouranos, then paused when he saw Cix. He watched a moment, closed his eyes, took a deep breath, then held a hand out to Matt.

"Clearly we have a lot to talk about."

CHAMBERS

Matt sat on one of the big stone chairs in the Assembly Chamber, keeping his gaze from the still-vacant Golden Guardian seats next to the Master Guardian. He had a bottle of water on the polished table. It caught the glow from the pinprick starlights on the ceiling, giving it a glittery radiance, but he hadn't touched it. His stomach screamed at him to eat something, drink something, but he couldn't concentrate.

All he could see in his head was Cix slipping away over and over again, frightened, helpless, Gemless. He flattened his ears, and forced himself to look around, to hear the conversations around him, to take in anything that would ground him in the present.

Izzy sat in the chair next to his, right on the edge of the seat so she could be as close to Matt as possible. She held his hand tight and refused to let it go. Matt didn't protest. He expected to hear a mess of Izzy's thoughts after that, but she seemed so exhausted. All he got was a distant bell jangling in his mind.

Charlotte walked into the room, padded up to Matt, and gave him a big hug. She tried to keep her face calm and stoic, but her efforts just made her look distant. Matt hugged her back and smiled at her. It was almost a whole minute before she broke the hug, but when she did, she managed a smile back.

But she didn't speak. She opened her mouth like she wanted to, and nothing came out. Instead, she shook her head, grabbed a foldable chair, and sat next to Natassa.

Roscoe and Darvin, who was also apparently a Cast and had somehow retained himself, lay on the floor near her. Roscoe had curled himself around Izzy's feet but Darvin managed to shape his Cast body so that it resembled a stag. His three blue eyes darted about on his "face." A bit unnerving.

Sami sat next to Izzy, nursing a Lexi acid injury in her right eye. Not as bad as Darvin's was, thankfully, but it'd need a week or two of healing therapy to get back to normal.

Larissa sat in the Domini Defender's chair next to Lance, with Kole at her side. Kole worked healing magic up and down Larissa's crushed arm. Matt flicked both ears back. He didn't understand healing magic the way Izzy did, but he once remembered Izzy telling him that crush damage wasn't an instant fix like a lot of healing could be. She might need a couple of weeks of healing therapy for that.

Which, he supposed, made Izzy's miraculous healing of Natassa even more impressive.

But Larissa ignored the healer, her face stoic and calm. She focused her attention on her wife standing next to her. Viri gripped her hand like Larissa would disappear if she let go.

Matt gave Izzy's hand another squeeze.

Ouranos sat on the other side of him, at Matt's insistence, with Natassa next to him. Natassa stared at the floor, though she gripped Ouranos' hand like a vice. The Athánatos prince leaned down in his chair, trying to make himself small, as if all eyes were on him.

In fairness, most eyes were.

The only one cleanly avoiding Ouranos' gaze was Lance himself. He sat on the Master Guardian's chair, studying a piece of paper through a spare set of glasses, while they waited for Aric and Jaymes to come back with what little information they had about the Cast.

The only sound in the room came from Kole's whining Gem as she healed Larissa.

After Cix's death, the Cast had gone completely docile. Lance had directed efforts to herd them up, and they'd gotten them into a pair of magic labs. The clear-walled rooms were made of some of the strongest material on Zyearth, so even if something riled them up again, it was unlikely that they'd be able to break free and wreak havoc.

There were a lot of Cast.

And a lot of dead.

Ouranos sunk deeper into his seat, staring at the floor, his ears pasted back. Matt frowned and squeezed his shoulder. *Sorry, I was projecting again.*

You were only speaking the truth, Ouranos said, avoiding Matt's gaze.

Aric and Jaymes walked in. Aric took a seat across the table with some papers, but Jaymes walked over and stood by Matt and Izzy. Jaymes kept his gaze forward and stood straight, but Matt could see him shaking. Matt chewed his lip. He lifted his and Izzy's hand toward Jaymes. The fire-red quilar watched it a moment before eclipsing their hands with his own.

Definitely shaking.

Lance stood now, quiet and calm, glancing at the paper in his hand.

"Two hundred and thirty-seven Shadow Cast now reside in our strongest magic labs." His voice echoed off the stone walls. He paused a moment, eyes closed. "And seventy-eight Defenders now reside in Draso's Palace."

373

Ouranos winced, shooting a spike of gray guilt through Matt's mind.

"The loss of any Defender, any life, is a tragedy," Lance continued. "But considering the circumstances and the number of Cast, I am grateful it's not more." He finally met Matt's gaze. Then slowly turned to Ouranos. But there wasn't anger in that gaze. Sadness more like. Regret. Worry. Relief. Lance sighed. "We have Matt and Ouranos to thank for the relatively low casualties."

Matt stared at the ground. *Only because we killed Cix...*

I killed Cix, Ouranos said.

We did, Ouranos, Matt said. *You're not the only one responsible and I refuse to let you take the full blame.*

Ouranos didn't respond, but Matt felt the shame still bubbling. He tried filling the space with light in their heads, hoping it helped.

"Medics are supervising the cleanup, both here and at the colony plane site," Lance continued. "They've been instructed to retrieve both Caesum and Pilot. Initial numbers are sketchy, but right now we're estimating at least a hundred injured, but most not serious."

Likely because the serious ones died of their injuries, Matt thought. *Fire and ice, what a disaster...*

Lance turned to Aric. "What do you have to report?"

Aric stood carefully, flicking his black, yellow spotted tail and twitching his whiskers. "Honestly, not much, sir. These Cast behave just like Darvin on the scanners. Devoid of magic. They are completely docile now that... that the Basileus has lost his connection to Zyearth."

"Speaking of," Lance said. He turned to Ouranos. "There is no chance the Basileus can possess someone new, right?"

Ouranos shifted in his chair. "I do not believe so. For him to possess me, he had to physically gain control of my magic. I assume it was the same with Cix. He has no connections on Zyearth now, so he has no way to physically sever anyone's magic bonds."

"Hmm," Lance said. He turned back to Aric. "Please continue."

"Yes, sir," Aric said. "We're hoping that the Basileus' absence will give us an advantage while we try and figure out how to fix them. They should remain docile." He managed a small smile. "I have faith that they're fixable, though. We gathered up their Gems and all of them are still bound, and in full color. The fact that the transformation didn't sever those bonds is encouraging."

"Any thoughts on how to fix them?" Larissa asked.

Aric glanced over at Darvin. "We have a lead at least. Cast appear to be created by shoving a black shard of some substance in the eye of a zyfaunos victim."

"Elixir," Matt muttered. Everyone turned on him. He frowned. "I guess you could call it Black Bound Elixir." He explained about how the liquid appeared and why the Basileus wanted it. "If he freezes that elixir and breaks it apart, he can use those shards to create Cast. I saw it on the battlefield."

Cast charms, Ouranos muttered in Matt's mind.

"Ouranos calls them Cast charms," Matt said.

Jaymes frowned. "You think this is because you are Black Bound?"

"Have you ever seen a black liquid form on anyone else's hands before?" Matt asked.

"I have," Izzy said quietly. "When I healed Natassa."

Natassa drew her knees to her face and shuddered.

Izzy pressed her lips together and gave a brief description of Natassa's injuries and her poor attempts to heal her. "But then my Gem flashed white and I got that black liquid on my fingertips and healed her instantly."

"I saw the liquid on her hands too," Sami said. "I've never seen healing like that. When I went to go get Kole, I knew Natassa wouldn't make it. But then she did. Izzy practically brought her back from the dead."

Izzy met Matt's gaze. "We always said being Black Bound didn't actually make us different, but I think it does."

Matt perked both ears now.

"I am grateful then, for your bond with your Gem," Ouranos said quietly. "Thank you for saving Natassa."

"Of course," Izzy said. She and Natassa exchanged small smiles.

"But how does that create Cast?" Larissa asked.

Matt shrugged. "I think the elixir suppresses stuff. It might suppress the Lexi acid I should produce when I'm overusing my magic, and we used it to suppress the Basileus' hold on Ouranos." He shifted. "Admittedly, that also nearly broke his bond with his focus jewels."

"Water *above,*" Izzy said. "Cix's Gem was covered in that stuff when we found him in the woods. Is that how the Basileus got in his head? By breaking his Gem bond?"

"Since that is technically how he controlled me in the first place, I believe this is correct," Ouranos said.

Matt's eyes widened, and Ouranos sunk lower in his seat, filling Matt's head with a sickly green. "Good Draso, that's why Cix's Gem bond had broken," Matt muttered.

"Natassa," Larissa said. "You said Cast were created by suppressing the soul."

Natassa nodded, ears flat. "I did."

"Then if the Black Bound elixir does suppress things like Matt thinks, that explains how it creates them," Larissa said.

"Lightning and air…" Matt muttered. Maybe he really was as dangerous as the myths suggested. Damn it all. He'd have to really keep his powers under control after this. Who knew what else that elixir could do?

Lance cleared his throat. "Back to Aric's lead."

376

"Yes, sorry," Aric said. He nodded to Darvin. "Darvin is the only Cast to fully retain himself after transformation. To clarify, which eye did the Basileus use when he turned you?"

Darvin shifted, his body gurgling and rippling. "The left one."

"The one recently damaged with Lexi acid, yes?"

Darvin's inky body stood taller, one of his "antlers" falling into the puddle below at his movement. "Good Draso, it was wasn't it?"

"We think Lexi acid might be the key to curing the Cast," Aric said with a nod. "We're not sure how yet – we'll need time. But we'll be gathering acid and, if Izzy and Matt don't mind, some of that elixir from them and see what we can come up with. But we're hopeful."

"Cast have good chance," Jaymes added. He gripped Matt and Izzy's shoulders. "No worries, okay?"

Ouranos heaved relief, blowing flittered white particles through Matt's mind like snow, almost palpable. *It has been nearly a century and we have found no cure for Cast. If your people can do this…*

Have faith, Ouranos. Matt squeezed his shoulder.

"Matt, Ouranos," Lance said. Matt looked up. "This centers on you. Perhaps you ought to explain what happened."

Matt took a deep breath and launched in an explanation of everything – his fight with Ouranos, the time travel, their social bond, the attempt to gather the elixir, Roscoe's transformation, Matt's encounter with the Black Cloak, and finally his attempts to sever the strings the Basileus held on Ouranos. Ouranos occasionally spoke, clarifying things and filling in the gaps when Matt hadn't been with him. He ended with a short explanation of his encounter with Cix and Ouranos' merciful killing.

The longer Matt spoke, the more ridiculous the whole thing sounded. Time travel? Accidental jewel bonds? The Black Cloak himself? It'd be a wonder if they didn't just drop him in a psych ward.

Lance sat back in his chair when Matt finished up, rubbing his snout thoughtfully. "I'm not sure where to start here."

Matt shrugged. "I'm not sure either, if I'm honest, sir."

"Let's... let's start with Roscoe. We have some idea of why Darvin retained himself after the transformation, but what about Roscoe?"

"I ah, have a theory," Ouranos said quietly. "When I first fought with Matthew during the fair, I retrieved a precious few droplets of the Black Bound elixir. My father attempted to freeze the liquid and create Cast charms, but I was able to pull back enough on my magic that I stopped it. The charms were only semisolid. I suspect the Basileus used one of those charms to turn Roscoe."

"Hmm," Aric said. "That's important data, honestly. Thank you for sharing, Ouranos."

Ouranos gave him a slow nod and sunk back into his chair.

"If I may confirm a part of Matt's story," Izzy said. "I met the Black Cloak too. Not face to face, but he took over one of Natassa's summons and spoke with me directly. And he all but confirmed he was a time traveler."

Ouranos shifted in his chair at the name Black Cloak. Matt glanced at him, but Ouranos said nothing.

Lance pinched the fur between his eyes. "Let's not get into this supposed time travel right now." He met Matt's gaze. "You say you have a social bond with Ouranos."

Matt nodded.

Lance leaned on the table. "I'm having a hard time believing that. Social bonds don't happen by accident."

Matt bit his lip, chancing a glance at Izzy. Izzy flicked an ear back and looked off.

"They *don't,*" Lance said, crossing his arms.

"I don't know what to tell you," Matt said.

378

"Can you prove it?" Larissa asked.

"We can speak telepathically with each other," Matt said. "And we see each other's moods as colors in our heads. I don't see how we could do that without a social bond."

Lance raised an eyebrow. "That's not exactly proof since we can't see inside your head."

Matt shrugged. "Sorry, I don't really know how to prove it."

"Ouranos," Larissa said, looking him in the eye. Ouranos frowned, but met her gaze. "Ask Matt about the injury he had when he was twelve and have him answer you telepathically."

Ouranos lifted a brow, but turned to Matt, swirling yellow curiosity in Matt's mind.

Matt winced slightly. *Broken leg,* he said. *I fell down the stairs in our building and broke the leg in six places. I needed a week of healing therapy to repair it because the break was so bad and had to stay in bed the whole time.*

"Matthew tells me he broke his leg in six places falling down the stairs and he needed a week of healing to mend the damage," Ouranos said.

Lance stared, wide eyed.

Matt leaned on his hands. "I told you."

Lance ran a hand down his snout. "That complicates things."

"Does it?" Larissa asked, turning toward Lance.

"Social bonds are *dangerous,* Larissa," Lance said.

"They seemed to have handled it well," Larissa said, twitching a badger ear. "It didn't impede their ability to fight and stop the Cast. I dare say it gave them an advantage if their abilities on the battlefield are any indication. And they seem to have it relatively well under control after only a few days."

Lance twitched his tail. "But the long-term effects--"

"--Are something we'll have to study," Larissa said. "Everything we know about social bonds have been between two Lexi Gems. And, I might add, what we know is very little, as many of the records no longer exist. I would have to do some research, but I have never heard of a bond between two different types of focus jewels. This is not a 'normal' social bond." She met Ouranos' gaze, her eyebrows slightly furrowed in concentration. "For that matter, this gives us a distinct advantage."

Matt raised an eyebrow and perked an ear. "It does?"

"You can see in Ouranos' head," Larissa said. She leaned her head on her hand. "You can tell us how much of a villain he actually is."

MERCY

Matt's red-hot anger blossomed in Ouranos' head at Larissa's words, making him wince. Matt managed to stay in his seat and remain physically calm, but his anger dripped through his words and practically burned Ouranos' mind.

"Ouranos is *not* a villain."

"Matthew," Ouranos said. "After everything I have done--"

"After everything *your father* did, using you," Matt spat.

Ouranos flattened his ears. "It was still my hand that did the damage." He turned to the Master Guardian, Lance. "Master Guardian, I take full responsibility for your lost Defenders and I insist on the harshest of punishments."

"Ouranos!" Natassa squeaked.

"Ouranos, *please,*" Matt said.

But Ouranos stood and lowered his head. "I am at your mercy, Guardian."

Lance tapped his foot, his toeclaws echoing on the hard stone. "Then mercy you shall have."

Ouranos lifted his head, eyes wide.

Lance took a deep breath. "Ouranos, it's very clear this was not your doing. I admit I didn't believe you could somehow be physically puppeted by your father, but seeing Cix, one of our most loyal Defenders, behave the way he did, I believe it now." He flicked an ear back. "In some ways, this is my responsibility too. Matt suggested from the very beginning that you were being physically controlled by your father, against your will, and needed help, and I dismissed it. If I had listened to him and sent my team with that in mind, we might have had a very different outcome. I was so concerned with the fact that you attacked that I dismissed your need for help. We are Defenders. We help those in need." He shook his head. "I cannot hold you responsible for the actions of your father."

Ouranos swallowed hard. He did not deserve that level of mercy. "I value your pardon, but I am unworthy of it. While my father did have physical control over me, there were times I escaped that control and behaved selfishly, knowing my actions could be damaging. I still hold myself responsible for the deaths of your Defenders."

Lance leaned on his hands. "It's very brave of you to admit that. Can I ask why you behaved in such a way?"

Ouranos leaned back, surprised. "I, ah." He flattened his ears. "I… hoped to escape my father's hold on me."

"And all your actions reflected that."

"Yes," Ouranos said. "My only goal was to regain my freedom." He rubbed his arm. "I have been my father's prisoner for a very long time."

Lance eyed him. "So, did you set out to step on others while you fought for your freedom?"

"Heavens, no!" Ouranos said, raising both palms.

"And you rushed into every decision, not caring who you hurt in the process?"

"Of course not!" Ouranos said. "I questioned every action. It was never my intent to *harm.*"

"Then that is the difference between you and your father," Lance said. "The Basileus' whole purpose for coming here was to build an invincible army designed to cause death and destruction. He didn't care who he hurt or killed to get what he wanted, even if that meant killing his own children. He never looked beyond his own selfish goals and never questioned his actions." Lance offered him a tiny smile. "You did."

Ouranos sat down, unsure how to respond.

Lance leaned back in the chair. "Sometimes circumstances force us to take risks, Ouranos. I'm sure Matt took several risks in helping you to escape your father in the first place."

Matt flicked an ear back, but said nothing.

"But there's a significant difference in taking a risk while trying to help someone and taking a risk for your own selfish goals. You and Matt were trying to help someone."

"Myself..." Ouranos muttered.

"You're allowed to want to save yourself," Lance said.

Ouranos sunk deeper into the chair.

"Ouranos," Matt said. "The whole reason you were in this position in the first place was because of your father. That's not your fault. No one could blame you for wanting to escape him." He gripped Ouranos' shoulder, his rosy dawn filling Ouranos' mind with warmth. "You said it yourself on the battlefield. You don't have to feel guilty for the Basileus' destruction."

Ouranos rested his head on his hand, shaking.

These Defenders had no reason to grant him this much mercy. This much compassion. Tears filled his eyes and he let them fall, relishing in his ability to live in his emotions, free of his father's poison. After a moment, he lifted his head and met Lance's gaze.

"I have no words for your act of mercy," Ouranos said. "But I ask that I do something, anything, to reconcile my hand in these deaths."

"I think you should," Lance said. "And in fact, I can think of no better way to do that then to assist in the burial of the dead, if their families will have you. In the meantime, I will insist you be under tight watch until we know for certain the Basileus has no chance to repossess you. And I'm sorry, but until we have a better sense of your social bond with Matt, I can't send you and Natassa home. I hope you understand."

Ouranos shifted. That should bring a sense of dread, but considering everything waiting for him at home, there was peace instead. He looked at Natassa, who nodded, teary-eyed, but smiling. Ouranos nodded back and turned to Lance. "We do."

"Good," Lance said. He shook his head. "I don't know why the Basileus came here, or why he wants to create the Cast. Natassa has been very secretive on that front."

Natassa flicked an ear back and looked away.

"But I assume that just because he failed here, doesn't mean he'll stop trying." Lance looked back and forth between Ouranos and Natassa. "When we send you home, I intend to send you with help. My military is at your disposal. The Basileus is too dangerous to leave him to his own devices.

Ouranos sighed relief.

"However," Lance continued. "We'll do so only after we know how to fix the Cast. There aren't any Black Bound Gem users on Earth, if there are any Gem-bound at all, so we shouldn't have to worry that the Basileus will overrun the planet with Cast. But I think it'd be unwise to go back to Earth without that knowledge."

"I agree," Ouranos said.

"I'm glad we see eye to eye," Lance said. "Now." He eyed Matt and Izzy. "It's time we address your ultimatum."

CHAPTER 58

GUARDIAN OATH

Matt stiffened. Hell. He knew this was coming.

Lance narrowed his gaze. "Matthew Azure. I had very specific rules for you to follow. Obey my orders. Be a partner to Izzy. Work with your pack." He bared a fang. "You disobeyed every one of them."

Matt took a deep breath. The Black Cloak's words came back to him. He claimed that if Matt helped Ouranos, he'd be granted the Guardianship, even though it was at the expense of someone's life.

Cix's life.

But that was horse spit. These things didn't happen just because strange time traveling cryptics claimed they did. Despite the Cloak's words about Cix coming true, Matt didn't trust a damn thing he'd said.

After everything Matt had done, he didn't deserve the Guardianship and he knew it. He met Lance's eyes, determined to keep his emotions under control.

This was it. Time to let go.

"Sir, I make no excuse for my actions. I willingly disobeyed your orders and frequently justified that disobedience to seek only my own goals. My actions hurt myself, my team," he glanced at Izzy, and flicked back an ear, "…and my partner. I may have achieved my goal of helping Ouranos, but in doing so, I disregarded your orders and caused irreparable damage. I also take responsibility for Cix's death." He stood straight, though he shook. "I fully accept that at best, I did not live up to expectations on this mission and I've lost my chance at Guardianship, and at worse, I should face punishment or dismissal for my disobedience and the destruction that caused."

Lance perked his ears and lifted an eyebrow, almost confused it seemed. But a ghost of a smile graced his lips. "Here I was about to apologize, and I get this. I suppose that solidifies my decision then."

Matt flattened an ear. "Sir?"

"You're right that you disobeyed every order," Lance said. "Which is definitely something we need to work on. But I also need to work on listening. I meant it when I said that if I had listened to you about Ouranos, we could have avoided a lot of this mess. You've been training to be my Golden Guardian for a long time. But I haven't been training myself to accept you as that Guardian. I'm supposed to be willing to listen to your judgement calls. That's literally part of the job. And I didn't. That was unfair of me."

Matt flattened his ears.

Lance crossed his arms. "I need to learn to listen. You had a better understanding of the situation than I did, and I refused to see that. You acted based on that understanding, and I'm grateful. Frankly, if you hadn't saved Ouranos, the damage could have been far worse. Imagine the Basileus possessing *two* zyfaunos. I don't think we would have survived it."

Ouranos shuddered, sending a nasty brown wave through Matt's mind.

"I think this has proven to me that I can, in fact, rely on you when you act on your own," Lance said. "That doesn't mean you have the right to go do whatever you please, mind you. We need to learn to work together. But the mistake was as much mine as it was yours. I think we can both accept that."

"I… yes sir," Matt said. Who was he to argue?

"You do still need more discipline, however," Lance continued. "We'll start with structure. For the next year, you will forego any unnecessary duties and teach a full cache of fencing classes. Jay damaged their paw last semester and I need someone to take their classes. Can I count on you to fulfill that duty?"

Matt saluted. He wasn't a huge fan of teaching, but considering everything he'd done, he'd gotten off light. "Yes, sir!"

Lance rubbed the white fur on his chin. "And clearly, you need to be a better team player. I'll have to work out the specifics, but I think some wargames are in order. Specifically wargames where you aren't in command. I'll set things up and send them your way once we've got the time. Understood?"

Matt chewed his lip, but Lance was right. He saluted again. "Yes, sir."

Lance nodded. "And Izzy."

Izzy stood straight up.

Lance flattened both ears. "You have spent the majority of your Defender career believing you have no place in the Guardianship, despite everyone around you, including me, telling you otherwise."

Izzy wrinkled her snout and furrowed her brow.

"However," Lance continued. "During this battle, you have proven yourself a thousand times over. You've been a leader, a fighter, a healer. You covered the gaps in your team, you led when no one was there to lead, you continuously put yourself in danger to protect those around you, you healed with a skill and speed that no other Defender can, and you saw the value in making Natassa your ally when everyone else was quick to dismiss her. I

388

would say this entire event has been an exercise in proving just how ready for Guardianship you are. Would you agree?"

Izzy's eyes widened, and she glanced at Matt.

Matt kept his thoughts to himself. This wasn't for him to decide for her, as he practically had when Lance had given them the ultimatum in the first place. It was on her to recognize how much she had grown. He gave her an encouraging smile.

She blinked, her thoughts a jumbled mess in Matt's mind, accompanied with tiny, jangly bells in his ears. She looked past Matt at Natassa. Natassa smiled widely, waving a hand at her.

Izzy smiled back, her thoughts calming, taking the bells with her. She turned to Lance, putting on a determined, serious face. "Yes sir, I would agree."

Lance smirked. "It's good to see you finally see yourself as the rest of us do." He waved to Izzy and Matt. "Stand with me."

Matt exchanged a glance with Izzy, but they both stood.

Lance folded his hands behind his back. "Fellow Defenders. While the circumstances are not ideal, I nevertheless feel this moment is far past due." He faced Matt and Izzy. "Before your Master Guardian, your Domini Defender, and these witnesses here, recite with me the Oath of the Guardian and take your place as our Golden Guardians."

Matt's bones buzzed. They got the Guardianship? *Seriously?* After everything he had done these past few days, his mind screamed at him to reject the offer, to admit he didn't deserve it.

But you do, Ouranos said, as white flooded Matt's mind. Joy, he realized. *You saved me and my sister. You banished the Basileus. You have given us hope that the Cast can be restored. You are every bit the Guardian Lance sees you as.* Matt chanced a glance at Ouranos and found the Athánatos prince smiling at him. Smiling! *You deserve this, Matthew. Take it with honor and use your position to help others as you have always wanted.*

Matt blinked at Ouranos, then smiled back. *Thank you.* He stood stiffly at attention, as did Izzy. This moment was too important to mess up.

Lance raised a hand and together, the three of them spoke the Guardian Oath.

"I solemnly swear to support my fellow soldiers, protect the innocent, defend all creatures, and uphold the Defender Spirit. I swear to put my charges and my mission first. I understand and am willing to put my life on the line to abide by the code of the Guardian. I take this obligation of my own freewill and will faithfully perform to the best of my ability from now until the end of my service or until death takes me. I swear this before Lord Draso, and his sacrificial offspring Kai. *Tel rasta separit vasa bayfore Draso.*"

Lance smiled and waved a hand at the empty Golden Guardian seats. Izzy glanced once more at Matt, a sad smile on her face, and the two of them took their places in front of the chairs.

"Fellow Defenders," Lance said. "May I introduce our newest Golden Guardians -- Matthew Azure and Isabelle Gildspine. May they hold their positions long and may they do unimaginable good during their careers."

Despite everything, every zyfaunos in the room stood as one and clapped.

BITTERSWEET

After the impromptu ceremony, Lance dismissed everyone with a promise to commission Matt and Izzy's new golden Defender pendants as soon as possible. Larissa and Viri left with Kole for more healing therapy, and Sami followed to get more treatment for her eye. She shared a hug with Matt before she left.

"I'm so glad you're safe," she said. "Don't scare us like that again."

"No promises," Matt said, trying to sound flippant, but failing. Izzy smacked his arm, which got a laugh out of Sami.

Good, Matt thought. *We need to work on getting back to normal.*

Aric planned to escort Darvin and Roscoe out to the labs. Darvin managed a guise of a smile and a congratulations to Izzy and Matt.

"I'll keep Roscoe under my watch," Darvin said. "We'll get back to normal in no time. You'll see."

Izzy couldn't hug him, but she gripped a tentacle like "hand" and smiled. "Thank you."

Darvin turned to the two Athánatos and lowered his inky head. "Ouranos, Natassa, I want to apologize for my behavior toward you. I should have trusted Matt and Izzy, and I should have been willing to see the shades of gray instead of black and white. I hope we can be friends while we try and fix this mess. I know that'll be awkward, but..."

Ouranos placed a hand on his chest and took a short bow. "It would be my honor. Thank you." Natassa nodded, smiling.

Roscoe gurgled politely. Darvin chuckled, a deep, rippling sound. "I think Roscoe feels the same." He met Ouranos' gaze. "And Ouranos... I don't blame you for this. This wasn't you. This was your father. Okay?"

Ouranos perked an ear. "Ah, thank you. I appreciate that." He rubbed the quills on the back of his head. "It may take time for me to believe that myself, but that helps."

"Good," Darvin said. He managed a decent salute. "We'll see you all later." Aric took them out.

Once Aric left, Jaymes walked over and pulled Matt and Izzy into a big hug. He held them for a full minute before he spoke.

"Your fathers would be proud," he said quietly, his accent showing through thicker than normal. "Of your Guardianship, but also your growth." He stood back and smiled. "They would have acted same as you. Throw themselves in danger to help others. Is a Guardian trait, I think." His smile faded slightly. "But please, take care. Okay?"

Matt exchanged a glance with Izzy, and they nodded.

Jaymes hugged them again. "I love you both." Then he followed after Aric.

Matt watched Jaymes go, pressing his lips together.

Charlotte walked up to him now. She actually smiled. "Well. You got it."

Matt flattened both ears. "Char--"

"Don't start," she said, holding a hand up. "There's no reason to try and comfort me. This is what you always wanted and it's not fair of me to hold you back. And this whole event has shown me that it doesn't matter whether you're a Guardian or not. You're always going to put yourself out there to help others. And I think you should. It's what Dad did. He'd be proud of you." She took a deep breath. "Just… please think of me while you're out there fighting the good fight." She paused, like she wanted to say more, but nothing came out.

He hugged his sister. "I will. Thanks for understanding."

"Of course." Charlotte gave him another squeeze, then followed Jaymes out of the room.

Matt's tail drooped. He always expected his rise to Guardianship would be joyful and exciting. A big ceremony, maybe a celebration party, or at least a nice dinner with friends and fellow Defenders.

But the circumstances had left it bittersweet. He'd finally gotten what he had been wanting for so long, but he had lost so much to get it.

He should have been celebrating his promotion with Cix.

He watched Ouranos speak with Natassa, both of them looking more relaxed and at peace then Matt had ever seen. Natassa gripped Ouranos' hand, chatting excitedly about the prospects of fixing the Cast and what that could mean for their people back home. Ouranos watched her, smiling slightly, nodding at appropriate places, and clearly just enjoying something normal again.

Matt perked his ears. Maybe there was more of a silver lining to this battle than he thought.

Izzy walked up to Matt and gripped his hand. "Well. We made it."

Matt gripped her hand back, but then flicked an ear back. "At quite a cost."

"I know," Izzy said. "It makes this whole thing feel wrong. But," she squeezed Matt's hand. "This is how it happened. We can't change it. All we can do is work on fixing the Cast and accepting what we can't fix. Right?"

Matt squeezed back. "Yeah, I suppose you're right." He stared at Ouranos again.

Ouranos glanced back, smiling. But then his eyes widened. "Matthew."

Matt raised a brow. "Something wrong?"

"Isabelle said we need to accept what we cannot fix," Ouranos said. "But... Cix... we could fix him."

Matt narrowed his eyes. "Ouranos, he's dead."

"Now he is," Ouranos said. "But not in the past..." He nodded to Matt's Gem. "Could we perhaps travel to that past and save him?"

Matt's eyes grew wide. He glanced down at his Gem too. Ouranos had a point. They *could* time travel.

But could they do it on purpose? Did they know how to make it happen at all? And if they did, could they actually get to the right place and fix things? If they saved Cix, what effect would it have on the future? How would their past selves react seeing copies of themselves? Just thinking about it made him dizzy.

More than that, what effects would it have on him and Ouranos? They had woken up damaged and broken. It would take practice to learn how to time travel on purpose, and more to get to the right spot and who knew what physical damage that would do to them while they tried. Not to mention the psychological damage.

No, there was too much risk, as much as Matt didn't like to admit that.

"I don't think so, Ouranos," Matt said, and he briefly explained his reasons. "I worry we'll do more harm than good, you know? What's done is done. I think it'd be better if we just work on accepting that instead of killing ourselves trying to change it."

394

Ouranos heaved a sigh. "I suppose you are right."

"I think he is," Lance said, walking up to them. "Part of being a Guardian is learning to accept loss. It's not how I would want for you to learn it, but this is a good lesson for you. And I'm proud to see you growing in that respect."

Matt smiled. "Yes, sir."

Lance walked up to him and gave his shoulder a squeeze. He smiled back. "This was a hard road. But you and Izzy finally got to the end of it. You earned your Guardianship. Seriously *earned* it, at quite a cost. But you rose above unimaginable strife and challenges. I'm proud of you for that. I know there's precious little to celebrate right now, but once things calm down, let's plan something, okay? And in the meantime," he nodded to Ouranos and Natassa. "You should help our new friends get settled in. They're in it for the long haul. Consider that an order."

Matt paused a moment, then snapped to attention. "Yes, sir!" Izzy followed his example.

"Good," Lance said. "Dismissed." He left the room.

Matt flicked an ear back. Another chance to save Cix slipped through his fingers, but he knew this was for the best. *But it'll take some time to accept that Cix died at my hand.*

"Well, at least we have that time now, yeah?" Izzy said.

Matt flicked his ears back and twitched his snout. She was hearing him again. He turned to Izzy. "Izzy, I need to apologize."

Izzy frowned. "No, you don't."

"Yes, I do, and don't stop me," Matt said. "I treated you horribly through that whole mission. I dismissed your concerns, I abandoned you multiple times, I insisted you follow orders without even explaining why, and while it was mostly by accident, I made you believe I was dead. I caused you a lot of stress and I didn't act like the partner you deserve." He lowered his head. "I won't make excuses. But I hope you'll forgive me. And I hope we can work

395

on being better partners." He bit his lip. "That... that might start with admitting we have a social bond and trying to work on ours, too."

Izzy furrowed her brow. "Matt, I still don't think we have a social bond."

Matt raised an eyebrow. "After everything we've been through?"

"Yes, and I'll tell you why," Izzy said. "I don't see colors in my head like you do with Ouranos. I don't hear your voice in my head."

"But you do!" Matt said. "The other day--"

"Was me being stressed," Izzy said. "Here, let me prove it." She eyed him in silence a moment. Matt listened for her voice in his head, but he heard nothing. "So did you hear me?"

Matt lowered his gaze. "...No."

"Then we clearly don't have a bond," Izzy said. "Look, we've both been stressed. We hear things when we're stressed. We don't have a bond." She looked off, somewhat nervously. "We don't, okay? Don't worry about it. Focus on your bond with Ouranos."

Matt pressed his lips together. He really didn't believe Izzy. She knew what they had. But she was in denial. And frankly, he couldn't blame her. He sighed. Let her deny it now, while he worked with Ouranos. Once he knew more there, he could approach the subject again. "Okay, I'll concede that. But regardless. We're Guardians now. I need to work with you, not against you."

Izzy smiled. "I forgive you, and thank you." She gave him a big hug. "Maybe we could start with some food? I'm starving, and you never did get me breakfast like you promised."

Matt smiled. "Sure." He turned to Ouranos and Natassa. "Come join us?"

Ouranos shifted, but nodded. The group walked out of the Assembly Room.

They had a long road ahead of them. But at least they weren't tackling this alone.

Epilogue

Ouranos stood to the side of the large funeral pyre, close enough to feel its heat through his fur, focusing on the embers floating above the flames. He wore a black Defender novice uniform, which covered far more fur than he was used to. It protected well against the autumn's emerging cold, but also trapped the heat of the fire before him. The soft burning smell mingled with the earthy scents of the woods just outside the Defender Academy where the majority of Defender funerals were held. A gentle chill cooled his back as he kept his gaze on the embers. He told himself it was because he needed to make sure the flames did not catch on the pines surrounding them.

In truth, he knew, he simply did not want to see Cix's body as it burned. Nor did he want to concentrate on the large gathering of friends, family, and Defenders who had come to see Cix's killer perform burial rights.

Apparently most Zyearthling burial rituals involved elements of some kind. For the warrior, that element was fire.

Cix was quite the warrior, Matt said, standing next to Ouranos.

Ouranos chewed his lip. Matt had insisted on being next to Ouranos with every burial he helped at. The families of the dead were surprisingly sympathetic and forgiving, traits apparently common on this planet. He had faced adversity, yes, and some families simply did not want him there, but he would have been surprised at any level of mercy.

You did not have to be with me at every funeral, Ouranos said.

Yes, I did, Matt countered. *I had a hand in these too. It was my Black Bound elixir that caused this. And besides, I can't have you wallowing in despair because of something that isn't even your fault. It keeps us up at night.*

Hmm. Ouranos forced his gaze to the center of the blaze. A thin outline, barely visible, was all that remained of Cix.

It had been a hard three weeks. Adjusting to the modern living of the Zyearthlings, navigating the campus, performing funeral pyre after funeral pyre for the dozens of Defenders dead at the destructive power of the Cast. Cix was, at last, the final funeral left to perform, postponed to give Domini Terrill and his family time to get their affairs in order and travel to be here for the memorial. He was thankful this chapter of his life was finally coming to a close, but he had a rough future ahead, all while dealing with the stares and behind-the-back whispers of Defenders who thought he had "gotten off too easy."

They're hurting still, Ouranos, Matt said, blowing soft white particles like snow through Ouranos' mind. *Give it time. Meanwhile, stay by your friends. We'll help you get through it.*

Ouranos sighed. "I know." He met Matt's gaze. "I am honored you call me friend."

Matt smiled. "Of course."

"Guardian Azure? If I may trouble you a moment?"

Ouranos turned, his heart racing. A flash of memory not his own ran through his mind - Cix saying the same words to Matt. The memory felt distant, faded, dead, but Matt's thoughts indicated it was actually only a few weeks ago. The very same day Ouranos had attacked the campus.

For half a second, Matt's presence in his head insisted the voice belonged to Cix, though this thought fled instantly at the sight of the zyfaunos speaking.

The wolf before him was unmistakably Cix's father. Tall, mostly black with white streaks through his fur, bearing the same strong yellow eyes as his son. A gray wolf who Ouranos suspected was his wife stood near him, holding onto the hand of a young white wolf with icy blue eyes.

Fear flooded Ouranos' chest.

Don't worry, Adalwolf is a good zyfaunos, Matt said, though sickly yellow fear invaded the edges of Ouranos' mind anyway. Matt stood tall and offered the wolf a salute. "Domini Terrill."

Adalwolf saluted back and, despite everything, actually smiled. "Technically that was unnecessary as you outrank me now, Guardian."

"Respect should be shown where it is due, sir," Matt said.

"I appreciate it." Adalwolf shifted a bit. "You were Cix's sword partner."

Matt flicked an ear back. "I was, yes."

Adalwolf closed his eyes a moment and took a deep breath. "Cix talked about you a lot. You were the reason he streaked blue through his fur. Strictly nonregulation, but it did a good job showing his personality and it was a reminder of how much you meant to him. I'm grateful you were with him in the end."

Ouranos took a step back and stared at the ground, ears flat.

Adalwolf whined quietly. "Ouranos, I am grateful you were there as well."

Ouranos lifted his head. "I beg your pardon?"

"The reports were very clear that his death was an act of mercy," the wolf said. "Lance actually praised your quick and painless method and said you blessed him in Draso's name before he died."

"I... this is how it has always been done with us," Ouranos said.

Adalwolf smiled. "And I'm thankful for that."

399

Tears formed in the corner of Ouranos' eyes. "Sir, it is my fault your son had to die in the first place."

"It is the Basileus' fault, and Cix would agree with me," Adalwolf said. His eyes glistened, and he shook slightly, but he still held an air of dignity. "My son died as he lived – a Defender. He was never happier than when he was helping others. He would have been a willing sacrifice."

The words struck Ouranos as surely as if he had been assailed by lightning. "I… I will never be able to repay such a sacrifice."

"I would say different," Adalwolf said. "You're still alive, aren't you? You have a lifetime to do good. Longer even then ours, if I read Lance's report correctly." He gripped Ouranos' shoulder warmly. "That was a gift. Use it wisely."

Ouranos took a shuddering breath. "Your grace in this situation is immeasurable, sir."

"Grace and mercy will allow us to heal," Adalwolf said. "Anger and hate only serves to fester and damage."

The young white wolf walked up to Matt and tugged on his pants. "Guardian Azure?"

A dark wave blew through Ouranos' mind betraying Matt's discomfort, but the quilar smiled and crouched down to the wolf's eye level. "You're Robert, right? Cix spoke about you a lot."

Robert offered a shy smile. "Cix told me he had all kinds of adventures as a Defender."

Matt sniffled slightly. A rain of dark blue dripped in Ouranos' mind. "He did, yeah."

"I want to have adventures too!" Robert said. "I want to be a Defender some day!"

Matt perked his ears. He glanced up briefly at Robert's parents.

Both of them smiled at him. Adalwolf nodded.

Matt turned back to Robert. "Then I look forward to seeing you in the Academy someday."

Robert grinned at him.

"We would be honored to have you visit us on the Archipelago once things settle down," Cix's mother said.

"I look forward to it," Matt said. Adalwolf offered another salute, which Matt reciprocated, and the family walked off.

The flames of the pyre had cooled, and with it, Ouranos' adrenaline. He turned back to the dying fire.

"Ouranos," Matt said carefully. Ouranos could feel the hesitation in the colors. "I know Natassa wouldn't explain, but maybe you would. Why does the Basileus want an army of Cast?"

Ouranos pressed his lips together. He supposed this was inevitable. "I will explain his intent, but I am not ready to divulge the reason. Is that understandable?"

Matt nodded. "Sure."

"The Basileus has a deep, unquenchable grudge against humanity," Ouranos said. "And he intends to use the Cast to eliminate them on Earth."

Matt's colors turned black and his quills stood on end. "All of them?"

"If he has his way, yes," Ouranos said. "And you and I both know that they would be powerless against the Cast. They do not possess innate magic. It would take time, but even a small army of Cast could do irreparable damage."

Matt shifted his weight. "That's a problem."

"Indeed."

"We'll get back to Earth someday soon, Ouranos," Matt said. "We'll learn how to fix the Cast and take down the Basileus. We'll save your people and stop his genocide. It's what we do. And in the meantime, you're safe. You have support. You don't have to do this alone." Matt gripped Ouranos' shoulder. "Okay?"

Ouranos stared at the flame, taking a shuddering breath. He reached up and gripped Matt's hand. "I hope so."

The End

About the Author

R. A. Meenan was born in London during the golden age of science fiction, but somehow time traveled to the Modern Era (some say a mad man with a blue box was involved). She was dropped on the doorstep of a house owned by anthropomorphic cats and though they were disappointed she didn't have furry ears and a tail, they took her in to teach her the ways of elemental magic. After setting fire to her furry cat friends' tails one too many times (final score – fire: 2612, cat's tails: 0) they called an exterminator and sent her out on her way.

Now an adult (physically, not mentally), she ride-hops intergalactic military spacecraft, combing the outer reaches of space and time, writing science fiction and urban fantasy stories based on her experiences. She's also hoping to find the perfect cup of coffee and a better way to grow dinosaurs. Humans kind of look at her funny, but she's managed to make herself an honorary ambassador for furry and anthropomorphic aliens and space dragons.

She carefully feeds and brushes her wonderful husband Joe and the pair have four furry children (which are really cats, but don't tell them that) and a human child named after a video game character. She also spends her spare time teaching essay-writing haters, molding them into people resembling Actual Students and Lovers of English.

She may not win the hearts of stiff military men or students who want good grades for no effort, but she certainly captures the spirit and imagination of time travelers, magic users, nerds, Students-In-Training, and fantasy lovers. Welcome to her nonsensical world. We hope you like it here.

You can email R. A. Meenan at r.a.meenan@zyearth.com. Check out more of her works at www.zyearth.com. You can also follow her on Facebook at https://www.facebook.com/zyearthchronicles or on Twitter at @sammieauburn or on Instagram @zyearthdefender, where she posts snippets and artwork from the Zyearth chronicles.

If you enjoyed this book, consider reviewing it at the retailer where you purchased it!

Enter the World of Zyearth

Liked this book? Read more Zyearth stories for FREE for signing up for the newsletter! Join now at Zyearth.com or by scanning the code below.

Matt has earned his long-coveted Guardianship, but it wasn't always in the bag. When Matt's Gem first broke, his powers spun out of control -- and he took drastic action to get them back under control.

Read about Matt's first encounter with his magic for FREE for signing up for the newsletter!

Izzy knew she would be a Guardian. It was in her blood. She just had to break her Gem and earn her magic. But she didn't expect the cost of that Gem break to be so high.

Read about Izzy's first encounter with her magic for FREE for signing up for the newsletter!

Glossary

Learn more about the World of Zyearth at Zyearth.com!

Zyfaunos: Zyfaunos are anthropomorphic animal-like bipeds. All zyfaunos have similar characteristics -- plantigrade or near plantigrade legs, human stance structure in the spine, humanlike eyes and sometimes lips, generally short snouts, and have humanlike, five fingered hands, usually with tiny, somewhat sharp retractable claws instead of fingernails. Zyfaunos tend to have the same height range as humans, with a few extreme examples of very short or very tall species. All zyfaunos can interbreed regardless of the individual's species. Unlike most faunos, zyfaunos are not always "traditionally" colored, and often have unnatural colors in their fur, such as red, blue, green, purple, and others. Though relationships are rare, humans and zyfaunos can produce children. Zyfaunos are named as such because the DNA strain originated from the planet Zyearth and Zyearth has the purest forms of this species.

Quilar: Quilar are perhaps the most unusual of all zyfaunos, as it is unclear what animal they evolved from. They have several key characteristics -- catlike ears and snout, slightly humanlike lips, though usually black or dark pink, humanlike feet and hands, tails, and quills of various lengths on their head in place of hair. Quilar quills are hard, though not usually sharp like a porcupine or hedgehog. Instead of fingernails, quilar have tiny retractable claws on each hand. These claws are not very sharp and are mainly used for scratching. Quilar can be divided by color and physical characteristics into three different categories.

Zyearth Quilar: Zyearth quilar have very short, very soft fur and generally longer, thicker quills on their heads. Their snouts are short and flat and many even have human-like lips. They tend to have catlike ears and human-like eyes. Quilar are the most human-like of all faunos. Human-faunos relationships usually involve a quilar. Zyearth quilar tend to have browns, whites, blacks, and grays for their colors.

Jason is modeling a Zyearth quilar. Jason's fur is soft golden brown.

Earth Quilar: Earth quilar are physically very similar to Zyearth quilar, though their colors tend to be more vibrant. They also generally have streaks of color in their fur and quills while Zyearth quilars tend to be one solid color.

Trecheon is, reluctantly, modeling an Earth quilar. His fur is vibrant red.

Athánatos Quilar: Athánatos quilar are typically taller than their Zyearth and Earth kin. They have ears that bend backwards and more animal-like tails and feet. Their snouts are short and flat and like other quilar, they can have human-like lips.

Ouranos is modeling an Athánatos quilar here. His fur is jet black.

Focus Jewels: Focus jewels are found on many different planets throughout the universe. The term refers to any jewel that can be bound to a user's skin, soul, or lifeforce that grants supernatural powers. Sometimes focus jewel power only grants simple powers, such as long life, but others exhibit more extravagant powers.

Lexi Gems: Lexi Gems are focus jewels bound to the user's soul and grants users several powers. Average Gem users are granted long life, up to four hundred Zyearth years, and slow aging. Advanced users develop "Gem

Specialties" through the Gem "breaking" usually after a stressful, dramatic, or difficult event in the user's life. Military personnel are the most likely to have broken Gems and most Gems break in training.

There are a variety of specialties that users can develop. The most common specialty is healing, followed by elemental fabricators and manipulators, and a select few specialize in cloaking and shielding. Users are usually granted only one specialty, though a rare few have two. In the case of a duel specialist, both specialties are significantly weaker than those in a single specialist.

Lexi Gems are usually about the size of a user's fist. Gems often take on the colors of their users in one of several forms, but they lose their color if the user doesn't touch their Gem for extended periods of time or if the user dies, which also results in the Gem's bond breaking with their user. Gems can be used again by another user after a previous user has died.

Ei-Ei Jewels: Ei-Ei Jewels, like Lexi Gems, are focus jewels and are the source of magic and power for a member of the Athánatos tribe. Ei-Ei jewels are small and they are fused to the skin of the user just around the edge of their eyes. Ei-Ei jewels also come in pairs. Each eye has one set of the pairs. There are three jewels, but all of them work together to properly function.

The first jewel, the Mind Jewel, is yellow, representing the sophia flower, a symbol of wisdom. This jewel set keeps the user's mind fresh and free of deterioration. They even protect against mind aging issues like Alzheimer's and dementia.

The second set, the Body Jewel, is red, representing the purity of blood and flesh. This jewel set keeps the body from deterioration. Athánatos tribe members are immortal because of this jewel, but they are not invincible.

The final set, the Soul Jewel, is the color of the users eyes, representing the user's soul. This jewel set keeps the soul pinned to the body. Together the three sets make the user immortal.

Defender: The Defenders are a military group run by a small country called Zedric on the continent of Yelar on the plant Zyearth.

Guardian: Guardians are an essential part of the Defender military. Guardians are high ranking, highly trained individuals that perform tasks that average Defenders aren't trained for. There are two important types of Guardians.

Master Guardian: The role of Master Guardian is usually held by two people at the same time, often a former Golden Guardian pair. Master Guardians have a duel task – they are both the head of the Defender army and the leaders of the country of Zedric. Master Guardians must be smart, strong, courageous, and influential. Master Guardians are usually in office for life, though there are checks and balances that can remove a Master Guardian if the governing Assembly or the people of Zedric feels like they are not properly performing duties, and some Master Guardians choose to retire. Master Guardians are generally considered by most Defenders to be the most powerful zyfaunos of their time.

Golden Guardian: Golden Guardians are a team of two Defenders specially trained to handle delicate situations and complete covert and difficult missions that need small strike teams. Golden Guardians are selected by the Master Guardian of their era, and are given an extra five years of special training beyond typical Defender training. Usually the team has one healer and one elemental user.

Defender Pendant: Defender pendants are worn by all Defenders, regardless of their position in the army or Academy. They carry holographic identification cards and are the most common means of communication among Defenders. The pendant also carries several symbols. On Zyearth, a legless dragon is a sign of peace, so the Defenders made the legless dragon the center of their pendant. The dragon's neck is tucked under, a classic move that prevents strangulation in

411

battle. This represents defense. The outstretched wings are a sign of openness and welcome. Finally, the Gem at the dragon's side represents the world of Zyearth, since all native Zyearthlings are bound to Gems.

Made in the USA
Las Vegas, NV
07 May 2021

22637286R00239